*To anyone who has ever been
hurt by someone they love.*

*Remember, there's no weakness
in forgiveness.*

FUEL

A BLACK KNIGHTS INC. NOVEL

FOR FIRE

JULIE ANN WALKER

sourcebooks
casablanca

Published by Sourcebooks Casablanca, an imprint of Sourcebooks, Inc.
P.O. Box 4410, Naperville, Illinois 60567-4410
(630) 961-3900
Fax: (630) 961-2168
www.sourcebooks.com

Printed and bound in Canada.
MBP 10 9 8 7 6 5 4 3 2 1

*Courage is being scared to death...
and saddling up anyway.*

—John Wayne

Prologue

London, England

"Christ in a cardigan sweater, if Ace ever tries to talk me into binge-watching *Ray Donovan* until oh-three-hundred in the morning again, remind me to tell him to go take a flying leap, will you?"

As far as Chelsea could figure, Dagan Zoelner—or "Z" as she liked to call him—was talking to no one in particular. This was confirmed when he didn't wait for an answer, simply stomped across the living room of their rented fourth-floor flat toward the kitchen.

Even barefoot, grumpy, and wearing a rumpled T-shirt, he was still a spectacular superhuman creature. And he had a voice like fine Southern moonshine, all smooth and distilled. Hearing it warmed her insides ten degrees.

So what else is new? she thought sourly, taking a bite of her morning bagel and adjusting her glasses to get a better look at his phenomenal denim-clad ass—*oh my!*—before he disappeared through the kitchen doorway.

Dagan had been screwing with her internal temperature for... Well, sometimes it felt like forever. Back when they were both working for the CIA, it hadn't been so bad. She'd been a counterterrorism analyst, which kept her chained to her desk. He'd been a field agent, which meant he had been away in parts unknown far more than he had ever prowled the halls of Langley with that loose, long-legged stride of his. But fast-forward eight years—and throw in an odd twist of fate—and now they were both working for Black Knights Inc., the most clandestine government defense firm in the United States. Which meant that now it was *impossible* to avoid him.

Just to be clear, as the official "liaison" between the CIA and the Black Knights, Chelsea was still *technically* employed by the Central Intelligence Agency. But she'd been living and working exclusively with the Black Knights for months in an attempt to uncover the true identity of the head of one of the world's most nefarious crime syndicates. A man responsible for human trafficking, illegal weapons sales, piracy, and so much more. A man who went by the bone-chilling nickname of Spider.

That meant she'd been on a body-temperature roller coaster for a heck of a long time.

Think that sounds fun? Well, you'd be wrong. And to make matters worse—*Yup, it gets worse*—Dagan had grown out his beard.

Before the dark, sleek pelt of facial hair had appeared, she'd thought his face was...*nice*. All-American-male nice. Guy-next-door nice. Nondescript nose, high brow, and solid jaw nice—his heavily lashed, storm-cloud eyes being his best feature. But after the beard? The Beard? Well, it took his *nice* face and made it hotter than Southern summer nights. That would be hot spelled H-A-W-T. All severe and foreboding and...*hubba, hubba.*

Combine his new visage with wicked tattoos and a body that was broad of shoulder, lean of hip, and made for sin, and that subtle *fsssss* anytime he got near was the sound of Chelsea's panties melting.

That seemed to happen a hundred times a day too.

It was pathetic. *She* was pathetic. Especially since he had never expressed similar feelings for her.

Although, come to think of it, perhaps it was better he *hadn't* expressed any interest. After all, there was the Big Bad Secret she was keeping from him, and—

"You should just invite him to come meet your cat and get it over with." Emily Scott took a seat on the sofa next to Chelsea. Emily wore silk sleep pants and a ratty sweatshirt that looked like Methuselah might have had it made during his younger years.

"Huh?" Chelsea frowned, slathering a fresh spoonful of cream cheese onto her bagel. She enjoyed her food, and it showed in the extra fifteen pounds she hadn't been able to shake since she was sixteen. Not that she had tried all that hard. According to the chart in her doctor's office, her BMI was in the healthy range. So who cared if she jiggled when she wiggled?

Not me. She took another happy bite of bagel and thought, *Life's too short.* "What cat? What are you talking about?"

Emily rolled her eyes. "It's a euphemism, silly."

"For what?"

"For a little sideways hi-how-are-ya."

"Oh, you mean…" For some reason, the word stuck in Chelsea's throat like it came with a set of barbed hooks.

"Sex," Emily finished for her far too loudly.

"Shh." Chelsea glanced toward the kitchen where the three BKI men who had crossed the pond to provide support for her and this mission were gathered, talking in low tones as they waited for the second pot of coffee to brew. "What makes you think I want *that*?"

Emily shot her a look. "Uh, maybe because every time you see him, you aggressively eye fuck the hell out

of him?" Emily's South Side Chicago accent emphasized the *a* sounds of her words, drawing them out.

"I do not." Chelsea felt her cheeks burst into flames.

"Oh yes. You do."

Usually Chelsea enjoyed a no-bullshit, speak-her-
mind kind of gal. But right then she'd have sold her left
boob if Emily would shut up. Unfortunately, it appeared
the market for left boobs was woefully saturated. No
one was buying.

"I don't see what the problem is." Emily adjusted
herself on the sofa, taking a sip of coffee. "You're not
seeing anyone back home, are you?"

"Just Junior Patrick." Chelsea figured the straight-
up, honest-to-God truth was the most expedient way to
extricate herself from the conversation.

"Who's Junior Patrick?"

Chelsea gave Emily's words back to her. "It's slang,
silly. Don't you ever watch the BBC? Junior Patrick is
another name for a lady's best friend."

"Ah. Right. Good to know I'm not the only one in an
intimate relationship with that guy."

Chelsea chuckled and stood to slip out of her favorite
Dobby the House Elf slippers—she was an avid reader
and collector of all things fantasy-related and nerdy—
and into her kitten-heel pumps. Draining the last of her
coffee, she set the empty mug on the table and sighed.
"I'm off. Another day, another dollar."

"And hopefully another chance to plant that bug in
Morrison's computer." Emily grinned up at her, showing a set of crossed fingers and an expression of true
sympathy.

Right. Roper Morrison. Otherwise known as…Spider.

The name was enough to make Chelsea's skin crawl.

Chapter 1

"THERE MUST BE A BETTER WAY TO GET THIS JOB DONE."

Dagan Zoelner noted his own thunderous expression in the mirror hanging on the wall near the front door before returning his attention to Chelsea, sullenly eyeing her when she leaned close to her reflection to apply lipstick in a shade that could only be described as take-me-big-boy pink.

When she blew a kiss at him in the mirror, a coiling awareness tightened his gut. Then she turned and gifted him with a look that would have made a lesser man instinctively reach to protect his balls.

"Lands sakes alive, Z! You're going to whip out your misogyny *every* morning?" That husky voice of hers... it *did* things to him, and she planted her hands on her fantastically curvy hips. The woman was built like a Kardashian, no doubt about it, but the familiar stance reminded him not of Kim or Khloé, but of a pint-sized Wonder Woman.

All she's missing are the gold cuff bracelets and the flowing black hair.

Because while Chelsea's hair was dark and shiny, it was as short as a little boy's. A *pixie* cut, he thought it was called. And that word described Chelsea Duvall perfectly.

With her smooth café-au-lait skin, her copper-colored eyes that frequently glinted with mischief, and the sprinkling of freckles like cinnamon across the bridge of her button nose, she was an ethereal creature. One he

wanted to put in a gilded cage so he could keep her safe
from the cruel world. And, more importantly, from the
likes of Roper fuckin' Morrison.

"It's not misogyny. It's a cold, hard fact. You're not
qualified for this kind of work."

"Oh sweet Jesus!" She tossed her hands in the air.
She was unaware that the movement caused her blazer
to gape open, revealing a set of spectacular breasts
that stretched tight the fabric of her lavender blouse.
"It's déjà poo. As in, I've heard this crap too many
times before."

"Frequency doesn't make it any less true." He ripped
his eyes away from the vast landscape of her chest
because…you know…he refused to be *that guy*.

Even so, it didn't escape his notice that her amazing
rack was partly to blame for the position Chelsea currently found herself in…the position of pretending to
be Morrison's personal assistant when, in truth, she was
waiting for an opportunity to plant a virus in one of his
computers. Once she did that, the Black Knights back
at headquarters in Chicago would hack into Morrison's
systems and get the information they needed to prove,
once and for all, that he was the notorious Spider.

For months, they had tried to ferret out Spider's
true identity with no luck. Then, with the release of
the Panama Papers, the detailed attorney-client information for more than 200,000 offshore companies and
the identities of those companies' shareholders and
financial transactions, they had found the proverbial
needle in the haystack. The papers had uncovered a
tie between Morrison and a diamond mine in Angola.
Which wasn't all that unseemly on the surface, right? A
man of Morrison's means—estimated net worth four-
teen billion dollars—who owned a media empire of a

hundred newspapers and dozens of television stations in both the United States and the UK, had investments all over the world, Africa included. But it just so happened that the Black Knights and the CIA had reason to believe that that *particular* diamond mine was owned by the shadowy Spider.

It had been a clear case of a transitive relationship as far as everyone had been concerned. If A equaled B, and B equaled C, then A equaled C. Morrison was Spider. The trouble came in trying to prove it. They hadn't been able to hack into Morrison's systems from the outside because, according to BKI's hacker extraordinaire, the renowned Ethan "Ozzie" Sykes, "Morrison's firewalls have firewalls." So that had left them with only one option: Get someone on the inside.

Enter Chelsea Duvall.

She had volunteered for the job with one unforgettable sentence: *I'll get so close to Morrison, he won't be able to take a piss without me giving it a shake.*

Dagan had exploded. He'd told her and everyone else at the early-morning meeting, "There's not a snowball's chance in hell Chelsea will be the one to do this. She's an analyst, not a fuckin' field agent!"

But he'd been outvoted.

Apparently Chelsea was the perfect pawn to use in the chess match with Morrison because the man was known to hire and surround himself with women who possessed certain…physical attributes. Read: Ladies built like brick shithouses. And Chelsea's backstory about wanting to quit her job with the Bureau of Land Management—that was her CIA cover—move to England, and go to work for Morrison was exceptional for two reasons. One, it was believable. And two, it happened to be one hundred percent true.

Less than two weeks after that fateful meeting at BKI headquarters, it became known that Morrison had fired his PA. Twenty-four hours later, Chelsea's résumé had been in Morrison's hands. Forty-eight hours after *that*—time no doubt used by Morrison's security team to vet Chelsea top to bottom—she had been on a plane to London to sit for an interview.

Just as had been predicted, Morrison had taken one look at Chelsea—and her…uh…*myriad* delightful features— and hired her on the spot. That was the good news.

The bad news? Well, on top of being an evil and lecherous old fart, Morrison was incredibly paranoid. In the four and a half weeks Chelsea had worked for him, not once had she been allowed to enter either his home office or the office he kept in downtown London to use the thumb drive she meticulously sewed into the lining of her jacket or slacks or whatever other item of clothing she happened to wear to work that day.

Morrison not only *locked* the doors to his inner sanc- tums, but gaining access to the rooms required a retinal scan and voice recognition. Getting around the voice recognition part wasn't too hard. Chelsea had already made a secret recording of Morrison saying the pass phrase. But the retinal scan? Short of offing the asshole and plucking out one of his eyeballs, they were at a loss. *Something has to give.*

Dagan was convinced that *something* should be Chelsea's job with the handsy bastard. They could prove that Morrison was Spider some other way. One that didn't involve her subjecting herself to Morrison's unsubtle leers, roving hands, and blatant sexual innuendos.

"I'm just saying"—he eyed her mulish expression— "if you were going to get the chance to plant the virus, it would've happened by now."

"Says who?" She thrust out her chin. It was small and pointy, and he had the oddest urge to bend down and kiss it.

"Says me."

She rolled her eyes and adjusted her glasses. "And you're the ultimate authority…uh…*why*?"

"Let me see. Maybe it's the hundreds of successful missions I've—"

"Lord have mercy," she interrupted, slipping into the unhurried drawl that revealed her Southern roots. "You realize if I wanted to commit suicide, all I'd have to do is climb your ego and jump down to that place where you keep your humility."

Before he could think of a good comeback, she continued. "And, sure, okay, let's stand here and go through all the reasons I'm not qualified for this kind of work. *Again*. No, really. I love beating a dead horse. You go first. And when your arm gets tired, I'll jump in. Ready? Go."

"Bloody hell!" Christian, a former SAS officer who, for reasons known only to a few, had left Her Majesty's Army to go to work for Black Knights Inc., called from the kitchen. "Would you two stop trading verbal punches? It's too early in the morning. I've yet to finish my first cup of tea, and all that blathering is giving me a sodding headache!"

"Oh, now you've done it. You've gone and angered the Brit," Colby "Ace" Ventura said, sauntering up beside them and planting a kiss on Chelsea's cheek.

Before coming to work for the Black Knights, Ace had been a crackerjack Navy pilot, hence the nickname "Ace"—although there was some speculation that his last name and the Jim Carrey movies had played a part in his nom de guerre. Dagan respected the shit out of the guy. But right now? Well, he was hard-pressed not to punch the fucker in the mouth. If the guy's lips were busted, maybe *then* he'd keep them to himself.

But the dude's gay, one might argue.

Didn't matter. When it came to a man's mouth on Chelsea, Dagan's green-eyed monster made an appearance. Because the fact of the matter was, despite their daily verbal boxing matches, he *liked* her. Had since the first time he met her back at Langley all those years ago when she'd given him an Intelligence report. Looking at her, he had seen nothing but soft curves. Listening to her had revealed a sharp mind.

It was a wonderfully complex juxtaposition, and Dagan had determined to get her in bed on the double. But since he had rarely been stateside back then, the opportunity had never arisen. And just as he had been poised to return to the United States for a good, long stint, an op in Afghanistan had gone horribly wrong, and five people had paid for his mistake with their lives. Afterward, he'd been fired from the CIA quicker than you can say, *Clear out your locker, dickhead*. And as if all *that* wasn't bad enough, following his expulsion from the Company, he'd briefly gotten himself involved with a corrupt senator.

Both of those screwups were black stains on his character. He was convinced that a woman like Chelsea, a woman who was upright and true, wouldn't give him the time of day. Not knowing what she knew about him.

"Do you have everything you need?" Ace asked Chelsea, handing her a travel mug of coffee. "Perhaps you could use some Mace? Or electric underwear so every time that old bastard *accidentally*" — Ace made air quotes with his fingers — "rubs your ass, he gets a nasty shock?"

"Thank you, Ace honey." Now it was Chelsea's turn to smack a kiss on Ace's cheek. "I don't know what I'd do without you."

Dagan's inner six-year-old stomped his foot and sullenly shouted, *What about me? I'm* always *looking out for you!* But he quickly reminded the little brat of Afghanistan and Senator Aldus. *She wants nothing to do with the likes of us, and you know it.*

"My pleasure. Teamwork makes the dream work, am I right?" Ace winked at Chelsea. He really was a handsome bastard. All blond hair, sea-blue eyes, and a physique that looked like it belonged in an underwear advertisement.

Dagan's jealousy was ridiculous. But that didn't stop him from wallowing in it when Ace opened the front door and Chelsea walked into the hall that led down four flights to the hustle and bustle of London's streets.

After the door shut behind her, Ace took one look at Dagan's face and sighed. "Come with me, Werewolf of London." It had been a running joke since they'd taken up residence. The town. The beard. Dagan got it. He just didn't think it was nearly as funny as the rest of them did. "Let's get some of Christian's tea in you. Maybe it will settle your nerves."

"If only it were that easy," Dagan muttered, allowing Ace to pull him through the living room and into the kitchen.

Sitting at the small circular table in the corner was Christian. The three of them made up the team that had volunteered to move to London to provide Chelsea with support. And after living together in such close quarters—the flat only had two bedrooms, so all three men were bunked in one room—and with no real purpose except spending their days poring over every bit of Intel and research they could find on Morrison, a.k.a. Spider, they'd taken to busting each other's balls more frequently than usual.

Case in point...

"What happened to my bagel?" Ace demanded after opening the toaster oven and peering inside.

Christian glanced at the remains on his plate and grinned.

Ace spied the half-eaten bagel. "You shit-swizzling breakfast stealer!" He had a rare talent for coming up with imaginative insults. "I had that toasted perfectly!"

Christian picked up the bagel, studied it from all sides, then took a considering bite. "Indeed it was," he said around a mouthful. "Thank you."

"I should rip off your dick, shove it down your throat, and feed you your own ball sac for dessert. But rumor has it, you sport a microwang, and I don't want to strain my eyes trying to find it."

Aw, yes. The attack on the size of a man's meat. Classic.

Dagan jumped into the fray, happy for the distraction. Anything to take his mind off Chelsea. "You going to let him dis your doodle like that, Christian?"

"This rumor is easy to refute." Christian stood and reached for the top button of his jeans.

"I'll thank you to keep your man stick to yourself." Emily Scott sauntered in from the living room.

Whoops. Dagan had forgotten to mention *her* as part of the team that had come to provide support for Chelsea. Although for the life of him, he couldn't understand how. Emily, the former secretary to an FAS—a foreign area specialist inside the Central Intelligence Agency—and current BKI office manager, was the one who had kept the refrigerator stocked these last few weeks in London and the one who twisted their ears when the laundry piled up. Without her and her mother hen ways, they'd likely be living on pork and beans and wearing three-day-old underwear.

"Hand to God, I'd rather have my right eye gouged out with a toothpick than see Christian's dick," she continued, projecting a toughness that he knew covered a soft, gooey center. Emily *cared* about all of them. She just didn't like to show it. "There's enough testosterone floating around this place without the addition of naked wagging wangs."

"Once again," Christian said, "let me point out that you didn't *have* to come with us. No one twisted your arm." His hoity-toity English accent made it sound like *yoor ahm*.

"And leave poor Chelsea to fend for herself among you three animals?" Emily snorted. "Not likely."

And great. Dagan had enjoyed a brief reprieve, but one mention of Chelsea and his brain was firmly fixed on her. He *hated* that she was alone in that big penthouse with Roper fuckin' Morrison. He hated worse that he couldn't come up with a better plan to prove Morrison was Spider so that she wouldn't *have* to be alone in that big penthouse with Roper fuckin' Morrison.

"And speaking of Chelsea…" Emily continued. When she turned to Dagan, she rocked the eye daggers of doom. "I really wish you would refrain from giving her grief every morning. The poor innocent woman has enough on her plate without you piling it on."

Innocent? There was a word. When it came to Chelsea, Dagan's thoughts didn't live in the same zip code as innocent.

"All that shit on her plate is precisely the point," he insisted. "She's not—"

"Qualified or trained to do this kind of work. Blah, blah, blah. But news flash: she's doing a bitching job regardless. And instead of sending her off every morning feeling like a can full of squashed assholes, maybe you could try sending her off feeling like she can conquer the damned world. Step up your game or keep showing up as lame, man. Jeez."

"And how would you suggest I make her feel like she can conquer the damned world?" He took a sip of the tea Ace passed him. The Earl Grey wouldn't do a thing to soothe his nerves, but it *would* soothe the roiling in his stomach at the thought that his words to Chelsea, meant to be cautionary and to express his concern, were instead making her feel bad about herself. *Shit*.

"A dozen body-shaking orgasms should do it," Emily said.

Dagan choked on his tea. "*Excuse* me?"

"It's as obvious as the nose on your face."

"What is?"

"That you're hot to trot for our resident undercover CIA liaison."

Was it just him, or had someone cranked the heater up about twenty degrees? "How do you figure that?"

"Oh, I don't know." Emily rolled her eyes. "Maybe because if it were possible to impregnate someone with a look, Chelsea would be carrying around octuplets?"

"I don't know what you're talking about." That's what he said. What he thought was *fuuuuuuck*.

"Oh, for the love of Shoeless Joe Jackson." As a born-and-raised Chicago South Sider, Emily's White Sox fangirl was never far from the surface. "You're so full of manure that if you laid in the dirt, you'd start growing little versions of yourself. How you're always sniping at her? That's your inner six-year-old's way of getting her attention."

Emily knew about his inner six-year-old? Double *fuuuuuuck*.

"And here's an idea," she continued. "Instead of walking around like a boy in a man suit, how about just manning up and telling her how you really feel?"

When Dagan got good and pissed, or when he was homed in on a target, he went completely still. *Spooky* still, some had said. And following that stillness was always some sort of explosion. "Are you calling me a coward?" he asked quietly.

"I'm not calling you a coward. I'm calling you a fool and a man suffering from unappeased lust. They are often the same thing."

"So by your logic, verbally sparring with Chelsea is just a cover for me wanting a little push-push-in-the-bush, huh?"

She wrinkled her nose. "Well, I wouldn't have described it *that* way, exactly. But, yes."

He had her. Target locked. Time to let the lead fly. "That must mean you're aching to knock boots with Christian then, right? I mean, you chew his ass every chance you get."

"Uh…" All the color drained from Emily's face, and for a beat or two, silence reigned in the kitchen.

It was Ace who broke the tension. "I swear." He shook his head. "I start my days in a good mood. But within ten minutes of being around all you heteros, I have a serious desire to kill someone."

Emily ignored him, glaring at Dagan. "S-stop trying to change the subject."

"I'm not trying to change the subject." That was a lie. "I'm just pointing out that your accusing me of fighting with Chelsea to cover up the fact that I want to sleep with her is a little like the pot calling the kettle black."

Now Emily's cheeks were fire-engine red. "For the record"—she stole a quick look at Christian—"I fight with Christian because *someone* has to. It's the only way to keep his ego in check."

Christian's eyebrows slammed into a scowl. "Bloody hell. How did this get turned on me?"

Before anyone could answer, their phones came to life. The combined sounds had Dagan's spine going ramrod straight. Pulling his cell from his hip pocket, he thumbed on the screen. They had received a group text message from Chelsea, and a dizzying mess of emotions tumbled through him when he read her two simple words: *I'm in.*

Chapter 2

I'M IN! I'M IN! TAKE THAT, DAGAN ZOELNER!

Chelsea slid her cell phone into her pocket after sending the text and glanced around before pushing the door to Morrison's office wider. At this time of the morning, the only staff members in Morrison's fancy-schmancy Mayfair penthouse were her and Juanita Gonzalez, Morrison's chef. But Chelsea still felt as if a thousand eyes were peering at her. When the door hinges creaked, she winced.

Toeing out of her kitten heels, she slipped into Morrison's office. She'd only caught a few glimpses of the room over the past month, but they had been enough to familiarize herself with the layout. His large mahogany desk—and the laptop that was her ultimate target—were over by the west wall. Too bad that in order to get there, she'd have to pass a passed-out Morrison.

The clang of her heart in her chest was so loud, she was surprised the sound didn't wake the sleeping man as she tiptoed across the room. She missed her shoes quite desperately. The hard marble tiles were cold enough to freeze the tits off a frog—one of her father's favorite Southern-fried sayings, God rest his soul. And the frostiness seemed to slip through the soles of her feet and up into her body, turning her lungs into two blocks of ice.

Was Dagan right? Was she really *not* cut out for this kind of work? The fact that the room was spinning seemed to point to *yes*. Of course, not being able to breathe probably had something to do with her stupid frozen lungs. *Damnit!*

Tugging on the collar of her blouse, she forced herself to suck in a ragged breath. The air felt hard and sharp, but it was enough to crack the sheet of ice in her chest and make the room stop doing its best impression of a merry-go-round.

Better. She nodded to herself with satisfaction and crept farther into the room. When she passed the red leather sofa, she glanced down at the old man. He was still wearing the tuxedo he had changed into before she left yesterday. The smell of bourbon and cigars wafted up from him in a cloud so thick, she thought if she squinted she might be able to see it.

Apparently, the fund-raiser he'd gone to had turned into quite a party. Then again, everything Morrison was involved in eventually turned into a party. He acted like he was twenty-one, not seventy-one.

Lordy, he even had a mun—that would be a *man bun* for the untrendy—like he was a hipster or some shit. Which, at his age, was pathetic enough. But the mun was made worse by the fact that his thinning white hair meant the little knot at the back of his head was no bigger than a cherry tomato.

Chelsea could *not* understand how his stylist let him out into the world looking like that. Then again, when you were a multibillionaire media mogul and a secret underworld crime boss, you did what you wanted and damn the naysayers.

And everyone else, come to think of it.

She took comfort in knowing that once she used the thumb drive sewn into the lining of her blazer to upload the virus, Morrison wouldn't be damning anyone anymore. His "party boy" persona was just a ruse to cover up the true depths of his depravity. She was certain of this because sometimes, when he thought she wasn't looking, she saw his lips thin, his eyes narrow, and an ugly look of malice would slide over his face. At those times, she felt she was seeing the *true* man. *Spider*…

Morrison's mouth slid open, and out came a mighty snore that reminded her of her father's ol' bluetick coonhound—who'd had the uninspired name of Blue and was now buried beneath the willow in the backyard of her childhood home—and how the dog used to fall asleep on the front porch, snoring loud enough to wake up half the county. Only ol' Blue had been a good boy. Roper Morrison on the other hand…

The thought hastened her journey across the room. After reaching her destination, she slid a hand inside her blazer and tugged a loose string in the lining. The thread unraveled, revealing the pouch that held the thumb drive.

If she'd thought her heart was racing before, now the damned thing was trying to break the land speed record. Every muscle in her body clenched, and her teeth threatened to explode beneath the pressure of her jaw. Closing her eyes and counting to three, she forced herself to relax and inserted the thumb drive into the USB port on the side of Morrison's laptop.

Done!

Now, all that was left to do was wait. Wait as the program on the drive automatically booted up Morrison's computer. Wait as it went through the algorithms necessary to break through the password. Wait as the virus began to upload. Just wait, wait, wwwwwait.

She hadn't realized she'd curled her hands into tight fists until one of her nails pierced the skin of her palm. Sucking the sting away, she thought of Dagan. No doubt about it, he *never* got this nervous. He was Mr. Calm-Cool-and-Collected. And if he could see her now, he'd shake his head and say, *I told you so.*

Well, he could take his I-told-you-so's and shove them where the sun never shined. John Wayne supposedly said once that true courage was being scared to death and saddling up anyway.

So…giddyup.

She glanced over at Morrison, happy to see him still out cold and sawing logs. Then a flash on the screen drew her attention to the computer. The virus was in, and the laptop powered down.

It's done!

A ragged breath leaked out of her, and she gave herself a second to fully appreciate the magnitude of what she'd accomplished. Then she quickly unplugged the drive, slipped it back into its hidey-hole inside her blazer, and pulled her cell phone from her pocket. She texted two words to the group at the flat: ***Virus loaded.*** She thought about adding *booyah,* but ultimately decided against it.

Her teammates would make sure to pass her text on to the Black Knights in Chicago, then they would pack their belongings for a fast retreat across the pond.

I did it! I really did it! Chelsea Duvall, master spy! She liked the sound of that. *Now, to get the heck out of Dodge…*

She was halfway across the room when Morrison called her name. Her spine snapped to attention one vertebra at a time. Slowly turning to him, she ignored the ice water running through her veins and donned a pleasant smile. "I, uh, I hope you don't mind, sir." She adjusted her glasses. "I just came in to check on you. That must have been one heck of a party last night, huh?"

"Come here, Chelsea." He beckoned her with a flick of his bony fingers.

Despite every instinct telling her to run, she continued to play the part of the dutiful and long-suffering PA. Walking to the edge of the sofa, she gritted her teeth when Morrison's hot, clammy hand curled around her bare calf.

She *knew* she should have worn slacks today instead of the pencil skirt that ended just below her knees. "Can I get something for you, sir? Some aspirin? A glass of water, maybe?"

"A little fur from the cat that scratched me." His voice sounded rusty, but he grinned up at her, waggling his eyebrows. She was convinced the hair on his head had migrated south. His brows were thick and bushy and seemed to march across his forehead like two gray caterpillars. "There's a bottle of bourbon in my top drawer. Fetch it for me, would you, darling?"

She smiled down at him, despite her clenched jaw. When Christian said *dahling* in his English accent it was downright swoon-worthy. When Morrison said it? Yup. She had to fight the urge to retch.

"Of course," she told him, happy for any excuse to escape his marauding hand. His fingers had slowly inched up her leg until they were behind her knee, caressing softly.

Gag a maggot.

Roper Morrison was the lowest, most vulgar man the good Lord ever strung a gut through, and as she hustled over to his desk, Chelsea thought she could still feel his hot, sweaty fingers on her skin. However, a quick glance at his laptop reminded her that all the indignities she'd suffered in his employ were worth it. She'd planted the virus, and Morrison…er…*Spider* was going down. *Booyah!*

On second thought, she *should* have added that to her text message. Who cared if it would have made Dagan point and say, *See? What kind of trained field agent texts something like that?*

Her. That's who. The impulse to shoot a fist in the air and indulge in a hip shake was strong. Instead, she satisfied herself with grabbing the bourbon. Her eyes caught on the myriad cheap phones in the drawer. *Burner* phones. If she didn't already know that Morrison was a slimy, criminal piece of dog shit, that would have been enough to convince her. He probably had a different phone for every awful venture he was involved in.

Shutting the drawer, she walked back to the sofa and handed him the bottle. The old man reclined against the leather cushions like some sort of over-pampered sultan.

Which makes me what? One of his harem girls? She'd sooner swallow a bag full of rusty nails, thank you very much.

"You really should eat or drink something to restore your electrolytes, sir." One thing she'd learned was that Morrison liked to be fussed over.

Fussing was an easy enough thing to fake. All she had to do was ask herself, *WWMD? What would Mom do?* Because her mother, bless her sweet soul, was the queen of doting and fussing.

Morrison waved her off, then twisted the cap on the bottle of booze.

"I'm going to run and fetch something for you anyway," she lied.

Turning on her heel, she padded out of his office, stopping to toe into her shoes before making her way through the massive penthouse toward the front door. The opulence of the place still got to her. Vintage

Limoges vases, gold-leaf detailing on picture frames, the Picasso painting hanging on the dining room wall… Just a few of those pieces sold on the black market would net her a sum bigger than the debts that had made her backstory so believable.

Her daddy would have said that Morrison was shittin' in high cotton. *She* said he had more money than any one man should. And oooh, the temptation to grab a few pieces of wealth on her way out was strong. But she was no thief. And besides, the twenty G's Morrison had already paid her for her first month's work would go a long way toward reducing her remaining student loans. Once those were paid off, she would use *every* extra cent she made to pay off the mortgages. And then… *then* she would finally be able to rest easy, knowing her parents' house had been saved, knowing their *home* had been saved.

She made a left at the half bath with its antique marble pedestal sink and passed the kitchen where Juanita was busy making Morrison's breakfast. "Bye, Juanita!" she called cheerily. "I'm off to run some errands for Mr. Morrison!"

Juanita absently waved her hand, and Chelsea felt a little kick of excitement. She was almost home free. She'd done it! She'd really done it!

Scurrying across the foyer, she pulled her favorite trench coat from the hall tree. Her hand was on the knob of the front door when it turned inside her grip.

Steven Surry, Morrison's head of security, burst in so quickly, she stumbled back, dropping her coat. He caught her arm before she could ass-plant, and the expression he wore was the facial equivalent of a thunderstorm. Every hair on her body lifted in warning of a potential lightning strike.

"Where the bloody hell do you think you're off to, huh?" he demanded.

"I…" Chelsea's throat was as dry as the fruitcake her father had always made for Christmas. She had to swallow to gather enough spit to try again. "I was going to run some errands, and—"

"What errands would those be?" he cut her off, cocking his head and eyeing her suspiciously.

"M-Mr. Morrison is nursing a hangover. I'm going to buy him some coconut water. It's packed with electrolytes and—"

Surry held up a hand and she gulped. *Audibly.* When he heard the noise, his gaze narrowed further. Steven Surry had eyes as dark as the pits of hell and ebony hair that seemed to absorb all light. In another life, one where he wasn't working for Morrison, Chelsea might have considered him handsome.

"You're not going anywhere." Since he still held her arm in a hard grip, it was easy for him to spin her around. With a not-so-gentle nudge, he herded her back through the entryway.

She considered making a break for it. Maybe if she darted around him, she could get out the door. But then what? Wait patiently in the hall while the elevator arrived?

Sure. That'll work out wonderfully well.

Her other option was the emergency stairwell. But as soon as she ran, Surry would *know* she was up to something and he would immediately give chase. She harbored no fantasies that she could outmaneuver Surry—who looked like an NFL running back—down twenty flights of stairs.

Nope. Better to retain my cover and wait to see what's happening.

She didn't have long to wait. "We've had a security breach, and you're staying with me until I determine whether or not you're involved," he grumbled.

Security breach…

Those two words made her gulp again. Surry pulled her to a stop, pinning her with a stony-eyed stare.

Okay, so now she was starting to come around to Dagan's way of thinking. She really *wasn't* cut out for this shit. The fact that she was giving herself away left, right, and center was proof positive.

She had just enough time to reach into the pocket of her blazer and press the volume-up button on her cell for a three-second count before Surry grabbed her hand and extracted her phone. He looked down at the black screen. "What are you up to with this, huh?"

"Nothing," she lied, her heart pinwheeling inside her chest. The stupid organ banged into her stomach, making her nauseous. "I was just putting my hands in my pockets."

And hoping I held down that button long enough to activate the distress call.

Ozzie, BKI's techno-geek extraordinaire, had programmed all of their cell phones with an emergency feature. If they held down the volume-up button for a one-Mississippi, two-Mississippi, three-Mississippi count, their phones would automatically text a Mayday to the rest of the group. Then the cell would send out its GPS location. Pretty brilliant. Chelsea only hoped she'd used it correctly.

"We'll see about that." Surry pocketed her phone before grabbing her arms and tugging her wrists behind her back.

"Hey! What the heckfire do you think you're doing?" She hoped to cover her terror with bravado, and she was insanely grateful that she'd learned early on in her CIA training to wipe the call and message log on her phone after every call or text, and to make sure to keep her contacts encrypted. "Take your damned hands off me!"

"Please," Surry scoffed. "After a month with Morrison, no doubt you're accustomed to a bit of man-handling. I'll apologize for any ill treatment later. Once I know you're innocent."

She'd be waiting the rest of her life for that apology.

Oh, holy friggin' crap. She should have bolted when she had the chance. Maybe, just maybe, she could have beaten Surry on those stairs. A smart operator might have taken the chance. A *brave* one certainly would have. But here she was, marching past the kitchen and toward the scene of the crime, all without lifting so much as a pinkie to fight her way free.

She really *wasn't* cut out for this. She hated proving Dagan right.

Dagan…

Just the thought of him gave her hope. Because if anyone could get her out of this mess, it was him.

Chapter 3

DAGAN HAD LIVED IN FEAR OF THE DAY CHELSEA FOUND herself in an ungodly mess. And now that day had come. Good thing he was just the man to get her out of it.

"We going in or what?" Ace asked from his hiding spot in the alley next to a stack of crates. "I mean, I can continue to do my best impression of the Little Match Girl, but my feet are going numb."

"Wait for it," Dagan whispered. He was crouched beside a dumpster behind Morrison's condominium building. The air was ripe with the smells of garbage and damp concrete. Little puddles left by the recent rain shower reflected their strained faces and the steel-gray sky overhead.

No joke. March in London was dreary as hell. Even if the day was unseasonably warm at a little over sixty degrees Fahrenheit, Dagan couldn't wait to grab Chelsea and hop the first plane home. Not that Chicago in late March was anything to cheer about. Far from it. Winter tended to hang on until well into April. And the ice and snow—to mention nothing of the damned wind—were enough to slice a man to his bones. But at least there the sun peeked out occasionally.

"Wait for what, pray tell?" Christian hissed from beside him. "Why are we messing about here? Every second counts, yeah?"

Dagan gusted out a martyr's sigh. "For fuck's sake. *Yes*." Every second that had passed since they received Chelsea's Mayday had felt like an eternity. "But going in half-cocked could screw our chances of pulling this off without a hitch. Considering it's Chelsea's neck on the line"—her smooth, decidedly lickable neck—"I'd like to avoid hitches at all costs."

Ace grinned over at him. "You really *do* have a soft spot for her, don't you?"

No. What he had for Chelsea was a heart-on. It was like a hard-on but with feelings and shit. "Believe me, when I think about Chels, *nothing* is soft." He figured he might as well admit it. After this morning's ass-chewing from Emily, it wasn't like there was any use denying it.

"I *knew* it," Ace whispered to Christian, turning his hand palm up. "Pay up."

"I left my wallet back at the flat," Christian said.

"Likely excuse," Ace told him before turning back to Dagan. "But seriously, why aren't we marching up to that door and hot-wiring the security pad?"

"We're waiting for the maintenance man," Dagan whispered, trying not to let it get to him that his friends had been making bets on…what? His love life? Or his decided lack of anything resembling a love life? "He always comes out for a smoke break at this time."

Ace skewered Dagan with a narrow-eyed stare. "And you would know that…*how*?"

Busted. "All those times I said I was going to the gym or the library or the park?"

"Don't tell me." Ace raised a hand. "You were here, surveilling the building."

"And Morrison's downtown offices, too," Dagan conceded. As they say, in for a penny, in for a pound.

"I thought we agreed surveillance might draw unwanted attention to Chelsea. You know, odd if suddenly there were men skulking about right when she started her employment."

"We agreed not to do any *group* surveillance. But I never said I wouldn't go out on my own and—"

"Never mind." Ace waved him off. "You're sweet on her, which makes you paranoid and overprotective and apparently a liar-liar-pants-on-fire."

Dagan *did* feel bad to have misled them. But if he'd admitted what he was up to every day, they would have tried to stop him. And he *could not* have allowed that. He had needed to know everything he could about the places Chelsea spent her days. It was the only thing that had kept him sane.

"We'll kick your ass later," Ace promised. "Right now, I want to know what happens *after* the maintenance man comes out for a smoke. What's the plan?"

"We tranq him. We take his key fob. And we enter the building without hot-wiring the security pad and potentially setting off an alarm. The building is rigged with security cameras, but if we take them out as we pass, we should be able to get in and out without anyone the wiser."

"Bob's your uncle," Christian said, which Dagan had learned was the British equivalent of *there you go* or *sounds good*.

Dagan pulled the wrist of his black jacket back to glance at his watch. "Any second now, the maintenance man should—" That's as far as he got. Right on cue, the guy in question pushed through the back door, fresh cig dangling from his lips.

Dagan pulled on his ski mask and, from the corner of his eye, saw his brothers-in-arms do the same. Quietly sliding the dart gun from the holster on his hip, he took aim. The world around him slipped into a fog. The only thing he could see or hear was his target.

The little pistol was loaded with six rounds of

thiopental. The stuff wasn't lethal. At least not in the
dosages they used. But it could put a grown man down
in about three seconds flat. Trouble was, it generally
only kept him down for somewhere between ten and
fifteen minutes. After that, the victim would be groggy
and nauseous, but nonetheless functional. Which meant
after they tranqed the guy, they needed to get in and out
in short order.

Blowing out a breath, Dagan squeezed the trigger.
The dart left the barrel with a muffled-sounding *thwack*
and flew true. It embedded itself in the meaty part of the
maintenance man's shoulder.

The guy yelped, dropping his lighter as the unlit cigarette fell from his mouth and landed in a rain puddle. He
ripped the little dart with its fuzzy yellow tail from his
arm. "What the feck is—"

That's all he managed before his knees went weak
and he stumbled.

Shit. Maintenance Man was going to go down like a
sack of potatoes, and Dagan could just see him whacking his balding head on one of the two steps leading
from the back door to the alley. If he did that, *nighty-
night* could very easily turn into the *big sleep*.

Dagan holstered the dart gun and charged from
behind the dumpster. Half a dozen bounding steps
allowed him to catch the guy before he could go timber.
Dagan grunted. The dude wasn't a lightweight. But
Dagan managed to gently lower the unconscious man to
the ground, careful to keep him out of the cold puddles.

"Holy guacamole. That's some fast-acting shiznit,"
Ace said. He and Christian gathered around Dagan to
stare down at the man. "Next time, *I* want to shoot it."
Ace reached for the weapon on Dagan's hip.

"Hands off." Dagan slapped him away. "I'm the one

who thought to pack the dart gun for this mission, which means *I'm* the one who gets to use it."

"Stingy," Ace huffed.

Some people might think it strange to be joking at a time like this, but when you lived like they did, always on the edge, you learned never to lose your sense of humor. Because if you did, you might never find it again.

"Right, then," Christian said. "Let's go get Chelsea."

Chelsea...

Her name alone was enough to kick-start Dagan's heart.

After snatching the key fob from the retractable bungee cord clipped to the front pocket of the maintenance man's coveralls, Dagan tapped it against the security pad. A loud *buzz* was followed by a soft *click* as the door unlocked.

"Ready?" He glanced over his shoulder.

"Let's do this thing and blow this bloody island," Christian grumbled. Given what had happened to Christian before he left the SAS, Dagan couldn't blame the guy for having no love for the country of his birth.

"Yes. Let's go get our girl," Ace added.

Our girl...

Dagan figured that was as good a description of Chelsea as anything. With her clever mind, sharp tongue, and soft heart, she had become a favorite of the Black Knights. But if he was honest with himself, he knew he would like to exchange the word *our* for *my*.

"My girl..." That old song by the Temptations spun through his head, giving him an earworm as they pushed into the building. A long hall stretched in front of them. "There!" he hissed, pointing to the camera mounted in the corner of the ceiling at the end of the hallway. Its red light was a beacon in the gloom of the corridor.

Ace aimed a laser pointer at the lens of the camera, overloading its light-sensitive chip. Funny, people thought security cameras provided just that...*security*. But disabling them was cheaper and easier than getting a hand job from a masseuse at one of Bangkok's famous rub-n-tugs.

In a matter of seconds, they were piled into the staff elevator. Every *ding* of the passing floors going up all twenty stories corresponded with a dozen beats of Dagan's heart.

Come on. Come on.

It had taken fifteen minutes from the time they received Chelsea's Mayday to the time they got to Morrison's condominium building—five minutes gearing up and five minutes getting there. Another five minutes had been wasted waiting on the maintenance man to appear. And now more seconds ticked by as the elevator made its maddeningly slow journey toward the top floor.

A red haze crept into Dagan's vision. If Morrison or one of his goons had dared to lay a finger on Chels, so help the assface.

The elevator announced their arrival at the penthouse with a cheerily discordant *bing-bong!* But it took a couple of seconds longer—seconds during which Dagan bit his tongue to keep from screaming his impatience— before the silver doors slid open.

The three of them were out of the claustrophobic little box in a flash, creeping along the wall toward Morrison's front door. Once again, Ace made quick work of the surveillance cameras at each end of the hall by hitting them with the laser light. It took Christian only slightly longer to pick the lock. Then...

We're in!

The CIA had trained Dagan to control the speed of his pulse. But when it came to Chelsea, the usual tricks didn't work. His heart slammed against his rib cage like his little brother had slammed his shoulder against the locked passenger door of Dagan's truck the morning Dagan had forcefully admitted him to rehab. The memory of Avan that dreadful day was as unwelcome as it was crystal clear, and the only way Dagan could ignore it was to concentrate on the sound of his own blood thudding in his ears.

He led the silent charge into the penthouse, the dart gun up and at the ready. They weren't alone in the space. He picked up on that right away. Not because he could hear anything over the soft hum of electricity and his own racing pulse, but because the hair twanged on the back of his neck and his palms prickled.

Thanks to the software Ozzie had installed on their phones, they could easily see that Chelsea's iPhone was still inside the building. Of course, that didn't mean *Chelsea* was. It could be anyone making Dagan's instincts sit up and bark. A maid. A secretary. One of Morrison's many girls-of-the-month.

The possibility that Chelsea might have been removed to another location while her cell phone remained in residence was enough to have Dagan's stomach threatening a revolt. And since there was nothing stealthy about blowing chunks, he pushed the possibility aside. Then his toe caught on something. When he glanced down, he saw it was Chelsea's favorite trench coat, and he was suddenly thrown back in time, his mind ripped to a place of dust and danger and blood.

"Sonofa—" Dagan didn't finish the curse as he pulled his car to the side of the road, putting it in park

and glancing toward the café where the meeting was supposed to occur. All the players were in place, seated at tables on the gritty sidewalk.

All the players except him. He was late, thanks to having gotten stuck behind a vegetable merchant twenty blocks back. The man's horse-drawn wagon had tipped over, sending produce tumbling all over the street. An entire crowd had rushed to help the merchant right his cart and reload his cargo, effectively stopping traffic in all directions and keeping Dagan hemmed in for a full fifteen minutes.

Kabul was strange that way. On the one hand, it was a throwback to a gentler time. A time when people used animals for transportation and didn't hesitate to jump in and help each other out of a jam. On the other hand, it was the harshest place Dagan had ever known, filled with flinty-eyed zealots who didn't hesitate to "honor" kill their women for any perceived slight, or slit the throats of those they considered infidels.

Dagan had been in the country for four years, and if he hadn't needed to return home to help his little brother, he imagined he would have remained for at least a few more. He spoke the language, knew the customs, and had a nice network of assets who supplied him with Intel. But his brother came before flag and country. Since their parents had died—their mother of breast cancer and their father three years later of an aneurysm—Avan was all the family Dagan had left. Which brought him here, to this moment, handing off one of his assets, Abdul Waleed, to Agent Innes McShane, a black-bearded Boston boy with big shoulders and an even bigger smile.

McShane and Waleed looked uncomfortable sitting at the little iron table, neither truly trusting the other without Dagan there to act as a bridge between them. Agent Terrence Walker was a few tables over, pretending to read a newspaper, but actually keeping an eye on McShane and Waleed. In a chair pushed up against the wall of the cafe sat Jordy Moore, another agent on hand for the encounter. The CIA did nothing by half-measures. Even the simple passing off of an asset from one handler to another required backup and more backup, and both men were dressed in the local style, blending in seamlessly with the population.

When Moore took a sip of chai, a popular drink among the denizens of Kabul, and then blatantly looked at his watch, Dagan hastened his step. He had gone no more than half a dozen paces when Waleed suddenly reached beneath the front of his perahan tunban, *the wide, knee-length billowy shirt worn by so many men in Afghanistan's capital city. The move struck Dagan as odd.*

Then Waleed pushed to a stand, raised his face to the sun that turned the dust in the air to shiny specks of fairy powder, and yelled, "God is the greatest!" in Pashto.

"No, Abdul!" Dagan bellowed just as he was blinded by a flash of bright, white light and deafened by the roar of the bomb Waleed had strapped to his chest.

The percussive effects of the explosion knocked Dagan back two steps, but he remained on his feet. For a moment he was too stunned to do anything but stand in the middle of the street, blinking against the smoke and chaos around him, the screaming that seemed miles away, and the flurry of people that scattered and ran in all different directions. Then, reality set in and he sprinted to the smoldering ruin that was once the café, trying to find anything familiar, anyone familiar.

There was nothing but smoke and destruction and the smell of melted flesh.

The toe of his boot bumped something, and when he looked down, he saw it was McShane's baby-blue perahan tunban. *The shirt was deep crimson in spots and completely missing Agent McShane.*

Dagan leaned down, and the closer inspection revealed his mistake. The shirt wasn't *missing McShane. It was simply that McShane had been beheaded and dismembered by the blast. His bloody torso was still intact inside the shirt and Dagan felt as if his own chest had been ripped open, exposing his heart to the hot, dusty air. Bile burned the back of his throat like sulfuric acid. As he retched dryly, the only thing he could think was...* why?

A nudge on his shoulder yanked him back into the present. He turned to see Christian squinting at him, his ski mask obscuring what Dagan knew was a fierce frown.

Shit. He hated the flashbacks. They always came unexpectedly and at the worst possible times.

Waving a dismissive hand, even though he would swear the smell of charred flesh stung his nose, he stepped over Chelsea's coat. He could feel Ace and Christian on his heels, weapons drawn, and took comfort in the fact that his teammates were packing something more than little darts filled with thiopental. If whoever was inside the place wanted to get unfriendly, lead was far more likely to change their mind than a little tranquilizer.

The banging of a pot told them the room directly in front of them was the kitchen. And it was occupied.

Dagan jerked his chin. That was all the communication needed. After running countless ops together, they could pretty much read one another's minds.

Christian slunk around the corner, a soundless black

FUEL FOR FIRE   37

shadow. He grabbed the woman loading the dishwasher,
slapped a hand over her mouth, and spun her around.
A heartbeat later, Dagan squeezed his trigger. The dart
lodged in the woman's thigh, and the drug took effect
almost immediately. Her wide, dark eyes fluttered, and
Christian softly lowered her to the tiles. After straightening, he jerked his masked chin toward the back of the
penthouse, a wordless *Done. Let's get a move on*.

Dagan spared the unconscious woman a brief glance,
but it was enough to show him she had one of those
Bodies by Mattel. As in, she was more Barbie doll plastic than flesh and blood.

Morrison certainly had a type. But while the cook's
physique came courtesy of a good plastic surgeon,
Chelsea's curves were given to her by the Maker himself.

The memory of the time Dagan had accidentally
walked in on Chelsea in the bathroom when she'd been
wearing nothing but her bra and panties flitted through
his brain. No, really, he *hadn't* done it on purpose. But
accident or not, the fact remained that the sight of her
smooth, round ass and amazing tits encased in black
satin was permanently affixed to the backs of his eyes.
Hence all that arm-and-hand cardio he'd been doing in
the shower for the past few months.

A sound came from down the hall. It hit him like a
wrecking ball, and rage surged inside him.

On the one hand, he was grateful Chelsea was still
inside the penthouse. On the other hand, he was going
to kill whichever fuckhead had just made her cry out
in pain.

Chapter 4

*WELL, THIS IS ABOUT AS MUCH FUN AS A DADGUMMED THORNY
dildo,* Chelsea thought, wincing when Steven Surry
grabbed her jaw in a merciless grip and dug his fingers
into the hollows of her cheeks.

"Tell us who you work for, cunt!" he demanded
for what seemed like the millionth time. He held up
the thumb drive he had found after marching her into
Morrison's office and giving her a thorough pat-down.
"Tell us what you're trying to find!"

At first, Morrison had sputtered and demanded that
Surry release her, playing the good boss even though
Chelsea was certain she'd seen him eagerly lick his lips
while watching Surry shove his fingers into her every
nook and cranny. But the minute Surry pulled the drive
from her blazer—and especially after Surry had tried
to search her phone and found it encrypted out the
wazoo—Morrison's face had changed. Now, it was beet
red with barely suppressed fury, and the gleam in his
eye reminded her that he was far more than a lewd old
billionaire. He was…*Spider*.

"Tell us!" Surry demanded again, giving her head a
hard shake. Her brain banged around inside her skull,
making her see stars. Since she was tied with a length of
electrical cord to one of the chairs in front of Morrison's
desk, her hands duct-taped behind her back, there was
little she could do to defend herself.

Then again, she still had her smart mouth. "Screw
you, buddy," she snarled. Those three words were all

she allowed herself before she clenched her teeth and sealed her lips shut.

The violence that clouded Surry's face and glinted in his hell-black eyes made her want to curl into a protective ball. He leaned down so that his nose was an inch from hers. His hot breath smelled of coffee and buttered croissants, and the thought of him actually *eating* struck her as weird. She had assumed he sustained himself by devouring the souls of Morrison's enemies.

"You will bloody well tell us what we want to know, Miss Duvall." When he spoke all low and menacing in that thick English accent, she got the unsettling feeling that something dark moved in the shadows just out of sight. "Or I will jab this letter opener into your carotid." He pulled back to wield the weapon he had taken from Morrison's desktop. The sterling-silver letter opener glinted in the golden glow cast by the overhead chandelier.

Releasing her face, Surry cocked his head. "So, what shall it be? The truth? Or the knife? The choice is yours." There was an emptiness in his voice when he asked the questions. Like he didn't really care what the answers would be. Like he was tired or bored or maybe…resigned?

Oh, that doesn't bode well.

Of course, the truth was out of the question. She would never rat on the Black Knights. No telling what Morrison, a.k.a Spider, with all his power and connections, could do with that information. So that left… the knife.

But there's still so much I want to do!

She had never learned to make her mother's she-crab soup. She had never tried her hand at writing fiction like that of Tolkien or Rowling or Martin. She had never married the love of her life and given him two bouncing, chubby-cheeked babies.

A cold finger of terror dragged up her spine, and for a second she considered spilling her guts and saving her hide. But then, from somewhere deep inside, a well of strength erupted, filling her with determination and the will to do what must be done.

Her mind briefly touched on her mother, and a great sadness weighed down her heart. Grace Duvall would be devastated by the death of her only child. But Chelsea took comfort—cold comfort, but comfort all the same—in knowing that her life insurance policy would be enough to pay her mother's debts. That was something. Something to hold on to.

"Well?" Surry demanded. "What will it be?"

Chelsea licked her lips. Fear was a living thing inside her, crawling through her chest like a centipede on prickly legs. She shoved it aside and sealed her own fate. "Do your worst, you sorry, low-life sonofagun!"

Surry's beard-stubbled chin jerked back as if he couldn't believe the choice she'd made. Then his eyes narrowed, and grim determination transformed his face.

Closing her eyes, Chelsea waited on the inevitable. That centipede was going crazy inside her, making her chest ache and raising the hair on her head. She braced herself for the deathblow as a million regrets, a million joys, a million memories flitted through her brain.

Funny how many of those regrets and joys and memories feature Dagan.

She held her breath, savoring it, knowing it was her last and—

"Drop. The. Knife."

With a cry, she blinked open her eyes and craned her head around to see three figures dressed from head to toe in black. Each of them wielded a weapon as if it were an extension of himself.

The Black Knights…

Even had Dagan not spoken the three most beautiful words she'd ever heard in that smooth moonshine voice, she would have known the trio anywhere. There was no mistaking those broad shoulders or those defiant, cocksure stances.

Her eyes homed in on Dagan. He was in the middle and slightly forward of the other two. It wasn't his height or carriage that gave him away. It was his stillness. Ace and Christian seemed to vibrate with barely leashed power. But Dagan was a statue. Not a muscle quivered. Not a tendon or ligament cracked. Chelsea was reminded of a pair of tectonic plates under intense pressure. She knew what came next. The earth would rip open, and hell would spew forth.

Surry must have felt the doom behind Dagan's stillness, because his voice sounded wheezy when he demanded, "And who the fuck are you?"

"Worry less about who we are," Dagan snarled, "and more about what we'll do if you don't drop the knife."

Proving he had more balls than brains, Surry spun Chelsea's chair around and palmed her forehead to wrench her head back. The sharp tip of the letter opener nicked at the skin pulsing over the large vein in her neck. She hadn't had time to scream, and now she didn't dare breathe.

"Ring up the police, sir," Surry said.

From the corner of her eye, Chelsea saw Morrison/ Spider make a move toward the desk.

"Take one step in the direction of that phone, and you'll be eating a bullet for breakfast." There was no mistaking Dagan's words *or* his tone. He meant what he said.

Morrison must have come to the same realization. The old man stopped in his tracks.

"Good man," Dagan acknowledged. "Now, there's one thing you both need to understand. We're leaving here with Chelsea. That can be over your dead bodies or your live ones." Even though his words were calm and his body as motionless as a mountain, rage burned inside him. It was there in his eyes, glowing red like the fires of Mordor. "So what will it be? The choice is yours."

It was the same option Surry had given her, spoken in the same words. How long had the three of them been outside listening?

"You have no bloody idea who you're fucking with," Morrison snarled, his chest heaving with every furious breath. "I have—"

That's all he managed. In a flash, the statue, a.k.a. Dagan Zoelner, came to life. He moved faster than the human eye could follow, certainly faster than Chelsea could track with her head angled back in Surry's grip. One second Dagan was staring at her and Surry, and the next he aimed at Morrison and pulled his trigger.

The gunshot was oddly muffled and Morrison stumbled back, hitting his hip on the edge of the desk. Surry bellowed his outrage and released her head. Free from his brutal grip, she turned to Morrison and understood the strangeness of the weapon's sound.

It wasn't a bullet that had exploded from the end of Dagan's gun. It was a dart. She had just enough time to catch a glimpse of the fuzzy yellow end protruding from the center of Morrison's chest before Dagan fired again. This time the dart whizzed over her head. Surry made an awful gurgling noise. When she pulled her chin back, she saw the projectile sticking from his neck.

He reached for the dart, stumbling into her chair.

His hand hit the back of her head, looking for leverage and forcing her chin into her chest as every vertebra in her neck threatened to crack under the pressure. She couldn't see what happened next. But she heard it. Heard the boots that pounded against the tiles as the Black Knights raced into the room.

Surry released her head when Christian tackled him. From the corner of her eye, she watched Ace catch Morrison right before the old man toppled face-first onto the floor. And Dagan? Well, Dagan knelt in front of her.

She gasped when his big, warm hands cupped her cheeks, gently lifting her head. Her neck ached, but it wasn't broken. All her fingers and toes still worked when she gave them an experimental wiggle.

"Chels... Christ. Are you okay?" His stormy eyes searched her face.

She nodded. That's all she could manage because a giant lump was centered in her throat. She had put on a brave face throughout the entire ordeal, but now that it looked like she was saved, all her shock and terror rose to the surface, crumbling her mask of courage.

"Thank God." He wrapped his arms around her, pulling her close.

It was the first time he had hugged her. The first time she had been in his arms. Oh, how she wanted to hold him tight in return. But with her hands still trapped behind her back, the only thing she could do was turn her face into his warm neck and breathe him in.

She had always loved the way he smelled. A mixture of worn leather, dryer sheets, and shampoo. All clean and healthy and...*male*.

"I was afraid m-maybe I didn't press the button long enough to send out the Mayday," she said in a rush, her lips moving against the rough fabric of his ski mask. "And th-then they found the thumb drive. But they were so quick to stop questioning me and…and…" She had to stop. "Thank you. Thank you for coming for me."

His wide palm cupped the back of her head, holding her close. Was it trembling? "Always, Chels. Never doubt it."

Oh great. Now the lump in her throat had grown to the size of a Carolina pine.

She wanted the moment to last forever, to stay just like this, safe in his arms. But all too soon, he pulled back. "What were you thinking, telling them to do their worst? You were baiting them, egging them on. You stupid, stubborn, self-sacrificing fool."

And just like that, happiness and relief morphed into incredulity that slid quick as a whistle into anger. Seriously? He was going to stand there—er, squat there—and call her names?

He may be hotter than the door handles of hell, but when he gets all Me Tarzan, You Jane, I want to dump his limp body in the River Thames and feed him to the fishes. After she'd killed him with mind-blowing sex and multiple orgasms, of course. And she could probably cop to his last two accusations. She *was* stubborn, and in that instant she *had* been willing to sacrifice herself. But the first one?

"*S-stupid*?" she sputtered. And good news! The lump in her throat had vanished. "Screw *you*, Dagan! In case you've forgotten, I pulled off this op w-with…"

She stumbled to a stop because he'd ripped off his mask. And there it was. The Beard.

Looking at him dressed all in black, shoulders as broad as the Lowcountry, she couldn't help but think he resembled a god. One of the mythical beings she read about in her fantasy novels. Formidable. Powerful. *Gorgeous*.

And here I am, a mere mortal.

The look he pinned on her was one she recognized. She liked to call it his Clint Eastwood gunfighter squint. He tended to whip it out right before he laid into her for something. She braced herself, mentally running through her standard list of comebacks. But he didn't give her a tongue-lashing. At least not a *verbal* one. Instead, he took her face in his hands and sealed his lips to hers.

She was so surprised that her mouth formed a startled *O*. Dagan took advantage, his tongue surging between her teeth. His lips were firm yet amazingly soft, and his beard abraded the tender flesh of her cheeks.

Holy mother! Dagan Zoelner was...*kissing* her!

Oh. My!

Chapter 5

THE INSTANT CHELSEA'S LIPS TOUCHED HIS, DAGAN REALized *she* was the reason he had a mouth. So that he could kiss her. Taste her. Take her sweet, earthy essence inside himself.

"Aw, look at you two." Ace's voice broke the intimacy of the kiss. "You're making my ding-dong and my ping-pongs all tingly. But as the inimitable Short Round in *Indiana Jones and the Temple of Doom* would say, 'No time for love, Dr. Jones!' We need to get out of here before these dickheads wake up. So unlock those lips, untie Chelsea, and let's get on the stick."

Untie Chelsea...

Those two words were hammer strikes at Dagan's head. Jesus H. What was he doing?

Taking advantage of a woman who is handcuffed and hog-tied, that's what.

Nausea swirled low in his belly. With a snarl of disgust, he broke the kiss.

"Check their pockets," he instructed the others, rubbing a hand over his mouth to massage what remained of Chelsea's sweet kiss into his lips. "Find the drive."

"Aye-aye, Captain." Ace snapped him a sarcastic salute, then bent toward the sprawled-out Morrison...or Spider...or whatever the hell the man was called.

Turning back to Chelsea, Dagan didn't dare meet her eyes. Instead, he went to work on the knot in the electrical cord tying her to the chair.

He was such an ass. *Worse* than an ass. He was a cad,

a fiend, a low-life shit-for-brains who had taken advantage of a woman who couldn't give him a well-deserved swift kick to the dick.

"Sonofabitch." He cursed the knot when it refused to budge. He was working directly beneath her breasts. Given how he'd just mouth-raped her, he was doing his best not to come anywhere near either one of her amazing, soft, oh-so-round boobs.

Finally, he managed to grab a loop of electrical cord and pull it free. As he worked, Chelsea's words to Morrison's goon screamed through his overheated brain. She had been so brave, so selfless. And standing outside that door, listening to her willingly sacrifice herself, had made all his feeling for her, feelings he had been refusing to name for years, rise to the surface where they could no longer be denied. Then, when she had gotten all up in his grill, using his name? Not Z, but Dagan? Well, something had broken apart inside him.

I think it's called self-control.

The only thing he had wanted to do was claim all that was her—the incomparable *wonder* of her—for himself.

The knot finally came free, and he helped her stand by palming her shoulders. *Soft.* Chelsea was so infinitely soft. Her softness made him hard.

"Z, I..." she began huskily, then stopped and licked her lips.

For the first time since the Kiss—yes, it deserved to be capitalized—he allowed himself to look into her eyes. Shock and confusion and something more registered on her face.

Please don't let it be pity. He could handle anger. He could even handle disgust. But not pity. Never pity.

"Z," she said again, and he noted with no small

measure of disappointment that she was back to using his nickname. "I—"

"Save it for later, Chels." He skirted around to her back, pulling his tanto folding knife from the case attached to his belt. With a flick, the razor-sharp blade sprang free, and he easily sliced through the duct tape binding her wrists.

She turned to him then. She obviously had more she wanted to say, but she simply frowned, gnawing her plump lower lip.

That sensually innocent move sent a shock wave of lust down his spine. Chelsea had absolutely no idea what she did to him, what she'd *been* doing to him for years now.

"Besides the thumb drive, this is all the wanker had on him," Christian said, nudging Morrison's unconscious head of security with the toe of his boot and holding out a black Android and Chelsea's iPhone.

Dagan knew the latter was Chelsea's phone by the purple waterproof case. The woman was enamored with the color. Half her clothes were some shade of it.

"Am I the only one tempted to hoist this motherfucker over my shoulder, take him with us, and tie him up in some dark, damp place?" Ace asked, looking down at Spider's unconscious body with a lip curl of distaste.

"Not our mission." Dagan shook his head. "Our mission is to find the proof that ties him to his underworld operations and then turn that proof over to the proper authorities. They'll be the ones to tear apart every sorry thing he's built and then light a match and burn the rubble to the ground."

"So for us, it's all guts and no glory."

"As you Yanks are so fond of saying"—Christian made a face—"what else is new?"

"Workin' nine to five!" Dolly Parton's voice

suddenly blared through the room. Christian wasted no time pocketing the thumb drive and crushing the Android beneath his heel. It wasn't much, but taking out even one of the enemy's forms of communication was better than nothing. Then Christian tossed the purple cell to Chelsea.

They all recognized that ringtone. They'd heard it every day, twice a day, for more than a month. Chelsea's mother was calling. And even if hellfire was raining down on their heads, Chelsea would answer.

There were a lot of things that Dagan admired about Chelsea. Her commitment to family was a big one. And he got it. After all, it was his commitment to his brother that had forced him to put in for a transfer from Afghanistan back to the States all those years ago.

"Momma!" she hissed into the phone, her Southern accent coming to the forefront and stirring Dagan's heart—and *other* parts of him located decidedly south. "I told you not to call me 'til after six p.m. London time. I'm on the job."

"The job you took because of the money." The eerie quiet of the penthouse meant Dagan had no trouble hearing the other side of Chelsea's conversation. "But, honey, I'll say it again. I don't want you wastin' your God-given talents just so—"

"I can't go through that with you right now," Chelsea whispered, nodding her head that she was ready to go. Ace and Christian led the way. Dagan motioned for Chelsea to follow, then took his place at the rear of the pack, unholstering the dart gun.

Just in case.

As they made their way from the office, Chelsea's mother said something Dagan couldn't quite make out. Chelsea's response, however, was crystal clear. "It's not what you think, Momma! I'll explain everything once I'm home."

"Home?" He heard Grace Duvall's squawk.

"Yup. I'm coming home soon, Momma. Maybe today."

There was silence on the other end of the line. Then Grace demanded, "Chelsea Lynn Duvall, what haven't you told me?"

Chelsea had kept the true reason behind her quitting the "Department of Land Management" and moving to London a secret from her mother. Given Grace's propensity for *getting all up in Chelsea's business*—that wording was Chelsea's, not Dagan's—and given the lengths to which they had suspected Morrison might go to vet Chelsea, it had been decided that Chelsea's cover story should remain entirely intact. Only the president of the United States, the Black Knights, and the director of the CIA knew the whole truth about her undercover operation in London.

"Well, this one time in the twelfth grade when you thought I was at a sleepover at Lori Jackson's house, I was really on a coed camping trip with fifteen members of the senior class," Chelsea whispered into the phone as they passed the kitchen. Her eyes widened when she saw the cook lying on the floor, but she breathed a sigh of relief when she spied the dart sticking from the woman's thigh before Christian removed it and pocketed it. *Leave no evidence behind*. It was a tenet they lived by.

"Don't sass me, child!" Grace's bellow rang through the phone's speaker.

Despite himself, Dagan grinned.

Chelsea narrowed her eyes at him, shaking her head. "Momma, I have to go. I'll call you later. Love you. Bye."

Grace was still sputtering on the other end of the line when Chelsea thumbed off her phone and slid it into the breast pocket of her blazer. "Not a word," she warned Dagan before turning back to the duo in front.

Not a word? Good. Since words became impossible when he had an unencumbered view of her ass in that tight pencil skirt.

Chapter 6

THERE WAS A HEARTBEAT BEHIND HIS EYES.

That was the first thing Steven Surry noticed as consciousness slipped over him as softly and gently as his mother's long, dark hair had slipped through his fingers when the chemotherapy had begun to take her crowning jewel. She had been in so much pain. And the doctors had been at a loss on how to further attack the tumor eating away at her brain. Their last hope had been an experimental operation. The trouble was that the procedure was so new and so risky that it hadn't been covered by insurance, and Steven hadn't had the quarter of a million pounds necessary to pay for it from his own pocket.

Enter Spider. The man had approached Steven one dreary April afternoon with a deal. A deal, it turned out, that was made with the devil. Now Steven was stuck well and good in Spider's sticky web.

Spider…

The name prowled through his head on prickly feet. It was followed by a cascade of memories, each more disturbing than the last. The breach to the computer system. That stupid, lying twat of a PA. The three masked men who had stormed in to save her like the horsemen of the apocalypse. The dart gun…

Bloody hell!

He lifted a tentative hand to pat the small puncture wound in his neck—someone had been smart to remove the dart and any fingerprints it might have sported. A drop of warm blood smeared across the pads of his fingers. He wiped it on his shirt before digging into the front pocket of his trousers, searching for his mobile.

He wasn't surprised to find it missing. Trained agents knew to confiscate and/or destroy any hardware they found. And those three? They had definitely been trained. The way they had entered the room in formation? The way they had handled their weapons? The swiftness and accuracy of the one who had pulled his trigger? It all spoke of years of preparation, practice, and discipline.

And he would know. He'd done the same, after all.

In my other *life.*

His eyes sprang open to a world of mist and a room that spun in a slow circle. Despite this, he pushed to a seated position, blinking rapidly. That helped to clear the fog and right the world, but it did nothing to mitigate the terrible pulse at the backs of his eyes. And, brilliant. The sudden movement had his stomach threatening a revolt.

Whatever those daft prats had drugged him with was some seriously *un*-fun stuff.

Glancing at his watch, he was relieved to see very little time had passed. Which meant he wasn't completely buggered.

He groaned, pressing the heels of his hands to his eyes. When he pushed to a stand, he stumbled and retched. His stomach felt full of poisonous stones. He wished for nothing more than to toddle to that lovely red sofa and sleep for a year. But as the old saying went, *If wishes were fishes, we would all swim in riches.*

He wasn't a fish. He wasn't rich. And sleeping on the sofa would be the beginning of his doom.

Spider...

The nickname skittered through his brain again like the eight-legged horror it was.

Staggering to the big desk, kicking the shattered remains of his phone, he spared the old man a cursory glance, watching that scrawny chest rise and fall with deep, even breaths. Steven's hands shook when he picked up the phone, hesitating when he couldn't remember the number for Benton, the computer whiz kid Spider had hired straight out of Oxford University. His mind was sluggish, struggling to wade ashore through the waves of narcotic still swimming through his bloodstream.

Come on, man. Think!

He licked his lips, grimacing at the metallic taste the anesthetic had left on his tongue. Lifting the handset, he realized he'd dialed the wrong number when a woman's voice cheerily answered, "Halloo?" Slamming the handset back into the cradle, he blew out a breath and willed his hammering heart to slow.

He spared another glance at the man lying on the tiles, and picked up the phone again. Forcing his mind to go blank, he dialed the number by muscle memory. Benton answered on the first ring. *Thank bloody Christ!*

"Mr. Morrison?" Benton sounded harried. "Did you find it? Whatever she used to upload the virus?"

"It's Surry," Steven said, then immediately filled Benton in on recent events. His voice grew thick with fury when he recounted the part about the three men who'd had the audacity to break into the penthouse. "The thumb drive I confiscated off Miss Duvall's person is gone. They took it. Can you keep out whoever is trying to hack in without it?"

"Sodding mess," Benton grumbled. The sound of his fingers flying over the keyboard was a droning hum in the background. "I can delay them for a day or two.

Perhaps even three or four. But I can't keep them out forever." Steven's heart sank. "Not without the original virus. It's very sophisticated. Just when I think I've eradicated it, it changes form and attacks a new variable. I need to reverse engineer the nasty bugger if I have any hope of squashing it."

"Shite. Fuck. Damn and prick!"

"That pretty much covers it," Benton agreed.

Steven was breathing hard, his vision still a little hinky. But he forced calm on himself. *Work the problem*. That's what he had been trained to do. That's what he *would* do. "Okay. I understand. You worry about protecting the digital information for as long as you can. I'll worry about finding Chelsea Duvall and that sodding thumb drive."

The line went dead without Benton first signing off. The kid was odd, no question about it. But that didn't matter because he was the best hacker Steven knew—maybe the best hacker in the world—which meant that, for now, Steven could stop worrying about the data and turn his full attention toward finding Chelsea Duvall.

The first place he should look was her home. But he had no idea where she lived. His understanding was that she had been somewhat of a gypsy after moving to London, living with friends and acquaintances while she looked for a flat. And since her initial background check came back clean, he hadn't bothered to follow up on her living arrangements.

Plus, even if he *did* know where she lived, there were four of them and only one of him. Gathering Spider's vast group of henchmen would take time. Time he didn't have. So that meant…what?

And then he knew. It came to him in a blinding flash of inspiration.

Chelsea Duvall was a thief. She had stolen—or, more precisely, was poised to steal—private information from one of Great Britain's most influential men. And lucky for Steven, his boss was friends with *other* influential men, *government* men. Men who would be only too happy to help Steven find Chelsea and stop her, if for no other reason than to remain on Spider's good side.

Pulling the phone from the cradle once again, he dialed a number from memory—the cobwebs in his mind had begun to clear—and when a nasally-voiced assistant answered, he wasted no time. "I must speak with the deputy commissioner."

"I'm sorry, sir. The commissioner is—"

"He'll want to speak with me *now*," Steven interrupted, then delivered the coup de grâce. "Tell him I'm employed by a man who goes by the name of Spider."

Chapter 7

"So what you're saying is we're up Shit Street without a GPS."

As an Englishman, Christian Watson was a connoisseur of the finer points of the English language. That meant he had to give Ace credit for using it creatively when Emily informed them that while they were making their way back to the flat from Morrison's penthouse, Morrison had come to and called his contacts in Scotland Yard. Now there was an APW—similar to an American APB—out on Chelsea.

Apparently, for the last ten minutes—they had been stuck in blasted London traffic for nearly fifteen—Chelsea's face had been splashed across every telly in the country. She was Public Enemy Number One. The reports accused her of stealing private files from Morrison, files that were highly classified, files that could be "very dangerous to the sovereignty and safety of Great Britain."

The strategy was quite brilliant when Christian thought about it. Everyone in England knew just how powerful the media mogul was, and no one would doubt that a man of his stature and connections was in possession of damning or classified information.

"Damn, that was fast," Ace grumbled. "He must have come to and immediately started calling in favors."

"Or else it was that other bloke," Christian posited. "He was a rather large fellow, wasn't he? Perhaps the dose didn't work as well on him."

"Doesn't matter." Emily waved a hand. "We just need to get the hell out of here. Pronto. Like…*yesterday*. Morrison and his goons might not know about this apartment." Because they had treated it like a safe house. Chelsea had been careful not to list her address on any of the paperwork she signed, claiming she hadn't found a permanent spot and was couch-surfing until she did. And she had taken a different route to and from work every day, meticulously making sure no one was on her tail. It was just a normal precaution in their line of work. One Christian was incredibly grateful for, given the current state of affairs. "But that doesn't mean they won't find it sooner rather than later," Emily finished.

"And once we get out," Christian said, "what then?" He looked around the flat's sitting room as if expecting the answer to pop out from behind the settee. "We can't spirit Chelsea out of the country the usual ways. The authorities will be on the lookout for anyone fitting her description at all points of entry and exit."

Since Chelsea had an exotic complexion, an unmistakable figure, and lion-bright eyes, she wasn't the type to blend into a crowd and slip through the net tightening around the country.

Bollocks.

"So we lie low in some two-bit motel and wait for the heat to die down," Zoelner suggested.

The hair on the back of Christian's neck curled at the thought. He'd already spent too much time in England.

"Please." Emily gifted Zoelner with a look of pure disgust as she grabbed one of the rucksacks—or backpacks as she called them—from the pile. In the short time they had been rescuing Chelsea, Emily had packed their gear and a few items of essential clothing. And yes, the thought of her elbow-deep in his underwear drawer gave Christian the oddest little thrill. "Who do you think you're dealing with here? *C'est moi*." Emily hooked two thumbs toward her chest. "Roper Morrison might slam a door shut, but I know how to kick open the windows."

Emily Scott had a lithe, feminine figure, and her face was an exquisite mishmash of features that made her far more interesting than conventionally pretty. But beyond that, more importantly than that, she possessed a rapier-sharp mind.

Her job title might be office manager, but from all Christian had seen, he figured it was more accurate to call her a magician. She had an uncanny ability to pull rabbits out of hats and resources out of the ether. In addition to that, she was bossy. She was brazen. And she was altogether bothersome. Especially since she was a mother hen to all the other operators at BKI, but when it came to him, she seemed far more interested in blistering his ears than in—

"Morrison might be able to make things happen here in England," she added, "but he doesn't have nearly as much clout across the Channel. One of the boys back at BKI called in a favor from a former Armée de l'Air friend who left the French services to start his own private charter-jet company. A plane will be waiting for us at Paris–Le Bourget Airport. That way we can skip the cameras and most of the bureaucratic nonsense at Charles de Gaulle."

"The problem is *getting* to Paris." Ace frowned.

"Exactly," Christian agreed. He desperately missed the days when they had worked "unofficially" for the U.S. government. Black Knights Inc. had been covertly assembled and clandestinely run for the last seven years by none other than the president of the United States and his trusty Joint Chiefs of Staff. So in a situation like this, a quick ring to the president would have had strings pulled and an American military transport waiting to take them home. But the president had left office nearly three months earlier, and his successor had no interest in continuing to fund and run a personal defense firm.

So even though the Black Knights were still tasked with finishing their final mission to bring down Spider, they were doing it all on their own. *Unleashed* was the term the president had used to describe them on his last day in office.

They were supposed to turn over to the CIA whatever Intel and proof they found on Morrison/Spider, but before that, they were working outside the law, outside the protection of the good ol' U. S. of A. And even though Chelsea's boss, the director of the CIA, had agreed to let her help the Black Knights in this last hoorah, he had done so with the strict edict that no other CIA services or personnel would be used on a task he had come to refer to as the former president's "personal pet project."

Bugger it all.

"Not as much of a problem as you might think." Emily winked. "There's a guy in Dover who owes me a favor. He's agreed to smuggle us into Calais on his fishing boat. Once there, we'll meet up with Angel, who will drive us to Paris."

Christian frowned, thinking of the former Israeli Mossad agent who worked for BKI. Jamin "Angel" Agassi was a giant question mark. Had been since day one. And in all the weeks, months, and years since, the man hadn't done much to clear up the mystery surrounding himself. Angel spent very little time at BKI headquarters in Chicago. Instead, he was constantly on missions that kept him abroad. Missions only the president seemed to know about.

All that being the case, Christian supposed he shouldn't be surprised to discover Angel was in Europe.

Yet he was. "Anyone know what Angel is doing in France?" he asked.

"He's not in France. At least not yet anyway. When I called headquarters to tell them the cheese had hit the grater, I found out he was doing some work in Bruges. He's in his car right now. If he takes the highway the whole way and doesn't run into traffic, he'll beat us to Calais."

"Jamin Agassi." Ace shook his head. "International man of mystery."

"Better the devil you know than the one you don't," Zoelner said. "Which brings me back to this fishing-boat guy in Dover."

"Right." Chelsea exited the loo while still in the process of pulling on a jumper—or *sweater*, as the Americans called it. She had immediately set off to change clothes after they burst through the door of the flat, ready to grab their bits and bobs and jet back to the States.

Was that really only five minutes ago? A look at the clock on the wall confirmed that it was. *Oh, how time flies when you're not having fun.*

"That's *my* question," Chelsea continued, joining the group around the piled rucksacks. "How do you know this man, Emily?"

"He was an asset to one of the agents run by my FAS," Emily explained. "I helped him out of a pretty gnarly jam before I quit the Company to work for BKI. Now he's ready to do the same for me, for *us*." Her tough, South Side Chicago accent made the word *for* sound more like *fer*. That toughness encased inside such a tender-looking package had been making Christian's inner hound dog sit up and pant from the beginning.

"Dover is more than seventy miles away." He ran through scenarios in his head. "We'll need to rent a car."

They had been using public transportation to get around London to avoid the headache and the paper trail involved in purchasing a vehicle for the mission. But with the APW out on Chelsea, hopping a bus or riding the train was out of the question.

"Already taken care of." Emily grinned. "The minute my Dover connection agreed to sail us across the Channel, I called that motorcycle shop three blocks down. A couple of weeks ago, I noticed the sign in their front window said they rented bikes for day trips. So I got us three Ducatis." She made a face. "I wanted five. I hate riding bitch. But three was all they had, which means Chelsea and I will bow to your fragile male egos." She sighed like this was the greatest sacrifice ever. "The bikes should be delivered any minute now, and once they are, we'll bid a fond cheerio to merry ol' London."

"Ducatis?" Christian made a face. "Are you off your trolley? It's bloody cold outside. Would not a car or a van have been the better choice?"

Unlike the other Black Knights, he did *not* ride a custom Harley back in Chicago. Black Knights Inc. operated out of a custom chopper shop, a good cover since most of the Knights were burly, tattooed, and prone to sporting denim and leather. But Christian liked his wheels to count to four, thank you very much. And he far preferred a mode of transportation that provided a roof over his head should the weather turn inclement.

"And what if we encounter traffic on the A2?" Emily lifted a pert eyebrow. In fact, come to think of it, *everything* about her was pert. "We'll be a lot more maneuverable on bikes. And this is no time to dillydally. As for the cold, it's not *that* cold."

"But—" Whatever argument Christian might have made—and he *had* been about to make one, because the entire conversation wouldn't feel right if he hadn't at least had *one* go-round with Emily—was cut off when the sounds of street bikes echoed up from below.

"They're playing our song." Ace bent to lift his rucksack. He slung the straps over his shoulders, stopped to grab his coat and gloves from the hall tree by the door, and exited the flat without as much as a backward glance. The rest of the group wasted no time following suit.

Left with no choice but to shoulder his own rucksack, Christian grabbed his cold-weather gear and trudged down the four flights while shrugging into his coat. He glanced at his watch and realized only seven minutes had passed since they'd burst through the door to the flat. Seven minuscule minutes. And now they were out the door and on their way with a brand-new plan.

Emily Scott is a wonder, he admitted to himself. Of course, he would never admit as much to her.

Pushing through the building's front door, he found three exquisitely engineered Italian-made motorcycles waiting for them. Unlike the fantastical choppers the Knights designed back in Chicago, the Ducatis were built for one thing only: speed. And loads of it.

Watching his two teammates each chose a bike and shake the hand of the man dropping it off, Christian desperately missed his Porsche back in Chicago. All those lovely horses in her engine. Two doors. A rather wonderful sound system. And the smell of rich, hand-crafted leather.

"You do know how to ride, don't you?" Emily

asked. The sun chose that moment to peek through the clouds, running bright fingers through her brown hair and bringing out the gold and auburn highlights that wove through the darker strands. She really was quite an arresting-looking woman. And that beauty mark high on her cheek made him oddly excited.

"Just because I choose *not* to do something doesn't mean I'm incapable of it," he told her.

"Well, then, let's pretend for a minute that you're someone less uptight, someone who likes to get a little dirty, someone...*else*, and mount up."

To his complete bewilderment, and as had been the case since she'd set foot inside the BKI compound a few months ago, she was trying to get his goat. For once, he refused to let her.

"Oooh," he crooned and gifted her with a toothy grin. "I do so love role play, darling. Tell me more about my character."

"How about, just for today, you try *not* to be a wiener on a half shell?"

For a moment, he stared at her, drawing blank on a comeback to that little bon mot. Damnit! She had bested him again. He was overcome with the urge to either shake her or kiss her senseless. Both options would surely shush that wickedly quick mouth of hers, but only the second would give him any *real* relief. "Devil take you, Emily."

"Not likely." A smile pulled at her tempting lips. "The devil wouldn't know what to do with the likes of me."

Before he could tell her that he wholeheartedly agreed, Zoelner asked Chelsea, "Who do you want to ride with?" The words and tone were casual, but Christian could read the strain on Zoelner's face.

"I..." Chelsea blinked behind her glasses. She was

careful to keep her face turned away from the men who had delivered the bikes. Not that they looked like the kind of blokes to follow the news, but still… "I thought I'd just…ride with you. If that's okay?"

Zoelner's Adam's apple bobbed in his throat, and his chest expanded to twice its usual size. "I thought maybe after what I did in Morrison's office that you…" He trailed off. Christian watched him search Chelsea's eyes before firming his jaw and finishing with "Let's go, then."

Those two are the absolute worst, Christian thought.

Everyone could tell they were barmy about each other. But, for whatever reason, they refused to see it or acknowledge it for themselves. Pathetic. And annoying. And…*whatever*. He had his own pesky, misplaced lust to deal with.

Grabbing the remaining motorbike, he opened the seat to reveal the storage compartment inside. After shoving in his rucksack, he mounted up and rocked the steel beast off its kickstand. It felt heavy and cumbersome.

Turning the key, he listened to the massive engine purr to life. Then he tugged on the helmet that had been dangling from the handlebars. To his surprise, Emily swung her leg over the seat, scooting in close behind him.

He stiffened at the feel of her warmth seeping through his leather and wool-lined coat. Swallowing, he turned to find her slipping on the extra helmet that had been strapped to the back of the seat.

"Okay if I ride with you?" she asked.

For the first time ever, he saw uncertainty in her eyes, heard trepidation in her voice. Emily put on a good front, but she wasn't as confident and unflappable as she would have them all believe.

Given her closeness, given that look in her eyes, he could do nothing but nod. When he did, he saw relief flash across her face before she flipped down her visor. Then...the most amazing thing happened. Her thighs squeezed his hips, and her arms went around his waist.

Okay, so perhaps there's something to this motorbike thing after all.

Chapter 8

Dover, England

LLOYD AND HARRY FROM *DUMB AND DUMBER*…

That's how Chelsea expected to look by the time she and Dagan exited the highway toward Dover. But with Dagan in front of her blocking the wind, and with his blast-furnace body heat radiating against the length of her, instead of being chilled to the bone, she was all warm and tingly. *More* than warm and tingly. She was on fire.

So, not Lloyd and Harry from Dumb and Dumber, *more like Frodo and Sam on Mount Doom right before the Eagles saved them.*

Then again, maybe all that heat had something to do with her having just spent the last sixty minutes plastered around Dagan like human Saran Wrap while he maneuvered the sleek Ducati in a marvel of easy agility and fluid strength. Or maybe it was the memory of that kiss that had kept her toasty warm.

Talk about hot. Lord have mercy!

Never before had Chelsea experienced such a toe-curling, head-spinning lip-lock. He had mad skills. Unbelievable oral gymnastic skills.

No doubt perfected over many years and with many women. Ugh.

Normally, she would insist she didn't have a jealous bone in her body. But when it came to Dagan? Yup. She was pretty sure she had two hundred and six of them.

It didn't help that after he kissed her, he'd pulled
away with a look of utter horror contorting his face. It
had hurt. It *still* hurt. That look coming so close on the
heels of the best moment of her life. And all she could
think was…*why?*

*Why did he kiss me? And then why was he immedi-
ately horrified by it?*

She wasn't a bad kisser. She'd been assured of that
by her high school boyfriend who had once told her she
had the mouth of an angel, all soft and sweet and eager
to please. Then again, she'd been so shocked by the fact
that Dagan had been kissing her that she hadn't had the
time to really bring her A game, so maybe—

"Almost there!" Dagan turned to her when they
stopped at an intersection. He yelled to be heard over
the purr of the Ducati's engine. "You okay?"

No! Chelsea wanted to holler back. *I'm not okay! I
won't be okay until you explain what the heck happened
in Morrison's office!*

But she proved she was a chickenhearted cur when
she simply dipped her chin, the weight of the motorcycle helmet pressing the earpieces of her glasses into
the sides of her skull.

Dagan nodded and turned back to the road, throt-
tling up and making his way down the winding lane that
ran through the center of the seaside town. Dover was
perched beside vast, chalky cliffs, and brick four-flat
houses nestled next to their whitewashed counterparts
zoomed by on either side of the bikers. Locals turned
their heads, curiously watching the trio of high-end
motorcycles making their way toward the docks.

Chelsea breathed deeply of salt-tinged air. Having
been born and raised on the coast of South Carolina, she'd
always been partial to the sea. To the changing tides, the

beauty of a sunrise over open water, and the inherent spark of danger that lurked just below the surface.

Once, a long time ago, she had said something to that effect to her mother. Grace had smiled gently, shaken her head, and accused Chelsea of being a romantic. "Just like your father," Grace had added, a wistful gleam in her eye.

Chelsea's father *had* been a romantic. A man filled with a hunger for life and the belief that love really did conquer all. He had proved that belief by falling head over heels for Chelsea's mother during a time when white Southern boys were not supposed to marry poor black girls. And then he'd reinforced that belief every day for twenty-three years, through thick and thin, whether dealing with prejudice or acceptance. And always with a smile on his face and a wide-open heart— until one day that heart gave out on him and he died peacefully in his sleep lying next to the woman he had loved since the moment he saw her at a drive-in movie.

Being compared to him had always been a compliment. But now, sitting behind Dagan, still dazed by the power of his kiss and wounded by his horrified expression afterward, Chelsea wondered if being a romantic, if living with her heart wide open, would cause her to suffer more hurt than she could handle.

She was pragmatic enough to know that her parents had been incredibly lucky, and not everyone ended up with happily ever after.

Whoa. Had she really just gone there? Imagined a future with Dagan?

She closed her eyes, unconsciously squeezed his waist tighter, and admitted that she had. Which was ridiculous because…number one, the look on his face after the kiss did not bode well for a lifetime of repeats. And number two, there could never be any sort of forever for them because she was harboring the Big Bad Secret.

Oh, good night, nurse! Get out of your own head, Chels! It was just one little kiss in the middle of a tense, adrenaline-filled situation. It meant nothing to him!

Right. Good advice. Trouble was, no matter how much she tried to convince herself otherwise, it had meant something to *her*.

Chapter 9

DAGAN HAD BEEN CALLING HIMSELF AN IDIOT FOR THE LAST hour. But as he turned down the road leading to the Dover docks, he decided that was an insult to stupid people.

His reaction to the feel of Chelsea pressed against him, the warm weight of her amazing breasts on his back, the sultry heat at the junction of her thighs, not to mention the sheer delight of having her small arms wrapped around his waist, went beyond idiotic and veered helter-skelter toward insanity.

We're talking straitjackets, padded walls, and gurneys with straps attached, folks. Because even though his rational mind knew that a woman like her wouldn't want anything to do with the likes of him, and that he had already strayed *way* over the line with that kiss, that didn't stop his irrational mind—the base, instinctual, animalistic part of his brain—from wanting her.

He had been hard the whole ride, and the subtle vibration of the Ducati's well-made engine hadn't helped his situation one bit. It was agony times one hundred. And he was terrified her hand might slip down. If it did, there was no way she wouldn't notice the effect she had on him. Then he would have something *else* to apologize for, in addition to that ill-timed, ill-advised, all-consuming kiss.

A parade of images marched through his head: Chelsea seated at the conference table back in Chicago, admitting to having a monkey on her back and fearlessly volunteering for the job to infiltrate Spider's household;

Chelsea bent over her laptop, poring over Intel, her fierce mind hard at work; Chelsea sitting in that chair in Roper fuckin' Morrison's office, tied and helpless and willing to give her life for the cause.

Chelsea…

Jesus H, he was going to have to grovel for her forgiveness. Then again, perhaps grovel was too sanitized a word. What he needed to do was to get down on bended knee, kiss her feet, and beg her to absolve him for taking advantage of the situation, for taking advantage of *her*.

The trouble with that plan? Well, once he began kissing her feet, he would be tempted to continue the journey upward. Nipping her delicate ankles. Biting her lithe, muscled calves. Licking her smooth thighs until—

Oh, for God's sake!

"Look how pretty!" Chelsea yelled over the Ducati's engine, pointing at the towering cliffs of Dover when they finally came into full view.

The cliffs were composed almost entirely of chalk, a bright, blinding white. Dagan couldn't shake the feeling that they were angry teeth, snarling across the Channel at continental Europe and daring anyone with ill intent to set foot on the island. But it charmed him that after all Chelsea had been through in the last couple of hours— hell, what she'd been through in the last *month* under the employ of Roper fuckin' Morrison—she could still look at those bleached cliff faces with a sense of child-like awe.

"Don't you think that's just about the prettiest thing ever?" she enthused, her breath warm against the nape of his neck, sending a cascade of chills down his spine.

Instead of answering—afraid she would hear the lust in his voice—he simply nodded and followed the others into the gravel parking lot beside the docks. One by one, he and his teammates cut the bikes' engines. The sound of low, growling horsepower was replaced by the *shush* of waves lapping against rocks, the *clink-clink* of mooring lines against rigging, and the forlorn cries of the seagulls that dove and darted overhead.

Having grown up in Cleveland, on the banks of Lake Erie, and then having worked the last handful of years in Chicago, perched alongside Lake Michigan, Dagan thought there was just something about the water. He loved the fishy smell of it. The devastating…vastness of it.

Those rare times when he'd had a day off and had gone sailing with friends, he'd realized that he could only truly grasp his smallness, his infinitesimal worth in the grand scheme of the universe, when he was out in the middle of all that unrelenting water. And for some reason, that made him feel better. Made all his mistakes seem somehow less important, less grave, just…*less*.

"Emily Scott! As I live and breathe!" A big-chested man who looked like he should be playing cornerback for the Chicago Bears trotted across the lot toward them.

"Rusty!" Emily hopped from the back of Christian's rented motorcycle, tossed Christian her helmet, and turned to throw herself into the arms of the approaching man.

When she kissed the newcomer smack on the lips, Dagan was sure he heard Christian growl. He glanced over, brow raised, but was immediately distracted when Chelsea hopped off the back of the bike, taking all her feminine warmth and softness with her.

He felt the desertion like a physical ache. His body *longed* for the touch of hers.

Then he wasn't feeling anything but annoyance when she blinked at Emily's friend in wide-eyed wonder and

muttered, "Goodness sakes. That man is a specimen."
Now it was *his* turn to growl. "I swear. I feel like I'm in
some sort of sexy man laboratory. Each new experiment
is hotter than the last," she added.

Dagan didn't register that, in fact, Chelsea had just
called him sexy. He was too preoccupied by the latter
half of her statement. The part where she thought New
Guy was hot.

A sense of possessiveness he had absolutely no business feeling spread through him.

"You look good, Rusty!" Emily grinned up at the
fisherman. "The simple life agrees with you."

Rusty had wild, unkempt hair the color of black cher-
ries, and he wore dark foul-weather bib-and-brace pants
with yellow suspenders that stretched over massive
shoulders covered by an oatmeal-colored fisherman's
sweater. Seeing him standing there, smiling down at
Emily, Dagan changed his mind about that Chicago
Bears thing. Emily's friend belonged on the cover of a
Cabela's catalog. He was the epitome of every rugged,
wild seaman Dagan had ever seen. *The rat bastard.*

"Right back atcha, dollface." Rat Bastard winked.

Dagan hopped off the Ducati and opened the seat
to haul out his backpack. Shrugging into the shoulder
straps, he turned in time to hear Emily say, "Well, don't
you all just stand there looking like wet weekends.
Everyone, come meet Rusty Parker."

"You're American," Christian said, shaking Rusty's
hand. His tone made the observation sound like an insult.

"Born and bred in Pittsburgh." Rusty grinned. "But I
hope you won't hold that against me."

Of all the things Christian was likely to hold against
Rusty Parker, Dagan figured coming from Pennsylvania
wasn't one of them.

"When Emily said she had a fisherman friend who was willing to sail us across the Channel"—Ace shook Rusty's hand—"I expected missing teeth, an eye patch, and a hook for a hand."

Rusty's rat bastard grin deepened, revealing a set of dimples. Unless Dagan's ears deceived him, Chelsea sucked in an awed breath. Okay, and now he wasn't just feeling possessive, he was feeling downright murderous. His hands curled into fists. To keep himself from using them, he shoved them deep into the pockets of his coat.

"I'm a cod fisherman, not a pirate." Rusty chuckled.

"I don't think I was thinking pirate as much as eye cabbage." Ace tilted his head, eyeing Rusty up and down.

"Eye cabbage?" Rusty raised a brow.

"Opposite of eye candy," Ace explained.

"Okay, that's enough out of *you*, Romeo," Emily cut in. "Let's finish the intros and get moving. Dagan Zoelner." She turned. "Meet Rusty Parker."

Dagan had more than his fair share of calluses, but shaking Rusty's hand was like grabbing hold of an old leather shoe. And if Dagan squeezed with a little more pressure than was strictly necessary, you wouldn't know it by the impassive expression on Rusty's face.

"And last but not least," Emily said, "may I present Chelsea Duvall. The lady of the hour and the reason we need to bust ass across the Channel."

Rusty's big paw of a hand swallowed Chelsea's. The asshole had the audacity to bend and kiss her knuckles. "Hello, Hot Cocoa," he said with a wiggle of his eyebrows.

When Chelsea giggled—*giggled*, for God's sake!— Dagan was hard-pressed not to rip her hand from the fisherman's grip.

"Pleased to meet you." Chelsea dipped her head

demurely and looked at Rusty through the veil of her sooty lashes.

What's that sound? Oh right. It was Dagan's back molars being ground to dust.

"I don't know about you, mate," Christian whispered from the corner of his mouth after coming to stand close to Dagan's side, "but I should think I hate him already."

Dagan grunted his agreement as Chelsea gushed, "And thank you so much for doing this for us, Mr. Parker."

"Please, call me Rusty."

"Okay...*Rusty*," Chelsea said in that husky sex-operator's voice of hers.

Dagan had had all he could stand. "Yes, thank you, Rusty." Why did it sound like he had been swallowing rocks? "Now, if it's not too much trouble, let's go. The longer we stay in this country, the more I feel the Earl Grey and incessant rain seeping into my bones, making them soggy."

"You grow to love soggy bones after a while." Rusty winked at him.

Like we're best buds or some shit? Just because I didn't pop you in the puss the moment you laid those filthy lips on my... Dagan wasn't certain where he was headed with the rest of that thought, but whichever direction, he decided it was best to hang a swift left.

He found himself sorely tempted to challenge the fisherman to a wrestling match so he could...what? Prove to Chelsea that between the two of them *he* was the better man?

Christ in a cardigan sweater!

"Come on, then." Rusty motioned over his shoulder. "Grab your gear, and leave me the keys to the bikes. I'll make sure they're returned to the rental agency."

"Rusty, my love," Emily said as she followed him across the gravel lot, "you're a lifesaver."

"Anything for you, dollface." Rusty threw a beefy arm over her shoulders, and Dagan glanced at Christian. The poor man's florid face pretty much summed up what Dagan was feeling.

"Let's go." Chelsea grabbed Dagan's hand to give him a tug. "Quit lollygagging." When she tried to release his fingers, he instinctively tightened his grip.

Turning back, she looked at him, then down at their joined hands, then back up at him. "What in the world has gotten into you today?" A seagull darted overhead, its desolate cry calling to something inside Dagan's soul. Some lonely, aching part of him.

What had gotten into him? *Her!* She had gotten into him!

After years of denying himself the taste of her, like an anorexic denying himself food, he had finally caved. And now all he wanted was to gorge himself on her. Binge again and again, over and over until he couldn't take any more.

Of course, he said none of that.

With a shrug and a roll of her eyes, Chelsea turned to traipse after the others, who were already making their way across the parking lot toward the dock and the waiting fishing boats. Still, he didn't release her hand.

Why? Well, probably because he wanted to mark his territory in front of the oh-so-dreamy Rusty Parker. Which just proved he was an even bigger idiot than he had suspected.

Chapter 10

Dagan Zoelner had kissed her and then immediately been horrified by it. Now he was holding her hand as they made their way up the stairs to the docks, and Chelsea couldn't help but wonder if in two minutes, he would be horrified by that too.

Okeydokey. Forget two minutes.

Dagan dropped her hand like a hot potato when Christian turned from his spot at the top of the steps, looking down at them with a raised brow and a knowing smirk. She frowned as she climbed the treads and made her way down the wooden dock toward the large twin-engine catamaran Rusty had stopped beside.

The fisherman had a presence as big as all outdoors and a smile to match when he offered her a hand aboard. She thought she heard Dagan mutter a profanity but couldn't be sure. She was too busy getting her footing on the wide gray deck as it shifted gently up and down with the tide.

It occurred to Chelsea that the entire day had been like a bad episode of *The Twilight Zone*. One minute, Dagan was suffering an invasion of the body snatchers, acting uncharacteristically affectionate. The next, he was back to his solemn, annoying self. And the change from one state to the other kept happening so fast that she was suffering from emotional whiplash.

"Set your stuff anywhere you like inside, and grab a seat," Rusty instructed after they were all aboard. He threw off thick, heavy mooring lines as if they weighed no more than jump ropes. "We'll be underway in a jiff."

Dagan passed her, heading toward the wheelhouse. She scowled at his broad back before following him inside. The place was spacious and housed the electronics and steering for the vessel. The white walls were bedecked in bright-orange life jackets on hooks. And two rows of bench seats were bolted into the decking behind the captain's chair.

The boat was immaculate. Not a stray fish scale or vagrant speck of oil marred any surface. And the air spelled of bleach and industrial-strength soap. Rusty was obviously a fastidious boat captain.

What's his story? Chelsea wondered. Not many Americans became English cod fishermen, she would bet, and—

"Come with me." Dagan tugged her backpack from her shoulders. He set it beneath one of the bench seats, scooting it next to his own.

"Come with you where?" She lifted a brow. "Overboard? Because I reckon that's the only place left to—"

"Belowdecks." He grabbed her hand and towed her toward the stairs to the left of the captain's chair. "We need to talk."

"Oh goody." She made a face. "All truly awesome conversations begin with those four words."

Before descending the six metal steps that led into the catamaran's hold, she stopped to see the others settling onto the bench seats. All three of them were watching her curiously. Chelsea caught Emily's gaze, lifting her brows as if to say, *Any idea what the heckfire is up with Z today?*

Emily shrugged, and Chelsea was left with no recourse but to follow Dagan down into the belly of the ship.

He wanted to talk? Fine. Good. Because *she* had a couple of things she wanted to say to *him*.

"Here's good." He stopped next to a stack of boxes. Their labels read *Skimmer Clams*. Chelsea assumed they were the bait Rusty used to catch cod.

The hold was as clean as the rest of the boat: pristine floors, neatly stacked gear, and the aroma of strong soap mixed with the more common maritime smells of anti-fouling paint and marine fuel. A single bulb in a yellow plastic cage lit the space, creating long shadows, especially across Dagan's face. They made him look even more mysterious. Even more fierce. Even more…*delectable*.

Chelsea turned away, refusing to look at him, hoping to find something to distract herself from his nipple-tightening presence. Then he blurted, "I'm sorry," and she swung back to face him, blinking.

There were a few things to know about Dagan Zoelner. Number one, he had an uncanny ability to blend into a crowd. Number two, there was that odd statue-stillness that came over him right before he was about to do something of grave importance—or right before he was about to lay into her for something. And number three, in all their years working together, and all the times they had verbally tanned each other's hides, he had never, *not once*, apologized to her.

Which was probably why she stood there, her mouth opening and closing like the catfish her father had loved to catch out of Old Man Miller's pond. When she finally found her voice, it was to respond with an oh-so-intelligent "Huh?"

Dagan ran a hand over his beard, looking away from her into the middle distance before finally turning back. "For kissing you when you hadn't invited me to and when you couldn't push me away," he said.

Aha. Well, that explains the look of horror on his face.

Did he really believe for even one second that she might *not* have welcomed his kiss? Before she could speak the thought aloud, words gushed out of him like the water that had rushed out of the backyard spigot when she was fifteen and accidentally ran into it with the riding lawn mower. Holy Moses, her mother had been madder than a wet hen. But her father? He had just laughed at her soaked hair and clothes before shutting off the main water to the house.

"It's just that when you sent that Mayday, I was terrified what might've happened, what might *be* happening to you. And then to get to Morrison's penthouse and find that you had not only managed to get yourself caught, but that you were foolish enough to think you needed to sacrifice yourself and—"

Chelsea stopped listening right then and there. Probably because she couldn't hear over the blood pounding angrily through her ears.

"Damnit, Z!" she snarled. Her fisted hands landed on her hips as she thrust her chin up at his damnably handsome face. "Just once, just one friggin' time in your life, could you, oh, I don't know, say something *nice* to me?"

His chin jerked back. Or rather…the Beard jerked back. His gray eyes narrowed as he blinked at her. There it was again…his Clint Eastwood gunfighter squint. And he got very, *very* still.

She braced herself for a verbal assault. Thankfully, it never came.

"Chels, I…" He stopped and swallowed. The expression on his face morphed from an impersonation of ol' Clint into something he might have worn if she'd started growing a third nipple. On her cheek.

And, okay, so maybe she could understand some of his assessments. For most of her career, she had ridden a desk. She was only an inch over five feet tall, not an imposing figure. She was a woman in a man's world. And she made sure to speak to her mother twice a day. No doubt, he saw all those things as disadvantages, as...*weaknesses*.

He was flat-out wrong. Riding a desk had taught her patience and had given her the ability to view situations and Intel from all sides. Her small stature made people underestimate her. Her sex meant she was naturally sympathetic, which had allowed her to put herself into the shoes of America's enemies and accurately guess what their next moves might be. As for her relationship with her mother? Well, he might think *Time to cut the apron strings*, but the truth was that Grace Duvall made Chelsea a better person. She kept Chelsea honest. Made her strive for higher standards. But also reminded her to enjoy the little things in life.

Yup. Chelsea was stronger, smarter, *tougher* than he had ever given her credit for. And as far as she could figure, him not giving her credit stopped here. Today. As Hagrid said in *Harry Potter and the Goblet of Fire*, "I am what I am, an' I'm not ashamed!"

"Land sakes alive," she said through gritted teeth when he seemed fine and dandy just standing there looking at her like *she* was the crazy one. "Are you telling me you can't think of one single, solitary nice thing to say?"

"I... You're..." He stopped, his Adam's apple bobbing in his throat. "It's not that you're...*not* one of the most courageous people I've ever worked with." When the words were out of his mouth, he looked ridiculously pleased with himself.

She, on the other hand, was sorely tempted to slap

him upside the head. Really? After everything she'd accomplished today, *that* was the best he could do?

"I'm sorry." She seethed. "Was there a compliment buried somewhere in that double negative?"

"Oh, for fuck's sake, Chels." He lifted his arms impatiently and let them fall back to his sides. She did not notice how it made the halves of his thick leather jacket pull wide, revealing the broad expanse of his chest covered by a soft merino wool sweater. Okay, so maybe she noticed a *little*. "You know what I think of you. *How* I think of you. I've made it clear for years. Don't make me repeat myself."

Just like that, every one of her hackles was standing stick-straight. If she'd been a cat, her back would be bowed and the hair on her tail all fluffed out. She took a step forward and shoved a finger into the center of his chest.

"You're right," she snapped. "You've made it crystal clear that you have no respect for me. You've gone out of your way to block me from doing the jobs I'm assigned. You tell me all the time that I'm not good enough. And why in the good Lord's name should I think you might have the decency to come up with just *one* thing that…that…that…"

She was so worked up, she was tripping over her own tongue. Then she nearly *swallowed* that same tongue when he grabbed her shoulders in a hard grip and ducked down so that he was on eye level with her.

"Christ, Chels." His smooth moonshine voice had turned hoarse. "Is that what you think?"

She was tempted to shrug off his hands. But sweet Lord, she *liked* it when he touched her. "It's not what I think, you big, hairy jackass. It's what you *do*. It's what you *say*."

He straightened and stepped back, running a hand over his beard and shaking his head. "You could not be more wrong."

Ha! She rolled her eyes. "How in blue blazes do you figure that?"

"I respect the hell out of you, Chels. I think you're… *amazing.*" Just like that, he had suffered another invasion of the body snatchers, and she was back in *The Twilight Zone*. She looked around, half expecting to hear Rod Serling say, *You unlock this door with the key of imagination. Beyond it is another dimension…* "You have steel in your spine, fire in your brain, and grace in your heart."

Okay. And *that* wasn't just nice. It was the *nicest* thing anyone had ever said to her.

Dagan had always been an overachiever. *Damn him.*

"If I've tried to block you from doing the jobs you've been assigned recently, it's only because I know you weren't given the right fuckin' training for them."

Dagan was a born-and-raised Midwesterner, which meant he had no noticeable accent—a trait she had spent years trying to mimic since having an accent was a tell in and of itself. But anytime he used the word *fucking*, he always left the *g* sound off the end.

"And if I've made you feel like you're not good enough," he continued, "that wasn't my intention. I *care* about you, Chelsea. And that caring makes me absolutely terrified something could happen to you on my watch. So I've tried to remind you to always be careful, to be vigilant, to never lose sight of the fact that this is incredibly dangerous work and that you—"

He *cared* about her? Oh, how she had longed for this day. And dreaded it too.

Stepping forward, she wrapped her arms around his

waist and squeezed him tight. Never one to couch her words, she gave him the truth. *Her* truth. Even if she knew she would be damned for it. "I care about you too, Dagan."

Chapter 11

HEARING SUCH SWEET WORDS ON CHELSEA'S LIPS, HEARING his *name*, had warmth unfurling inside Dagan. Having her pressed against him turned that warmth into a blazing heat that melted his reason and burned away all his good sense. Or…at least that's what he blamed for what happened next, for what he *did* next.

Wrapping his hands around her shoulders, feeling her lithe muscles flex through the puffy down fabric of her coat, he walked her backward two steps.

With her back pressed against the boxes stacked next to the bulkhead, she blinked up at him in confusion. "Dagan?" And there it was again. His name spoken in that sexy, husky voice with just the tiniest trace of a Southern drawl.

After that scene in Morrison's penthouse, he should have known better, should have learned his lesson about taking without asking. But for the first time since Afghanistan, he dared to hope that maybe, just maybe he had been wrong.

She had just said she cared for him, hadn't she? She had willingly stepped into his embrace to hold him tight, hadn't she? So maybe there was a chance that an amazing, wonderful woman like her *could* fall for a shitheel like him. Maybe she was able to look past his bad decisions and see that he was doing his damnedest to… what? Not make up for what he'd done—he could never make up for that. But he had been trying to live his life in a way that counted.

Taking her face between his hands, he marveled at the delicate, satiny feel of her skin. Slowly, ever so slowly, he lowered his head, all the while keeping his eyes trained on her, searching for rejection.

He never saw any. Instead, her plump, pink lips trembled and fell open in an unconscious invitation. Her breath was warm and sweet against his mouth. And then... Oh, and *then* she closed her eyes, exhaling a shuddering sigh. *That* was all the permission he needed.

"Chelsea." Her name was a harsh whisper, torn from his throat by the power of his desire. Closing the distance between them, he took what she was offering.

Just as before, the instant his lips touched hers, he was sucker-punched with a sense of overwhelming *rightness*. As if *this* was what he had been born to do. As if *she* was the one he had been born to do it with.

"Mmm," she moaned when he slowly delved his tongue inside her sweet mouth. The low, sultry sound traveled from his ears down his spine and settled heavily in his stomach. And lower.

After a brief moment, her tongue tentatively sought his, tangling, darting, and daring to spear past his teeth into the hot welcome of his mouth. He wanted to howl his joy, his pleasure. In Morrison's penthouse, he had kissed her with abandon, but she had been too stunned to kiss him back. But now, oh, *now* she wasn't just kissing him back, she was making love to his mouth. With deep, wet tastes and soft, ball-tightening sucks.

That hope that had flared to life inside him, grew into an all-out conflagration that stoked the fire of his lust ever higher. His control shattered. His gentleness disappeared with it.

A possessive growl sounded at the back of his throat. Using his hands, he canted her head to the side to gain better access to her wanton, wicked mouth. Then he feasted. Like a starving man, over and over he went back to taste, to savor, to devour. Every suck of her plump lips made his thundering heart beat harder. Every stroke of her tongue made the blood rushing in his ears roar louder.

Her fingers tangled in his hair, pulling the strands in her effort to get closer. He welcomed the bite of pain and accommodated her by pinning her lush body against the crates.

She hummed her approval into his mouth, the sweetest melody he had ever heard, and rubbed herself against him. Her luscious breasts raked over his chest. Her hips canted forward, seeking the evidence of his desire.

She found it waiting for her, pulsing and painfully erect behind the fly of his jeans.

"You taste amazing," he told her, releasing her face to wrap both arms around her waist. The temptation of her ass was too much. He had dreamed about her butt for so long. Dreamed of kissing it, of spanking it, of watching it bounce prettily as he hammered into her from behind. But first…he wanted to *feel* it.

Palming a jean-clad globe in each hand, he was delighted to discover she was more than a handful. Chelsea…sweet, sexy, sassy Chelsea was all woman. And everything that made him a man reveled in the knowledge. Her lush curves turned him rock hard. The mewling sounds at the back of her throat had him answering with a low grumble.

"You *feel* amazing," he added between deep, plunging kisses while kneading her ass and relishing the firm, plump give of her flesh.

It occurred to him then, as he kissed her until they were both senseless, that the air had been sucked out of the room. He lived solely on her sweet breath. The world around him, the boat, the boxes, the stairwell, it all vanished. He saw nothing but her lovely face, *felt* nothing but her soft body moving shamelessly against him.

"Dagan." Her voice was huskier than usual when she ripped her mouth away and let her head fall back against the stack of crates. "Please."

"Please what?" He took advantage of her exposed neck. The skin there looked as smooth as latte and tasted as sweet when he pressed his lips against her pulse. He sucked and felt the beat of her heart pick up its pace.

Breath hitching, she tilted her head further to the side, inviting more. He didn't disappoint. He nibbled and sucked and kissed his way back to her ear.

"Please what, Chelsea?" he whispered again.

She speared her hands into the open halves of his jacket, fisting handfuls of his sweater. "I don't know." There was a hint of desperation in her voice.

A small smile curved his lips as he nipped at the delicate lobe of her ear. Man, she smelled as good as she tasted. Like strawberries warmed by the summer sun and dipped in vanilla.

"*I* know," he assured her.

And then he showed her that he spoke the truth by bending his knees to more fully align their bodies. He released one of her beautiful ass cheeks to slowly slide his hand down her thigh, stopping at her knee. Pulling her leg high around his waist, he opened her to him, stepping forward to put himself right where he wanted to be.

Bull's-eye!

All the hairs on his body lifted, his balls pulled up tight, and his dick throbbed when her sultry heat seeped through both their jeans to brand him. Knowing that *he* had done that to her, that *he* had made her hot and wet, was an erotic victory.

"You're so hot," he whispered against her ear. "So fuckin' hot, Chels."

Then she did the most amazing thing. She pushed his jacket off his shoulders, letting it fall to the deck at their feet before she wrapped her arms around his neck and hopped up, both her legs circling his hips. He supported her full weight, and despite her short stature, she wasn't a dainty thing. She felt solid and warm and alive and... like a deliciously sexy, grown-assed *woman* in his arms. Which was enough to have him threatening to shoot off like a damned geyser in his pants.

She made everything so much worse—*or better?*—by proceeding to *ride him*.

"Yes, Chels," he breathed between deep, tongue-twisting kisses. "Keep doing that."

He helped her by palming her ass and thrusting his pelvis in counter rhythm to her pumping hips. The boxes behind them rattled and banged against the bulkhead. He hadn't dry-humped a woman in...how long? Since freshman year in college, maybe?

Holy shit. He had been missing out.

"Oh my," she whispered against his lips.

Oh my, indeed, he thought. As in...*oh my God! Oh my, yes! Oh, my sweet girl, don't stop what you're doing*.

The friction was amazing. The heat of her. The sultry wetness of her was almost enough to—

The big engines came to life, cutting off the sound of Chelsea's moans of pleasure. Above deck, Rusty wasted no time piloting the catamaran away from the dock. The minute the boat hit the open water, the choppy currents of the Channel caused the deck beneath Dagan's biker boots to roll. With Chelsea's added weight, he was thrown off balance.

Cursing, he stumbled backward, tripping over his

jacket and hitting another stack of boxes. When the crates threatened to tumble over, he was forced to take a knee.

The deck heaved again as Rusty tacked strongly to the port side, and Dagan found himself flat on his back with Chelsea rising above him like a dark angel. Her golden eyes glinted down at him. Her hands flattened on either side of his head. And a smirk tugged at her kiss-swollen lips.

"Well, I'd say it's about damn time." There was laughter in her voice.

He wanted nothing more than to drag her down for another kiss, to thrust his hips against her and restart that delicious friction. Instead, he squeezed her thighs and asked, "About damn time for what?" For him to take off all her clothes and make hot, sweet love to her? If so, he most definitely agreed.

"About damn time *I* ended up on top after one of our duels." She winked saucily, and the freckles on her nose once again reminded him of flecks of cinnamon. He wanted to kiss every one of them.

The metal decking was cold against his back, but she was so incredibly warm against his front. Her ripe breasts hung down so that just the tips brushed his chest. "Is that what we're doing?" He quirked a brow. "Dueling?"

"I'd say that what we had going back there"—she hooked a finger over her shoulder toward the stack of boxes he'd pinned her against—"definitely qualifies as a good bit of thrust and parry."

He couldn't help it. He chuckled. Only Chelsea could make him hot as hell one minute and laugh out loud the next.

"Well, for the record, you're welcome to climb on top of me any time your heart desires. As for the thrust and parry…" He made sure the grin he shot her was wholly devilish. "Baby, you ain't seen nothing yet."

He expected her to come back with a witty quip. She rarely let him get in the last word. But instead, her smile dimmed as if she'd reached inside herself and flipped a switch. "What are we doing, Dagan?"

He gave her thighs another squeeze. "I would think that's obvious." But just in case she needed more clarification, he thrust his pelvis at her while using his hands to drag her hot, sweet cleft backward along his steely length.

Oh yes, he thought a little deliriously. *There's that glorious friction.*

"Holy Moses." Her eyes rolled back, and her throat worked over a hard swallow. "I can't think when you do that," she said.

"Isn't that part of the fun? Letting your body take over for your brain?"

"Lord, yes." Her voice was thick with desire. Desire that *he* had put there. He was tempted to beat his chest King Kong–style. "But I…" She stopped and opened her eyes. He was once more waylaid by the golden glow of her irises. Those eyes had always done a number on him, reminding him of a sleek, sexy jaguar. And now he knew how appropriate that comparison was. From what little they had already done together, he could tell she would be a wildcat between the sheets. "But I don't understand," she finally finished. "I always thought you didn't…well…you didn't *like* me."

What was she? Crazy?

"All evidence to the contrary," he told her, again rubbing his hard length against the sultry juncture of her thighs.

"S-stop that," she whispered. But he could tell her words didn't match her wants when she wiggled her hips the tiniest bit to get the angle just right. "I'm trying to have a serious conversation with you."

"Why?" He watched her through half-lidded eyes, loving how passion had brought a rosy blush to the apples of her cheeks.

"Because I don't understand," she said exasperatedly.

To his great dismay, she sat up, taking the weight of her glorious breasts with her. She went to fist her hands on her hips, but her knuckles bumped into *his* hands. And he wasn't letting go. Hell no, he was holding on for all he was worth. Which left her only one option. She crossed her arms.

Praise Jesus, he thought when the most delicious line of cleavage appeared above the V-neck of her purple sweater.

"Hey!" She snapped a finger in front of his face. "Pay attention."

"Sorry. It's hard to focus with all"—he waved in the general direction of her chest—"*that* going on."

She glanced down, saw what was holding him enthralled, and quickly uncrossed her arms.

"Damnit." He frowned.

"I swear, all you men are the same. Put a pair of boobs in your face, and your IQ drops fifty points."

"It's biology, babe. Propagation of the species."

"Whatever." She adjusted her glasses. She looked absolutely adorable when she was being sincere. "I'm serious, Dagan. I need to know."

"I'm sorry. My IQ is currently in the toilet… You need to know what?"

"Why you haven't given me the time of day for years, but now, suddenly, you've turned into a kissy, handsy, bearded Don Juan. What gives?"

He could have told her everything. How he had

wanted her from day one, but that Afghanistan had happened and his brother had happened and Senator Aldus had happened—and afterward he had never dreamed she would want anything to do with him. How he had continued to want her, to fantasize about her until his control had finally snapped back in Spider's penthouse. How he had been, and still was, shocked as shit that she could know all his secrets and still want him, too. Yes, he could have told her all that.

Something held him back.

Maybe it was pride. Maybe it was shame. Or hell, maybe it was just self-preservation. Because if he laid himself open—ripped his ribs apart and exposed his heart—and she brushed him off, he wasn't sure he would recover from the rejection.

"Professionalism," he said.

She wrinkled her nose, causing her delightful cinnamon freckles to meld together. "Huh?"

"I didn't make a move while we both worked for the Company because fraternization between employees was frowned upon. Same goes for after you became the liaison to BKI. We were coworkers. I had to respect that distinction."

She narrowed her eyes, head canted to the side. He liked to call it her "thinking pose." After a second she said, "But…aren't we *still* coworkers?"

He'd dug himself into a hole, and the only way out was to keep digging with the hope he could break through to the other side. "That's a negative. The minute you uploaded that virus onto Morrison's PC—and the minute the boys back at BKI began hacking his systems and finding the evidence to bring the asslick down—was the beginning of the end for BKI. I'd say I am now officially a civilian. And you, babycakes, are now officially back to being a CIA counterintelligence officer. So, no more conflicts."

   He winked even though he was sure to burn in hell for the lies he had just told.

Chapter 12

DEATH BY A THOUSAND CUTS.

That's what it felt like to sit there, straddling Dagan Zoelner, the man Chelsea had lusted after for years, and hear him admit that all that time he had wanted her too. Especially since there was no way she could act on all the chemistry bubbling between them, not with the Big Bad Secret flying around over her head.

The awful thing was always there. And when she least expected it to, it would dive-bomb her like the seagulls had that time her mom and dad took her to Hilton Head for Labor Day weekend. Back when there had been money for vacations. Back before hardship and struggle and *responsibility* became the be-all, end-all of life.

So, yup. She was going to have to do one of the hardest things ever. She was going to have to turn down the oh-so-sexy man of her dreams.

Trouble was, she cared about him too much to reject him outright. She didn't want to hurt him. He'd been hurt enough. So she racked her brain for a way to let him down easy.

There was always *It's not you, it's me*. But that was far too trite. She considered telling him she had an incurable, highly contagious venereal disease. But her pride wouldn't let her go that far. So, that left her with…what?

The truth, a little voice whispered through her head.

The truth? Well, the truth was that she *couldn't* make

love to him because she wouldn't be satisfied with a little bit of afternoon delight when what she'd fantasized about for years was a fairy-tale happily ever after. The truth was that they *couldn't* have happily ever after because the minute they started down that path, she'd be forced to come clean about what had really happened in Afghanistan. The truth was that she...*loved* him.

And there it was.

The *ultimate* truth.

A long time ago, Chelsea had shoved it down deep, where she had hoped it would either become part of the fabric of her being or else lead to septic shock that would put her out of her misery.

"So what do you say?" Dagan prompted when she had been quiet for too long. "Want to put that condom in my wallet to good use?"

Yes! So much. But I...can't.

Then the solution to her dilemma suddenly presented itself. She wouldn't have to reject him if she could get *him* to reject *her*. Which should be easy enough, given that she knew his weaknesses, his worries, the responsibilities he had shouldered and refused to unburden himself of. It startled her, actually, how well she knew him.

"And if we act on this...*thing*"—she waved a hand between them, staunchly ignoring the feel of his erection pulsing between her legs—"what then? Like you said, you're officially a civilian working at a custom chop shop in Chicago. And I'm back to being a counterintelligence officer at Langley."

Instead of answering, Dagan grabbed her hand and splayed it against his, measuring the difference in size and texture. His palm was large and hard and calloused. Hers was small and soft and unblemished. Threading their fingers together, he tugged her forward.

She could have resisted, she supposed. But if this was the last time she was in his arms, what harm could there be in allowing herself to revel for just a little longer?

With her breasts pillowed against his broad chest and the curve of her lower belly cushioning the steely evidence of his desire, his sweet breath fanned her face. She could have gone on just like that for eternity. Feeling him breathe. Feeling his heart beat in time with hers. Feeling his passion for her.

"Dagan." Her voice was so scratchy it sounded like she'd been swallowing cockleburs. "I need you to answer me and…"

Any remaining words died quick deaths when he carefully removed her glasses. She blinked at him until he came into focus, then frowned when he folded the earpieces and set her glasses aside.

"Chelsea." Once more, he settled his big hands on her hips and softly kneaded. When he said her name like that, she nearly had a mini-orgasm on the spot. "Don't draw a line in the sand you can't cross later."

Her brow knitted. "I'm sorry. Did you just pull a Gollum on me? Was that some sort of riddle?"

He laughed. The low, rolling sound made her ovaries explode. If she looked around, she was certain she'd see eggs lying everywhere, just waiting to be fertilized. The flash of his straight, white teeth against the backdrop of the Beard was enough to stop her heart, and in her head, she didn't hear Gollum's voice, but Yoda's saying, *The Devastating Grin Game is strong with this one*. She was obviously getting her odd, pointy-eared gnomes mixed up.

"I'm saying that for right now, let's forget about the past, stop thinking about the future, and just live in the moment."

And there it was. Her plan was falling into place perfectly.

So why does it hurt so much?

"Said every boy in the backseat of his car on prom night," she told him with a wry twist of her lips.

It was utterly fake, her grin. Because what she *really* wanted was to curl up in the corner and have a good cry. Just whimper and wail and curse the decision that had brought her here, to this moment, when she was presented with a dream—the dream of *him*—and forced to turn away from it.

"And like the backseat on prom night, let's make some sweet memories."

"I'm saying," she said, "that if you'll hold your horses and try thinking with your big head instead of Little Z's head—"

"Just FYI," he interrupted, "there's nothing little about Little Z."

Don't I know it, she thought. Because some things were obvious, even covered by a layer of thick denim. What she *said* was, "My point is that what we start here today is doomed to come to a quick and decisive end once we're back stateside and hundreds of miles away from each other."

His brow puckered. "Are you saying you *don't* want that, or you *do* want that?"

"I'm saying I'm thirty-two years old and way past the point of settling for a two-pump chump."

"Excuse me?" He could not have looked more offended if he'd tried. "I have *never* been a two-pump chump. Feel free to ask any of the women I've been with. They'll tell you I—"

She shoved a finger over his mouth because the last thing she wanted to talk about was the women he'd had.

His whiskers tickled her skin and reminded her of how those same whiskers had tickled her neck and her ear and… "Z, I'm trying to make you understand that what I want and what you want are two entirely different things. So it's better to stop this crazy train before it has a chance to go off the rails."

"What happened to Dagan?"

"Huh?"

"Since we came down here, you've been calling me Dagan. But just now you went back to calling me Z. Why?"

She sat up and frowned at him. "I didn't realize I was doing it, I guess. Dagan or Z, it's all the same to me. Both are *you*." Although that wasn't quite true. Calling him Dagan had always felt so…intimate. Too intimate. "Why? You have a preference?"

"I like the way my name sounds on your lips," he said. "With just the hint of that Southern drawl."

The words themselves were innocuous, taken one by one. But put them together and combine them with his deep, moonshine voice, and they were an invitation to sin. Her mouth went bone-dry.

Funny, considering other parts of me are the opposite.

"Stop trying to change the subject," she scolded him.

"Is that what I'm doing?" She felt his smile in her bones. Deeper. In her *soul*.

"*Yes*. You're doing everything in your power to detour this conversation straight toward Sexy Town."

"But it's such a nice destination, don't you think?"

Oh, how easy it would be to just let him have his way! But…then what?

"Look, I know Little Z is calling the shots right now, but just for a couple of seconds would it be possible for me to talk to Big Z?"

To ensure *both* their minds were focused on the conversation, she crawled off him. Sitting on the cold floor she immediately missed his fiery warmth. She tried to generate her own heat by pulling her legs up and wrapping her arms around her shins. A glint of purple from her discarded glasses caught her eye and had her reaching for them. Sliding them on, the world around her went from soft, fuzzy shapes to hard, sharp edges — including Dagan.

He was the human equivalent of a hard, sharp edge. And she studiously avoided looking at the fly of his jeans when he sighed and pushed into a seated position. His legs looked a mile long as he stretched them out and crossed them at the ankles. "First of all, I call a permanent moratorium on the phrase *Little Z*. And second of all, do you realize the expression on your face makes you look like you're about to give birth to an oversized, ill-tempered hedgehog?"

"Nice." Chelsea frowned at him. "Very nice."

He curled a big, warm hand around her ankle, all trace of humor gone. "Okay, babe, I give." *Babe*. A simple endearment. But it hit her so hard that she lost her breath. "Say whatever it is you need to say. Big Z is all ears."

Chapter 13

CHELSEA PURSED HER BEE-STUNG LIPS, AND DAGAN WAS sorely tempted to lean forward and take her up on the invitation she'd unwittingly sent him. But something was...*off* with her. So he remained where he was, satisfying himself with simply touching her, watching as her big, expressive eyes searched his face.

The longer she looked at him, the more he felt his chances of being with her slipping through his fingers. It reminded him of the mist that had crept over Lake Erie in the springtime. Or his brother's sobriety in those early years. Here one minute, gone the next. Impossible to hold on to.

His heart beat sickly. Maybe he had been wrong to hope. Maybe there really *was* no way a woman like her could—

"I'm done playing the field," she told him in a rush. That sounded fine by him. Just the *idea* of her with another man... Uh, *no*. Negative. No fuckin' way. "I want a man who's ready to take the next steps in life. Who's ready for marriage. Who wants children."

Marriage? Children? *Seriously?*

With Black Knights Inc. going civilian, he didn't know where he'd be in a year, *who* he'd be in a year. He was no mechanic, so there'd be nothing for him to do for the shop. Not to mention there was Avan.

Always, there is Avan.

His mind was ripped back to the day of his father's aneurysm. Dagan had been home on spring break from graduate school, and Avan was about to finish his freshman year at Ohio State University. They had all been in the kitchen, laughing over some ridiculous thing involving their batty neighbor who kept potbellied pigs. And then their father had suddenly stopped and sat down on the linoleum floor right beside the kitchen table.

Dagan remembered exchanging a look with Avan before squatting beside his father...

"Dad?" He squeezed his old man's knee. "What's up?"

His father looked up at him, and there was something funny going on with his eyes. "Head," his father said, sounding breathless, blinking quickly. "Pop."

Dagan didn't know much about human biology, other than what he had learned in his science classes, but he knew something was definitely wrong with his dad. Fear became a poisonous flower that bloomed in his chest as he turned to Avan. "Call 911!" he yelled, then swung back to his father. "Dad, hang on, okay? We'll have help coming soon."

His father stared up at him, but there was a haze in his eyes, as if he couldn't see clearly. The grip of his dad's hand when he grabbed Dagan's shoulder, however, was as strong as ever. "Take care..." His father shuddered. In pain? In fear? Dagan didn't know. He was so helpless. So wretchedly helpless.

"Yes!" he heard his brother yelling into the phone. "That's right! Come right away! I think my dad is having a stroke or a heart attack or—"

"Dagan." His father's hand squeezed tighter.

"Don't try to talk, Dad. Just—"

"Your brother." His father cut him off. "Take care of..." He shuddered again. "Your brother."

"I will, Dad. I—"

"Promise." The hand on his arm had become a vise.
"I swear it! But, Dad, you don't have to—"
That's all Dagan managed before his father's eyes
rolled back and he tumbled to his side, dead.

Dagan's flashbacks didn't always involve Afghanistan.
And that promise? The promise to take care of Avan?
Well, he'd failed to keep it at first. He had been too
busy in graduate school, then too busy being recruited
by and going to work for the CIA. But the day he had
received that call in Afghanistan that Avan was in the
hospital recovering from an overdose was the day he had
known he could no longer shirk his duty to his brother or
sidestep his promise to his father.

He had put in for a transfer stateside and had gone
about handing off his assets to other agents. Then
had come the bombing and his ultimate ejection from
the CIA.

With no job and very limited savings, Dagan hadn't
had the cash to book his brother into the ninety-day
recovery program Avan had so desperately needed. So
when Senator Aldus had approached Dagan about an off-
the-books job to find missing files, Dagan had jumped
at the chance to make some much-needed moolah. Little
had he known that the senator was corruption incarnate,
and the files Dagan had been hired to retrieve were proof
of Aldus's criminal endeavors. By the time he *had* found
out, it was almost too late.

Luckily for him, that job for the senator had put him in
the path of the Black Knights. They had seen something
in him. Something beyond the dishonorable discharge
from the Company. Something more than the man who'd
been duped by one of his own government officials.

They had offered him a job, and it had paid for

Avan's rehab. Both that first time, and then again two years later when Avan fell off the wagon.

And the rest, as they say, is history.

But it wasn't the past that was making Dagan's heart beat too fast now. It was the future. Where would he go? What would he do? How would he continue to keep an eye on his little brother or make the money it would take to put Avan through rehab for a third time, should he need it?

Dagan knew the answers to none of that. Was terrified of all those unknowns, in fact. And here was Chelsea talking about marriage and children.

"For God's sake, Chels." Dagan ran a hand over his beard. "Don't we get to have fun before we get serious?"

"That's my point." She speared him with a knowing look. "No. We don't. Or at least *I* don't. I know you, Z." He really wished she'd go back to calling him Dagan. "I know you haven't thought about what happens *after* we scratch our itch." The fact that she'd hit the proverbial nail on the head made him shift uncomfortably. "Are you going to move to Washington to be with me? Are you going to leave Avan in Chicago to fend for himself?"

"I…" He shook his head, unable to go on. He could hear the mad rush of blood in the hollows of his ears.

Her expression softened, and she reached down to pat the hand he still had wrapped around her ankle. She might have the curves of an Amazon, but she had the bones of a bird, so small, so fragile. "I know," she said. "Let's agree to be friends, okay?"

The sickly beat of his heart had turned positively bilious. "Naked friends?" He forced a smile he knew didn't come within spitting distance of his eyes.

She chuckled, but he noticed her smile didn't reach her eyes either. "You're a hard man to—"

That's all she managed before the sound of feet pounding down the metal steps interrupted her. "You two better come back topside," Emily said, standing on the second-to-last tread. "Looks like we could have trouble."

Chapter 14

"DON'T WORRY," BENTON SAID. "WE AREN'T SNOOKERED yet. I've written an algorithm that slaps the wanker in the face every time he tries to find a back door. But between you and me, he's good. Maybe the best I've seen."

Steven Surry wasn't keen on all the tech talk. He wouldn't know an algorithm from an apple, a back door from a badminton racket. But he knew he could rely on Benton to delay whoever was trying to hack into Morrison's system. Hadn't it been Benton's personal software, installed on all of Morrison's computers, that had alerted them to the breach in the first place?

That chap knows his onions, Steven thought. Aloud he said, "Good. That's good. But the question now becomes, *who* is trying to infiltrate Morrison's systems? And why? My first guess would be that someone is trying to bring him down for his…you know what." He glanced over at the old man. After Morrison had come to, he had cursed roundly and then demanded to know what Steven had accomplished while he was out.

Luckily, Steven's plan of attack had pleased Morrison. Now the skinny old wank was reclined on the red sofa, talking in hushed tones on one of the mobiles he had fished from a drawer in his desk where Steven was currently balancing a hip.

"But my worry is that those blasted Panama Papers

tipped someone off that not everything in Morrison's organization is precisely as one would expect," he added. He and his security team had been in the process of going through all twelve million leaked documents, hunting for clues that might link Morrison to the mysterious underworld crime boss known only as Spider, but so far, they'd come up clean. Still, that didn't mean someone *else* hadn't found some sort of connection.

"I suppose it's possible. I wouldn't put it past— Stupid knob! Sodding gobshite!" Steven knew Benton wasn't speaking to him, especially since the sound of Benton's fingers clickety-clacking over the keyboard increased their speed. After about ten seconds, Benton added, "That's right, you bloody wankstain. Eat my digital dust." Then, more calmly, he said, "Now what were we talking about?"

"Chelsea Duvall…who sent her and why."

"Oh right." Benton's voice seemed to shrug. "You know, it doesn't really matter why. The fact remains that she was bloody well *sent*. What does Spider want you to do?"

Again, Steven snuck a peek at Morrison. "Find her. Find the thumb drive. Whatever it takes."

Benton snorted. "Sounds about right." Then he added, "But have you considered what will happen if the authorities catch up to her before you do? If she is working for the Americans in some way, she could come clean. Where would that leave us?"

"Spider assures me he has contacts inside who will all-too-happily hand her over to us, should she be apprehended. But of course he prefers that we use the information the authorities share with us and then take care of the nasty business ourselves."

"And can you take of it yourself? Do you have any

idea where to begin looking for her?" The sound of Benton's rattling keyboard was almost hypnotic.

"It took some work and more time than I would have liked, but Scotland Yard forwarded CCTV footage that shows five figures on Ducatis racing out of the city a little over an hour ago."

"Five? I thought you said there were four of them in total. Chelsea and the three masked men."

"There were five on the motorbikes. Three men, Chelsea, and what looked to be another woman. They were all helmeted, so I couldn't see their faces on the film. But Chelsea was easily recognizable. That derriere alone…"

"Right-oh!" Benton chuckled. "I've seen photos of her. She is one well-padded woman."

Ignoring that, Steven continued, "They were heading south on the A2. I'm thinking Folkestone or Dover. They'll likely try for a Channel crossing by ferry or via the Chunnel."

At least he hoped that's what they were doing. He was *betting* that's what they were doing. Betting everything, in fact. Not just his own life, but his mother's as well.

In Spider's organization, there was no such thing as getting sacked. Failure equaled death. Pure and simple. And if Steven died, his mother would be transferred out of that posh facility Spider's paychecks allowed him to keep her in and sent to one of those dodgy government-run places where the patients were allowed to sit around in shat-filled trousers half the day. He suffered no illusions that she would last long in a place like that.

The surgery to remove her brain tumor had been a success. She was now cancer-free. But while recovering, she had suffered a debilitating stroke that had left her mostly paralyzed and completely unable to speak.

She was still alive and kicking inside the shell of her wrecked body, however. Her eyes lit up—the same dark eyes she had passed to him—whenever he went for a visit. And the little computer he had purchased for her, the one she could type on with the pointer finger of her left hand—which, miraculously, she had retained the use of—allowed her some rudimentary communication. She always asked how he was and then listened avidly before typing out the words: *I love you. I'm proud of you.*

If she only knew, Steven thought now.

He *would* do this thing for Spider, just as he had done a hundred other distasteful things for the man. Things that went against his morals and his training. Things that would make his loving mum weep if she ever found out.

"Our friend in Scotland Yard has teams waiting at the Chunnel and ferry terminals," he told Benton. "I'm headed there as soon as I get off with you."

"Well, good luck to you, mate." Benton signed off.

At the same time Morrison ended his call and turned to Steven. "It's confirmed. Cameras in Dover picked them up traveling through the center of town."

"Mother England's overabundance of surveillance equipment comes to the rescue once again," Steven mumbled.

It was said there was one CCTV camera for every eleven English citizens. That usually made the work he did a bit tricky. But in this case, those nasty little fish-eyed fucks—as well as the vast network of sources his boss had inside the British government—were coming in rather handy.

"Seems you were right about them trying for a Channel crossing," Morrison mused, fiddling with the ridiculous bun at the back of his head. "The noose is closing. Shall you and I head south?"

"You want to come with me?" Steven couldn't hide his surprise.

Red mottled Morrison's cheeks, and his bloodshot eyes glowed fiercely in the light from the office chandelier. "She came into *my* house with that sad sap story about her mum and the childhood home she was desperately trying to save, pulling at my heartstrings." Steven knew it hadn't been a story. The background check he had run on Chelsea was in depth. She *had* been trying for years to pay down the mortgages on her family's home, the house her parents had built themselves. Still, that didn't mean she wasn't *also* working for the American government.

"Then the duplicitous bitch turned around and poisoned *my* property and is poised to bring down *my* empire along with..." The old man didn't finished the sentence. Instead he swallowed and breathed heavily. "I want to be there when she's captured. I want to be there when she's turned over to you. I want to be there when you question her, and...whatever else might need to happen. In fact, I might fancy *helping* you with whatever else might need to happen. As my doddering old parish priest used to say, 'Vengeance is mine, sayeth the Lord!'"

Bile climbed into the back of Steven's throat.

Chapter 15

The English Channel

"SON OF A SHIT-SPECKLED FRAGGLE FART!" ACE BELLOWED when the catamaran tacked quickly to starboard, causing Emily to lose her balance and stomp all over his feet. Her arms pinwheeled, and the entire ship tilted.

Or is that just me?

She prepared her ass for a personal introduction to the deck, but she was suddenly pulled forward and into Christian's lap. Blinking and feeling a little dizzy, she glanced at Ace. He was bent down, rubbing his ill-treated feet.

"Sorry," she said. Then she turned to thank Christian for coming to her rescue, but the words stuck in her throat.

She'd never been this close to him.

Holy duck balls! To say he was smokin' was an understatement. He had a quintessentially English appearance. Handsome in a way that American men were not. His face was all sharp angles and hard planes. And his jaw? Well, his jaw appeared to have been hewn from granite, resulting in a stubborn, resolute slab of flesh and bone.

For the first time, Emily could make out the brown flecks in the centers of his light-green eyes and measure the bump on the bridge of his straight English nose. And then there was his body...his hard thighs beneath her ass. His chest like a steel wall along her side. She imagined she had jumped astride a machine made of pure muscle, something built solely for tensile strength.

Or, she thought, *in layman's terms, he's all that, a bag of chips, and a twenty-four-ounce soda*.

And here she was, on a boat with five other people and no place to give her kitty a quick spanking.

My kingdom for a little privacy! she silently railed.

"You all right?" Christian asked, his accent making the last two words sound more like *awl roight*.

For the love of Paulie Konerko, his warm breath smelled good, like teacakes and toothpaste. It brushed over her cheeks in a teasing caress, and she considered leaning in to take a quick taste. Of course, right after that wholly inappropriate thought rolled a tide of common sense.

No. No way. So much nope. Best that she keep on doing what she had been doing since she walked through the big doors of the warehouse back in Chi-Town. Namely, ignoring the fact that Christian should go by the name of Smokin' McHolyhot and that he made her pulse stutter any time he opened his mouth and out came that delicious English drawl.

Emily had never thought of herself as an anglophile before Christian. Now? Well, as they say, *God save the Queen!*

But she'd learned her lesson about fraternizing with coworkers. The last time she'd done so, her entire life had been turned upside down. And considering she quite liked the *new* life she'd built for herself, the one that included a move back to her hometown—*Go Sox!*—and a job with the Black Knights, she was determined not to make the same mistake she'd made before.

Therefore Christian Watson, with his hella hot bod and even hella hotter accent, was strictly off-limits for anything more than a little flirtation via a few well-placed verbal barbs.

Was that immature? Like the boys who had sat in the pew behind her at St. Mary's and pulled her ponytail when she was a little girl? Sure. But it was still damn good fun. And it helped soothe the ache she sometimes felt, knowing that she could never have a happily ever after, that she would never—

"Emily?"

She blinked and realized she'd been sitting there staring up at Christian like a slack-jawed idiot. If she'd thought riding behind him on that Ducati was heaven, it was nothing compared to sitting on his *lap*. The smell of his expensive cologne tunneled up her nose. It was both zesty and sweet and brought to mind two sweating bodies rolling around on cool silk sheets.

"Sorry!" She scrambled off Christian and plopped onto the bench beside him. "Thanks for the catch. I'd be flat on my ass if it weren't for your quick reflexes." When he lifted a brow, she frowned and demanded, "What?"

"Just…that may well be the first time you've ever thanked me for anything. Are you feeling a touch lurgy?" He pressed a hand to her forehead, feigning a look of concern.

Before she could answer, or ask what the hell *lurgy* meant, Zoelner demanded from the top of the steps, "What's all the ruckus up here?"

"I'll give you two guesses, and the first one doesn't count." Ace shot a quick, meaningful glance back and forth between Emily and Christian.

"I'm not talking about those two." Zoelner made a face, then seemed to get distracted by Chelsea who had come to take a seat on Christian's opposite side.

If Emily wasn't mistaken, that was beard burn

around Chelsea's mouth. She looked over at Zoelner and noticed that his hair stuck up every which way, like he'd plugged his finger into an electrical socket.

Well, it's about damn time, she thought with a smile.

"Hello?" Zoelner snapped his fingers. "Emily, mind filling me in on why you came down the stairs like your hair was on fire and declared we might be in trouble?"

How had she forgotten about the cutter that was three nautical miles off their port side? *Oh, of course. Finding myself sitting on Christian Watson's lap, that's how.*

"It's the HMC *Valiant*," Rusty answered for her, pointing at the tiny gray speck on the horizon. The sky was overcast, and the Channel was the color of wet cement on a Chicago sidewalk, so the cutter was only visible when one of its windows caught a stray ray of light. Rusty kept one hand on the wheel and lifted the binoculars to his eyes. "She's a Border Agency vessel. Think something along the lines of our Coast Guard back home. I've seen her patrolling these waters plenty of times before."

"So where's the trouble then?" Zoelner asked.

"The trouble is I've made two course corrections that the *Valiant* has mirrored. Unless I'm mistaken, she's following us."

"Oh. Well…fuck." Zoelner raked a hand over his beard.

"You said it," Rusty concurred.

"Why would she be following us?"

"Talk over the marine channels makes it seem like they're checking all the ships in the Channel that are coming from England." Rusty lowered the binoculars and glanced at the group sitting behind him. "Just who did you guys piss off anyway?"

"You haven't turned on your television or radio today, have you?" Zoelner asked.

"No." Rusty's eyes narrowed. "Should I have?"

"Probably best you don't," Zoelner assured him. Some men would pace back and forth, given the situation. Zoelner just got ghostly still and asked, "So what now?"

"Well"—Rusty shook his head—"as always happens when you're dancing with the devil, there *is* an alternative. But none of you are going to like it."

Chapter 16

"PLEASE TELL ME THAT WHAT WE'RE ABOUT TO DO WILL be the mint on the pillow at the end of this day," Emily muttered.

Chelsea glanced over at her with a sympathetic expression. They were hunkered down outside the wheelhouse, watching the shoreline race by them. The low-hanging clouds overhead seemed almost close enough to touch.

Rusty had been right. The cutter *had* been shadowing them. The minute he turned the catamaran back toward England, the Border Agency ship pursued, slowly closing the distance between the two vessels. Rusty was convinced they would be boarded the instant they put in to port. Which was why Chelsea was in the process of donning her courage like a suit of armor made by the Dwarves of Middle-earth. Or, in short, she was going to need every ounce of chutzpah she possessed for what came next.

"Because I have to admit," Emily continued, "I've had about all the excitement I can stand for one day."

"It's not just me, right?" Chelsea asked. "This hare-brained scheme feels like seven kinds of wrong to you too?"

The wind and sea spray coming over the side of the boat raised gooseflesh on her arms. The salty smell of the Channel reminded her of the Atlantic back home—and the endless winter storms that had fascinated her as a child.

She recalled the time she and her father stood on their back porch, and her father pointed at the heaving waves tipped in white and hurling themselves against the coastline of Port Royal Sound.

Look at that, sweet girl, he had said. *See how mouthy Mother Nature can be when she has something to say?*

Chelsea hoped Mother Nature went against type now, took pity on her, and had only *nice* things to say.

"More like seven*teen* kinds of wrong," Emily agreed, her long hair flying wild. "So help me take my mind off what we're about to do and tell me what happened between you and Zoelner when you two disappeared belowdecks."

Chelsea opened her mouth to deny that *anything* had happened, but before she could, Emily interrupted with "And don't try to say it was nothing. Because Zoelner's hair looked like it'd gone through hurricane-force winds, and judging by the rash around your mouth, you either gave him a good tongue tango, or else you spent the day lip-locking a porcupine."

Gritting her teeth, Chelsea wondered what would happen if she told Emily to mind her own damned business. On second thought, she *knew* what would happen. Emily would scoff and brush her off, and then wheedle until Chelsea eventually gave in. It was a well-known fact within the hallowed halls of Black Knights Inc. that Emily Scott had only a passing familiarity with the word *privacy*. Nosiness was just her nature.

Having no energy to withstand any wheedling—and still feeling drained and strangely disappointed by the way things had ended belowdecks—Chelsea admitted, "Yup. We did some…"

She racked her brain for the right words to describe the wonder of being in Dagan's arms. "*Adult* things," she finally finished, wrinkling her nose because *lame-oh!*

Turning back toward the railing, Chelsea concentrated on watching the coastline whiz by. Brick houses with white dormers came into view to the south. A gray stone building clung to the side of a hill, its tall, pitched corners giving it a vague castle-like feel.

The town of Folkestone.

If she craned her head around, she could see the long arm of the pier jutting out into the Channel. It was crooked as a dog's hind leg, a monstrosity of human construction that looked eerily out of place amid the brown and green vegetation of the countryside, the soft gray waves that lapped at its base, and the cheery English town at its back.

Her heart fluttered against her ribs. Tipping her chin back, she peered through the window into the wheel-house. The BKI boys were down on their knees, taking off their shoes and socks and stuffing them into the two waterproof float bags Rusty had graciously given them.

Chivalry at its finest, she thought as she watched Dagan slip her backpack into the float bag he would carry.

Turning back, she saw Emily eyeing her. "What?"

"So what happened *after* you did adult things?"

Sounded as lame coming out of Emily's mouth as it had coming out of Chelsea's.

Before Chelsea could answer, Emily drew her own conclusions. "Oh no!" She lifted her hand to her mouth. "Did it take a weird turn? Does he have dragon breath?" A look of horror came over Emily's face. "Is he one of those guys who tries to touch your tonsils with his tongue? He is, isn't he? Oh, *gross*!"

"First of all," Chelsea said exasperatedly, "he doesn't

have dragon breath. Second of all, it didn't take a weird turn, and he sure as shit didn't do that torpedo-tongue thing you're talking about. Just the opposite, it was... He was..." What? What was he? There weren't enough words in the English language to describe the glory of his kiss, the splendor of his unapologetic bump and grind. "*Wonderful*," she finally finished.

Too wonderful. She was ruined for all other men.

"So then what's the problem?" Emily's brow furrowed. "Why are you both acting funky around each other now?"

"We aren't."

"Ahem." Emily held up a hand. "In case it escaped your notice, while Rusty was laying out this plan, you and Zoelner didn't get up to your usual shenanigans. Zoelner didn't say one word about you not being cut out for this kind of stuff. And you didn't once tell him to shove a sock in it. In fact, it was nothing but crickets and tumbleweeds from the both of you."

Chelsea shot Emily a dirty look for being right. Then she admitted, "The *problem* is we want different things in life."

"Psshh." Emily rolled her eyes. "Don't we all? Compromise, baby. Isn't that what couples do?"

"Z and I are *far* from a couple." Chelsea did her best to ignore the ache that sad truth started somewhere in the vicinity of her breastbone. Figuring the only way out of the conversation was to turn the tables—and needing a distraction from thoughts of what she was about to do— she said, "But enough about me and Z. I want to know what's up with you and Christian."

Emily's expression shuttered like someone had drawn a set of blackout shades over her face. "Why does everyone assume something is up with us? Can't we just be coworkers who like to give each other crap? Does it have to be more than that?"

Chelsea sniffed the breeze. "Is that the scent of bullshit I smell?"

Emily's eyes narrowed.

"Oh, come on now." Chelsea shook her head. "Are you really sitting there trying to convince me you don't think Christian is hot?"

"Of *course* I think he's hot. How could I not? I got eyeballs, don't I?" When Emily got worked up, she whipped out her South Side 'hood girl grammar.

"So what's the problem?" Chelsea shot Emily's earlier words back at her.

"The *problem* is it'd turn into more than just a little wham-bam, thank you, man. I know from experience. I tried once before to have a thing with a coworker, and…" She curled her upper lip. "It blew up in my face. All that forced togetherness, all those shared experiences and mutual friends? Yeah, I suppose it was inevitable that he started to want more than the occasional desktop diddle."

"And you…*didn't* want more?" Chelsea prompted.

"Hell no." Emily made a scoffing sound, but Chelsea thought she detected something wistful in Emily's eyes. "For me, men are only good for recreational purposes. And since that's the case, I've learned not to shit where I eat. When it comes to coworkers, I'm on a strict man cleanse." Chelsea opened her mouth to demand more details, but Emily lifted a hand. "That's enough show-and-tell for now, don't you think?"

Chelsea harrumphed. The sound caught in the wind and melded with the growl and grumble of the churning twin engines. "Have you ever noticed you have no issue sticking your nose in other people's business, but the instant someone tries to get the four-one-one on *you*, you close up tighter than a clamshell? It's enough to make a preacher cuss."

Emily's grin was unapologetic as she gathered her dark, rioting hair into a ponytail. "And it's one of my better qualities, don't you think? Speaking of sticking my nose in other people's business, let's get back to you and Zoelner."

Chelsea groaned. "Nope." She adamantly shook her head. "Just hold that thought forever."

Emily feigned a pout. "Despite my current lack of a sex life and my utter lack of interest in a love life"— there was that odd, wistful look again—"you should know that neither of those things affects my judgment when it comes to matters of the heart for *other* people. I've been told I give excellent relationship advice."

Rusty was slowing the boat, which meant they were getting close to their destination. Chelsea's stomach clenched into a fist. "Would it offend you terribly if I said that right now I want your two cents about as much as I want a third nipple?"

"Who *wouldn't* want a third nipple?" Emily blinked in mock confusion. "I mean, you'd up your pleasure ante by fifty percent. Plus, a man has two hands *and* a mouth, so…" She let the sentence dangle.

Chelsea laughed. The two of them had become friends in the time Emily had worked for BKI, and Chelsea was going to miss Emily's boundless enthusiasm and no-holds-barred way of expressing herself once they finished this mission.

In fact, she was going to miss a *lot* once the boys and girls of Black Knights Inc. officially became civilians and she went back to piloting a desk at Langley. Like the smell of metal grinding as the Knights built the custom bikes that acted as their cover. Like the way they all teased and tormented one another, but when push came to shove, they banded together like family. But most of all, she was going to miss…Dagan.

It was as if the thought of him conjured him to life. He, Christian, and Ace crouch-walked out of the wheelhouse. The Border Agency cutter was still a good two miles behind them. Only if someone was out on her deck with powerful binoculars would they be able to see anyone aboard the catamaran. Still, no one was taking any chances.

Even all hunched over, Chelsea felt the impact of Dagan hit her smack in the solar plexus. She was mesmerized by the breadth of his shoulders and the way the wind caught his dark hair and ran loving fingers through the silken strands. He was a man who had danced with the Reaper and come out the winner, and it showed in the certainty of his movements, each one a lesson in economical grace.

"You ready for this?" His moonshine voice cut through the noise of the wind and waves as easily as a knife cut through her mother's famous flaky crab cakes. That was one thing they *hadn't* had to give up after her father's death when money became tight. The crab pots her father had left behind assured them that come crab season, they were well fed. "Anything I can do to help?" he finished.

Okay, so Emily was right. Before that scene down in the hold, Dagan wouldn't have asked, *You ready for this?* or *Anything I can do to help?* He would have grumpily informed her that she *wasn't* ready for this, and then he would have outlined exactly what he was going to do to help her.

Everything had changed between them.

And, oh! The irony!

For years, she'd wanted him to treat her like an equal, like an agent who knew what she was doing. Now that he finally *was*, she wanted things to go back to the way they were before. When they had snapped and snarled, poked and prodded. *That* had felt right. But this? Yeah. No.

Of course, she couldn't tell *him* that. Instead, she forced a wry grin, added a saucy wink, and gave him one of her daddy's Southern-fried favorites. "Am I ready for this? Does a farm dog have fleas?"

Rusty had managed to keep a good distance between his catamaran and the cutter. But he had assured them that wouldn't last for long, not nearly long enough for them to sail back to Dover, and then dock and unload before the Border Agency ship was on top of them. Instead, he had turned them south, piloting them full steam toward Folkestone, the town he had called home since moving to England.

"There's a long pier that juts way out into the water. It's called the Folkestone Harbor Arm," he had said, outlining his plan. "I can sail behind it, and you can all hop overboard. It's perfect because while we're back there, we'll be out of the cutter's line of sight."

Sounded easy, right?

Wrong.

Turned out, the pier was a massive construction that didn't have anywhere for a small boat the size of Rusty's catamaran to pull up to. Which meant they were going to have to *swim*.

Now, usually swimming wasn't a problem for Chelsea. Liquid locomotion was something she had mastered at the precocious age of three. But *that* had been in late June in the creek running behind her house with her father looking on. What Rusty proposed was a dunking in the freezing cold waters of the Channel in late March. And as if that weren't enough, they were supposed to use the pier's pilings as cover against any curious onlookers while battling the waves and the current on their way to shore.

When Rusty had told them *that* part of the plan, he had taken one look at the disbelief on her face and pointed a finger at her nose. "And see," he'd said. "That's why this plan is perfect. Those Border Agency boys won't think for one minute anyone would have the cojones to hop into the Channel right now. So when I sail back to Dover and dock, and they find nothing but little ol' me, they won't be the least bit suspicious."

Good. Great, Chelsea had thought. *Unless, of course, we all drown.*

"Is there nowhere *else* you could drop us ashore?" she had asked.

"The coastline around here is pretty straight and barren." The look Rusty had given her was sympathetic. "Our only hope for a few minutes of cover is the Folkestone Harbor Arm."

The massive shadow of that very thing suddenly loomed over the catamaran, dragging her back to the present. There was a lighthouse at the end of the pier. It towered above them as they made their way to the opposite side. She couldn't shake the sensation that it was a giant smirking down at them, laughing at the audacity of their plan.

Fee-fi-fo-fum, she imagined it chuckled. *I smell the blood of Americans.*

The waves gently rocked the vessel as Rusty sailed the boat closer to shore. He turned the catamaran suddenly, darting between the harbor arm's leggy pilings.

Ten seconds later, he cut the engines and ducked through the wheelhouse door, then ran to the bow of the boat and tied a rope from the catamaran to a huge, rusted metal loop on one piling. After the boat was secure, he joined them on the far side of the wheelhouse.

"Everybody ready to get wet and wild?" he asked, surveying the scene around the boat. "I noticed the pier is empty. I was hoping that'd be the case."

Right. Because March wasn't a month for tourists, and the day had turned too cold and windy for the local folks to latch on to the idea of an afternoon walk onto the unprotected Folkestone Harbor Arm. However, the five of *them*? Yup, they were about to jump in for a swim.

Holy Moses. Had Chelsea been Catholic, she would have crossed herself.

"I've sailed us as close to shore as I dare." Rusty glanced over his shoulder at the shoreline that looked to Chelsea to be about ten thousand miles away, through choppy waves and deep, dark shadows. The shade of the harbor arm turned what was already a cloudy day into full-on twilight. And the sound of the current pulling and pushing at the pilings created an eerie echo. "Thirty yards. Piece of cake." Rusty nodded.

"Says the only one of us not about to swim it," Chelsea grumbled, pulling off her boots and socks and handing them to Dagan to add to the waterproof bag. Her coat came next. The minute she shrugged out of it, she felt the bite of the breeze and refused to consider just how much harsher the bite of the water would be.

Watching Dagan shove her things into the army-green float bag, she wiggled her toes against the damp deck. Emily gave her socks, shoes, and coat to Christian to add to the second waterproof bag. Once they made it to shore, they would want to have dry things to change into.

If we make it to shore, Chelsea thought with uncharacteristic pessimism.

When they were ready, Rusty reached into his pocket and pulled out a set of keys. He handed them to Ace. "You remember the address I gave you?"

"Number Six London Street." Ace nodded.

"Home sweet home."

The two men eyed each other for just a second too long. Chelsea lifted a brow when Ace turned away, a slight blush on his cheeks.

Well, what do you know.

Clearing his throat, Rusty once again looked toward the shore. "There's food in the fridge, dry clothes in the closet upstairs if you need some, and if you hang your wet things over the radiators, they'll be dry in a couple of hours. I'll meet you back there this evening."

"Thank you, Rusty." Emily laid a hand atop Rusty's rubber boot.

If Chelsea wasn't mistaken, Christian cursed under his breath. She felt like whacking him upside the head and telling him to open his dadgummed eyes. He was a covert operator trained in the fine art of observation. Or at least he was *supposed* to be.

"My pleasure," Rusty told her. "Been a while since I've had this much excitement. Now get moving. All of you."

Dagan was still wearing that look Chelsea couldn't quite read. When he searched her face, she hoped she was doing a good job of hiding the dread and fear in her eyes. She realized she *wasn't* when he placed a comforting hand at the small of her back and leaned in to whisper, "You got this."

"Of course I do." She gnawed worriedly at her bottom lip.

His eyes focused on her mouth, and memories of all they'd done in the catamaran's hold filled the space between them. Even beneath the harbor arm, the wind played with Dagan's hair, tousling it around his head. It might have made him look boyish. You know, if it weren't for the Beard.

That thing was *all* man. All rough and tumble and deliciously abrasive when he kissed her lips and nuzzled her cheeks.

How good would it feel brushing against the insides of my thighs?

As soon as she had the thought, she willfully beat it back.

Fixing her mind on the task at hand, she scooted to the edge of the catamaran and poked her head between the rails. Below, the silvery waves lapped hungrily at the hull of the boat. Soon, they would be lapping hungrily at her.

She had the distinct urge to kick herself for not letting Dagan have his way with her earlier. Death from multiple screaming orgasms sounded so much nicer than death by drowning in the friggin' English Channel.

Chapter 17

DAGAN THOUGHT HE HEARD CHELSEA MUMBLE SOMETHING that sounded like, *Well, butter my butt and call me a biscuit* when a larger-than-usual wave momentarily tipped the catamaran at a precarious angle. He loved it when she got all *Southern-fried*, as she called it, on him. But even in the gloom, he could see her face had been leached of color. There was a slight tremor in her fingers where they wrapped tightly around the boat's railing.

He would give his left nut if there was a way to save her from having to make this swim. But for the life of him, he couldn't think of another option that would allow them to evade the Border Agency ship and avoid getting caught by Roper fuckin' Morrison.

"This is one of those good ol'-fashioned gut-it-out situations," he told her, hoping to convey comfort with his tone.

Her throat worked over a hard swallow. "Like Rusty said, piece of cake." He could tell she was trying to convince herself more than she was trying to convince him, and his heart swelled with pride for her. Then she snapped her fingers and said, "Lordy. I almost forgot."

Pulling off her glasses, she handed them to him so he could add them to the waterproof bag. After he did, she smiled her thanks. Just at that moment, the sun peeked out, throwing rays over the waves at the edge of the pier, which in turn reflected up to cast a golden glow over her pretty face. It made her look so…unguarded. And vulnerable. And not at all cut out for this kind of shit.

He was a second away from telling Rusty they needed
to come up with a new plan when Ace slipped over the
side of the catamaran into the choppy water. The former
Navy flyboy came up gasping, squeegeeing the water
from his eyes and shaking his head.

With one of his mercurial facial expressions, all
laughing eyes and perpetually smiling mouth, Ace
looked to Dagan as if he was on the verge of telling a
joke. Admittedly, most times he *was*. So Dagan wasn't
surprised when Ace grinned up at them and said, "Come
on in! The water's so fine it'll blow your dick off!"

Christian's mouth quirked before he also slid quietly
overboard. He dragged the waterproof bag with him,
and it hit the water next to the boat with a gentle *sploosh*.
The thing was buoyant. But just barely. A scant inch
of the army-green material showed above the waves.
Dagan did *not* look forward to dragging his own packed
bag through thirty yards of surf.

Never one to be outdone, Emily took a deep breath
and pitched herself over the side of the catamaran. She
hit the water with all the grace of a buffalo and came
up squawking.

"How bad is it?" Chelsea asked.

"Colder than a w-witch's t-tit in a brass b-bra."
Emily's teeth chattered. She wasted no time turning to
tread water toward shore.

And then there were two.

"Let me go first," Dagan told Chelsea when he saw
her gather herself to take the plunge. He wanted her in
the water for the shortest time possible. Blowing out two
big breaths and steeling himself, he said, "Screw it. Here
goes," and shoved overboard.

The instant he hit the water, his muscles contracted,
shrinking away from the shock of the cold. When he

surfaced, it was to find Chelsea bobbing next to him. The wonderfully willful woman must have waited a full half-second before following him into the drink.

She was always trying to prove herself. It made him absolutely crazy. The risks she took? The shit she volunteered for?

This entire mission, for instance? Anyone? Anyone? Bueller?

Then again, she'd demonstrated just how capable she was time and again, so maybe *he* was the one with the problem. Still, he couldn't help growling at her. "What happened to me going first?"

"B-best just to get it over w-w-with," she chattered. Her dusky-pink lips were already tinged with blue.

"Stubborn, confounding woman," he groused, motioning for Rusty to toss down the remaining waterproof bag.

Chelsea began stroking toward the others, but not before saying, "Oh, sh-shove a sock in it, Werewolf of London."

If his face hadn't been frozen, he would have smiled. There had been awkwardness between them after their conversation in the belly of Rusty's boat. But her words gave him hope that it was a passing phase.

Wasting no time, he tied the line attached to the float bag around his chest and swam after Chelsea. Instead of focusing on how cold he was, on how much he hurt, he turned his mind back to the catamaran's hold, to the flame Chelsea had become in his arms. Her passion had burned so hot, so bright that she had set something inside him ablaze. The fire burned still, slowly turning to ash all his fears of the future and the great unknown it held, all his reasons for not agreeing to her terms.

Chapter 18

CHELSEA WAS IN... WHAT WAS THE WORD SHE WAS LOOKING for? Oh, right. Hell. She was in hell.

But unlike what she'd been led to believe, hell wasn't a fiery pit filled with the shrieks of the damned. Oh no. It was thirty yards of frigid water. It was waves that lapped icily over her head and tried to grind her against the massive pilings. It was muscles that ached with effort, fingers and toes that had frozen solid. It was the inability to cry out when her shoulder raked against a clump of barnacles attached to a piling and her soaked sweater— along with the tender flesh beneath—tore free.

They were all struggling to fight the wave action beneath the giant shadow of the Folkestone Harbor Arm. So even if she had had the breath to exclaim or curse—which she *didn't*—she wouldn't have. She couldn't draw attention to herself. She knew that the second she did, Dagan would turn his efforts toward helping her. Considering he was already dragging what looked like a bazillion pounds of gear behind him, she reckoned the only person he needed to worry about helping was himself.

In a far, distant corner of her mind she registered that Rusty had engaged the catamaran's engines and was piloting the boat back to open water. She had a vague sense of Dagan beside her. Was he shortening his strokes to keep pace with her? She couldn't be sure. Her brain felt fuzzy, like someone had glued cotton around the inside curve of her skull.

"J-just a little f-farther," Dagan said, spitting water from his mouth when a wave washed over his face.

She couldn't respond. Her jaw was locked tight. Her arms and legs were completely numb, yet they continued to move. It was a miracle.

"That's it." Dagan's teeth chattered. "You d-did it. Now, p-put your feet down."

Blearily, she looked over to see his shoulders shedding water in sheets. The collar of his woolen sweater hung down to the middle of his chest, and the drooping neckline revealed the upper bulges of his pectoral muscles as well as a dark smattering of hair. Even without her glasses, she could see just how amazingly well put together he was. A man in his prime. Fit as a fiddle and wholly, unabashedly virile.

She was lost in admiring him, grateful for anything that took her mind off her misery, when he said her name.

"Wh-what?" Her teeth chattered so fast she reminded herself of a woodpecker. The shadow of the harbor arm lent the whole scene a time-slip feel. How long had she been swimming? Minutes? Hours? Had it been days?

"P-put your f-feet down," he said again.

The words made no more sense the second time than they had the first. She frowned dully.

"Damnit, Ch-Chels." He palmed her shoulders and dragged her half out of the water. "Put your feet down. You can touch."

She could? Had she really made it? Could it possibly be true?

Straightening her legs, she was amazed to find that it was. But the minute her feet touched the rocky bottom, she cried out in pain. Her frozen soles sent agony slicing through the bones of her feet, up her shins, and straight into her knees. They buckled.

She thought she heard Dagan curse. But between the
sting in her torn shoulder and the pounding ache in her
feet, it was hard to concentrate. Then, before she could
make another attempt at standing, she was lifted out of
the water and pulled tight against Dagan's broad chest.
Icy water sluiced off her in all directions, and she could
feel the immense power of Dagan's thighs displacing
waves as he surged through the surf.

The salty smell of sea life was overwhelmed by the
scent of his shampoo. Beneath that was the unmistakable aroma of strong, healthy man.

She knew she should tell him to put her down. But
she was so cold, and he was so warm. Of their own
volition, her arms wrapped around his neck, and the
words she heard tumbling from her frozen lips were
"Y-you're ridiculously s-sexy. You know that, r-right?"

His jaw was clenched against the cold, but when he
glanced down at her, there was unmistakable heat in
his eyes. "Th-that's a different tune than the one you
w-were singing earlier."

"I blame the c-cold." She attempted a grin, but
feared it probably looked more like a grimace. Her
shoulder was starting to bark at her like a rabid dog.
"Words are b-bypassing my brain on the way t-to my
m-mouth."

"Maybe you should turn off your brain more often."

She pulled back to look at him. He clocked her
interest with a raised eyebrow. How was it possible to
still want to jump his bones when she was colder than
a well digger's butt in January? That had been another
of her father's little gems. "And th-that's the *same* tune
you were singing earlier. If memory serves."

"What can I say?" He shrugged his shoulders, still
powering through the water. The float bag dragged

behind him, bobbing lazily in the surf. "I figure if I say it enough, one of these times it'll sink in."

And then he smiled, his teeth flashing brightly.

Once again, she felt his smile in some deeply fundamental place inside her. A place she dared not name. Following the impact was a hard fist of regret and shame. There was safety in his strong arms, but she suddenly remembered she had no right to claim it.

"Put me down, Z." She wriggled in his embrace. "I g-got it."

"And I've got *you*," he insisted, clomping through the waves that now circled his knees.

"Hey." She swatted at his chest, doing her best *not* to get distracted by the dark hair there. The hair that seemed to beckon the stroke of her fingers. Or her lips. "I might be short," she told him, "b-but I'm far from small. Put me down before you get a herniated disk."

The pilings loomed around them like giant, limbless trees. "Every single inch of you is…" He stopped and swallowed, his Adam's apple bobbing below his beard. She waited with breathless anticipation for him to finish. When he did, her heart grew so huge she feared it might exceed the limits of her chest cavity. "You're perfect, Chels."

H-h-holy wow.

His admission felt enormous. *Too* enormous. "Perfect, huh? Even when I'm volunteering for jobs I'm not qualified for?"

"Especially then," he whispered, trudging onto the pebbled shore. "Especially when you're brave and self-sacrificing and throwing caution to the wind. It makes me insane, but…that doesn't mean I'd change a damn thing."

She couldn't answer. She was too overcome.

Everything felt so right and so wrong as he slowly

lowered her to the ground. He didn't take his hands from her waist, and she became mesmerized by the droplets of water that clung to the sleek, dark strands of his beard, by the way his wet hair curled over his forehead and around his temples.

Her breath hitched at the fierceness in his stormy eyes when she sucked a drop of water from her bottom lip. The world shrank around them. Suddenly, the whole planet was reduced to the inches separating them, to the air they shared when he breathed out and she breathed in.

"Dagan." His name tumbled from her lips unbidden.

His nostrils flared. He leaned forward and she found herself going up on tiptoe, anticipation tightening her belly into a fist. Then Emily's voice broke the spell.

"Ah, Christian, I knew you muscle-bound meatheads were g-good for s-something!"

When Chelsea ripped her gaze away from Dagan, it was to find the others already gathered on shore. Emily and Ace looked like drowned rats—*frozen* drowned rats—with their arms wrapped around themselves for warmth. Christian was squatted among the multicolored pebbles, tearing open the float bag and handing them their dry things.

"R-right," Christian said. "I'm your b-bloke if you ever need help opening a s-stingy lid, have a burning desire to engage in a s-spitting contest, or need someone to haul your g-gear through thirty meters of s-surf."

Chelsea felt Dagan's hands leave her waist. The spots where his big, rough palms had been instantly cooled in the icy breath of the breeze.

Dagan wasted no time untying the cord around his chest and hauling in the waterproof bag hand over fist. Once it was on shore, he dragged it over the pebbles and out of the reach of the waves. After unrolling the top few inches of fabric, he ripped open the Velcro fitting and lifted out her dry backpack. Once he'd handed it to her, she fumbled to swing it over her shoulder without disturbing her wound any more than was necessary.

"Girls to the left." He waved a hand toward a piling in that direction. "Boys to the right."

On her way to the appointed spot, Emily stopped beside Dagan and teased, "Next time, it's *my* turn to be carried ashore."

"If there's going to be a n-next time, just shoot me now," Ace grumbled, shouldering his pack and traipsing toward another piling.

Dagan handed up Chelsea's socks and boots. Next came her soft, downy coat. The urge to shrug into its promised warmth was only overrun by the desire for it to still be dry once she peeled off her sopping clothes. Of course, just like always, her body temperature jumped ten degrees when Dagan's fingers accidentally brushed hers.

Or was it an accident?

When she glanced at him, there was a definite twinkle in his eye.

It was insane, this effect he had on her body. And now that he was in full-on seduction mode? It wasn't an exaggeration to say it was insanity raised to the power of ten.

How was she supposed to keep resisting him? How was she supposed to—

"Yo!" Emily called from behind one of the pilings. "Give a s-sister a hand, will ya? My zipper's stuck!"

Ripping her eyes away from Dagan's bold gaze actually made them burn. Or maybe unshed tears were backing up behind Chelsea's eyeballs. Tears for a dream that might have had a chance to come true if only—

She stopped her thoughts right there. *If only* was for suckers and fools, and she was neither.

Marching behind the piling where Emily was, Chelsea found the woman gritting her teeth and wrestling with the zipper on her…uh…jeans?…with fingers that looked clumsy and numb.

"Exactly what kind of jeans are th-those?" Chelsea asked, her teeth chattering again now that Dagan's nearness wasn't causing her temperature to spike. She eyed the false pockets stitched into the front of Emily's pants and the zipper that didn't run down the front of the garment like regular jeans, but down the side of Emily's hip.

"They're not j-jeans." Emily huffed out a frustrated sigh. "They're l-leggings made to look like jeans, but they're *way* more c-comfortable because they're made from cotton and elastane and… Ow! Damnit!" Her frozen fingers slipped, and she scraped her knuckles down the length of the metal zipper.

"Oh, for P-Pete's sake." Chelsea dropped her backpack on the beach, ignoring the dirty names her wounded shoulder called her, and fished around in her boot for her glasses. That's where Dagan had stored them to keep them safe.

Never accuse that man of not using his head.

After sliding her purple frames onto her nose—Mistake! Now she could see just how dingy and dirty it was underneath the pier—she approached Emily. "Let me give it a try."

"Thanks." Emily held up the hem of her dripping, long-sleeved T-shirt. The top sported a cartoon face with the words "Melk Man" printed below it. Chelsea knew the slogan was a reference to Melky Cabrera because it was impossible *not* to keep up with Chicago's South Side team while living and working with Emily Scott.

Come April, the woman ate, slept, and breathed White Sox baseball.

Squatting, Chelsea grabbed hold of Emily's slippery zipper and gave it a good tug. Nothing. It didn't budge an inch. She frowned and pulled the denim…er…*elastane* out far enough from Emily's hip to see that some of the thin fabric was caught in the teeth of the zipper.

"This wouldn't happen with r-real denim," Chelsea griped. If her fingers weren't frozen into ten little sausages, she might be able to pick the fabric free. As it was, she had zero dexterity. It was going to require brute force.

"But *real* denim is uncomfortable and hard to m-move around in," Emily insisted, rubbing her arms and shivering so that Chelsea had a hard time getting hold of the recalcitrant zipper.

That was another thing about Emily. She might have one of those slim, long-limbed figures that most women would kill for—Chelsea included—but she never flaunted it. In fact, Emily usually hid her lithe physique behind floppy T-shirts and yoga pants. *Comfortable* clothes.

How wonderful would it be to still look chic and sexy in comfortable clothes? Chelsea had to rely on a good pair of Spanx, a support bra, and tailored pants and shirts in order not to look like she was wearing a potato sack.

"And s-supportive," Chelsea argued around her chattering teeth. "Denim is supportive. It holds in all the w-wiggling. If I tried to wear these things"—she pulled at the elastic material—"it'd be ass and thighs and hips bouncing all over the place."

"Braggart."

Chelsea's chin jerked back. "You think that's *bragging*?"

"Have you looked in the mirror lately?" Emily asked,

genuine disbelief in her eyes. "You're a c-centerfold come to life, and I'm…" She wrinkled her nose.

"Slim and lovely," Chelsea finished for her. "I'd trade you bodies so fast your head would spin."

"Really? Where's a *Freaky Friday* dealio when you need it, huh?"

"Victory is mine!" Chelsea crowed, lifting a triumphant fist when, with a good, hard yank, Emily's zipper finally came free.

"Thank you." Emily groaned in relief. "I thought I was going to have to live in them."

Offering a hand down, Emily pulled Chelsea to a stand. The jerk on her injured arm made the wound there grumble with displeasure, but she ignored it as the two of them shucked their wet clothes.

The shadows beneath the pier created privacy from the outside world, and the thick piling provided privacy from the men. But Chelsea still hurried to get changed. For one thing, the place was pretty disgusting. A dead, bloated fish lay on the shore not ten feet away among the litter the tide had left behind: a beer can, part of a fishing net, half of a small Styrofoam buoy, and… Was that a fork glinting among the pebbles? The whole place had a smell like wet cement and old decay.

With her jeans and sweater lying in a soggy heap, she rummaged around inside her backpack, looking for her favorite sweatshirt and a pair of clean jeans. *Real* jeans. Made of denim. But before she could find either, she heard Emily snort behind her and say, "Jeez, Chelsea. That bra looks like something invented by the Holy Roman Inquisitor."

Chelsea glanced down at her flesh-colored bra with its one-inch-thick shoulder straps, industrial-strength underwire, and four heavy-duty hook-and-eye snaps that kept her girls both lifted and strapped in at the same time. Then she looked over at Emily's dainty black bra with its cute pink bow between the wee cups. The thing's straps were no bigger than spaghetti noodles. "*Now* who's bragging?"

Emily laughed, and Chelsea shot her a dirty look before turning back to dig through her backpack. She had no time to play tit for tat with Emily—Ha! *Tit* for tat. Get it?—because she was about sixty seconds away from succumbing to hypothermia.

Once again, she was thwarted in her endeavors when Emily yelped and said, "Oh my God! Chelsea, you're *bleeding*!"

"*What?*" she heard Dagan bark from somewhere nearby.

Glancing down at her shoulder, she saw that her encounter with the barnacles on the piling had resulted in a two-inch gash with ragged edges and sluggishly seeping blood.

"It's nothing a little Bactine and a Band-Aid won't fix."

"Oh, for the love of…" Emily sputtered. "My brain hates my eyes for what they've just seen."

"What?" Chelsea spun around, expecting a crab or a lobster or maybe another big dead fish to be rolling up the beach toward them. But what she saw instead was Emily in fresh black yoga pants with one hand covering her bra-clad chest and the other covering her eyes.

What in the world? Chelsea frowned. Then her frown slid into a slack-jawed, bug-eyed stare because she figured out what had caused Emily's outburst.

It was Dagan.

And he was naked.

Well, not *completely* naked. He was wearing his skivvies. And. Nothing. Else.

Just for the record—*God knows* I'm *mentally recording this*—his skivvies were a pair of black boxer briefs with a red elastic waistband printed with the letters SAXX. His shoulders looked impossibly wide, his various tattoos dark and menacing, and the smattering of hair on his chest was so crinkly and coarse-looking and... *male* that everything that was female inside Chelsea sat up and starting panting like a good little doggie waiting for a treat.

Gimme, gimme, gimme!

She followed the hair on his chest until it became a single line that traveled down the center of his abdomen, leading to her own personal apocalypse. And *speaking* of her own personal apocalypse, the briefs presented a rather large bulge that apparently even icy water couldn't shrink to a respectable size.

Blowing out a ragged breath, she shook her head and chuckled. Even to her own ears, it sounded weak and defeated. "Well, well, Z. The good Lord was just showing off when he made you, wasn't he?"

Chapter 19

THERE WERE TIMES IN DAGAN'S LIFE—AFTER AFGHANISTAN, after Senator Aldus, the second time he'd had to haul his little brother to rehab—when he had seriously considered dragging a knife over his skin just so he could feel something besides guilt and regret.

The moment he heard Emily scream that Chelsea was bleeding was the moment he knew the knife was no longer needed. He felt *so* much more.

In the two seconds it had taken him to race from behind the piling he'd chosen as his changing room to the piling behind which the women had stationed themselves, he felt terror. Then, when he spied Chelsea crouched next to her backpack, looking whole and mostly unharmed, he felt the kind of relief that made his knees weak.

As if those two emotions weren't proof positive that he was past the self-mutilation stage, the look on Chelsea's face when she let her eyes drag over him had filled him with lust. But more than that, when she'd made that remark about God showing off, grinning that Chelsea grin of hers that was enough to move the loss that was this shitty-ass day directly into the win column, he was overcome by a wave of affection. Soul-shaking affection. The kind of affection he had never felt for another living human. The kind of affection he thought might skate precariously close to that crazy little thing called...*love*.

Holy fuckin' shit, was he in love with Chelsea Duvall?

He searched inside himself and could find zero evidence to the contrary.

"Why do I suddenly get the feeling that I'm about as welcome here as a fart in church?" Emily muttered.

He was careful not to look directly at Emily. In fact, it occurred to him that he probably shouldn't be looking directly at Chels either. You know, given she was dressed in nothing but her bra and panties—her ridiculously *complicated*-looking bra and her far-too-sexy matching lace panties. Or were they called boy shorts? He thought maybe that was the right name for the scrap of lace that hugged her hips and rode high on her amazing ass to reveal the bottom half of each succulent, drool-worthy cheek.

In an effort not to spring a boner, he forced himself to stare down at his toes and concentrated on visualizing his middle-school gym teacher. Mr. Papazian had been three hundred pounds of hairy Armenian.

"How bad are you hurt, Chels?" Whoa. Was that his voice? It sounded like he'd run his vocal cords over sandpaper.

"Not bad," she assured him. "It's just a scrape, really. I didn't do a very good job of avoiding one of the pilings on my way to shore."

Movement from the corner of his eye told him Emily was shrugging into a sweatshirt, and he bit back the urge to tell Chelsea she could have avoided getting hurt altogether if she'd just manned a damned desk like she'd been *trained* to do. But Emily had said that comments like that didn't actually express his concern, and instead made him sound like a jackass.

"Mind if I take a look anyway?" He was careful to

pose it as a question instead of a demand. "Just for my own peace of mind."

"Aww!" Emily cried, batting her lashes and clasping her hands together. "Look at you, Zoelner. Being all sweet and concerned and accommodating. Give me a minute to clean myself up from the puddle I just melted into."

Convinced Emily was decent, he allowed himself to gift her with a steely-eyed frown.

"Ouch!" She stepped back. "Okay, okay. Stop shooting me with your eye bullets. I'll leave you two alone. Just let me grab my stuff." Her South Side accent turned it into *Just lemme grab ma stuff*.

After bending to snag her socks and shoes, she shouldered her backpack and ambled past him. But not before she stopped to whisper in his ear, "Go get her, lover boy."

As if *that* wasn't sophomoric enough, she actually had the temerity to give him a nudge. He didn't dare look at her for fear she'd add a wink.

"Do I want to know what she told you?" Chelsea asked after Emily had picked her way toward a distant piling.

Having pushed to a stand, Chelsea held a sweatshirt in front of herself. It was a crying shame to see all those luscious curves covered up, but Dagan took heart that he still had an unobstructed view of her sweetly turned legs and her delicate, unpainted toes. He had never been a foot man before, but the desire to kiss every one of those cute little digits was sharp.

And then work my way up.

No. *No*. None of that. He had more important things to deal with.

"Can I check your wound?" he asked again. He

wasn't sure why it was so important to him. Obviously she wasn't hurting *that* bad. If she was, he'd be able to hear it in her voice, right? Like he'd been able to see the regret on her face down in the hold of Rusty's boat when she gave him what amounted to an ultimatum.

Her mouth quirked. "How about we both put some clothes on first? Aren't you freezing?"

He was. Goose bumps peppered his skin, and his bare toes ached all the way to the bones. "Two minutes," he told her gruffly, then turned to trudge back to his gear.

After tugging on a dry pair of jeans and another thick wool sweater, he donned fresh socks and shoved his size twelves into his biker boots. *Clodhoppers*, Chelsea teasingly called them. He supposed that was as good a description as any. Though, for the life of him, he couldn't remember the last clod he had hopped.

He wasn't sure it had been a full two minutes by the time he finished wringing out his wet clothes and stuffing them in the front section of his backpack. Shrugging into his coat, he found himself back beside Chelsea's piling.

There was a part of him—the *guy* part—that hoped to catch her in the process of shimmying into her jeans. He could quite easily imagine the wiggle of her lovely lady bits. But to his disappointment, she had already slipped into her denims and had pulled on her sweatshirt and coat.

Well, she'd pulled the latter two pieces of clothing *half* on, anyway. She had left her damaged arm uncovered, the left side of the sweatshirt bunched up around her neck. "Here. See?" She presented him with her arm. "It's not so bad."

She was right. The wound didn't appear very deep.

Still… "Barnacles carry tons of bacteria. When we get to Rusty's, we need to clean this thing and slather it in ointment. Until then…"

He unzipped the side pocket on his pack and pulled out a roll of gauze. *Always be prepared.* He and Avan had gone through the Boy Scout program together, and that was one lesson that had stuck. "We'll wrap it so it doesn't ooze onto your sweatshirt."

She adjusted her glasses. "I feel like this is much ado about nothing."

Winding the gauze around her laceration, he tried his best not to look at the bottom edge of her bra or the smooth skin of her side where her waist dipped in dramatically before flaring out to her hips. When that didn't work, he thought it best to force his mind onto something else.

"Shakespeare?"

"Huh?" She blinked up at him.

Eyes like hers should be outlawed. They were hell on a man's self-control.

"*Much Ado about Nothing?*"

"Oh." She shrugged. "Never read it. Watched the movie with Emma Thompson and Kenneth Branagh about a hundred times, though. Love the language. But Keanu Reeves was a weird casting choice for Don John, don't you think?"

"The accent he used was pretty bad," Dagan agreed, thinking it a marvel that after the day they'd had, they could still carry on a normal conversation.

But that was Chelsea for you. She was a phenom when it came to reading Intelligence. She loved fantasy novels and, apparently, Shakespearean movies about love. And she was the only person on the face of the planet he could be himself around. Talking to her…

loving her—yes, he was no longer in denial about that—was just so easy.

What *wasn't* easy was trying not to keel over. Because when he leaned close to use his teeth to tear off the gauze, he was hit by the sweet strawberry-vanilla smell of her.

"You two lovebirds ready to rock and roll?" Emily called, stomping toward them as Chelsea tucked her bandaged arm into her sweatshirt and coat.

"Bloody hell, woman!" Christian complained. "Give me a moment to get into my shoes!"

Emily stopped in her tracks, her expression turning positively devilish before she swung around to smile at Christian, who was sitting on the ground, tying the laces on a pair of Italian-made ankle boots that probably cost more than Dagan's last car.

"Now why did you automatically think I was talking to you and Ace?" Emily asked. "Is there something the two of you would like to tell the rest of us?"

"He should be so lucky!" Ace called, trotting out from behind a piling, fully dressed and carrying his backpack and the two folded float bags.

Dagan turned back to Chelsea, offering his hand. "You ready?"

She looked down at his callused palm with a considering frown. For a moment, he thought she would balk—and that would tell him something, wouldn't it? Something he didn't want to know? Like maybe that whole *I'm done playing the field* shtick was just her way of letting him down easy? So when she slipped her fingers into his, he wanted to shout with joy.

Ace beelined toward the edge of the pier, and Emily and Christian wasted no time tagging along after him. Dagan pulled Chelsea into step behind the trio, keeping his fingers laced with hers. He realized that despite all the ways his day had gone wrong, holding hands with Chelsea made everything seem right. And for the first time in a long time he was…happy.

Which in his experience meant the proverbial shit was about to hit the fan.

Chapter 20

"WHAT DO YOU KNOW?"

A valid question, given that Steven had been on the phone he had borrowed from Morrison since they began their drive south. Still, he wished the demanding old bugger would give him a second or two to arrange his thoughts. There was something...

"What did they say?" Morrison added.

Steven glanced across the backseat of Morrison's SUV—just one of the *many* vehicles in the billionaire's stables—at the man himself, the one who had gotten him into this unholy mess. He fought to keep the scowl from his face. If he had learned one lesson in life, it was that it was always best to play his emotional cards close to his vest.

"There's no sight of them at the Chunnel entrance. And so far nothing on the water either. CCTV footage shows the Ducatis parked by the docks in Dover, but nothing more than that. The revolving cameras are set on a fifteen-minute timer, and they didn't catch the moment the group arrived or if they boarded a vessel. The Border Agency has tracked and searched every ship that has docked or disembarked from the Dover docks today. So far, nothing."

Morrison's top lip curled back, revealing a set of teeth that had been polished to perfection. Those stark white teeth had always made Steven uncomfortable.

They reminded him of sharks' teeth. And he couldn't help but picture those teeth sinking into the neck of some innocent—

"That's disappointing," Morrison said, interrupting Steven's thoughts. It was just as well. The images that had begun to form in Steven's head were enough to make him retch.

"It's more than disappointing. It's bloody frustrating," he grumbled.

Every hour that ticked by, he felt the blade of the guillotine hovering above his head slip a little more. Still, he couldn't focus on the fear living inside him. There was still work to be done. There was still a chance he could make it out of this unscathed.

"And suspicious," he added, running through scenarios. As a former SAS officer, he knew how operators like the three who had burst into Morrison's office thought.

"Suspicious?" Morrison lifted a bushy gray eyebrow, his eyes sharp. He might like to act the aging playboy, but Steven knew that was all smoke and mirrors. Morrison's parties, his ready smile, his boozy debaucheries and fat-bottomed women were just icing covering a poisonous cupcake. "Suspicious in what way?"

"Our friend inside Scotland Yard said that the HMC *Valiant* reported following a cod boat from Dover to Folkestone and back to Dover. According to the Border Agency blokes, the vessel kept making odd course corrections."

"Did they search the boat?"

"Yes."

"Well? What did they find?"

"Nothing but the captain and a fair bit of bait."

"I'm sorry." Morrison blinked. "Why is *that* suspicious?"

"I'm not sure as yet." Steven punched Redial on the borrowed mobile.

When the man from Scotland Yard answered, Steven wasted no time with pleasantries. "The captain of that cod boat you spoke of, what was his name?"

"Rusty Parker," came the reply.

"Rusty? Sounds American."

"*Is* American."

As Alice would say, curiouser and curiouser. "Thank you." Steven thumbed off the mobile and took a deep breath. The smell of Morrison's expensive cologne filled his nostrils, and he wondered how Morrison's driver, a man by the improbable name of Ramón, could stand being confined in such a small space with the evil old fart day after day.

He glanced at the rearview mirror to find Ramón concentrating on the motorway in front of him, piloting the SUV with easy efficiency. Ramón must have felt Steven's attention, but he never took his eyes off the road. Steven pictured him as one of those figurines depicting the three monkeys. Ramón saw no evil, heard no evil, spoke no evil.

Steven absently wondered if that might work for him too.

Too late, a little voice whispered.

"What are you thinking?" Morrison asked.

"I think something smells off." Lifting the borrowed phone, he dialed Benton's number. The hacker genius picked up on the first ring. "Who's this?"

"Surry," he said. "Are you too busy with things on your end to do a little online digging for me?"

"No." Steven could hear Benton slurping something noisily through a straw. "I just built a firewall so high it will take this wankstick hours to climb it. Tell me what you need."

"I need you to find out anything and everything you can about a man named Rusty Parker." He gave Benton the information he had on the bloke. That he was American, that he owned a cod boat anchored in Dover. "See if you can find a connection between him and Chelsea Duvall."

"Done."

The click of the line told him Benton had signed off.

Steven was still trying to figure out what was niggling at the edges of his instincts when Morrison interrupted his thoughts. "And while Benton works his magic, what shall you and I do?"

"Keep on 'til Dover."

"I feel a bit Bondish, even if I do say so myself." When Morrison smiled, all teeth and with a sick twinkle in his eye, Steven fought the urge to recoil.

Chapter 21

Folkestone, England

Rusty Parker's home wasn't what Emily would have expected from an outdoorsman.

It was three stories of blue-painted exterior, with an interior that managed to be both chic and warm. Neutral walls were covered in eclectic artwork—most having some sort of nautical theme. Big, comfy furniture was home to the occasional throw pillow. And the old oak floors were so heavily lacquered that she would swear she could see her reflection in the places not covered by brightly hued rugs.

She had chosen the top-floor bathroom to shower off the salt and foam from the Channel—neither smell had proved very pleasant when her body heat had begun to enhance them on the walk from the pier to Rusty's house. As she toweled her hair dry and made her way to the bottom floor to join her freshly bathed coworkers in the living room, she realized she was out of ideas on how to get them off this giant, pain-in-the-ass rock known as Great Britain.

Rusty had been her ace in the hole.

"So what's the plan now?" she asked before she'd stepped off the bottom tread.

Strategizing, preparing, taking action...those were her fortes. Sitting around twiddling her thumbs and scratching her ass had always made her feel twitchy. In fact, she was pretty sure that had there been such a diagnosis when she was a kid—or if her parents hadn't been so busy looking for love in all the wrong places—it might have been determined that she had a touch of ADHD.

Ace was on the phone and lifted a finger for silence. Never something Emily had been very good at, but she obligingly bit her tongue. Then, after a few seconds during which he said a lot of "okays" and "roger that's," he finally thumbed off his phone and sighed.

She didn't like the sigh. Sighs like that usually meant bad news. Paulie Konerko had heaved one very similar sigh when he told the press back in 2014 that he planned to retire from White Sox baseball—a loss she continued to mourn. Her mother had sighed like that when she told Emily she was divorcing her third husband, a man Emily had loved and adored. Richard, her FAS, had heaved a sigh that sounded a lot like Ace's when he had called her a heartless bitch and told her that he couldn't work with her another day.

When she thought about it, the list of times she'd heard sighs like that seemed endless.

"Ozzie's having trouble accessing Morrison's data," Ace said. "Something to do with another hacker throwing obstacles in his way."

"Ruddy inconvenient," Christian grumbled.

Ace shrugged. His wet blond hair looked almost brown in the low lights of the lamps parked on the big oak end tables. The gray day's mood had turned from mildly unhappy to full-on sulky. Rain was imminent.

March in England. Gotta love it.

"He says he'll beat the fuckhead—his word for the guy, not mine—but it could take some time," Ace explained. "In the meantime, Angel has changed his destination. Instead of Calais, he's on his way to

Le Touquet. Apparently he knows a guy who has a submersible we might be able to use."

Emily blinked, her mind stopping on the word *submersible*. "Is that covert operator speak for a flippin' *submarine*?"

"A small one." Ace nodded.

As if *size* made a difference…er…at least in *this* particular case? Big or small, a submarine was a submarine. Emily tried to comprehend how, from this morning until now, they had managed to veer off the road and career crazily toward that little place she liked to call O'Shitsburgh.

Or maybe that should be Underwater O'Shitsburgh.

"Do we, uh… Do we want to know what this friend of Angel's *does* with a submarine off the coast of France?" she asked.

"Probably not." Ace made a face. "This is Angel we're talking about."

Right. Jamin "Angel" Agassi. Not his real name.

In point of fact, Emily didn't *know* his real name. She wasn't entirely sure anyone back at BKI did either. What she *did* know was that Agassi was a former Israeli Mossad agent who had run into a heap of trouble. Trouble so big and bad he had been forced to abandon his post, abandon his country, undergo extensive plastic surgery to completely change his looks, and then, you know, have his vocal cords scoured so that voice recognition software couldn't identify him.

As if all *that* wasn't intriguing—or *spooky*—enough, after he had come to work for BKI, he had taken on a string of blacker-than-black assignments that had mostly kept him overseas. Emily had only met the man twice. Each time, she had been taken aback by his near-flawless beauty. Whichever plastic surgeon had done the work on him had been a Rembrandt. A true artist. No joke. She thought the Black Knights had been right to give him the nickname *Angel*.

With black, wavy hair and piercing eyes that looked like they held a thousand secrets, he was downright otherworldly. Which, quite honestly, creeped her out. And made her not trust him.

Not entirely, anyway.

Then again, beggars couldn't be choosers. If Angel and his friend with the submarine could get them off the island, she'd thank her lucky stars *and* him.

"So then the plan will be to hop onto...er...*into* this dude's submarine and Captain Nemo our asses across the Channel?" She tried not to imagine the giant squid from *Twenty Thousand Leagues under the Sea* wrapping its long, muscular tentacles around the vessel and dragging it down to the black depths until the hull buckled and—

Squeeeeeeeee! The kettle on the stove began singing its ear-piercing tune. On the heels of the giant squid imagery, it made Emily jump.

"Pretty much," Ace agreed. "Assuming Angel can find this friend of his, and also assuming this friend of his will be willing to help. Angel says it could take an hour or two to locate the guy. He'll give us a call once he does. But there's a catch."

"There always is," Christian muttered on his way past Emily. He sauntered into the kitchen where Zoelner was busy washing and redressing Chelsea's wound. After pouring himself a cup, Christian dropped in a teabag and strolled back to the living room.

Emily couldn't help but notice he carried himself with an easy, almost lazy confidence. It stirred something deep inside her. Something she promptly ignored.

Once bitten, twice shy, baby. She would *not* mess up the good thing she had going with the Black Knights. Although one look at Christian, and she was sorely tempted.

"The submersible is only big enough for the pilot and two passengers," Ace said. "So sneaking us all across will take hours."

Emily frowned. "But really it's just Chelsea who needs to sneak across, right? Spider and his contacts inside the British government don't know about the rest of us."

"Thanks for the all-for-one and one-for-all attitude, Em!" Chelsea called from the kitchen.

"You know I love you like my luggage!" Emily called back. Then, "But seriously, we could load Chelsea into the submarine, and then the rest of us could grab a ferry across or else take the train through the Chunnel. All on the up and up. Easy as you pleasy."

Plus, the plan had the added benefit of allowing Emily to avoid a chance run-in with a giant squid. And yes, she knew that particular concern was ludicrous, but that didn't mean it went away. Obviously she'd read *Twenty-Thousand Leagues* when she was too young and too impressionable.

Where had her parents been?

Oh yeah. *Out.* They had always been out. Each of them more concerned with finding the next love of their life—and the next, and the next, and the next—than looking after their own daughter.

"Good point." Christian's eyes darted to his watch. "On that note, and since it seems like we'll have a while to knock about regardless, what say we toddle over to the local pub? I don't know about the rest of you, but it's going on sixteen hundred, and I haven't eaten since breakfast. I'm getting peckish."

"Chelsea can't go out." Emily glanced over her shoulder at the woman under discussion, giving her a wink that said, *See? I got a sister's back.* "Not with her mug splashed all over the news."

"We'll fetch her back something," Christian insisted.

"But Rusty said there was food in the fridge."

"Tuna salad, a block of cheddar cheese, and a carton of milk do not a meal make, darling." Just like always, the endearment gave Emily a little thrill. "Besides," he continued, "if we go 'round to the pub, it'll give us a chance to have a pint and see if we can come up with a viable alternative, should Angel's friend not come through for us. You know, drink things through, as is the custom of my people."

Christian Watson was English through and through, right down to his love of Earl Grey and beer. Both served warm. *Bleck!*

"You guys go," Zoelner called from the kitchen. "I'll stay here and keep Chelsea company."

I just bet you will, Emily thought, hiding a smile. She knew the two of them needed time alone to work out their shit, so she was quick to jump on the bandwagon and add, "Come to think of it, I could really benefit from a plate of fish and chips."

"Good girl!" Christian clapped his hands and plucked his coat from the hall tree on the way to the door.

And *that* was how, two minutes later, Emily found herself walking down a quiet Folkestone street while all of England was on the hunt for her friend and coworker.

Life as a supersecret agent was weird indeed. People expected that it was all gas, no brakes. But the truth of the matter was that between bouts of chasing down the bad guys and running for their lives, there were long stretches of the everyday. Laundry. Bills. A walk to the pub for fish and chips because, you know, *a girl needs to eat*!

She contemplated the surrealism of it all as a light drizzle began to fall.

Gotta love England, she thought again. Chancing a glance at Christian, she admitted the man had more jawline than any mortal should. *Gotta love Englishmen too*, she silently added.

Chapter 22

CHELSEA WATCHED DAGAN TAPE THE ENDS OF A FRESH length of gauze around her arm. He had cleaned, medicated, and redressed the wound. All very carefully. All very precisely. All very *slowly*. And it wasn't an exaggeration to say the entire procedure had wreaked havoc on her respiratory system.

She was dizzy. The room spun around and around. In the center of all that tumult? Him. Z. *Dagan*.

Who knew being close to a man could actually make you hyperventilate?

He stepped back, eyeing his work, and managed to look both rakish—it was that damp curl of hair over his brow—and ridiculously pleased with himself. "Well?" he asked. "What do you think?"

She gave the fresh bandage only the most cursory of glances. She was too busy watching his eyes in the low glow of the glass pendant light above the sink.

Dear Lord, why *did you have to go and make him so irresistible?*

"It's good," she allowed with a dip of her chin, pulling the sleeve of her sweatshirt down. "Thank you for taking care of it. For taking care of me. You tend to do that, don't you?"

He smiled at her. Oh, how he smiled at her! It felt like the most beautiful gift, but also like a slap in the face. If he ever found out about the Big Bad Secret, he might never smile at her again.

"If you think *that's* good"—he waggled his eyebrows—"you should see my moves in the boudoir."

In the last handful of hours, their chemistry had managed to bust down the walls he had built around himself. He was still as formidable and bullheaded as ever, but now there was a side of flippancy and playfulness too. Basically, he was back to acting like the man she had met all those years ago when she was a wet-behind-the-ears CIA recruit.

It was *that* side of him, the irreverent side, that she had desperately missed. The side that had disappeared after Afghanistan.

Afghanistan…

The thought made her ache as if her bones were covered in bruises.

Fearing he might see, she adjusted her glasses and donned her best reproachful look. "First of all, I don't cotton to cocky men."

"Sure you do." He winked.

"Second of all, we've been over this." She clung to the decree she'd made inside the catamaran's hold like she clung to the memory of her father and the responsibility she had to her mother.

"True." He rubbed a hand over his beard—the Beard—and his callused palm rasped against the hairs. The sound had warmth coalescing in her core. Then he made it so much worse when he suddenly stepped between her legs and placed his wide-palmed hands on her waist.

She had dutifully sat on the kitchen counter while he tended her wound, and she had yet to jump down. *Oh, why didn't I jump down?* It would have been so much easier to avoid his advances if she had been flat on her feet so she could…what? Run?

That would have been really mature.

Dagan pulled her to the edge of the counter. Not gently. But not hard, either. Just...*authoritatively*. A man in charge.

Weak-willed ninny that she was, she experienced a rush of pleasure. That pleasure only increased when he pressed against her and she discovered he was hard. And pulsing.

Oh my! Dagan Zoelner in full-on seduction mode rated an F5 on the Fujita scale for nipple-tightening, panty-slicking, knee-loosening damage.

"Okay," he said. "Okay, Chels."

She didn't know what the heckfire he was okaying. "Okay what?"

"I'm willing to give it a try."

"Give...uh..." She had to swallow. "Give *what* a try?"

"Us," he said the word simply. But it was *not* a simple word. It was a crazily complex word. And it was enough to send her heart plummeting into her churning stomach where acid immediately went to work on it.

Her plan, her glorious plan, had backfired. *Big time.*

"I think we should give *us* a try," he added. "I mean, I'm not asking you to marry me this instant. And I have no idea how we're going to work out the details. My future is a huge question mark. What happens after BKI shuts its clandestine doors? Am I really supposed to be satisfied building bikes for a living? I'm a trained Intelligence agent, for God's sake. And what about Avan? What if he falls off the wagon again? If I'm not making good money, I won't be able to afford his treatment. All of this terrifies me, Chels. I *hate* the unknown. Always have. But wanting you...it's the one thing I do know, the one thing I'm sure of. So for now, I say let's let the future happen when it happens. For now, I say *okay*."

Oh no. Oh *no*! The time had finally come. She would have to do what she had hoped and dreamed and prayed she would never had to do. She would have to tell him the truth. Expose her guilt and shame and dishonor and finally face the consequences she had spent years avoiding.

"Dagan…"

Something dark and exciting sparkled in his eyes. "Say it again."

"Dagan, I—"

That's all she managed before he groaned, the sound low and male and deliciously sexy. He cupped her jaw in his rough hands. Then his lips claimed hers.

Her mouth formed a surprised O, and he took that as encouragement to dip his tongue inside. Slow, savoring licks… That's how he tasted her. It brought to mind how he'd attend to other parts of her body if only…

If only she had made a different decision all those years ago. If only she had been braver or less desperate. If only she had been able to see into the future to this moment, when he was offering her the world.

Her mind drifted back to the exact second when she could have changed it all. Changed her *fate*…

Agent Zoelner was in the building. She had seen him shuffle into her boss's office for a brief moment before he'd made his way down the long hall to knock on the door of the director of the CIA. His head had been low, his shoulders hunched, looking like he had aged ten years in the two days it had taken him to return from Afghanistan.

Chelsea sat at her desk on the edge of a veritable sea of desks, and the sound of her fellow analysts click-clacking at their keyboards was a constant chatter that

*matched the racing beat of her heart. Her legs quiv-
ered. Muscles in her thighs twitched with an eagerness
to stand.*

She almost did it. She almost jumped from her desk
to follow Dagan into the director's office and spill the
whole sorry, sordid tale. But something held her back.

She recognized that something as fear. Pure and
simple. Fear that what Ted Edens, her boss and the
director of the Office of Advanced Analytics, had threatened her with would come true. Then where would she
be? Where would her *mother* be?

Some place other than the house she adored, that
was for sure. Some place that didn't hold the mementoes
and spirit of the man they had both loved to distraction.
Some place that had no meaning, no memories, no soul.
Some place that wasn't...home.

It was that fear, fear of losing what she and her
mother were working so hard to keep, that held Chelsea
in her chair.

The seconds dragged by like hours. Her own saliva
soured in her mouth. And then the director's door
opened and Dagan walked out. He was white as a ghost,
a muscle sawing in his jaw.

Two security guards converged on him. One of them
indicated with a hand that Dagan was to follow them.
Chelsea suffered no delusions that their destination was
beyond the walls of Langley, and that Dagan Zoelner
would never set foot in the hallowed halls again.

Edens had convinced the director to fire *him!* How
could he have done that? How *could* he?

Curling her fingers around the edge of her chair,
Chelsea watched with burning eyes as Dagan was
escorted down the hall and across the room. When
he walked by her desk, she suddenly found herself on

her feet, her mouth open and two words spilling out:
"Agent Zoelner?"

He stopped to look at her. The fluorescent lights
overhead were no friend to the bags beneath his eyes.
She absently wondered if he had slept since it had
happened.

"Agent Duvall?" he asked absently. "Something I
can do for you?"

"I—" she began but was cut off by one of the security
guards.

"Sorry, Agent Duvall." His name was Larry...
Something. "I'm supposed to escort Agent Zoelner from
the building immediately. He's to go nowhere and talk
to no one along the way."

Chelsea swallowed past the mountain of a lump in
her throat. The words were there, the confession *was*
right there, poised on the tip of her tongue.

Then the sound of someone clearing his throat had
her turning. Her boss leaned against his office door-
jamb, arms crossed, eyes narrowed. And she knew...He
would make good on his promise. He would ruin her as
easily as he had just ruined Dagan.

She turned back as a wave of horror engulfed her.
It was followed quickly by a swell of disgust. And then,
right behind those two soul-crushing tsunamis, came a
tide of self-loathing.

Dagan stared at her for a long moment. She thought
she could actually hear the clock on the wall ticking
away the seconds, even above the rattle of fifty key-
boards and the sound of her own blood rushing through
her ears. The look on his face broke her low-down,
no-good, cowardly heart. Just broke it in two and then
stomped on the pieces until they shattered.

"Good knowing you, Agent Duvall." Dagan tipped

his chin, allowing the guards to accompany him from the room.

She watched him go, watched his broad back disappear behind the opaque glass doors. It felt like her world had been turned upside down. She had the sneaking suspicion it would never be set right again.

"Chelsea," Dagan breathed her name against her lips, dragging her back to the present, to the *amazing* present when he held her so tightly in his arms.

She could feel the raging beat of his heart against her breast, the gentleness of his hands as he canted her head to gain better access to her mouth. Tears burned behind her eyes. Tears of regret, tears of heartbreak. Oh, she wanted so much to give in, to let him take her and make her his own.

And really, what was stopping her?

He never had to know. If she kept the Big Bad Secret, she just might be able to keep him too and—

She squashed the thought before she could finish it. "Dagan." She turned her head to break the kiss. The *last* kiss. "I…have something to tell you."

He nuzzled her cheek, the Beard wonderfully scratchy and warm. "What is it?" He dropped his hands to her hips, his long fingers flexing against her flesh, testing its resilience. He must have liked what he found because she felt him throb against her.

Her eyes screwed shut. Her toes curled. For a moment, she forgot what she needed to say. Forgot her own *name*.

Was it possible to die from want?

He licked her earlobe into his mouth and groaned. "You taste as sweet as you smell. I've wanted you, wanted *this* for so long, but I never thought you…"

His voice hitched. She felt that hitch in her soul.
"After Afghanistan, I never dreamed that you might
want me too."

Afghanistan.

The word was a sledgehammer strike to her overheated brain, cooling her ardor and allowing her to focus
on what she had to tell him. Allowing her to remember
why she had no business being in his strong, warm,
wonderful arms.

"I did s-something." Her voice was shaky.
"Something...unforgivable."

He pulled back to look at her just as the first tear
slipped past her defenses and slid, salty and wet, down
her cheek. A look of gentle sympathy softened his harsh
warrior's face.

With a tenderness that stole her breath, a tenderness
that she would later reflect on with a bone-deep ache, he
removed her glasses and set them on the counter. She
blinked until he came into focus, breath sawing out of
her when he thumbed the tear from her cheek and stared
into her eyes. "Everyone, and I do mean *everyone*, has
something in their past they're not proud of, something
they think is unforgivable."

He was killing her with kindness! "But—"

He stopped her words with a kiss, his lips warm and
gentle. "Shh. I don't care. Whatever you've done, whatever you think you have to tell me, it can wait. Because
I *ache*, Chels."

He grabbed her hand and guided it to the source of
his pain, then groaned and tilted his forehead against
hers. His breath was hot when he said, "I've dreamed
about getting you naked for so long, dreamed about
making love to you in so many ways. Make my fantasies come true. Let me make *your* fantasies come true.

And afterward, if you still feel the need to confess, I promise I'll listen."

He lifted her hand, kissing the end of each finger.

What could she do? The man of her dreams, the man she had loved for so many years that she'd lost count, the man she had *betrayed* was asking one thing of her. And even though it was going to be her undoing to make love to him, to revel in the glory of his arms just this once and then never again, she couldn't deny him. She *wouldn't* deny him. Her mistake all those years ago had been to put herself—and her mother's needs—first.

Now it was his turn. She would give him what he wanted. *Everything* he wanted with a smile on her face and a song of love in her heart.

And then afterward?

Well, afterward she would finally, irrevocably destroy herself.

Chapter 23

"YES, DAGAN." CHELSEA CUPPED HIS FACE IN HER COOL, delicate hands and brought her mouth to his. "Yes."

If he'd had a voice, he would have cried out. But the instant he heard that first *yes*, the ability to speak eluded him. This woman…this beautiful, vibrant woman…was proof that God existed and was smiling down on him for no good reason.

There was a storm in his heart, a hurricane of happiness and love and desire and need. Whatever Chelsea wanted to tell him, whatever wrong she had committed, stood no chance against all of that. And he realized it didn't matter that his future was a giant question mark. Because whatever he did, wherever he was, *whoever* he became once BKI was no longer in operation, one thing was for certain: he would be by Chelsea's side.

"My sweet girl," he murmured between kisses.

Praise be! His voice had returned. Just in time too. There were a hundred naughty things he wanted to whisper in her ear.

Her tears added a salty zing to the sweetness of her kiss. And he couldn't quite believe that Chelsea Duvall, Queen of the Snarky Comebacks, Reigning World Champion of Counterterrorism and All-Around Ace at keeping herself in check—*don't forget the love of my life*—had cried in front of him. Had allowed herself to be vulnerable.

More than anything, *that* was what had whipped the whirlwind inside his heart into a frenzy. Because while he loved that she trusted him enough to be completely, emotionally exposed, he knew he would spend the rest of his days making sure she never had reason to shed another tear. He vowed then and there that he would make it his life's work to bring her nothing but happiness.

And he knew just where to start.

Palming her exquisite ass with one hand, he used the other to cup her head and hold her still for his assault. And it *was* an assault. He pillaged. He plundered. He waged a war of teeth and tongues and deep, wet sucks, kissing her with all the pent-up passion inside him. *Years* of pent-up passion. He wanted to set that earthy, unapologetic life force of hers on fire and then watch it burn.

She growled her approval, her hunger, and fisted his damp hair in her hands, meeting him kiss for kiss, suck for suck, sweet teasing bite for sweet teasing bite. She rubbed her breasts against his chest, unabashedly seeking the friction of his sweater against her nipples.

"I want to see you, Chels. I want to look at you," he whispered against her devilishly talented mouth.

The woman knew how to kiss, that was for sure. When she let herself go and stopped holding back? Holy shit, did she know how to kiss!

Another time, when he wasn't so eager to do everything, to see everything, to *taste* everything, he vowed to spend hours just making love to her mouth. But for now, he needed more.

"Seems I'm not in the mood to deny you tonight," she panted.

When he met her lusty gaze, there were still tracks of tears glinting on her cheeks. He kissed them away even as he pulled her sweatshirt over her head and tossed it over his shoulder. It landed in a heap on the kitchen tiles.

Her hair was still damp. It had a frizzy curl he found adorable. She usually spent thirty minutes in the morning using thick styling cream and some sort of wand-looking iron thingy to straighten her hair. But he preferred her like this. Au naturel. Because she was perfect just as she was.

And speaking of perfect, he was delighted to discover that the bra she was wearing was in her favorite hue. A purple so deep he might have called it eggplant. It set off her bronze skin and emphasized the stark white of the bandage circling her arm. She was so smooth, so silky-looking, especially the tops of her magnificent breasts where they bulged above the cups.

A faint sheen of perspiration dewed her mile-long cleavage. The knowledge that he had caused that heat, that he had been the one to stoke her fire made his cock thrum.

Breath held, he did what he had been waiting a lifetime to do. He raised a hand and gently, with just the tips of his fingers, brushed the silky skin atop one bulging mound. Goose bumps followed in the wake of his caress.

"You're gorgeous, Chels. I've dreamed about having you, seeing you just like this."

"Have you?" She raised a coquettish brow. "And after seeing me like this, what did you dream about next?"

He wouldn't have thought anything could drag his eyes away from the visual feast that was her boobs, but *that* did. He stared into her hypnotic copper gaze. Her lids flew at half-mast, but there was no mistaking the avid gleam behind them.

She wanted him to tell her. She wanted the *words*. Chelsea Duvall, vixen in purple, liked dirty talk.

Well, babe, you came to the right man.

"I dreamed of pulling the straps of your bra off your shoulders and kissing the sweet skin beneath." He watched her eyelids sink lower. "Bathing it and soothing it with my tongue."

"Mmm," she hummed. Then, when he did exactly what he had described, she purred—actually *purred*! Holy hell!

"I dreamed of unhooking your bra and feeling your breasts spill into my hands," he murmured against her smooth, delicious shoulder. "Will they be warm, Chels? Will your nipples be hard?"

"Find out for yourself." Her naturally husky voice had roughened with passion.

"Dirty girl. You've dreamed of this too, haven't you?"

"You have no idea."

That simple admission made him feel like he'd won the lottery. To know that she had wanted him like he had wanted her, that she had fantasized about him like he had fantasized about her, was the ultimate ego stroke. Had she lain in bed and touched herself like he had?

The visual that bloomed in his head had him wasting no time. He reached behind her back to unhook the clasp of her bra. Or…at least he *thought* he had unhooked it. But then there was another clasp. And another.

Growling in frustration, he looked over her shoulder at the recalcitrant piece of lingerie. "Just how many hooks and loops does this thing have?"

She wrapped her arms around his neck. "Four. Keep going. You're almost there."

Another snap of his fingers proved her correct. *Hallelujah!*

The halves of her bra sprang apart and he pulled back, hesitating. Like a kid opening his last birthday present, he wanted to draw out the moment, to savor it. Then he couldn't stand it and slid the straps down her arms, slipped the cups away, and...*looked.*

At this point, he fell to his knees. Or at least he *felt* like he should. Because Chelsea was flawless. From the soft slope of her shoulders to the lithe length of her arms. From the large, round globes of her breasts with their puckered brown nipples to the tininess of her rib cage.

Her bra dangled forgotten from his fingers and then quietly fell to the floor as he stood and stared, his heart thundering.

"Well?" There was timidity in her gaze. He couldn't miss the sound of her throat working over a dry swallow. "What's the verdict?"

"Sweet fuck-all, you have the best tits I've ever seen." He grimaced. That had come out more crass-sounding than he had intended. But, really, he was a dirt-and-sweat-and-calluses kind of guy when you got right down to it. And with most of his blood circulating down south, starving his brain cells of oxygen? Ten-four. He reverted to form.

Didn't seem to bother Chelsea. Her plump lips quirked. "No, silly. I meant are they as warm as you dreamed? Are my nipples hard?"

He lowered his chin and looked at her through the fan of his lashes. "Let's find out."

Cupping her breasts, he weighed them, tested their firmness. She hissed and let her head fall back when he used the rough pads of his thumbs on their tips.

Fascinating, he thought, watching her dark areolas

contract and crinkle. They pushed the centers up into round, hard points that begged for the attention of a mouth. *His* mouth.

"Better than I ever imagined," he murmured, leaning forward to wrap his lips around the place where her pulse hammered in her throat. He felt it jump at the first pass of his tongue.

"Yesss," she hissed, moving her hips slightly, seeking more friction where she was hot and wet and aching. He planned to give her plenty of friction. And soon.

But first...

"I dreamed of sucking your tasty nipples into my mouth and bathing them with my tongue until you were completely at my mercy. Until you were wild for me," he whispered in her ear, catching the tender lobe and giving it a delicate bite.

"Oh please," she begged. "Yes, please."

Southern girls... Even when they were being naughty, they were still polite. How adorable.

He plumped her heavy breasts high. The moment his mouth was on her, he tongued the hard pebble of her nipple. She gasped his name, not his nickname but his *name*, and cupped her hands behind his head to hold him in place.

As if I'd go anywhere?

Alternating licks with sucks, treating first her left breast, then her right breast, he was rewarded when she made a low mewling sound and dug the balls of her bare feet into the hollows behind his knees. She needed the traction to increase the bump and grind of her hips. The friction was off the charts. Better than it had been before. So much better, in fact, that if she kept it up, he was going to go off like a damned bottle rocket. *Bang! Zoom!* To the moon! The end.

"I dreamed of unbuttoning your jeans and pulling them from your pretty legs," he whispered around one taut nipple, or rather...*growled*. His voice had gone completely guttural. "Then I dreamed of taking off your panties, spreading your thighs, and tasting you."

Now the sounds issuing from the back of her throat were thick and raspy. Her nipple popped free of his mouth with a wet-sounding *plop* when he looked up to find her kiss-swollen mouth slack.

He wasn't the *only* one about to go off.

Damnit!

"Oh, no you don't." When he stepped back, both to stop her from rubbing herself to completion against him and to give himself room to work on the snap and zipper of her jeans, she howled her dismay and frustration.

"Uh-uh," he scolded. "When you come, it's going to be with a piece of me inside you. That piece can be my fingers or my tongue or my cock. I'm willing to negotiate. But you *will* wait for me."

Her eyes sparked. Her gorgeous boobs bobbed prettily as she panted. "Good to know your pushy, autocratic attitude extends to the bedroom."

Autocratic? She thought *that* was autocratic? *Well, babycakes, you ain't seen nothin' yet.*

He wasn't gentle when he pulled her jeans from her legs and tossed them over his shoulder to join her discarded sweatshirt. She squeaked and blinked at him. But he could see the intrigue twinkling in her eyes.

So, in addition to dirty talk, she prefers it a little rough. Good thing, since that was exactly how he liked to ride.

Gripping the waistband of her panties, he sent them the way of the rest of her clothes. Once again, he stepped back and...*looked*.

She attempted to close her legs, but he stopped her with a hand on either knee.

"No, babe. Don't hide that spectacular view from me." And it was spectacular. Swollen lips. A little triangle of trimmed black hair covering her plump mound. "You're so pretty and red and juicy."

"Dagan…" There was self-consciousness in her voice.

He couldn't understand why. Like the rest of Chelsea, that part of her was perfect. And this time he really *did* fall to his knees. Partly because his legs were jelly. And partly because the move put his face right where he wanted it to be.

Without hesitation, he draped her legs over his shoulders. The musky-sweet scent of her filled his nose and detonated inside his brain like an H-bomb. His mouth watered. He was a starving man looking at an all-you-can-eat buffet. And you could bet your ass he planned to savor each taste, each lick, every bite.

"Dagan." Her hand landed in his hair, tangling there. "You don't have to."

"And that's where you're wrong. I have to. I'll die if I don't."

He rubbed a thumb up her soaking seam, then brought the pad to his mouth, licking it clean. His eyes fluttered closed. His nostrils flared wide.

Her taste. *Jesus H*. It was salty and sweet, whetting his appetite for the enviable task ahead.

Bending, he pressed his lips to her. Chelsea hissed, and against his tongue, he felt her throb like a beating heart.

"Oh my," she moaned, her passion-darkened eyes watching him.

Smiling up at her, he set about his business in earnest. For long moments he loved her, treating her to the talents of his lips and tongue. Every moan she made, every whimper ripped from her throat taught him more about her.

She liked it when he sucked on her. But she *loved* it when he flicked the nerve-rich bundle at the top of her sex with his tongue. Fast and hard, then slow and steady. Then fast and hard again.

"Dagan!" The hand in his hair fisted tighter. Tight enough to make the strands pinch and protest.

His Southern girl was forgetting her nice manners. And he loved it.

When her thighs clamped around his ears, he redoubled his efforts. Bringing up his thumb, he place it over her clitoris, giving it a good, rough rub that made her pant and howl. Once he was satisfied she was good to go there, he thrust his tongue deep. His reward was the clenching of her inner muscles.

She's close.

The knowledge made his balls buzz. Idiots were just begging for release. But he resolved to teach them a lesson in patience. Right now was all about her. *Her* pleasure. *Her* release.

Moving his lips back to her clit, he sucked and flicked at the same time he pressed his thumb inside her.

Once more, her inner muscles contracted. Good God, she was a tight little thing. And for another thirty seconds, while he licked and flicked and sucked, he tested her limits. Tested his own too.

Then her whole body began to tremble like she was riding out an earthquake. He considered pulling back and letting her come down before bringing her back to the edge again—he didn't want this to stop; he wanted it to go on forever—but who was he kidding? The desire to see her come, to feel it and taste it, was stronger than anything else.

So he brought her home.

She stiffened when she reached the pinnacle, muscles locked, head thrown back, a loud scream that might have been his name lodged in her throat. Then she turned boneless on the way down, collapsing back on her elbows. Her listless legs slipped from his shoulders even as her sweet cleft continued to throb against his tongue.

Turning his face, he kissed the inside of her silky thigh, then sucked the pulse point there. Hard. Marking her as his woman.

"Mmm," she moaned languidly, the hand in his hair gentling until she cupped his face. "You—" She tried to talk but had to swallow. "You really brought your A game today, didn't you?"

"Nothing but the best for you, babe."

Standing, he shucked his clothes in record time. All the while, he watched her watching him with those lazy, sexy, jungle-cat eyes. She looked smug. *Sated.* Then came the moment when satiation gave way to new hunger. Hunger…and maybe a little trepidation.

"You have a preternaturally huge dick," she blurted, grabbing her glasses from the countertop and slipping them on.

He didn't know about *that*. What he *did* know was that his aching cock needed some attention. The dumbass was literally weeping for it.

Putting his own hand to work, he tried to soothe the poor bastard while Chelsea caught her bottom lip between her teeth, eyeing every stroke, every pull, her breaths coming faster and faster until she was panting.

She likes to watch, too, he realized.

If he needed further evidence of their sexual compatibility—which he didn't—*that* would have been it.

Then she grinned and said, "You need a little help with that bad boy? Maybe a little quid pro quo? I'd be happy to return the favor."

The thought of her on her knees in front of him, her pretty mouth wrapped around the head of his dick, had his hard-on jerking in his fist. Pre-ejaculate rolled over his knuckles, hot and slick.

"Later," he promised her, promised *himself*. "The first time I come, I want to be inside you."

Her lips formed a soundless *oh my!*

Chapter 24

CLEARLY, HAVING BEEN TENDED TO BY AN ORAL VIRTUOSO had turned Chelsea's mind into Swiss cheese.

It was either that or the fact that Dagan Zoelner was huge and horny and standing in front of her in nothing but his birthday suit. Because for the life of her, she couldn't remember why there was a hard stone of remorse lodged in the center of her chest, why there was a rough, sooty kind of sadness swirling around the edges of her brain.

Her eyes drank in the sight of his broad shoulders. His heavy chest with its crinkly hair. His washboard stomach that flexed with every breath. The tattoos on his body that stood out in thick, black ink.

On his inner right forearm were the words *To Thine Own Self Be True*. He had once told her he got the ink after unwittingly becoming Senator Aldus's puppet, a reminder to never be taken in again.

A huge Grim Reaper decorated the meaty bulge over his left shoulder. It was a snarling, hooded creature with the traditional scythe. *To emphasize that death is always near and that I should live each day as if it's a gift*, he'd said when she'd asked him about it.

And then there was the list of initials inked into his flank. Three sets. One for each agent who had died in the café in Kabul. A memorial to them that was far more personal than the stars carved into the lobby wall back at Langley—and a way to never let himself forget.

As if he would.

Seeing the tattoo made that hard stone of remorse grow larger, made that rough, sooty sadness spread deeper. But then he stepped between her legs, pulling her against his broad chest, and all rational thought became impossible.

She could smell the spicy scent of her own release clinging to his beard. The hairs on his chest were wonderfully abrasive against her nipples. And after a few minutes of kissing her to within an inch of her life, he cupped one sensitive globe and plumped it high, thumbing over the taut tip.

Blood that had cooled burned hot once again. He gently removed her glasses and set them aside before he slipped a finger into the place where she was slick and hungry and beginning to ache anew.

This man... This big, bearded, bossy man was everything she had ever dreamed he'd be and more. So much hotter. So much sexier. So much *dirtier*. And for this moment, for this brief bit of time out of time, she would forget everything but making him happy, giving him joy and pleasure and anything and everything he wanted.

He inserted a second finger, stretching her tight. "You have the sweetest, hottest little pussy I've ever tasted. I can't wait to get my cock in it. I'll fill you so full." His lips moved relentlessly against her own. "I'll hit all those spots inside you. The ones you know about and the ones you don't."

She didn't doubt it. She hadn't been joking about that whole preternaturally big dick thing. Not to put too fine a point on it, but Dagan was hung like a horse. Long and thick, with heavy veins and a bulbous crown that was so red and swollen it was shiny.

In all honesty? She was a little nervous.

Of course, any hesitation was forgotten as soon as he began to pump his fingers. In and out. Slow and steady. Using his thumb to thrum the knot of nerves at the top of her sex.

She squirmed and pressed against his talented, marauding fingers like the shameless hussy she was. She wanted more. She *needed* more.

He gave it to her by curling his fingers inside her and rubbing against that spot that only Junior Patrick, her battery-operated boyfriend, had touched in… years now.

Really? Years?

She searched her memory and realized that it had actually been *over* two years. Twenty-six months to be precise since the last time she had gotten a little sumpin'-sumpin'. And, truth be told, she wasn't sure that last time really counted.

Number one, she'd had a third glass of wine, which had pushed her over the county line of Tipsy into that little town known as Slightly Drunk. Number two, the guy she had gone to bed with was a friend of a friend, and not someone she was all that attracted to. He had reminded her a bit of Peregrin Took, short with elfin features and boyishly curly hair. She had only agreed to go out with him because she'd been desperate to stop longing for a man she could never have. And number three, the whole business had been over before she'd had the chance to come.

And speaking of coming…

Dagan was building the sensation inside her. It was becoming an intense burn that rose higher and flashed hotter as his fingers down below kept time with his stroking tongue up above. Then he pinched her nipple, and white lightning flashed across her skin.

Her toes curled. Her head fell back on her neck. She might have cried out his name, but she couldn't be sure since she was coming and coming and coming some more.

Chapter 25

"HE'S A BIG BASTARD. THAT'S FOR CERTAIN," MORRISON muttered, and Steven flicked him a look.

They were sitting in the gravel lot beside the Dover docks, watching the man they had come to know as Rusty Parker as he went about tidying his boat. Rusty couldn't see them through the SUV's deeply tinted windows, but they had no trouble observing him as he stowed gear and washed the hull and deck of his catamaran with a hose.

"He might put up a jolly good fight, were you to have to knock his head about," Morrison added.

"And why would I have to do that?" Steven didn't like the gleam in the old man's eyes. In point of fact, he didn't like the old man. Unfortunately, he was stuck with him. For better or worse. And the longer this day dragged on, the more he feared it would be for the worse.

"To get information from him, naturally." Morrison shrugged.

Not that Steven was opposed to bloodshed. In his previous line of work and his most recent endeavors, bloodshed was just a part of life. A part of *the* life. But he didn't *like* it, and he tried his best to avoid it when possible.

"Why don't we wait to hear back from Benton before we break out the Chinese water torture, hmm?"

And right on cue, his borrowed mobile came to life inside his trouser pocket. After glancing at the number, he thumbed on the device and held it to his ear. "Tell me something good."

"It took a lot of digging," came Benton's reply, "but when I looked into Rusty Parker, I found something you'll probably think interesting."

"Let's have it."

"Parker came into some scratch a few years back. Not an inheritance or anything, but a deposit of a quarter of a million dollars into his personal checking account."

"Who gave him the money?"

"That's the interesting part. It appeared to come from the National Marine Fisheries Service, but I couldn't find out what the payment was for. Since the CIA likes to hide payouts to its players inside the budgets of other government entities, I followed a hunch and hacked into their database."

All the hairs on Steven's neck twanged upright. "You hacked into the bloody CIA? Have you lost your marbles?"

"Nothing fancy. Nothing deep enough to set off any alarm bells. But I tell you, even a rudimentary surface scan was difficult enough. Our government could learn a thing or two from the Yanks when it comes to cybersecurity."

"Benton—"

"But that's neither here nor there." Benton pressed on quickly, reacting to the impatience Steven couldn't keep from his tone. "I found a reference to Rusty Parker. His name is attached to a CIA file I didn't dare attempt to download. But it was a big file. That much I could determine. Given the file size and the sudden influx of cash into Rusty's account, I would say the gobshite did some work as a CIA asset."

"Bollocks!" Steven snarled, his mind gathering all the pieces of the puzzle and trying to fit them together. "So the facts of the case are as follows: Number one, Rusty Parker likely worked for the CIA in some capacity. Number two, Chelsea Duvall planted a virus too sophisticated for you to overcome without first reverse engineering it, a virus the likes of which the U.S. intelligence agency has been known to construct. Number three, Miss Duvall was snatched out of my hands by what I'm sure were trained agents. And number four, the Ducatis Miss Duvall and her trained agent mates rented are parked right beside the docks where Rusty anchors his boat."

Their friend in Scotland Yard had agreed to hold off on sharing the information about the location of the Ducatis with any law enforcement agencies until Steven gave him the go-ahead. It was no secret that Spider was using his pull with the authorities to apprehend Chelsea Duvall. But it was also no secret that Spider would far prefer that Steven take care of the situation himself if possible. "Is it just me, or does that all sound a bit too coincidental?"

"Right-oh," Benton concurred.

"Did you happen to find Parker's current address in all your digging?" It was obvious that Steven's quarry wasn't on Parker's boat. But his intuition told him the same might not be true about Parker's house. "Does he live in Dover?"

"Nope. Over in Folkestone." Benton rattled off an address.

Folkestone, huh? The border agent *had* said Rusty led them on a merry chase from Dover to Folkestone and back again. Had Chelsea and the others been on Rusty's catamaran, only somehow to slip under the Border Agency's radar and make it back ashore before Rusty's boat could be boarded and searched?

Steven supposed it was possible. Then, the memory of the way those blokes had moved when they barged into the penthouse had him moving that *possible* straight into the *probable* category.

"Thank you, Benton." He thumbed off the phone and leaned between the front seats, quickly giving Ramón the address to Rusty's house. Adrenaline burned through his blood. He was on to something; he could feel it. "And step on it," he told the driver. "I want to have a look around before he"—he shot a finger gun toward Rusty—"gets there."

Ramón glanced at Morrison in the rearview mirror, asking permission to follow Steven's order with nothing more than a raised eyebrow.

"Do as he asks." The old man flapped a consenting hand that made Steven grit his teeth.

Chapter 26

Folkestone, England

IN CHRISTIAN'S EXPERIENCE, PLACES LIKE THE BLOODY Bucket, places serving free music, cheap beer, and marginally edible baskets of fish and chips were the world's leading purveyors of hangovers.

Unfortunately for him, he had limited himself to one pint of the local brew. A brew that Ace had decreed was the sudsy nectar of the gods, and Christian couldn't agree more. Beer was just better in Britain. None of that flat piss served ice-cold and guzzled by the twelve-pack.

Yet, despite the sad state of his near-empty pint glass, Christian was grinning as he swirled his last chip through a pile of mayonnaise.

That was another thing. He could not fathom the fuss about ketchup. If one didn't shake a ketchup bottle or ketchup packet properly, one was left with an unappetizing slick of ketchup water. Disgusting.

There were loads of things he did not miss about England. A good, noisy, wood-paneled pub wasn't one of them.

Popping the mayonnaise-dipped chip in his mouth, he hummed his contentment. Things could fall to shite faster than he could snap his fingers—that was just the way of the world in their line of work—but for now he was happy. As a spec-ops soldier, he had learned to appreciate life's little moments.

Across from him, Emily halted with a forkful of fish

halfway to her mouth. She cocked her pretty head. "Now *that's* a new smile." She pointed her fork in his direction. "I'm not sure how to read it."

Usually he tried to avoid going quip for quip with her. Especially since her quick mind always surprised and delighted him, which in turn made him incredibly horny. The latter was a problem since she had given him no indication that her constant taunting and teasing would lead to anything other than *more* taunting and teasing.

But the devil got the better of him—or else it was simply a case of masochism—and he feigned an amazed expression. "Oh, you read? The surprises today...they just keep coming, don't they?"

Ace snorted, but didn't look up from his basket of food.

"Don't let my occasional lapse into poor grammar fool you, mister," Emily declared. "I'm a card-carrying member of Oprah's Book Club. And speaking of reading..." She held up one of the Bloody Bucket's laminated menus. The history of the establishment was printed on the back. "So what if two hundred years ago on this very site a local went to the town well and pulled up a bucket full of blood because someone had disposed of a murdered body in there? Does that make it okay to name a place that serves food and drink the Bloody Bucket? What is *with* you Englishmen?"

"Skewed senses of humor?" Christian suggested.

"I vote for lack of imagination," Ace said, dragging a chip through a mound of ketchup. *Bleck!*

"You're one to talk," Christian scoffed. "If memory serves, your favorite place to eat in Chicago is Downtown Dogs, which serves hot dogs...say it with me...*downtown*."

Emily opened her mouth to add something that

Christian was sure to find wonderfully scathing or snarky. But before she uttered a word, her eyes focused over his shoulder and her lips sealed shut. He was instantly on edge.

They had chosen a four-top table near the southern wall. The location allowed him a view of the front window while Ace kept an eye on the back door. Watching the exits was one more thing they did naturally, *instinctively*. But the arrangement proved disadvantageous because it meant Christian's back was to the bar. He had to crane his head over his shoulder to see what had snagged Emily's attention. The moment he did, he wished he hadn't.

Oh brilliant, he thought, watching the woman headed their way.

When they arrived, the pub had been mostly empty. But the clock on the wall now read half past five, and the place had filled up. Locals packed the bar area, and the tables around them had not one seat to spare. Which brought him back to the woman…

She had been sitting alone at the bar when they entered. One look at her outdated, frizzy blond hairstyle, her two-sizes too-tight clothes, and her blatant leer had told him everything he needed to know. She was the town drunk and the town score.

Every little borough had one. A woman who dolled herself up and hit the local pub in the afternoon, drinking her government support check away by evening, which was when she would start chatting up others to buy her another round. Sometimes she would blow a stranger or a local just to get her next glassful. And all the while she lived with the hope that one of the men would see past her smudged eye makeup and whiskey-sour breath to the good-hearted woman beneath.

Christian knew all about her kind of woman. His mother had been one.

"Oh snap," Emily muttered. "My craydar is going nutso."

"Craydar?" Ace asked, unaware they had company coming.

"The ability to spot crazy," Emily explained from the side of her mouth just as the blond-haired woman sat in the extra chair at their table.

"Well, you three look flush and full of fun," she said, fiddling with the cheap silver cross attached to the chain around her neck. Christian had thought she was pushing forty, but up close he could see she was probably a good decade younger.

Hard living had a way of aging the body.

A memory of his mother stumbling home and stinking of well gin tried to invade his head, but he quickly shoved it away.

"How 'bout lettin' me join the fun, eh?" The woman's words slurred together. "What say you all to another round?"

"Care to give us your name first, luv?" Ace asked, eyeing her curiously.

"Oh." The frizzy blond blinked. "I'm Jenny." She extended her hand. "And you're the most delicious thing what's come 'round here in a fortnight."

Christian assumed she was attempting to look seductive when she pursed her lips at Ace, but it only served to make her look more drunk.

"Hi, Jenny." Ace shook her hand. "Nice to meet you. I'm Ace. I'm gay. And we're all on the clock, so another round is out of the question."

Well, that's *cutting to the chase*, Christian thought with surprise. Ace was usually the epitome of politeness.

But apparently he had known women like Jenny too, and wanted to nip the situation in the bud before it had a chance to bloom into a toxic flower.

A rather ugly expression contorted Jenny's face. She hooked a chip-nailed thumb toward Christian. "I thought *he* was gay, but not you," she told Ace. Then she added, "Damned poofs," before spitting on the ground and pushing from the table. She wobbled back to the bar.

Just like that, all the happy was sucked out of the evening. Their brief reprieve was over, and it was back to the grind.

Emily's mouth was set in a moue of disgust as she watched Jenny retreat. But her brown eyes were liquid soft and full of concern when she turned to Ace, laying a gentle hand on his arm. "I'm sorry she called you that. I'll go drag her out back and kick her ass. Just say the word."

Ace shrugged. "Sticks and stones, luv. Sticks and stones."

"Well, you might be able to brush it off, but I can't," Christian snarled. A vague film of red covered his vision. "I'm going to march up to that bar and tell Drunk Jenny a thing or two."

"And what would that accomplish?" Ace's smile was grim. He shrugged his shoulders, and there was such resignation there that Christian felt a pang in his chest. He'd survived some pretty bad shit. But he hadn't the first clue what it was to be judged on the color of his skin, or the god he'd been raised to worship, or the gender of the people he chose to love. He couldn't fathom it. "It won't change her ways," Ace added. "Besides, she's just a sad alcoholic lashing out at people to try to make them as sad as she is. Misery loves company and all that. I feel sorry for her."

"That makes one of us," Emily grumbled. And for the first time, Christian found himself agreeing with her.

There was no way to rekindle the happy atmosphere, but he hoped at least to end the evening on a lighter note. Self-immolation usually worked for that, so he sighed and donned a hurt expression. "But let's get back to the *real* issue here." Ace glanced at him curiously. "Why did she think *I* was gay?"

Mission accomplished, he thought when Ace and Emily burst into laughter.

"What?" he demanded, feigning a deep scowl.

"Please," Emily scoffed. "The clothes? The hair?" She waved a hand in his direction.

"What's wrong with my hair?"

"Nothing. That's precisely the point. It's all thick and wavy and styled so perfectly. There's even a well-placed whorl over your left eyebrow. Tell the truth… You do that intentionally, don't you?"

"That's a load of tosh."

"I don't know what that is."

"It means bullshit, darling."

"Why do you always gotta use fancy English terms on me? Speak American, why doncha?"

She could really pull off the tough South Side 'hood girl thing when she wanted to. Why that should intrigue him, Christian had no idea.

Wait a tick-tock. Yes, he bloody well did! It was because every time she got tough, his instinct was to tame. More than once, he had fantasized about dominating Emily until she turned pliant and submissive in his arms.

You can thank my childhood for that one too! he thought with a scowl.

He might as well have been raised by wolves. He'd had no structure. But worse than that, he'd had no power

over what happened to him. Helpless, that's what he'd
been. Bloody, buggering helpless. And *that* had informed
his adulthood. It was why he was fastidious about everything. His clothes, his hair, his car, his *world*. Control…
It was the only way he felt safe. Felt *sane*.

"Before you two start trying to tear each other's
throats out again, how about we head back to Rusty's?"
Ace looked at his watch and added, "He should be
home soon."

"Anxious to see him?" Emily waggled her eyebrows.
The beauty mark high on her cheek caught the light and
taunted Christian.

"I don't know what you're talking about." Ace
feigned boredom.

"Oh, sure you do. I saw the looks passing between
you two. And just for the record, Rusty's a really good
guy. I say, get your groove on, my man. We're all down
with the rainbow."

Hold the phone. Looks? Rainbow? "Wait." Christian
blinked. "Rusty's gay?"

Emily frowned. "How the hell did you miss that?
Aren't you supposed to have eyes in the back of your
head and a sixth sense about people?"

"I—"

Before he could answer, she pushed ahead. "Didn't
you *see* the way he and Ace were ogling each other? It
was so hot and dirty. Why do you think we had to take
showers? It was to wash off the residue of all that eye
sex they had while on the boat."

"There was no eye sex," Ace insisted. "There was
maybe a little…eye foreplay."

"If by *foreplay*, you mean *just the tip*. Then yeah.
Sure, okay."

"And on that note"—Ace pushed to a stand—"I'm out."

"Party pooper," Emily declared. But she too rose from the table, leaving Christian to follow suit.

When he skirted the table, Ace frowned at him. "What are *you* grinning about?"

"Nothing," Christian lied, carefully rearranging his features. "Just happy to have a belly full of good English food."

"I'm pretty sure the phrase *good English food* is an oxymoron," Emily shot over her shoulder, winding her way through the pub.

A group of blue-collar city workers eyed her passage with such interest that Christian was tempted to knock their heads together. But he kept his cool by focusing on the fact that Rusty Parker was…da-da-da-dah!…*gay!*

Now he could stop imagining Emily naked and in the big fisherman's arms. Never in his entire life had he been so happy to learn of another man's sexual preferences.

Chapter 27

"YOU'RE BEAUTIFUL WHEN YOU COME," DAGAN WHISPERED, gently sliding his fingers from Chelsea's body.

She would have reckoned speech was impossible, so she was surprised when she managed to pant, "Nobody is beautiful when they come. It's all weird noises and awful faces."

"*You're* beautiful," he insisted, pressing a long, deep kiss on her. After two explosive orgasms, she'd have bet her bottom dollar she was spent. But to her amazement, his talented lips and agile tongue had rekindled an unknown ember still burning inside.

"But let's make you come again," he said, "just to be sure."

"I'm not sure I'll be able to—"

"*I'm* sure," he declared.

There was a devilishly *arrogant* gleam in his eye when he smacked another quick kiss on her lips. Then he bent to retrieve his wallet from his jeans. After fishing out the leather trifold, he extracted a wrinkled foil packet.

That ember inside her became a spark when he ripped the foil open with his teeth and placed the condom's latex ring around his plump, bulbous head.

"Mmm," he groaned and fisted the condom down his length. His pulse beat heavily in his neck—and even heavier down below when he unabashedly gave his cock a couple of tugs.

A knowing smirk twitched his lips, causing a blush to steal into her cheeks. He had caught her looking and *liking*. But he didn't say anything, just stepped forward, cupped her face, and caught her mouth in another mind-melting kiss.

For long, tortured moments, he played with her lips, played with her breasts, plumping them and thumbing her nipples into sharp points of sensation. He had once more managed to stoke the flames of her desire. And all the while, she could feel him there.

Against her.

So hot, even through the latex. So hard. So... *tempting*.

"Please, Dagan," she begged when she couldn't stand it a second longer. "I need you inside me."

He growled deep in his chest and opened two of the lower cabinet doors. She cocked a brow, curious. Then she realized his intent when he hooked his hands behind her knees and positioned her feet atop the open doors. When he swung the doors as far as they would go, she was wide open to him. *For* him.

She could feel her heartbeat between her legs.

"Relax, babe," he whispered against her lips, his beard rasping against the soft skin of her cheeks. "Let's take this nice and easy."

She didn't want nice. She didn't want easy. She wanted hard and fast and hot. Then again, with the size of him...

Using his thumb, he angled his porn-star dick toward her and gently probed. Hot, hard skin met soft, wet flesh. She realized she was holding her breath in anticipation when little white lights strobed in front of her eyes. She blew out a ragged sigh when he dipped inside. Not much. But it was enough to have her body instinctively clenching around his intrusion.

"This is never going to work if you keep doing that,"

he whispered. Or rather panted. His thick chest heaved with effort. She knew his instincts were screaming at him to plunge inside. But out of concern for her, he held steady.

Steady…

That word described Dagan to a T. Besides her own father, he was the steadiest man she had ever known. The bravest. The most loyal. And for this one brief moment, he would be hers.

"T-try again," she managed, eyes still glued to the place where they were connected. To the length of hard, turgid flesh that bridged their bodies.

"Breathe this time," he commanded, gripping her hip in one hand, the base of his dick in the other.

She sucked in a steadying breath and released it, nodding her head. And just like that, he slipped inside. Not too much, just an inch or two. But it was enough to make her feel uncomfortably full.

"Fuck me, that's a pretty sight," he grumbled.

And it was. Him, so thick and hard, buried inside her. Her, so slick and soft, welcoming him in.

"Easy now," he coached, taking a few unhurried passes. In and out. Deeper each time. Stretching her. Preparing her. "How does that feel?"

"It feels amazing. *You* feel amazing. Now, give me all of it."

His breath hitched, and then he did. With one forceful jab he seated himself to the hilt. She gasped when his hot, heavy balls smashed against her ass at the same time the cushiony tip of him pressed hard against the entrance to her womb.

She was stretched as far as she could go. It was pleasure. It was pain. It was some sort of delicious combination of both.

"You okay?" His voice didn't sound like his own. It was so low, so guttural. "You're clamped down tighter than Fort Knox."

Inexplicably, a smile curled her lips—*Fort Knox?*—and she forced her body to relax. Pressing her forehead against his, she caught her breath. "Go slow at first, okay?"

And he did that too.

A gentle retreat was followed by a slow, slick advance. Over and over again, until nerve endings she hadn't been aware she possessed began to scream for fulfillment.

"You okay?" he asked again.

Okay? She was better than okay. Better than good or even great. She was... There was no word for it. Transcendent, maybe? Overcome? Undone? Blissfully on the verge of another orgasm? All were true, but none captured what it was to make love to the man who had stolen her heart so long ago.

"Faster, Dagan," she commanded, searching for his mouth with her own. "Harder."

And just as with all her demands, he didn't hesitate to comply. His hips pistoned. Sweat broke out over the skin of his shoulders where she was holding on for dear life. His mouth mimicked the motion he created below.

She could feel him straining to hold back even as her own twice-sated body labored toward another completion. For long minutes he kept up the crazy rhythm, refusing to go over without her. His stamina was amazing. Not that she ever doubted it would be, but—

Every thought was incinerated by the explosion of her orgasm. Once again, she was coming so hard, coming so good, just coming and coming and coming.

Dagan ripped his mouth away. "Yes!" he cried through gritted teeth. "Squeeze me just like… Oh fuck!"

She opened her eyes to see him fling himself over the edge. His eyes screwed shut, his jaw clamped down tight, and his mouth formed a soundless, animalistic snarl. Tendons popped out on the side of his neck, his stomach muscles contracted over and over again, and she felt his hot release even through the barrier of the condom.

She had been wrong. Some people *were* beautiful when they came. Dagan Zoelner was one of them.

Chapter 28

FOR YEARS, DAGAN HAD KEPT HIMSELF APART, DETACHED. Focusing on the missions and closing himself off from true happiness.

But it was impossible to remain detached in Chelsea's arms.

"Chels." He rested his forehead against hers as they both came down from the glorious high of physical release. "Chels, I—"

He wasn't sure what had been on the tip of his tongue. *I love you*, maybe? That was a pretty clichéd confession after sex, wasn't it? *You complete me*, perhaps? But that was just as bad. Luckily, neither had the chance to slip past his lips because the knob on the front door jiggled, interrupting him.

Without missing a beat, he filled his hands with her amazing ass, lifted her from the counter, and shuffled them into the pantry in the corner. He kicked the door shut behind them just as the front door opened and Emily called in a singsong voice, "Stop playing, little mice! The cats have returned!"

Except for the sliver of golden light visible around the edge of the door, the little cubby was pitch-black. The smell of flour, maple syrup, and boxed cereal was strong. And the feel of still being connected to Chelsea, *inside* her, was more distracting than the sound of footfalls traversing the living room and entering the kitchen.

Chelsea shifted in his arms. He realized she had caught the cord hanging down from the single bare bulb when she gave it a yank and dim yellow light flooded the pantry. It revealed canned goods, a whole shelf of cereal—a staple of the single man's diet—and let's not forget…Chelsea's bodacious boobs.

With her arm over her head, the left boob was looking up at him, taunting him and tempting him to bend his head and take a taste. Inside her, his softening erection throbbed with new life.

Chelsea blinked at him in astonishment. "Really? So soon after that performance out there?"

"What can I say?" He gave her ass a squeeze. "I can't get enough. As for that performance out there…" He bent close, buried his nose in the hair beside her ear, and dragged in the warm strawberries-dipped-in-vanilla scent of her. Now it was mixed with sex. "I must admit I think that was some of my better work. And on a kitchen counter, no less." Because he couldn't help himself, he gave her a shallow stroke that made them both moan with pleasure.

"Yoo-hoo!" A loud knock sounded on the door. "Would you two like me to hand in your clothes? Or would you prefer to come talk to us with your naked bits bobbing?" Emily made the word *naked* sound more like *nekkid*. "We have an update on the situation."

"Clothes, please!" Chelsea called, wiggling to be let down.

Dagan sent her a disappointed look.

She answered him with come-on-we-can't-very-well-make-love-again-with-an-audience-listening eyes.

He begged to disagree. *He* could be quiet if he really had to be. On the other hand, he wasn't so sure about her. The woman clawed her way to the pinnacle each time, hissing and snarling. And then when she finally reached the top, she howled her pleasure.

Sighing in resignation, he gently lowered her to the floor. They both groaned when he slipped out of her. Compared to the sultry heat of her body, the air inside the pantry was freezing cold. All he wanted was to get warm again.

Another knock sounded at the door. With a growl of frustration—or was it disappointment? Maybe both?— Dagan reached behind Chelsea, opened the door, and thrust out a hand. Pulling in a pile of clothes, he looked at Chelsea and hesitated.

She was so damn sexy standing there naked among the soup and the cereal. Her chest and cheeks were flushed from their recent exertions, her phenomenal curves on full display. It was a crying shame to cover any of that up.

"Uh-uh." She lifted a finger. "I recognize that look. Wipe it off your face this instant, or we're never going to leave this pantry."

"Would that be such a bad thing? Far as I can see, we've got everything we need. Food. Drink. You and me sans clothes." He waggled his eyebrows.

"Condoms?" She lifted a haughty brow, sure she had bested him.

He gave her his wickedest grin. "I can think of ways we can improvise."

"You're impossible." She shoved her hands on her hips, donning her patented pint-sized Wonder Woman stance.

He had always loved it. Little had he known how much *more* he would love it when she did it naked.

"And there's that look again," she said exasperatedly.

"What look?"

"You know good and well what look. Your Big Bad Wolf, come-a-little-closer-so-I-can-eat-you look."

He licked his lips and gave her his best growl.

Shaking her head, she stomped over, boobs jiggling in the most delightful way. But before she could snatch her things from his hands, he held the whole pile over his head. Since he was a foot taller than she was, it effectively put everything out of her reach.

Do the Wonder Woman thing again.

She fisted her hands on her hips, and it took all he had not to pump a fist.

"I'm not going to jump for them," she informed him with a sniff.

"Oh, please. Pretty please with a cherry on top?"

"You're *such* a pervert."

"Guilty as charged. And you love it."

"Ugh!" She tossed her hands in the air. "You are *impossible*!"

"You said that already."

"The truth bears repeating!"

Acting completely dejected—and having way more fun than he'd had in a long time—he sighed. "Fine. Have it your way."

Handing over her clothes, he watched her pick out her bra and panties. Seeing her shimmy into them had him growling in earnest. And without conscious thought, he advanced on her.

"No. No, no!" Up went her finger again—her delightful, biteable finger. This time, she added a wag. "Back up three steps, sir. And once you've finished doing that, I suggest you put that thing away." She made a vague motion toward his dick, which had regained its former glory. The condom was once more stretched tight around him. "Liable to put someone's eye out," she muttered under her breath.

He laughed. *Really* laughed. And, man, it felt good.

Alas, since his fun was over—*for now*—he looked around for some place to dispose of the used condom.

Chelsea, ever polite, pulled a new roll of paper towels from the shelves and handed him a square. "There's a trash can behind you in the corner." She pointed over his shoulder.

He turned to see she was right. When he swung back, he thought he saw something drift across her face. A fleeting shadow. But then she pulled her sweatshirt over her head, and when her expression was visible once again, she was all smiley lips and twinkly eyes.

Still, he *had* seen something, hadn't he? However brief it had been?

His mind turned it over as he disposed of the condom and dressed. But before he could question her about it, she put her hand on the door handle and asked, "Ready to face the firing squad?"

"Is that what we're calling them?"

"You think it's an unfair description?"

Knowing the Black Knights? "Not at all."

She pushed open the door, revealing the trio parked outside. Ace, Emily, and Christian stood in the middle of the kitchen. They formed a neat line, and when Dagan and Chelsea emerged from the pantry, they began clapping.

Chelsea blushed to the roots of her hair. But in typical, smart-ass Chelsea-style, she didn't let them get the best of her. Instead, she took a theatrical bow complete with rolling hand gesture.

Her upthrust ass in those jeans had Dagan's brains leaking out of his ears. Which was why he forgot about the shadow that had passed over her face and the fact that she needed to tell him something.

Chapter 29

"OKAY, OKAY." CHELSEA PATTED THE AIR AFTER STANDING from her bow. She retrieved her glasses from the kitchen counter. Not that she really wanted to see the tormenting looks on the faces of her coworkers. "You've had your fun. Now cut the crap."

"Aw, look at them." Ace threw an arm around Emily's shoulders. "Our babies are all grown up and finally getting jiggy with it. I've been hoping and praying for this day for so long. Brings a tear to the ol' eye, doesn't it?" He mimed wiping away a tear.

"It does," Emily agreed, grinning like a fool. "My only question is why the pantry? Unless…" She glanced behind Chelsea and Dagan at the open pantry door. "Is there whipped cream in there? Chocolate syrup? If so, I can completely understand—"

"We weren't in the pantry," Dagan interrupted. "At least, not originally."

Chelsea turned and widened her eyes. Her expression screamed *Ix-nay on the etails-day!*

He ignored her. "Before you guys stomped in like a herd of elephants, we were here in the kitchen." When he pointed to the counter—*their* counter—Chelsea prayed the floor would open up and swallow her whole.

"Remind me not to prepare food in here until the whole place has been sanitized." Ace's lip curled.

"Speaking of food," Dagan said, brow furrowed, "I thought you guys were supposed to bring us something to eat. I see no to-go bags."

"We left the bar in a bit of a hurry." Christian had the grace to look guilty. "A run-in with a mean drunk. Nothing major. But still, sorry to leave you in the lurch. If it's any consolation, the fish and chips would have been a soggy mess by the time we got them here."

"Guess it's cereal for us," Dagan lamented.

"Or tuna salad," Chelsea allowed.

They looked at each other, grimaced, and said in unison, "Cereal."

"Brilliant," Christian declared. "And while you're having a bowl, we'll catch you up on what we know."

Dagan ducked back into the pantry. He held out a box labeled "Shreddies." One would naturally assume that meant shredded wheat. But no. The picture on the box looked more like Chex.

Chelsea shook her head.

His next offering was Frosties, which—*hallelujah!*— were apparently the UK version of Frosted Flakes. There was even good ol' Tony the Tiger on the box. She nodded, and he got down two bowls from the cupboard. She did her bit by grabbing the milk from the fridge.

Christian, Ace, and Emily had taken seats around the small kitchen table. Chelsea joined them, but Dagan chose to stand. He leaned back against the countertop— *their* countertop—cereal bowl in one hand, spoon in the other.

"All right." He nodded, spooning Frosted Flakes— correction: *Frosties*—into his mouth. "Proceed."

"I got a call from Ozzie on the way home," Christian relayed. "He's made some headway on the data, but it's still slow going. Also, Angel has managed to locate his…uh…shall we call him *friend*?…in Le Touquet. You know, the one with the submarine?" Chelsea was still trying to wrap her mind around that one. "He's agreed to take you across the Channel, Chels. ETA is eighteen hundred."

"So that means we have"—Emily consulted the glowing numbers on the microwave—"a little less than an hour to sit around twiddling our dicks."

Ace leaned over the table as if to get a gander at Emily's crotch. "Something you'd like to share with the rest of us, luv?"

Emily thumped him on the shoulder. "It's an expression."

A little less than an hour, Chelsea thought, her stomach dropping like she was riding one of the Khaleesi's dragons in a steep dive. That was plenty of time to tell Dagan what she needed to tell him. Too much time, in fact. Because...then what? Sit there and look at him while the disillusionment on his face slowly turned to disgust that would eventually morph into hate?

The thought had her shoving her half-eaten bowl of Frosties away. She couldn't take another bite.

Chapter 30

"OY! WHAT'RE YOU DOING THERE?"

Steven hung his head and muttered a curse before quickly gathering his wits and fiddling with the laces on his shoe. He had been sure he had seen…

But no. Christian Watson was dead, right? After he'd left the SAS, he'd vanished without a trace, which everyone assumed meant he'd met a bitter end. And *that* meant the tall, dark-haired bloke who had sauntered into Rusty Parker's house was nothing more than a look-alike. A phantom from Steven's past come to bite him on the ass when he least expected it or, for that matter, *needed* it.

"Hey, you!" the young man in the baseball cap cocked at a rakish angle called again. Baggy jeans, bad skin, and patchy facial hair put him anywhere from sixteen to twenty. "I asked what you're doing there!"

And by *there*, the little shite meant crouched beside the Vauxhall Corsa parked across the street from Parker's townhouse.

"New shoes." Steven shrugged and offered the kid a wan smile. "The bloody laces won't stay tied. Seems I'm kneeling to redo them every other block."

The young man's expression softened. "Try double knots," he offered, fishing in his trousers for a set of keys. Once he found them, he pressed a button and the car chirped to life, its lights flashing.

After showily double knotting his laces, Steven stood and moved away from the car, careful to keep an eye on the house across the way. He could see nothing through the shuttered windows. The louvers were open, but it would take getting up close and personal with the property to see in.

"Sorry I yelled at you, mate," the kid said. "But I've had my rims nicked once already. I'm not looking to replace them again. They cost a bloody fortune."

Steven glanced at the rims under discussion. They sparkled in the light of the setting sun, looking like something a rapper would put on his tricked-out Cadillac, not something that belonged on a lime-green hatchback.

"Bad luck, that," he commiserated, shoving his hands deep in his pockets and trying to look unthreatening.

"Mmm." The kid nodded. "Well, I'm off to the market. Mum's screaming mad that Dad didn't replace the milk after he had the last of it this morning. She's to bake fresh biscuits for some party at my baby sister's school tomorrow."

"Mums. What would we do without them, eh?"

His mother's own sweet face flashed through his mind. Even after the stroke, she was still a beautiful woman. Her unlined face full of the grace and kindness she had shown him growing up. If she knew what he was doing, she would—

He ripped the thought out of his mind and tossed it away like a cancer.

"I'll tell you what *I* would do." The kid's lips twisted into a wry grin. "I'd stay out late every night getting pissed."

Steven laughed. "Well, there's that, I suppose."

"Right. Later, then." The kid waved, hopped into his eye-bleeding monstrosity of a car, and quickly drove away.

Steven glanced left and right down the quiet street. A few blocks up the way, Morrison and his driver sat in the black SUV. Steven could feel the old man's eyes on him, boring into him, even though the tinted windows reflected nothing but the deepest, darkest black.

"Nothing for it," he muttered to himself, pulling up the collar on his mac. To Americans, that word meant a brand of computer; to Brits, it was a kind of trench coat. Then he tugged the brim of his black wool newsboy cap low on his brow. Careful to keep his chin down, his eyes on the ground, he crossed the street.

Getting close to Parker's house was easy. The three-story structure sat on the sidewalk, a set of white-washed steps leading up to the front door. Getting a gander into the first-floor windows was another matter entirely. It required that Steven belly up to the house and rise on tiptoes.

And that *won't be conspicuous at all*, he thought sourly.

With another look around at the merry golden glow in the windows of the houses, he hoped the neighborhood's residents were too busy preparing dinner to take notice of a Peeping Tom. Blowing out a breath, he grabbed a windowsill and did a quick up-and-down peek-a-roo. Nothing but comfortable furniture, deeply polished floors, and a big flat-screen TV that sparked an ember of envy.

Fecking hell. The empty room meant he had to check the next window.

Trying to keep up casual pretenses was impossible. So he hurried around the front steps and over to the only other first-floor window. *Bingo!* A low murmur of voices hummed from behind the glass. The conversation was too muffled to make out, but no matter. He wasn't there as a spy. He was there to ascertain whether Chelsea Duvall and her merry band of masked men—and *hopefully* the thumb drive—were on the premises.

Up and down he went again. But this time, the downward motion took him all the way into a crouch. Fear and confusion made his heart beat out a rabbit-fast rhythm.

It *was* Christian Watson he had seen. *The* Christian Watson. Not that he had ever met the man in person, but he had seen Watson's picture plenty of times. The man was famous inside the ranks of the SAS. He was supposedly one of the greatest officers to ever wear the Special Air Services sand-colored beret. Tough. Ruthless. Brilliant—although there was some speculation that he'd been part of that bad business in Iraq known as the Kirkuk Police Station Incident. Regardless, he was... *assumed dead*!

Holy shit! What's he *doing mucking about in all this?*

Steven's mind buzzed around possibilities like a bee in a garden. A *poisonous* garden. Because every reason he could imagine for why and how Watson would be there was worse than the one before it, and—

The rumble of a car muffler in need of repair snagged his attention mid-thought. Even though the sun had set, it threw ambient pink and purple light into the sky. It was enough to show the approaching vehicle was a pickup truck. The kind of hulking monstrosity that ate petrol by the liter. The kind of thing Rusty Parker drove.

You can take the man out of America, but you can't take the American out of the man, Steven thought bitterly, quickly pushing away from the house and heading up the block toward the waiting SUV.

His adrenaline-filled veins urged him to hurry. But training and self-control kept him at a steady pace. He was careful to pass Morrison and his driver and continue up the block. Only after he heard the truck's big engine quietly ticking as it cooled, and the squeak of the front door to the house, did he turn around and start back toward Morrison's vehicle.

He hopped into the backseat, and the old man wasted no time demanding, "Well? Is she in there?"

Steven nodded, his mind still racing.

"Go get her, then. Get that bloody thumb drive and be done with it."

It was difficult to keep the incredulity from his face, but Steven managed it. Or, at least, he *hoped* he did. "And how would you suggest I do that? There is only one of me, and there are five of…no, correction…there are *six* of them."

"So call the local constable." Morrison flapped his hand through the air in that way that made Steven want to throttle him. "Tell them about the APW, and let them apprehend her and turn her over to Scotland Yard. Then we'll get her."

"These local authorities aren't equipped to deal with the men in that house," Steven said, his tone brooking no argument. "Those bastards are well-trained, which means they know all about escape and evasion." *Especially Christian Watson.* "They'll find a way to outmaneuver the backwater police force here. Mark my words. And then they'll know we're on their trail. Our element of surprise will be lost."

Morrison narrowed his eyes, considering. Then he shrugged. "So then you know what to do."

"Yes." Steven nodded and fished the phone from his trouser pocket.

He hadn't wanted to do it. He'd wanted to solve the problem himself. But now… Well, now he was forced to admit he needed help. With fingers he was disgusted to note were trembling, he dialed the number sure to have backup headed his way.

Chapter 31

CHELSEA TOOK HER HALF-EATEN FROSTIES TO THE SINK, dumped the remains down the garbage disposal, and tried to screw up her courage while she placed her bowl in Rusty's small European-sized dishwasher.

Now that the agenda was set, the others had wandered into the living room to welcome Rusty home. She heard them filling him in on the new plan and thanking him for his hospitality. She knew she should probably go add her voice to theirs—Rusty Parker really had gone above and beyond—but she wasn't sure how convincing she would sound. Not because she *wasn't* grateful for all Rusty had done, but because she was wholly preoccupied by the fact that the time for the truth had come. Here in a few minutes, the sweet, seductive smile on Dagan's face would turn hard and ashy.

Hang tough, her father's ghostly voice whispered through her head. It had been his go-to phrase anytime things got hard. It was so much simpler than *This too shall pass* or *Life's full of ups and downs* or any of those other trite sayings that always sounded as if they'd fallen straight out of a dog's ass.

Hang tough, she coached herself. *Do what has to be done.*

Bracing her hands on the edge of the countertop—*their* countertop—she closed her eyes and allowed herself a brief moment, just one more second to enjoy the fantasy that this could be the beginning of something.

Then she quickly reminded herself that it *was* the beginning. Of. The. End.

When she turned to face Dagan, her movements felt sluggish, as though she were wading through the Dead Marshes from *The Two Towers*. To her ears, her voice was a tiny, broken thing when she finally said, "Dagan?"

Maybe it was her tone, maybe it was her face, or then again maybe it was the fact that Dagan Zoelner was no slouch when it came to reading people. Truly, when she considered it, she was surprised that after all these years, he hadn't intuited that something was seriously wrong between them. But regardless, his expression sobered. "Chels? What is it, babe? What's wrong?"

If he kept using that endearment, she might lose her ever-loving mind.

"I need to talk to you." She glanced toward the living room where the others were gathered. Apparently, Ace had told a joke because everyone was laughing while Ace looked on, pleased with himself. What Chelsea wouldn't give at that moment to trade places with any one of them. But she had made her bed all those years ago, and now it was time she lay in it.

Hang tough.

"In private," she added. "Will you come upstairs with me?"

The frown line deepened between Dagan's sleek, dark eyebrows. "Of course." He dumped the discolored milk from his bowl and added it to the dishwasher.

She could feel him behind her like she could feel her own heart beating in her chest as she made her way to the stairs. It was as if he were part of her. Something fundamental, something crucial, something...she couldn't live without.

Well, we shall soon see if that's true.

"And just where do you two think you're going?" Emily asked, a mischievous gleam in her eye.

"To talk," Dagan answered for them both. Chelsea was glad. She wasn't sure she could speak around the Carolina pine–sized lump in her throat.

"Oh, is *that* what the kids are calling it nowadays?" Emily asked.

"Guest bedroom is the first door on your right after the landing," Rusty told them after elbowing Emily.

"Thanks," Chelsea managed. Not brave enough to meet their eyes and see their amused looks, she turned and made her way up the stairs. Each tread felt like a climb up the Wall at the northern border of the Seven Kingdoms.

She tried to think of a way to spin her tale to save Dagan from hurt. But no matter how she rearranged the events in her head, she always ended up in the same place. *Total devastation.*

By the time she reached the landing, her knees were shaking. When she grabbed the knob on the door to the guest room, she was not surprised to see her fingers trembling.

Hang tough. It became a mantra. *Hang tough. Hang tough. Hang tough.*

Opening the door, she saw the bedroom was as tastefully decorated as the rest of the house. A big oak four-poster bed took center stage, dressed in a cool cream spread and seafoam throw pillows. The air smell oddly of hibiscus. She assumed that was due to the bowl of potpourri sitting atop the chest of drawers.

She wondered if she would associate the smell of hibiscus with heartbreak for the rest of her life.

"Nice bed," Dagan said from behind her. "How about we put it to good use and then talk after?"

Before she could turn and answer, he'd booted the door closed and caught her around the waist, pulling her back against him. He used the Beard to nuzzle the juncture of her neck. Goose bumps erupted over her entire body.

For just a second, she allowed herself to lean against him. To feel his heat and strength and unflinching power. She was both lost and found inside his embrace. Torn apart and re-formed into a new whole. It felt wonderful. And awful.

Gently extricating herself from his embrace, she turned to face him. Her voice was a hoarse, strangled-sounding thing. "Z…" She used the nickname intentionally, giving up the intimacy of his name. "We have to talk about Afghanistan."

Chapter 32

DAGAN HEARD HER WORDS, BUT IN A DETACHED SORT OF WAY.

He was too distracted by the fact that after he had agreed to her terms, after all they had *shared*, she was back to calling him Z. And then there was the look on her face. It was one he remembered well. The same look she had worn that awful day he had been told the American people in general, and the Central Intelligence Agency in particular, no longer needed his services.

She had stopped him to say something when he had been escorted from CIA premises—which was just a nice way of saying he'd been booted out on his ass—and he had seen in her face all the things he had felt. Confusion. Sorrow. Regret.

Words hadn't been necessary that day because her expression had said it all. But words were *definitely* needed today.

Obviously, he'd been wrong to hope she might want him for the long haul. Obviously, she'd given him that ultimatum as an excuse, never dreaming he would actually take her up on it. Obviously, she had made love to him because... His brain stalled on that one.

Why did she make love to me?

Pity, perhaps? Or maybe it was as simple as wanting to extinguish the fire that burned between them. Because there was no denying their explosive physical chemistry.

Of course, whatever her reasons, there was that look. The look that told him it was over.

But *before* it was over, he would have his say. He would swallow his pride, bite the bullet, and take out his heart and show it to her. That way, when he walked away, he would never have to wonder, *What if?*

"Afghanistan." He sighed. "Sometimes I think the best part of me was killed that day. Other times I think I've become a much stronger, much *better* man since." He rubbed a hand over his beard and laughed. "Maybe it's true what they say. The worse things bring out the best in us. Know what I mean?"

She searched his face. "N-not really."

"Men…*died* because of me," he explained as best he could. "Because I got complacent. Because I dulled my own edges when I should have stayed sharp and frosty. And since that day, I've tried to live my life with honor and integrity, with virtue and service. I've tried to give some small measure of meaning to their sacrifice." He blew out an unsteady breath. "And for the most part, I think I have. The work I've done for the Black Knights has made the world a better place, a safer place."

"You are a good man, Z," she whispered. "Under all those scowls and beneath all that macho superiority"— *Macho superiority?* Emily was right. He really *did* come off like an ass—"is a truly good man. I knew it the first time we met."

Even though a deep fissure had formed in his heart, he still found himself smiling. "If memory serves, the first time we met, you ripped me a new asshole so big I could have fit a pizza box into it."

She shook her head. "As my daddy would have said, you're lucky I didn't cream your corn. You were cracking jokes while I was trying to give an Intelligence report. What did you expect?"

"To get you naked at the first available opportunity,"

he admitted, surprised that even while they were saying their good-byes—that *was* what they were doing, wasn't it?—they could still be friends. It was a testament to all their years together. And even though it would never be enough—he would never be satisfied with anything less than *everything* when it came to Chelsea—he supposed it was something. Something to hold on to. Something to cherish.

"Really?" She blinked. "Even then?"

"Then and every day since."

"You're making this so hard on me. You have no idea."

With that, the fissure zigzagging through his heart gave way, and the silly organ broke in two. "It's okay, Chels. You don't have to say anything more. I understand if you don't want…" His voice broke on a sharp edge. "Me," he finally finished.

"Oh, Z. I *do* want you." Her voice was thick with emotion. "I've wanted you for…*forever*. I still want you, but—"

"Workin' nine to five!" The sound of Dolly Parton's distinctive voice crooned from the cell phone in Chelsea's back pocket.

Dagan wanted to crush the damned device, especially when Chelsea squeezed her eyes closed and dragged in a deep sigh. She opened them, and there was no mistaking the resignation and *pleading* in her eyes. "Just…give me a minute, okay?"

What could he say? He knew all about the burden of family, so he nodded his head. But that *but* at the end of her previous sentence seemed to hang in the air between them.

Chapter 33

CHELSEA WAS OBVIOUSLY IN THE WRONG LINE THE DAY THEY distributed guts. Because like a yellow-bellied coward, the sound of her cell phone ringing filled her with relief.

She had known this...*confession* would be the hardest thing she'd ever done. But Dagan's earnestness, his bravery and honesty were making it all *so* much worse. He was killing her with kindness one sweet word at a time.

Pulling her cell from her back pocket, she watched him watching her. His stormy eyes did a number on her already-shattered heart. Maybe because there was resignation there. And she recognized that it wasn't anything new. Dagan Zoelner could be confident and cocky. He could be provocative and infuriating, but underneath all that, deep in the hot, beating heart of him, was always resignation. It was as if he thought his past shadowed him like a cloud he couldn't escape.

Well, I'm going to give him a way out soon enough, she thought. She had shot a hole in her own boat all those years ago, and now she was finally sinking. But first, she would take this reprieve. Chicken liver that she was...

"Momma," she answered without salutation. "This isn't a good time. Can I—"

"I don't think so, Chelsea Lynn!" her mother shouted in her ear. Grace Duvall so rarely raised her voice that Chelsea was shocked into silence. "Your face is all over the news over there! They're sayin' you stole something from your boss, and now you're a…a… *wanted woman!*"

The hysteria and fear in her mother's voice had Chelsea screwing her eyes closed and pinching the bridge of her nose. Her mother had downloaded the BBC news app the day Chelsea moved to England and had taken it upon herself to follow the British headlines. How could Chelsea have forgotten?

Shit on a shingle!

"It's not what you think, Momma. I promise you that."

"I'll tell you what I think, Chelsea Lynn. I think your daddy and I didn't raise no thief. I think all these years I've kept my Lord-lovin' mouth shut about your job 'cause I knew the only reason you wouldn't be straight with me was if you *couldn't*. I think your telling me you quit and uprooted to London to be some scrawny billionaire's glorified secretary just to make a little extra cash—cash I swear on your daddy's grave I don't need—was a lie. I think you're still workin' for the… uh…*government*."

Chelsea had never come out and told her mother she worked for the CIA. Not only was it company policy to keep such matters on the DL, but it was also for Grace Duvall's own good. Her mother couldn't give information she didn't have to a foreign power or to one of America's vast collection of enemies. Still, Chelsea's momma was one smart cookie. She had added two and two to get four a long time ago. Yet, the truth had remained unspoken between them. Chelsea's cover with the Bureau of Land Management was the eight-hundred-pound gorilla they had allowed to stay in the room.

"Chelsea, baby, what has the…" Her mother let the sentence dangle. She took a deep breath and then finished more quietly with "What has the CIA gotten you involved with?"

And there it was. Spoken aloud for the first time.

"It's a mistake," Chelsea assured her mother as calmly as she could, trying to inject certainty into her tone. A touch difficult considering that right then the only thing she was truly certain of was that she was minutes away from hurting a good man, the *best* man. "Everything will be cleared up soon. I promise you that when I get home, I'll explain it all."

Her mother dragged in a ragged breath, and Chelsea realized her tough-talk, take-no-guff momma was on the verge of crying. Chelsea wouldn't have thought she was capable of withstanding more pain.

"Momma, don't cry. Everything will be all right."

"You have someone there with you, child?" her mother asked. "I hate thinkin' of you over there all alone. Please tell me you have someone helpin' you through this."

Chelsea glanced at Dagan. If there had been any doubt he'd heard both sides of the conversation, that was squashed by the sympathy in his eyes. She wanted to rip her hair out. She wanted to scream. He had no business offering the likes of *her* sympathy. Yet there it was, all the same. Offered freely because he was Dagan. Because despite his my-way-or-the-highway, high-handed ways, he was the sweetest, most selfless man she had ever known.

"Give me the phone." He gently pulled the cell from her hand. "Let me talk to her."

Should she have stopped him?

Probably.

Given all he didn't know, it was wrong of her to depend on him for anything, even for what comfort he could offer her mother. But the truth of the matter was that if it was wrong, Chelsea didn't want to be right. When it came to Grace Duvall, she would do anything.

Just like always.

"Ms. Duvall?" Dagan said. "My name is Dagan Zoelner. I've known your daughter for many years now, and if there's one thing about her, it's that she doesn't need help from anyone. She's the smartest, bravest, most capable woman I know."

Chelsea wanted to die right then and there. If she were in her grave, six feet under and food for the worms, his sweet words wouldn't be able to hurt her.

"But if it's any consolation," he continued, "I'm here with her. And I promise you I'll help get her home to you just as soon as possible."

"Dagan Zoelner?" Chelsea heard her mother ask. "You're the one she calls Z?"

Dagan shot Chelsea a look, eyebrow raised. That eyebrow said, *You told your mom about me?*

Yup. She sure had. One night over a bottle of wine she had spoken of her heartbreak, of a man she had wronged—she'd left out the specifics—and her fear that she'd never love another as much as she loved him.

Her mother had advised her to come clean, to confess. *It's good for the soul*, her mom had said. *And even if he can't forgive you, perhaps you'll start to forgive yourself.*

That was, what? Two years ago? And here she was, still un-confessed.

"Yes ma'am. That's me," Dagan said.

"My girl speaks highly of you." Her mother's voice was tinny sounding through the connection. "I'm so glad you're there with her. And Dagan?"

"Yes, ma'am?"

"Once you get my girl home, why don't you stop on by and see me. I want to meet the man who's stolen my Chelsea's heart."

Oh, Momma, Chelsea thought. Never had that coffin and two yards of dirt looked better.

When she glanced at Dagan, she saw the skin on his cheeks go so pale it looked almost waxy. His voice was strangled-sounding when he said, "Yes, ma'am," and passed Chelsea the phone.

"Momma?" she said into the receiver.

"I like him, Chelsea Lynn. Man's got a good, strong voice. And he obviously thinks the world of you." Only because Chelsea had yet to take her mother's advice and reveal the Big Bad Secret. "Bring him 'round once you're home, you hear? I'm tired of tiptoeing around the perimeter of your life."

"I love you, Momma. But I need to go now."

I need to pull up my big-girl panties and finally come clean like you told me to.

"I love you too. And remember what your daddy always said: keep a weather eye out."

"And hang tough," they both finished in unison. "I will. I promise," Chelsea added. With that, her mother said good-bye and the phone went dead.

Chelsea thumbed off the cell and shoved it into her back pocket. Her reprieve was over. Time to face the music.

Blood-thunder. That was the sound in her ears as she took a deep breath. "Z, I—"

"Is it true?" He cut her off. He was doing his eerily still shtick.

"Is what true?" she asked, but she already knew. Her mother had let the cat out of the bag. There was no way to shove the little shit back in.

"Have I stolen your heart?"

She could have lied to him, she supposed. But there were already too many lies between them. So she gave him the truth, as plain and as unvarnished as she could make it. "You didn't need to steal it. I willingly gave it to you a long time ago."

Chapter 34

DAGAN HAD SPENT THE LAST HANDFUL OF YEARS KEEPING his heart encased in Kevlar. But Chelsea's confession blew through the protective armor and pierced deep.

She loves me! Chelsea Duvall loves me! He couldn't fathom it. And yet, the proof was there in her copper-colored eyes, shining up at him as brightly as a promise, as sweetly as a dream.

Pulling her into his arms, he buried his nose in her hair, loving the way it tickled his cheeks. She wiggled against him, trying to escape, but he just tightened his hold. Now that he had her, *really* had her, he had no intention of letting go.

She loved him. He loved her. As for anything else? Well, love conquered all, right? They could work it out. Together they could overcome anything.

"Chelsea," he whispered into her hair. "Babe, if only you could take my heart out and look at it. It's covered in scars. There are scars from those I've lost. Scars from the times I've failed. And…a big ol' scar from you."

"Me?"

"Yeah. The scar from where you wiggled your way inside."

He was prepared for a lot of things after that admission. What he wasn't prepared for was Chelsea falling apart. She'd always been so stubborn, so tough, and seemingly unbreakable. But as she clung to him, her entire body shaking, he realized that what he had long suspected was true. At Chelsea's core, she was as soft and tender as a butterfly. Someone to be cherished. Someone to be protected.

"You've always made me the best version of myself." He palmed the back of her head, loving how it was a perfect fit, as if she'd been made just for him. "With you, I can let down my guard. I can't do that with anyone else. Not even with Avan. Chels, you have always been like…*home* to me."

Saying the words out loud made him realize just how true they were. No matter what, he had always run to her, depended on her, *relied* on her. Wasn't she the one who had helped him figure out what Senator Aldus had really been up to? Hadn't she always had his back, even when he hadn't been worthy of her loyalty?

She loves me! Chelsea Duvall loves me!

"Dagan." Her voice was muffled by his sweater. But hearing her call him by name had never sounded so sweet. "I—"

"Chels," he interrupted, scared that she was going to bring up the past or the future again before he had a chance to arrange his thoughts on the subjects. Before he had a chance to think about what he wanted to say. "I believe that love is the strongest force on the planet. I believe that it really can conquer all. Do you?"

"Of *course*, but—"

"No buts. I know you want to talk about things. I do too. But for right now, would you just let me hold you? Will you stop thinking, stop scrutinizing and analyzing, and just allow us this moment?"

He desperately wanted time to wallow in the knowledge that she loved him, bumps and bruises, scars and warts and all, before reality and the past—or the future—came crashing in.

"Tall order." She sniffed. "I *am* an analyst, after all.

Thinking and scrutinizing comes with the territory. But, okay. I can give it the ol' college try. It's just that… No, no. Never mind. I was about to start analyzing again. *Damnit*. This is harder than I thought. Maybe we should…but no. That's more scrutinizing. Please help me stop talking, will you? I can't do it on my own." There was genuine pleading in her voice, and something more that he couldn't put his finger on.

"It's an easy enough problem to solve," he assured her. "All it takes is an ultimatum."

"An ultimatum?"

"Unless the next words out of your mouth are 'Let's put that big four-poster bed to use,' I'm going to kiss you until you can't think straight."

"That's not much of an ultimatum." He could still hear that *something* in her voice. "Either way, we end up in bed."

"Let no one ever accuse you of being slow on the uptake."

She softened in his embrace, all her muscles loosening. And *hello!* Her softening succeeded in making him hard.

Her breasts cushioned heavily against his chest. Her thighs pressed tantalizingly against his legs. And the sweet heat of her seeped into his bones, warming him from the inside out, chasing away the chill of too many long, lonely years.

She loves me! Chelsea Duvall loves me! He would never tire of that refrain. And he planned to show her just how much *he* loved *her* in about two seconds.

Glancing at his watch, he calculated how much time he had. Not enough to do it the way he wanted. But enough for Chelsea. The wonderful woman was like a bottle rocket. When it came to sex, she had a quick fuse, burning hot and fast before the final explosion which, by the way, was really loud and—

A knock sounded at the door.

"*What?*" he barked, unable to keep the frustration from his voice.

"Sorry to interrupt!" Emily called, not sounding the least bit sorry. Damn her. "But once again I'm going to ask you kiddies to get your clothes on. Angel arrived early, and he's itching to get you both loaded into his buddy's sardine can. Something about tides and currents and what have you. So, chop-chop!"

Chelsea pushed out of Dagan's arms, taking her soft curves and delicious feminine warmth with her.

"That woman has the worst timing," he muttered, adjusting his hard-on into a more comfortable position.

"I heard that!" Emily called through the door.

"Go away!" he bellowed. "We'll be down in a second!"

"I don't trust you, Romeo! I know just how single-minded you men can be. Chels? Can you hear me? Do you need me to come in and wrestle that big gorilla off you?"

Chelsea caught her lower lip between her teeth and shook her head. She looked a little…what? What was that expression? He narrowed his eyes, trying to see what was going on inside that souped-up brain of hers, but before he could get a bead on it, she slipped around him and pulled the bedroom door wide.

"I'd be more than happy to—" Emily cut herself off when she was suddenly staring him square in the face. "Oh, how disappointing. I thought for sure you two were…," She trailed off, narrowing her gaze at the look on Chelsea's face. Emily turned to him then, attempting murder with her eyes. "What did you do to her?"

"Emily…" Chelsea tried.

But Emily just barged ahead. "What did you *say* to her?"

"Down, mother bear." Dagan lifted a staying hand. "I didn't *do* anything to her. As far as what I said to her, that's simple. I told her I love her."

He was usually a private person. But in this particular instance, he didn't bother. First of all, because he wanted to wipe that accusing look right off Emily's face. And second of all, because he wanted to shout his glorious news from the rooftops.

Hear ye! Hear ye! Let it be known far and wide that Dagan Zoelner loves the amazing, talented, and gorgeous Chelsea Duvall. And miracle of miracles! She loves him too!

"Oh." Emily blinked. Then she said louder, "Oooohhhh. Wow. I just thought you two were visiting Pound Town. But sure, okay." Emily turned to Chelsea. "Another one bites the dust, huh? I wish I could say I'm happy for you, Chels. But the truth is that I'm jealous as hell. I'll be the only one left seeing Junior Patrick."

"Who's Junior Patrick?" Dagan demanded.

Emily opened her mouth, but Chelsea beat her to the punch. "Never mind that."

"No. Not never mind that. Who the hell is *Junior Patrick*?" It was amazing how quickly jealous rage consumed him. Had Chelsea been seeing someone? Had she and Emily *both* been seeing someone? The same guy?

Chelsea didn't seem the type. Back up. Rewind. Chelsea *wasn't* the type. So what was Emily talk—

"It's another name for a lady's best friend," Emily said.

Huh?

"A battery-operated boyfriend, numb nuts." Emily rolled her eyes. "Don't get your boxers in a twist. Jeez."

"Oh," he said. Then, "Oooohhhh."

"Is there an echo in here?" Chelsea demanded, hands on hips Wonder Woman–style.

Dagan lifted a brow, imagining her in bed, pleasuring herself with a vibrator. His little downstairs buddy liked the imagery very much. Too much.

Damnit. He glanced at his watch. He should've still had thirty minutes to screw her brains out. He'd have to have a talk with Angel when he saw him. Not sticking to the schedule was wreaking havoc with Dagan's sexual ambitions.

"And why are we talking about any of this anyway?" There was no mistaking the two red flags of color in Chelsea's cheeks. She might be one tasty little wildcat in bed, but out of it, she was still a Southern girl. Talk of her adult toy collection—he hoped it was vast. *Please let it be vast*—embarrassed her. "We shouldn't keep Angel waiting."

Dagan tossed an arm around her shoulders. He thought he felt her tense and wondered what *that* was all about. They'd cleared things up, hadn't they? They were on the same page, weren't they?

"Fine," he said. "We'll be on our way. But at some point in the future, I expect you to introduce me to Mr. Patrick. I'm curious to meet my competition."

"Gag me with a very large spoon." Emily threw her hands in the air. "You two are so adorable that you're making me sick to my stomach." She turned and flounced down the stairs.

Chelsea glanced at him through the fan of her sooty lashes. There it was again, that *something* in her eyes.

He was done trying to figure it out on his own. Best just to sac up and ask. "What is it, babe? What's bothering you?"

"You really believe love conquers all?" She gnawed on her lower lip.

He gave her the words she needed to hear, promising to prove them to her every day for the rest of his life. "I do, Chels. I really, really do."

Chapter 35

CHELSEA FOLLOWED DAGAN DOWN THE STAIRS ON RICKETY legs. She was old enough to know that words were cheap. It was easy to say something in the heat of the moment. But it was another thing entirely when the chips were down and the truth was revealed.

Dagan reached the bottom step and turned, offering his hand. Scratch that, his *paw*—the man's hands were too large and scarred and callused to be called anything else.

She reached for his fingers, and the instant they were skin to skin, a jolt of electricity zapped her system. Was it her imagination, or did the lights flicker? Would she always feel that white-hot frisson of awareness? If he were to touch her every day for the next fifty years, would she still feel a shock at the brush of his fingertips?

Please, Lord! Let me find out.

"In case it isn't obvious," Ace said when they walked into the living room. Joy of joys, the whole gang was gathered, grinning at them like a bunch of nitwits. "These two have finally admitted they're hot to trot for each other."

"More like ass over teakettle," Emily chimed in. "According to Zoelner, they're in love." She made the word into two syllables. *Luh-uv*. "And as I said upstairs, another one bites the dust. It's nearly enough to make a single girl want to scream and pull out her hair."

"Mmm," Angel hummed noncommittally. "I suppose congratulations are in order, then."

The former Israeli Mossad agent looked at Chelsea with his dark, uncanny eyes. The man gave new meaning to the phrase *Riddle wrapped in a mystery shoved inside an enigma*. In all the time she had worked as the CIA liaison to Black Knights Inc., Chelsea had only met him on a handful of occasions. Each time, she had come away feeling slightly unsettled.

There was just something about Angel.

"Thank you for doing this, Angel," she said. "You're saving my bacon."

"No thanks necessary." He spoke with a precision that would make an English teacher weep with happiness and an accent that was impossible to place.

Chelsea reckoned both affectations were intentional.

"Well, now that the social niceties have been concluded, let's get this show on the road, shall we?" Emily said. "This has been one long-ass day, and I, for one, can't wait to hop on that swanky private jet and catch some z's. Adrenaline is hell on the body." She shouldered into her backpack. When she had trouble with one strap, Christian obligingly helped her on with it. "You know"—she turned to the Brit and smiled—"you're really not so bad."

Christian clutched his chest. "My God! I'm having that put on a T-shirt."

"Like you'd *wear* a T-shirt." Emily rolled her eyes, then turned to Angel with a hand on the knob of the front door. "Say, Angel, what *does* this friend of yours do with a submarine in the English Channel, anyway?"

Angel's face was expressionless. "He is not a friend. He is a…contact. And one would not necessarily call him a law-abiding citizen." *Drug smuggler*, Chelsea thought, her stomach sinking. "Are you certain you wish to know the what, why, and how of his operations?"

Emily curled her lip. "Well, not when you put it *that* way. Jeez!"

"Very good." Angel nodded. "Shall we go?"

"Uh, Angel?" Chelsea didn't like the hesitation in her voice. But, lovesick puppy that she was, she *really* liked the way Dagan gave her fingers a reassuring squeeze. How was it possible he could be so attuned to her and not know she was hiding something huge and life-changing from him? *Please don't let it be* love-*changing too!* "How, um, how long will it take?"

She didn't need to clarify. Along with being spooky, Angel was sharp as a tack. "Gautier's vessel is small, but it is fast. He can have you to Calais in ninety minutes. Barring any course corrections he might need to make to avoid the tanker and cargo ships that pile through the Channel, of course."

Gulp. She hadn't considered *that*.

A series of images bloomed to life inside her head. A propeller striking the submarine. A loss of pressure. Her, Dagan, and Gautier—that sounded like a drug smuggler's name if ever she'd heard one—sinking to their watery deaths.

"Right-oh." Christian nodded. "It's a piece of cake."

"You'll be in and out before you know it," Ace added.

Rusty winked. "Easy breezy."

"Says everyone who isn't about to be squeezed into the vessel of a criminal named Gautier," Chelsea groused, giving them all dirty looks. "And how will the rest of you be crossing?"

"It is my hope that Mr. Parker will be good enough to take his truck with us through the Eurotunnel," Angel said. The train that ran beneath the English Channel was equipped to carry both passengers and vehicles. "Once we are on the other side, he can give us all a lift to Paris."

"No problem," Rusty assured him. "Done and done."

"Thank you." Angel nodded. Then he added, "If the online schedule is correct, Chelsea, you and Zoelner will beat us across by approximately thirty minutes. You will wait near the beach until we can come and get you. It is all very simple."

Simple? That's not a word she would have used. Not with a French drug runner and a submarine involved.

"You will want to wear coats," Angel advised in that raspy, scoured-vocal-cord voice of his when she and Dagan had moved to don their backpacks. "The Channel…she is very cold."

"Tell me about it," Chelsea grumbled. The memory of that afternoon's swim was all too clear in her mind's eye. Then a terrible thought occurred. "We don't have to *swim* out to the sub, do we? Where is it?"

"It is beneath the end of the pier." Right. The pier. Good. Great. Her wounded shoulder chose that moment to throb dully. "I swam to shore," Angel continued, and she noticed his jet-black hair was wet. His clothes on the other hand? Bone dry.

Huh. She wondered how he had managed *that*. Something similar to what they had done with the waterproof float bags, she hoped. Though she had the sneaking suspicion that he might have swum to shore—either clothed or naked—and then stolen dry threads off someone's clothesline or out of someone's dryer.

Stories of Angel's deft hand when it came to five-fingered discounts abounded back at BKI. And if she needed further proof that those stories were true, Angel finished with, "But not to worry. I appropriated a dinghy for you." *Appropriated. Right.* "It is tied on the beach beneath the pier. All you need to do is boat to the end of the harbor arm. Gautier is there waiting."

Okay. So…she was about to hop into a stolen dinghy to row out to a drug-smuggling submarine, which she would then take across the busy English Channel, all while telling the man she loved that once upon a time, when she had been scared and dumb and faced with an impossible decision, she had chosen her mother's happiness and memories of her father over him.

You know, just your ordinary, average day.

Chapter 36

STEVEN SAT FORWARD IN THE BACKSEAT OF MORRISON'S SUV when Rusty Parker's front door opened. A whole horde of people piled down the front steps. Seven, to be precise. He couldn't help but notice they were all dressed for traveling. Parkas, rucksacks, an air of furtiveness and impatience hanging around them.

Bloody hell. He glanced at the glowing green clock numbers on the console and grimaced. His backup wasn't due to arrive for another twenty minutes.

"Who is the new bloke, do you suppose?" Morrison frowned as the group gathered on the sidewalk beside Rusty's monstrous, king-cab pickup truck.

The streetlight cast the crew in an odd glow. It created sinister shadows and made them look more menacing than they really were. Then again, perhaps they looked *exactly* as menacing as they really were. Christian Watson numbered among them, after all.

"Another operative, if the economical way he moves and the covert way he catalogs his surroundings is any indication," Steven answered, eyeing the dark-haired gent who had entered the house not five minutes prior. Then Steven's attention returned to Watson. He had not told Morrison about the famous SAS officer. He wasn't sure why. Maybe because to admit that the great Christian Watson was on the premises would highlight just how far Steven himself had fallen.

"Economical way he moves. Catalogs his surroundings." Morrison parroted Steven's words, flashing his shark teeth. "Oh, how very droll. I do so love the way you clandestine types speak. It's all so...*shaken, not stirred*."

Steven was glad one of them was having a good time.

On second thought, no, he wasn't. He was annoyed that Morrison wasn't taking this more seriously. After all, weren't *both* their arses on the buggering line?

"Oh, sodding hell," he hissed when five of the seven piled into the pickup truck. The other two, Chelsea Duvall and the big bearded bloke, set off down the lane.

"Who should we follow?" Morrison asked.

"Both." Steven checked the clip on his SIG Sauer P230, the same make and model he had used while with the SAS. "You and Ramón will follow those in the truck. I will follow Chelsea and her hairy companion."

"Not bloody likely," Morrison growled.

"Pardon?"

"I *told* you. Chelsea Duvall wormed her way into *my* life and *my* home. She planted some insidious virus onto *my* computer to try to bring *me* down. I want to be there when that cunt is brought in."

"Sir—"

"Don't sir me." Morrison's usually pale face was livid. "Give me your spare weapon. I know you carry one."

Steven wanted to argue, but Morrison's mulish expression told him he wouldn't win. To save time, he took his Ruger LCR from the holster on his ankle. But before he handed it to Morrison, he narrowed his eyes. "You *do* know how to handle this, yeah?"

"Oh, piss off." Morrison snatched the gun from Steven's hand. "I was taking shooting lessons while you were still wetting your nappies. Don't let the luxury condos and sports cars fool you. A man doesn't get to where I am without knowing how to protect himself."

Steven clenched his jaw. "Remember there are only six rounds in the cylinder."

"If it comes to that," the old man sniffed, "six rounds are more than I will need."

Now *that* made Steven decidedly uncomfortable. Or perhaps it was more accurate to say he was now decidedly *more* uncomfortable, because he was always uncomfortable around Morrison, given the man's…predilections.

"It *shouldn't* come to that," Steven stressed. "Remember, we need Chelsea alive. She might not have the drive on her person, which means we need to be able to interrogate her to find out where it is."

The roar of the engine on Rusty's ridiculous vehicle had Steven glancing at Ramón. "Follow them," he instructed. "Then text us their whereabouts."

Ramón glanced at Morrison in the rearview mirror, waiting for permission to follow Steven's order. When Morrison nodded regally, Steven hoped neither man could hear his back molars creak.

As they waited for Rusty and the others to drive by, Steven kept an eye on Chelsea's progress. She and her companion turned southwest on a road that led to only one place. Back to the beach.

"I'll trail behind them," he told Morrison. "You circle the block and stay to the west of them. Once we have them boxed in, we can both advance with our weapons drawn. But *no* shooting to kill," he felt compelled to stress. "Not unless absolutely necessary."

Morrison just glared at him.

"Here." He took the borrowed cellular phone from his trouser pocket and dialed Morrison's mobile number. "We'll leave the line open and communicate that way."

Morrison's phone buzzed. The old man thumbed it on before depositing it into the pocket of his leather jacket.

When Ramón cleared his throat—did the man never speak?—Steven realized the pickup truck was pulling out of sight.

"Right." He nodded to Morrison. "Ready?"

"Please." Morrison snorted. Steven knew what the evil old twonker was going to say before he said it. "I was born ready."

It took some effort, but Steven managed to keep the disgust from his face as he pushed from the vehicle into the chilly night. Morrison followed him out and, without a backward glance, started up the block. Steven watched him go, feeling a strange sense of foreboding. *Or is that doom?* Then he turned and headed after his quarry, desperately missing the backup he had been promised.

Chapter 37

THE STOLEN DINGHY...ER...RATHER, THE *APPROPRIATED* dinghy was right where Angel had said it would be.

Chelsea wasn't sure what she had expected. Okay, she *was* sure. She had expected a modern-day inflatable equipped with one of those little outboard engines. But what she *got* was a rough wooden boat with peeling paint and two large oars.

Old school. As in she feared the last time this boat had seen the water was around the time her mother had given birth to her. Was it even seaworthy?

I guess we're about to find out, she thought, breathing deeply.

The smell beneath the pier, that moldy concrete and old decay smell, was stronger at night. She wondered absently just where the dead, bloated fish had gone. Glancing around, she didn't hold out much hope that she would be able to see it. If she'd thought it was dark beneath the pier in the afternoon, then at night it was downright stygian.

As if the smell and the darkness weren't enough, the echoing *shush-sushhhhhh* of the surf over the beach pebbles created a truly eerie effect. A crow called from somewhere overhead. It sounded like a scornful laugh.

Chills stole up Chelsea's spine.

"Hey," Dagan whispered. "You okay?"

"Yup." She forced certainty into her voice. "Just ready to get this show on the road."

You'll go to hell for lying just as fast as for steal-ing chickens, her father's voice whispered through her head.

"Me too, babe. This entire day feels like it'll never end."

He touched her earlobe, and her entire right side burst into flames. Her heart felt soft and squishy, huge inside the confines of her chest. And when he gently adjusted her backpack so it didn't ride so low on her shoulders—So solicitous. So caring. So *wonderful*—her eyes suddenly felt like two hot lumps of coal.

"Climb in," he instructed.

Taking a seat on the wooden bench at the back of the rickety little boat, she watched him push the dinghy toward the waiting surf. Then two things happened simultaneously. The first was that she saw his shoulders bunch and strain beneath his coat, and she thought once again that the way he moved was very primal. The *second* was that a loud report split the dense air overhead, ruining the relative peace of the night. The piling to the left of the dinghy exploded. Chunks of algae-covered concrete rained down.

She didn't have time to register more than a single thought: *Someone is shooting at us!* before Dagan gave the dinghy a mighty shove and yelled, "Go! Get out of here and get behind cover!"

Chapter 38

THE *BOOM* AND *POP* OF THE WEAPON'S FIRE SOUNDED AGAIN.

The *boom* was the initial shot followed by the *pop* of the bullet breaking the sound barrier as it whizzed by Dagan's head and bit into the pebbled beach beyond. For an ordinary man, that double report would cause chaos and terror. For him, it generated white-hot anger and stone-cold determination.

Thanks to that second muzzle flash, he knew the shooter's location. Thirty feet away, where the pilings ended and the solid base of the pier's retaining wall jutted up against the beach.

Chancing a quick glance at the surf, he was relieved to see that Chelsea and the dinghy were well hidden behind one of the big pilings. For the first time in her life, the stubborn, confounding, delightful woman had done what he had asked her to do.

Good. Trained to be a fully operational army of one, the last thing he needed was her "help." Plus, he could keep his mind on the task at hand if he didn't have to worry about her.

Adrenaline was fuel for the fire in his veins as he scrambled up the beach, darting from piling to piling. He bent briefly to snatch the only weapon available to him since they had left their sidearms and tactical knives back at Rusty's. Even if they were flying out of a private jet terminal, since it was an international flight, they would still have to clear customs once they reached the states. There was no way they would be able to do that with semi-autos, tranq guns, and pig stickers in hand.

When he reached the back of the pier where a huge brick wall connected the road above to the harbor arm, he bolted out from under the pier on the opposite side of the shooter. Compared to the darkness beneath the harbor arm, the starlight above and the lights of the town behind cast the beach in a twilight glow.

His heartbeat was metronome steady, and his lungs drew deep, even breaths as he jumped to grab the top of the retaining wall on the side of the pier. Hauling himself up took some effort, especially with the weight of the pack on his back. His boots scrabbled for purchase on the rough face of the wall, but with a mighty heave, shoulder muscles burning, he pulled himself over the top.

Halfway there.

He trotted the few feet to the railing running the length of the pier. The retaining wall on which he stood was still a good five feet below the pier's walkway, so he had to grip the railing's bottom rung and once again pull his full weight up and over. Once he'd done that, he crouched low and scanned the length of the harbor arm. Ears cocked for any sound. Eyes narrowed and slightly unfocused. It was a trick to catch minute movement.

A black shadow flitted farther down the way, near the middle of the pier. But it was just a crow pecking at what were likely the remains of a dead fish or a pile of bait left behind by a fisherman.

With stealth honed over many years and during too many assignments to count, Dagan ran on silent feet across the walkway. Stopping at the opposite railing, he noted the subtle smell of spent cordite that tinged the night air and turkey-peeked over the edge.

That's Roper fuckin' Morrison down there! Or
Spider. Or Shit for Brains. Or the Seventh Horseman
of the Douchepocalypse. Or any other colorful moniker
that might apply to the evil old bastard.

Morrison appeared to be alone, which Dagan thought
was highly improbable. A man like Spider wouldn't do
his own dirty work, much less do it by himself.

Where was Morrison's backup? Dagan scanned the
pier again, then turned his attention to the beach. Look.
Listen. Unfocus and look again.

Nothing.

He didn't get that lifted-hair-on-the-back-of-his-
neck, prickly-palms feeling either. The one that usually
happened anytime he found himself in the middle of
someone's crosshairs.

The tinny echo of a voice came from below. It
sounded like someone was saying, "Hop smooting," but
that didn't make any sense. Dagan strained harder to
hear when the voice came again, this time with a long
string of hissed syllables.

If he wasn't mistaken, Morrison's backup was com-
municating through an open telephone line. Not exactly
high tech or clandestine, but it could get the job done in
a pinch.

He saw Morrison lift his hand, and the small revolver
glinted malevolently in the starlight. Since there was
only one thing Morrison could be aiming at, Dagan
made his move.

One graceful leap had him over the railing. He
scampered quietly over the top of the retaining wall
and didn't hesitate to launch himself off it once he was
directly atop his target. The cool air teased him, kissing his cheeks and tousling his hair on the way down.
The smell of sea and surf was overwhelming. And the

white glow of the lighthouse at the end of the harbor arm seemed to shine with sinister glee.

He landed beside Morrison with a mighty *thud*, his knees screaming with the impact. Karate-chop style, he brought his arm down on Morrison's outstretched hands, and the little revolver hit the beach and skittered toward the waves lapping under the pier. As for Morrison? Well, the blow was enough to knock the evil old man to his knees where he howled in alarm and fury.

Dagan made a grab for him, getting his arms around the bastard in a bear hug that had nothing to do with affection and everything to do with his mad desire to squeeze the life right out of the fucker. Morrison had *shot* at Chelsea. As far as Dagan was concerned, that was reason enough to put him six feet under.

Morrison surged to his feet, biting and hissing and scratching and kicking. Dagan had to give it to the scrawny old fart. He was strong for his age.

And slippery as a fuckin' eel!

Morrison managed to get an arm free and…*wham!* He elbowed Dagan square in the jaw. Dagan's teeth clacked together. Stars flashed in his field of vision. The blow loosened his grip, and Morrison was able to scramble away.

Sonofa—!

The old man made it three feet before Dagan pounced. Simultaneously reaching into his pocket for his weapon and grabbing the ridiculous knot of hair at the back of Morrison's head, he yanked the old man against him. Without an ounce of care, he shoved the sharp tines of the fork he had grabbed from the beach against Morrison's wrinkled neck.

"Don't move, motherfucker," he hissed.

"Fuck you, you bloody fuck!" Morrison yelled, his

voice traveling over the beach and echoing across the water.

"Now I ask you, is that any way to talk to the man who holds your life in his hands? Where's your backup?"

With his front against Morrison's back, Dagan could feel every ragged breath the man took. Morrison was trying to act brave, but it was obvious he was scared shitless.

"You should be afraid," Dagan assured him. "The missions I've run? The men I've killed? It's like a drug, an analgesic that enters the bloodstream and numbs a man to the worst of life's horrors." Was he laying it on a little thick? Maybe. But there was also truth in every one of his words. "I could dispatch you to the next world without an ounce of regret. The only thing holding me back right now is that I want to know where your backup is."

Particularly if that backup had a bead on Chelsea.

The thought was enough to make Dagan sick to his stomach. He regretted that hasty bowl of Frosted Flakes…er…whatever they were called on this side of the pond.

Straining his ears, he listened for her. But the crashing surf and Morrison's wheezy breaths made it impossible to hear anything else.

"If I tell you, you'll just kill me," Morrison snapped.

"Maybe. But I can promise it'll be quick and painless. On the other hand, if you *don't* tell me, I'll stab this fork into your carotid. Believe me, it will hurt like hell while you slowly bleed out. Plus, you know, the posthumous humiliation of the mighty Spider having been taken out by silverware."

Morrison, who had continued to put up a weak struggle, stilled against Dagan. Then the old man did

the strangest thing. He threw back his head and roared
with laughter. "You think *I'm* Spider? That's rich!"

Dagan suddenly had that lifted-hair-on-the-back-of-
his-neck, prickly-palms feeling. He dragged Morrison
toward the pier until the side of the thing was at his back,
Morrison acting as a human shield at his front.

"I hate to be the one to break it to you, mate,"
Morrison said. "I'm just the weather vane. I don't make
the wind blow."

"I don't have the time to translate fuckwit into
English. Speak plainly."

"You want plain? I'll give you plain. You have the
wrong man. I'm not Spider."

Now it was Dagan's turn to go stock-still. Morrison
wasn't Spider?

For a moment, he considered that the old man was
lying. If Morrison *was* Spider, it wasn't like he'd go
around admitting it, right? Then again, Dagan had
always recognized the truth when he heard it. And the
truth rang loud as a bell in Morrison's words.

"Then who *is* Spider?" he demanded.

"Is he the one you're truly after?" Morrison panted.

"Yes."

"Tell me where you've hidden the thumb drive you
used to plant the virus inside my systems, and I'll tell
you the real identity of the man you seek."

As far as deals went, it wasn't too bad.

"The thumb drive isn't with me," Dagan told
Morrison. He could have lied or prevaricated, but in
situations such as this, he'd learned the truth was always
the better bet. "But it's safe. And I could have it here in
twenty minutes with one phone call. I'll give it to you,
and you can stop the hack job into your systems, but you
have to tell me who Spider is."

"Even if you know his name"—Morrison shook his head and that ridiculous man bun brushed Dagan's cheek, making his jaw clench—"you'll never catch him. He's too bloody smart. Too sly. He hides himself behind powerful people. Hides his businesses behind shell company after shell company. And if he knows you're coming after him?" Morrison laughed again and the sound was uncanny, sending a chill up Dagan's spine. "You're as good as dead."

"I'll take my chances."

"Oh yes?" There was a hitch in Morrison's voice. "But I don't think *I* will. You see, if I tell you who Spider is, I'm as good as dead too."

Red tinged Dagan's eyesight. "You lying piece of shit. We had a deal!"

Morrison tilted his head, bringing his lips close to Dagan's ear. When the old man's hot breath brushed Dagan's cheek, he grimaced. "And I'll keep it too." Morrison whispered so quietly that Dagan had to strain to hear him. "But first, shut off the mobile in my pocket."

Dagan thought perhaps it was all a giant ruse to get him to loosen his hold. Then Morrison continued, "And you have to promise me protection. You're American, right? Working for the CIA?" Close enough. "I want in the witness protection program. If I give Spider up, I *must* be protected."

That Morrison was willing to give up his fortune to go into hiding spoke volumes about what it must be like to be stuck under Spider's thumb.

Instead of agreeing—no need to chance Morrison's backup hearing—Dagan simply nodded. Then, still keeping the fork against Morrison's neck, he reached into the man's jacket pocket and pulled out the device. It was warm from having been on for so long, and he was only too happy to turn it off. Once he did, a sense of relief washed through him, knowing they were no longer being overheard.

"Now." He was careful to keep his voice low. "Who is—"

That's as far as he got before Morrison's head flew back and hot, wet blood splattered across Dagan's face. A single report sounded a split second later.

Chapter 39

Steven watched the bearded bloke drop Morrison's lifeless body and took aim once again. Squeezing his trigger, he grimaced when he missed the man's head by mere centimeters, his bullet slamming into the side of the harbor arm. Before he could get off another shot, Beard had thrown himself under the pier and out of sight.

"Bloody hell. Fucking Morrison," Steven swore.

The old man had managed to make it to the pier before Steven, relaying that Chelsea Duvall and Beard were about to hop in a dinghy and head to who knows where.

"I'll keep them here," Morrison had hissed.

It hadn't mattered that Steven had told him not to do a fecking thing, told him to simply hold his position, because not ten seconds after Steven made the demand, the sound of Morrison's first shot boomed across the beach. The second had followed a scant moment later.

Should have known better than to give him a gun, Steven thought from his position behind a fishing boat some distance up the beach. Since the tide was out, the little vessel rested on dry land and provided him with adequate cover from which to assess the situation.

He was completely dumbfounded that Morrison had tried to make a deal. Spider's identity for the thumb drive—he had known all that noise Morrison made about not giving Spider up was a bunch of tosh the instant the line had gone dead. So he'd put a round into the old man's head. Because even though on paper he technically worked for Morrison, in truth he had been Spider's man from the beginning.

Roper Morrison put on a good show by hiring bombshell birds and flirting and manhandling them so much it was enough to make a good man gag. But Morrison's true proclivities ran far afield. To pubescent girls with barely budding breasts and boyish figures.

Somehow Spider had found out about the child pornography that abounded on Morrison's personal computers and had even gotten his hands on photos of Morrison and some poor, clearly underage girl in Thailand. That's all it had taken for Spider to pull Morrison into his sticky web.

Spider had promised not to reveal Morrison's debauchery to the world. But in return, Spider expected Morrison to use his legitimate billion-dollar media empire to launder cash from Spider's very illegitimate businesses.

Of course, Spider hadn't gotten to where he was by trusting people to do their jobs. His motto was *Keep my enemies close but my friends closer*. Enter Steven. Hired to keep an eye on Morrison. Make sure the old man didn't muck up the good thing Spider had going by following his particular immoralities.

It had been ridiculously easy to kill Morrison, considering Steven had never cared for the bloody bugger to begin with. It didn't get much worse than a kiddie molester in his book. Morrison was far better off rotting in hell.

Steven considered ringing up Spider and telling him what he'd learned, but he held off. He knew what the next steps should be without Spider confirming them. Since the incursion into Morrison's systems was, in fact, a hunt for none other than Spider himself, the only course of action was to kill everyone involved. Total annihilation was Spider's go-to method when threats were leveled against him.

Steven darted from behind the boat, holding his SIG up and at the ready.

Chapter 40

THE MINUTES AFTER DAGAN SHOVED THE DINGHY INTO THE surf were foggy for Chelsea. But not the good kind of fog, not the sweet-smelling, first-of-fall fog. She was talking industrial spill, evacuate-the-area fog. Noxious fog. Fog tinged with terror and the haunting knowledge that Dagan had gone off to confront their enemies.

Alone!

She didn't remember precisely what she had done. Time had gone all wonky on her, becoming fast and slow all at once. But given she, or rather her backpack, was pressed against one of the pilings supporting the harbor arm and her booted feet were sunk into the pebbles of the beach, she must have rowed to shore. And given she was gripping the cold metal of the revolver, she must have retrieved the weapon when she saw it skitter over the beach. And last but certainly not least, given Dagan was sprawled at her feet, facedown and cursing roundly, he must have escaped being hit by any of the shots she'd heard fired.

Praise the Lord and all his angels!

The dark shadows that had filled her vision were chased away when he looked up at her, blinked in astonishment, then growled, "Damnit, Chelsea! I thought I told you to get out of here."

"When have you ever known me to do anything you say?" She offered him a hand up and then quickly transferred the revolver to his grip. She wasn't too proud to admit he was the far better shot.

"There are only four rounds left in the cylinder," she told him, surprising herself.

Did I check?

She must have. But for the life of her, she couldn't remember. Besides, she was distracted by the dark flecks dripping down his cheeks.

Had one of those bullets found its mark?

"Are you hurt?" She lifted a finger, touching the sticky substance.

"It's not mine," he assured her. "It's Morrison's. He's dead. I think his own man shot him."

"What? *Why*?"

"Because he was about to tell me who Spider is."

"Wha—"

"Apparently Morrison isn't Spider. But that's news to be dealt with later," he said in a rush. "For now, we need to get out of here. I think there's only one guy out there, probably that black-haired fuckwad who tied you up and threatened you with the letter opener."

"Steven Surry."

"Yeah. Him."

"How did he find us?" They had been careful, hadn't they?

"Who knows. CCTV cameras, maybe? And if Spider's network is as vast as we suspect, no doubt he has spies and informants inside law enforcement as well as the government. Could be he pulled some of those strings. Now, where's the dinghy?"

She pointed to the place where the little wooden boat rested on the beach. It was behind another piling.

"We're making a run for it." Dagan grabbed her hand. "Stay behind me." He jerked her into a run made awkward by her bouncing backpack.

They'd gone no more than three feet when a bullet

slammed into the beach in front of them, sending pebbles in a stinging, shotgun spray. Instinctively, they both jumped back, racing to the safety of a piling.

"Damnit!" Dagan cursed. "He's coming!"

Her heart sputtered like the old outboard engine that had been on her father's ancient aluminum johnboat. Before she could ask him, *What now?* Dagan pulled her out from under the pier and up to the moss-and-algae-covered retaining wall at the end of the harbor arm.

Dead end. A worm of terror wiggled through her chest, winding itself around her lungs and making it impossible to breathe.

Shoving the revolver in his jacket pocket, Dagan bent and made a basket of his hands by threading his fingers together. "Up you go!"

She looked at him. Looked at the wall. "Go sell crazy somewhere else. I got all I can handle here."

"Hurry, Chels!"

She slipped her foot into his waiting hands and jumped at the same time he gave her the ol' heave-ho.

Weightlessness.

Vertigo.

Dread.

She experienced all of those as she sailed through the air until...*wham!* She slammed into the retaining wall, her arms over the top, her hands digging for purchase, and her boots scrabbling against the surface.

"Just hang on!" Dagan hissed.

Right. Because it didn't seem she could do much else. Her arms didn't have the strength to pull her over the top.

Oh, *why* hadn't she hit the gym a little more? Or, for lands sakes, laid off the peanut-butter crackers? Dangling there, her backpack doing everything in its power to yank her backward, she felt as useful as boobs on a man.

In contrast, Dagan jumped, caught the top of the wall, and hoisted himself up and over so easily that she cursed. Then he grabbed her by the armpits and dragged her up next to him. She marveled at his strength. The whole of him was like steel forged in fire. She imagined his bones were made of the same stuff used in Tolkien's High-Elven Swords. Would he glow blue if an Orc were near?

And great. Wonderful. Fear had made her a little batty.

"Up you go, Chels," Dagan said again, pointing to the railing on the side of the pier.

Planting her foot in his hands, they repeated the jump-and-toss maneuver. But this time she was able to not only grab hold of the lowest rung on the rail, but also swing her leg up and over, which allowed her to hoist herself onto the pier.

Praise Jesus!

Ridiculously pleased with herself, she turned in time to see Dagan leap and latch on to the railing just as Surry raced onto the beach below. A dark newsboy cap was pulled low over Surry's brow, making it impossible to see his face. But she had no trouble making out the evil black eye at the end of his pistol. It was staring straight at them. Or, more precisely, at *Dagan*.

"Look out!" she screamed just as Surry's gun belched up a round.

The muzzle flash was blinding. The roar of the weapon deafening. But the bullet smacked the side of the pier six inches from where Dagan dangled, and she nearly fainted with relief. She might have done exactly that, had she not been looking around for something to throw at Surry, something, *anything* to distract him from taking another shot.

But she needn't have worried. Dagan didn't need her help.

Moving so quickly she could barely track him, he one-handed the pistol out of his pocket, aimed, and fired. *Bam!*

A bark of pain sounded from below. Surry dropped his weapon and grabbed his shooting arm, his cap slipping off his head and landing on the beach. She wasn't certain if the bullet hit him square or just grazed him.

"Here!" Dagan handed her the revolver.

The weapon was hot from its recent work. The barrel singed her fingers as she turned the gun and aimed for Surry who was already running for cover beneath the pier, pistol back in hand.

Dagan hoisted himself over the railing and wasted no time yelling at her to *run*!

Yup. Good plan. But which way?

Back into town where more of Spider's or Morrison's or whoever's goons probably waited? Or worse, the police? The cry of sirens sounded in the distance. The gunplay had obviously been overheard and reported. And yessiree, given Chelsea was a wanted woman, and given that the guy she was supposed to have stolen something from lay dead on the beach somewhere down below, getting apprehended by the local law was something she should probably avoid at all costs.

But that left…*what*? What else could they do? Where else could they go?

Dagan must have realized she was caught on the horns of a dilemma because he snatched the revolver from her hand, threaded their fingers together, and gave her a tug down the pier.

"We'll jump," he said as he broke into a run, dragging her with him. "And hope Gautier is still there."

What are the chances? she thought, racing beside him. Then she figured since straws were all they had, they might as well grasp at them.

It wasn't until a few seconds later, when the lighthouse loomed large, that she remembered the first thing he'd said. *We'll jump*.

Lord have mercy! *Jump?* As in off the end of the friggin' pier?

If memory served, it had looked to be a least a two-story drop. Now, with the tide out…what? Three stories? *Four*?

Her legs felt like pinwheels, spinning, spinning, *spinning* until her thighs screamed in protest. But *finally* they made it to the lighthouse. The motor atop buzzed as it spun its white lights over the Channel, warning away passing ships.

Peering into the dark water below made Chelsea dizzy. "Holy crap," she breathed, gripping the railing so hard her fingers ached. "Are we crazy to even consider this?" Three. It *had* to be three stories.

Before Dagan could answer, they both saw it.

A submersible bobbed just beyond the pier. It was torpedo-shaped and painted black as pitch. They may have missed it altogether if not for the fact that the hatch was open and standing in the center of it was a man with the face of a medieval monk, all long and pale and slightly foreboding.

"Bonjour!" He waved up at them. "The problem on the beach has been eliminated, *oui*?" His French accent made it sound like *zee problem on zee bitch*.

Dagan didn't answer, just lifted his hand. And that's when another shot boomed through the night.

The round hit the railing two inches from Chelsea's fingers, and the *ping* of the bullet against the metal sounded louder than a gong. Since she was holding on to the rail, the reverberation traveled up her arm and rattled her brains inside her skull.

Once again, Dagan was lightning fast. He swung around and fired.

Now, when taking a shot, a shooter had to consider environmental factors. Like wind and elevation. But Dagan was so skilled—or so battle-tested—that he did it all automatically. She couldn't see where his bullet buried itself into Surry's body, but Surry yelped and hit the deck.

Before she could do more than blink, Dagan was climbing the railing, holding a hand down and pulling her up beside him. Another bout of vertigo hit, the world doing a fast spin. But before she could get her bearings, Dagan squeezed her hand, his fingers so strong, his palm so warm and rough, and together they *jumped*!

Chapter 41

HE WAS DYING.

He knew it as surely as he knew his mother had named him Steven Jonathan Surry.

The dark, nearly burgundy color of the blood on his hand when he lifted it away from the gruesome wound was highlighted by the relentless revolution of the lighthouse. His liver had taken the deathblow. And the pain... Oh, the pain was unlike anything he had ever known.

Pressing his blood-soaked hand back against his wound, he struggled to stand. His thoughts focused on his mother. He had failed her by failing Spider. But if, before he succumbed, he accomplished this one last task, then maybe...just maybe Spider would take pity on him.

He had heard stories of such. That if one were to fight for Spider 'til the end, Spider would have mercy.

The first step toward the end of the pier had Steven crying out. There was a breathtaking agony so deep inside. But he gritted his teeth, palmed his SIG, and pushed forward. His heart fluttered in an effort to pump what blood remained in his poor, ruined body. And by the time he made it to the railing, his boot was full of the stuff. It was warm and squished between his toes.

His vision blurred when he peered over the rail into the undulating water below. To his surprise and dismay, what he saw wasn't the couple treading water back to shore. It was Beard. He was climbing into an oddly shaped vessel that rode low in the drink.

A submarine? If Steven hadn't seen it with his own eyes, he would not have believed it. As for Chelsea? Regrettably, she was nowhere in sight. But he would take what he could get.

Lifting his SIG, he was disheartened to see his hand shaking. *Needs must*, he thought and stopped applying pressure to his wound so he could use his free hand to support his firing hand. He could *feel* his liver leaking faster.

Closing one eye and sighting down the barrel, he gathered his strength to fire. Oddly, his muscles refused to obey, and before he could force them to his will, the hatch on the vessel slammed shut with a loud *gong*! Then the whole thing sank beneath the waves. A quiet *glug-glug* and a faint eddy were the only things proving it had ever been there.

"No. *No!*" he cried, collapsing onto the pier.

Pain and anguish filled the spaces his leaking blood left empty. The echo of sirens was louder now. But he suffered no illusions that the local authorities would get to him quickly enough to save him.

He decided to use his final minutes to call Spider and beg. Not for his own life—that was already forfeit—but for his mother's.

The mobile was hard to grip in his blood-slicked hands, but he managed to enter Spider's number. When the man himself answered, his bored tone worked over Steven's raw nerves like sandpaper.

"Sir." Was that Steven's voice? There was barely anything left of it. "I'm dying, sir. Sh-shot in the gut." There was silence on the other end of the line, and Steven hurried to finish his report while he still had the breath to do it. "Morrison and I followed Miss Duvall from the fisherman's house back to the Folkestone

Harbor Arm. There was confusion. A gun battle. Miss Duvall and her partner escaped in a…a *submarine*. But not…" He panted against the pain. "Not before I killed Morrison. Had to. He was going to give you up."

Finally Spider spoke. "Give me up? What do you mean?"

"They th—" Steven gasped when a sharp pain arrowed through his gut, making him nauseous. He thought it possible he might die while tossing his cookies. But then the sickness subsided and all that remained was unimaginable agony. "They thought Morrison was y-you. That's why they infiltrated his systems. They were looking for proof to bring you down."

He could hear Spider fumbling with the phone. Gone was any boredom in his voice when he said, "Any idea who *they* are?"

"CIA? I don't know. Maybe an…interagency effort." Between gasping breaths, Steven managed to tell Spider about the supposedly dead but surprisingly alive Christian Watson. "He is with four others. They left in the fisherman's truck and are being followed by Ramón, Morrison's driver. I think they have the thumb drive because I heard the man with Duvall admit that the device wasn't on him, but that he could get it. It would just take a little while. There—" Another pain lanced through him, the blackness closing in. "There might still be time to locate the others and find the drive."

"Yes. Yes, there might. Even so, I need to begin transferring and emptying any accounts tied to Morrison."

A herculean task, Steven knew. But if anyone could pull off making millions of dollars disappear without a trace, it was Spider. "Please, sir," he finished with a crackling wheeze. "My mother… She is innocent. She—"

"Not to worry." Spider's voice was calm, almost blasé. "You did as well as can be expected, I suppose. I knew Morrison was a liability from the beginning, but..." Spider's voice trailed off. Or at least Steven thought it did. It was becoming difficult to hear. Steven's eyesight was almost completely gone now. He suspected his ears were next. "Miss Duvall and her companion are likely headed to France," Spider continued as if they were having no more than a friendly conversation, as if Steven wasn't, in fact, *dying*.

"I would suspect they will be putting in at Calais as it is the closest point on the French side. I'll have men waiting to take them out there. As for this Christian Watson fellow and the group traveling with him, I'll ring up Morrison's driver myself. Once I know the location of the rest of the group, I'll send your backup to deal with them."

Steven had never doubted Spider could right his own ship. The man gave new meaning to the word *resourceful*.

"I thank you for your service this day, Steven," Spider added, but Steven didn't want thanks. He wanted bloody *assurances*.

"Sir?" His voice was a bare whisper. "Please, my mum?"

"Will finish her days in the luxury she's grown accustomed to," Spider said, and Steven nearly fainted with relief. Or blood loss. Probably both. "Like I said, you did well today. I reward my loyal employees."

"Thank you, sir," he managed, though his mouth had filled with blood. The iron-rich smell assaulted his nose. He hadn't the strength to spit it out, instead letting it slip unheeded from the corners of his mouth.

"You're welcome, Steven. Now, be a smart chap and toss your mobile and your weapon into the Channel before you go. Best not to leave more evidence behind than necessary. Good-bye."

The line went dead, and the last of Steven's strength left him. He dropped the phone and his gun to the pier. It took him forever to nudge them over the edge but somehow, eventually, he accomplished it.

With his final task for Spider complete, he surrendered to gravity and toppled onto his side. The pain was less now. Which he knew meant his time was short. He wished he could still see. He would have liked to gaze one last time at the stars above. But he satisfied himself with visualizing his mother's beloved face.

As he lay struggling to breathe, feeling his heartbeat go thready, he tried not to think of her coming heartbreak and disappointment. He had always been her little hero. Her good boy. But sometimes, due to circumstances beyond their control, even good boys turned into bad men.

He was a bad man. He could admit as much to himself. But it hadn't always been so. Once upon a time, he had been one of the good guys, fighting to bring the criminals of the world, men like Spider and Morrison, to justice.

He wondered if a lifetime of doing right had been obliterated by the last three years when he'd done nothing but wrong in the almighty name of Spider.

What is *the measure of a man?*

He would never know. Because with that thought, his heart ceased to beat, his laboring lungs ceased to draw breath, and Steven Surry, once an honorable and decorated member of Her Majesty's Special Air Service, died.

Chapter 42

"I REGRET THE TIGHT SQUEEZE," GAUTIER SAID FROM HIS place in the front of the sub. The pilot's seat appeared to be little more than a legless beach chair. And the only lights inside the vessel came from the control panel, which Gautier watched with eagle-eye scrutiny. "Better to lie down, *oui*? More room this way."

Chelsea's limbs shook uncontrollably. She wasn't sure if it was from fear or cold.

The jump into the icy Channel had nearly knocked her unconscious. It didn't seem possible that *water* could be that hard. Had it not been for Dagan, the collision with the surface, combined with the shock of the cold and the weight of her pack, might have been enough to do her in. She had been in the process of attempting a few feeble kicks when he had gotten an arm around her and dragged her to the surface. A second later, before she even had time to catch her breath, he had boosted her aboard the sub.

Now they both sat hunched in Gautier's vessel. The space was barely three feet high and not much wider. But it was at least nine feet long, tip to tail. So that was good. And the floor seemed to have a bit of padding thanks to a series of... What were those? Rubber yoga mats?

It was difficult to see in the dusky interior and...

Shit. She realized she had lost her glasses in the jump. Luckily, she kept an extra pair in her bag. Unzipping the front pocket, she fished out her spare glasses case, surprised to find it mostly dry, and slid on the frames.

Blinking the space into focus, she realized it *was* yoga mats lining the floor. They had been stitched together and fitted against the dark hull. Even though there was little light to see by, it was still enough to show the whole vessel looked like it'd been built by someone using the wrong end of a hammer. She instantly regretted donning her glasses.

"Good Lord have mercy," she muttered beneath her breath.

"Let's take Gautier's advice and get comfy." Dagan shrugged out of his backpack. "It's going to be a long ride." Twisting around, he got his feet pointed toward the back of the sub and stretched out, using his soggy pack as a pillow. "Come on, babe." He beckoned with his fingers. "Come down here with me. We'll share body heat and warm up. You're shaking like a leaf."

Right. But the question remained...*from fear or from cold?*

If it was fear, it had nothing to do with the residual effects of the jump. Or the terror of being underwater in a submersible that looked like it'd been pieced together with Elmer's Glue and Popsicle sticks. Oh no. If she was shaking from fear, it was because the time had finally come to reveal the Big Bad Secret.

On the walk to the pier, she had promised herself she would use the trek across the Channel to finally come clean. And even when she and Dagan had been running for their lives, her mind had kept coming back to the inevitably of that. *Like a dog to its own vomit*, as her dad would have said.

Here goes, she thought, wiggling out of her backpack and setting it beside Dagan's. Maneuvering herself around in the small space was awkward, but she managed it. She pressed her head against her pack and was surprised when the first words out of her mouth weren't the truth. Instead they were, "Do you think he's dead?"

"Who?" Dagan pulled her close. She allowed it because she was absolutely freezing and he was so very warm. Soon enough, he might turn his back on her, but for now she'd memorize every detail of what it was to be held in his arms.

The smell of the soap on his skin tantalized when she ducked her head under his chin, her shivering lips pressed close to the hot, beating pulse in his neck. "Surry. Is he dead?"

"If not now, then soon. I think I got him in the gut." She felt him grimace. "Those wounds are generally fatal. And I wish I could say I'm sorry, but he took a shot at you, Chels, tried to kill you, so I'm not. I'm *glad* he's dead. Does that..." He swallowed. His Adam's apple moved against her lips. "Does that shock you? That I can...that I can kill a man without remorse?"

"No, I...I'm..." She stuttered to a stop. *I'm just stalling* was what she should have said. Lord help her, she didn't want to lose him. Not yet. She had ninety minutes, right? And the Big Bad Secret wouldn't take more than ten to tell.

I have time, she assured herself. *Time to love him a little more and let him love me.* "I guess I was just worried he might..." She shrugged. "I don't know. Follow us across somehow. I mean, he *did* find us in Folkestone."

"You don't have to worry about him. I guarantee you that. Now come closer." He pulled her tighter against him, scissoring their wet, jean-clan legs together and slipping a hand inside her sopping coat. His flattened palm against the small of her back was warm and possessive. "This sub is hard and cold, but you're soft and warm. And since we have an hour and a half to kill, I'd like to do it snuggling with you. We never got the chance to snuggle. You know...*after*. And that's my favorite part. Well, *one* of my favorite parts." He chuckled. The sound was low and seductive and did familiar things to her belly.

A thumb under her chin had her lifting her head. Even in the semidarkness, even listening to the eerie *pop* and *creak* of the vessel as it dove to depth, she was mesmerized by his stormy gray eyes.

Lovely eyes, really. So soft and steady and...*quiet*.

Yes, there was an inner stillness to Dagan that was not to be confused with the stillness that sometimes came over him when they were arguing or when the world around them was threatening to end. *That* was the calm before the storm. But this? This came from a well of inner certainty. He was a man who had made his place in the world and was comfortable there.

Not that he didn't have regrets. She knew he did. She saw the shadows of them lurking in his eyes sometimes. But he had come to terms with them. Learned to live with them. And she could only hope that in the near future, she could do the same with *her* regrets.

She hadn't realized she'd been silent until Dagan said, "You're quiet, but you have an unquiet mind. I can smell the wheels burning up here." He tapped her temple. "What's up, babe?"

"I was just thinking about...my mother." It wasn't a total lie. Her mother was never far from her thoughts.

"Your mother?" He cocked his head. There it was. That Clint Eastwood gunfight stare. "You think she'll be embarrassed or ashamed because of the news stories? Chels, you know that'll clear itself up. It may take a while since Morrison isn't Spider and everything. But he *knows* Spider. I mean, he *knew* Spider, which likely

means he was tangled up with him in *something* illegal.
Ozzie will figure out whatever it was from Morrison's
files. Then the CIA will claim the credit for exposing the
old sonofabitch, with you as their agent, naturally, and
your reputation will be free and clear. Of course, then
your cover will be blown. I'm sorry as hell about that; I
really am. But at least—"

"Wow." She shook her head. "You've really thought
this through, haven't you?"

His chin jerked back. "Of course." The hand against
her back rubbed up and down, up and down, somehow
soothing and scintillating at the same time. "It's your
life. And since I plan to be a part of that, I—"

She closed her ears to what he said next. She knew
the words, those *wonderful* words, would flay her. And
she already felt like she'd lost a layer of skin.

"My mother isn't embarrassed or ashamed," she said
after he'd grown silent. "If she'd ever been the kind to
care about what people thought or said, she never would
have married my father."

"You know, you never told me what happened."

She tucked her head back beneath his chin. Some of
her hair got stuck in his beard, which was no big surprise
since she knew her 'do had to be a frizzy, kinky mess.
But oddly enough, Dagan seemed to like it. He palmed
her head and rubbed a lock between his fingers.

"What do you mean?" she asked.

"I mean, you were able to secure the position with
Morrison partly based on your background, on your
need for money and his belief that that need made you
desperate and vulnerable and likely to put up with his
pawing. But you never said exactly what was going on.
Will you…will you tell me now? Tell me why you need
money? Because maybe I could—"

Before he could offer to help her, which would crush
to dust her already broken heart, she interrupted him.
"Money. That word…it just…sticks in my craw. I mean,
it sounds so harmless, doesn't it? Rhymes with *honey*
and *bunny*. But when you don't have any, it's an insidious thing that impacts everything you do."

*From the smallest decision, like whether you buy
brand-name cereal or the generic stuff from the bottom
shelf,* she thought with disgust. *To the biggest decision,
like whether you give up paying a double mortgage and
let the bank take the home you grew up in or you keep your
job, keep a Big Bad Secret, and keep on paying the bills.*

"For years now, my mom and I have…uh… We've
been slowly trying to dig ourselves out of the debt left
by my father's passing," Chelsea told him. Even with
her chin tucked under his chin, she could *feel* his frown.

She never spoke about this part of her life, and it
showed in the puttering way the words left her mouth. It
wasn't that she was ashamed of her situation. More like
she had always reckoned it was nobody's damned business that she and her mother were *too poor to paint and
too proud to whitewash*, as her father would have said.

"My mom never wanted to be anything but a wife and
a mother. So that left my dad as the breadwinner of the
family. Not that there was a *ton* of bread. Public school
teachers make jack shit, but he made enough to buy a
piece of land after he and Momma married. He went
to the local banks to try to secure a construction loan,
but no one would lend him the money. Apparently, the
loan officers had all sorts of reasons why they couldn't
take the risk, but the truth was they simply didn't want
to lend money to a…a *mixed marriage* couple, I think
was the term they used. Remember, this was the South
in the eighties.

"Anyway," she continued, "Mom and Dad saved up during the school years, living on rice and beans so that they could purchase the supplies and equipment they needed. For five summers before I was born, brick by brick and nail by nail, they built their dream house. My *home*. We all lived there together for seventeen glorious years." She swallowed the lump in her throat and took a breath. "And then Dad died."

Dagan's hold tightened, his arms so warm and strong. She closed her eyes at the comfort his embrace provided, comfort she had no business feeling.

When she continued, her voice was hoarser than usual. "Dad had a life insurance policy, but that didn't cover much more than funeral expenses. Mom needed a job. But she didn't have any schooling or training past high school so she was forced to take out a loan on the house to pay for dental hygienist school. Then I went to college, and she had to take out a second mortgage to help cover the cost my scholarship and student loans didn't. Suddenly, the banks were all too happy to lend her money. Go figure."

Taking a deep breath, she told him the rest. "Fast-forward a few years to the bursting of the real estate bubble and…" She shrugged inside the circle of his arms. "Every extra penny I've made goes to my student loans and the bank that holds the mortgages on the house. And even at that, sometimes Mom and I are late on our payments."

It was hard to fathom that in all the years since she'd graduated summa cum laude with a double master's in statistics and international studies that she had barely made a dent in her and her mother's combined six-figure debt. Working for the Central Intelligence Agency was exciting, but the pay sure wasn't.

"I'm so sorry, babe. If it's any consolation, I know what it's like to be desperate for money."

"I know you do."

For a few minutes neither of them spoke, then Dagan said, "You know, I'm really looking forward to meeting your mother, even if I do take exception to her taste in music."

Chelsea ignored the first part of his statement—after she revealed the Big Bad secret, she suffered no illusions that he'd want to meet her mom—and focused instead on the second part. She pushed up on her elbow. "What do you mean her taste in music? How would you know what her taste in music is?"

"Her ringtone. She likes Dolly Parton, right?"

Chelsea narrowed her eyes.

"Uh-oh. I know that look. You're about to let me have it, aren't you?"

"And what the heck is wrong with Dolly Parton?" she demanded.

"Yep." He sighed. "Let me have it."

"She is one of the greatest songwriters of the last century. She's had dozens of hits. And did you know she turned down Elvis Presley when he wanted to record *I Will Always Love You*? Elvis Presley, for heaven's sake! And—"

He dragged her down and melted her brain with a soft, seductive kiss.

When she was thoroughly breathless, he released her and said against her lips, "I take it back. Dolly's awesome."

"Damn straight." She felt more than saw his smile. "But for the record, it was my dad who was the big Dolly Parton fan. Mom and I…we each have a different Dolly ringtone because it… Well, every time we call each other, it reminds us of him. That's also why we wear so much purple."

"Was that his favorite color?"

Her brow puckered. "You know, I don't know what his favorite color was. I just know that he thought Mom looked beautiful in purple. Every Christmas, he would buy her something new. A lavender scarf one year. An eggplant-colored summer dress the next. After he died, I started wearing purple too. Sort of a..."

"Memorial," he finished for her.

"Yeah. I guess so."

"He must have been an amazing man for two amazing women to love him and miss him so fiercely."

"He was the best. He had the biggest laugh you've ever heard."

"Wish I could have met him."

A lump formed in Chelsea's throat. "He would have loved you and hated you at the same time."

"Hated me? Why's that?"

"Loved you because you're a wonderful man. Hated you because you're diddling his daughter."

"Diddling?"

A smile twitched her lips. "I picked that one up from Emily."

"That woman has *such* a way with words."

"Doesn't she, though?" Chelsea snorted. "So what about your folks? I mean, what were they like when you were growing up?" *Stall much, Chels?* Yes. Yes, she did. But if this was the only time she would ever have to talk to him like a lover, to get to know him, then she was taking it. "You've never told me much— read: anything—about your childhood."

Dagan's voice had turned sleepy, the warm hand rubbing her back becoming slow and lazy. The strain

of the day, both mental and physical, was catching up
with him. It was catching up with her too now that she
was warm—more than warm, *steamy*. Their body heat
had combined with their soggy clothes to leave beads
of condensation glittering dully around the hull. Her
eyes threatened to drop closed, and her body loosened
until her muscles felt liquid.

"I guess you could say we were your all-American
family. Dad was an accountant for a wire mesh manu-
facturing plant. Mom was a librarian at the Union
Branch of the Cleveland Public Library. We lived in
a three-bedroom house on a cul-de-sac. Little League.
Boy Scouts. Summer barbecues with the neighbors.
Pretty standard stuff, really." He stopped abruptly, and
she could tell he was gathering his thoughts.

"And then your mom got sick?" she prompted.

"Yeah. I was away at college, but Avan was still
at home. He watched her go through it, watched *Dad*
having to watch her go through it. After she died, Dad
was really never quite the same. And then before Dad
could truly heal from his heartbreak, he had the aneurysm." She heard Dagan's throat work over a swallow.
"Maybe it was a blessing. I don't know. I'm not sure
there's an afterlife, but if there is, I like to think my
parents are together sharing it."

Her heart broke for him. "I can't imagine losing
both of my folks in such a short time. It was awful
enough losing one."

"It was tough. No doubt about it. But I was so busy
trying to conquer the world, you know? College, grad
school, applying to the CIA. I missed my parents, but I
didn't really miss the sense of security they provided.
The sense of *home*. Or at least I didn't miss it like
Avan did."

"He was still young enough to need them."

"I guess that's it. He's never said as much, but I'm pretty sure that's why he turned to drugs. He was self-medicating, trying to fill the empty spaces inside him where family and home used to be."

There was a hole in Chelsea's heart. It was in the shape of Dagan Zoelner. "I'm so sorry." They were the only words she knew to give, but they didn't seem like enough.

Her hand lay on his chest. He brought it to his mouth, kissing the tips of her fingers. His lips were warm and soft, but his beard was wonderfully scratchy. "I guess that's why I get it," he said, flattening her hand back over his heart.

"Get what?"

"Get why you've been fighting so long and so hard to save the house your parents built. To save your *home*. I didn't realize how much home meant until I didn't have one anymore, until *Avan* didn't have one anymore."

The tears that were suddenly behind Chelsea's eyes felt sharp enough to cut glass. Would he "get it" once he knew the truth? Would he understand then?

He let out a mighty yawn, stretching so that his big body tightened. Once he relaxed, she felt the hand rubbing against her back slow and then stop altogether. His breaths grew deep and even. A minute later, he was asleep.

It had always amazed her how agents and operators could do that, just drop off at a moment's notice. She suspected it was a learned habit. If, in the midst of a mission or a battle, you were forced to stay awake for hours or *days* even, it behooved you to learn to go out cold the minute things calmed down.

She usually envied that ability. But not now. The

last thing she wanted was to succumb to exhaustion. Instead she would spend what little time she had left listening to his heart beat, feeling his big chest rise and fall, and cherishing every second she was in his arms.

Chapter 43

CHRISTIAN HAD BEEN ARGUING WITH EMILY SINCE THE moment they hopped into Rusty's truck. He acted highly offended by her constant berating, but the truth was, he *liked* it. Sick shite that he was, it got his blood pumping. Made him feel alive and excited and...*horny*.

Emily's last comment had been a real zinger. He wasn't sure how to come back from it. Telling her to *piss off* was his first instinct, but it sounded so completely inarticulate compared to her most recent offering. So, instead, he satisfied himself with images of bending her over his knee and paddling her sweet ass as punishment.

And damn the bloody woman. She knew she had rattled him. It was well past dark, but the truck was lit up like Christmas by the streetlights on the road where cars waited in the queue to be loaded onto the train, so he had no trouble seeing the delight that sparkled in her dark eyes and the victorious smile plastered on her pretty mouth.

"You're doing a happy dance on the inside, aren't you?" Christian made sure to wreathe his face in a fierce frown.

"Color me Rose on the lowest deck of the Titanic." Emily waggled her eyebrows.

"In case I haven't mentioned it before, I find you as irritating as a housefly. Be gone. Shoo."

Since the two of them were crammed into the stiff

backseat of Rusty's pickup truck along with Angel, there was nowhere she could go. Which, of course, Christian was secretly fine with. Having her pressed all along his right side as they waited to have their passports checked was one of his fonder experiences of late.

Well, that and the motorbike ride.

"Holy hobbling Christ on a crutch!" Ace complained from the front passenger seat. "As usual, you two are making my head hurt."

"Are they always like this?" Rusty asked him.

"Always." Ace let loose a long-suffering sigh.

"Heteros." Rusty shook his head.

"Exactly," Ace agreed.

For Ace's sake, Christian wished they could spend a little more time in England with Rusty. Ace hadn't expressed an interest in anyone since coming to work for BKI. And it didn't take a psychic to see there was a well of sadness inside Ace that needed filling and maybe, just maybe, Rusty Parker was the man for the job.

"Sorry about the headache, mate." He leaned forward to clap a conciliatory hand on Ace's shoulder. "But as usual, she started it."

"And I'll finish it too," Emily declared.

"Always have to be the one with the last word, yeah?" Christian raised a brow.

"Only when the situation warrants."

So tough, he thought, hiding his smile. *But there is tenderness in her too.*

He longed to explore both. Unfortunately, she seemed immune to his masculine wiles.

He opened his mouth to continue the fun, but Angel stayed him when he hissed. "Quiet." That one word was followed by another. "Look." Angel pointed out the window.

Christian followed the line of Angel's finger and immediately spotted what had drawn his attention. A man dressed in civilian garb walked casually down the line of parked vehicles. But despite his leisurely stroll, his eyes never stopped moving.

"Looking for Chelsea, do you think?" Emily asked, watching the man approach the pickup truck.

"Maybe," Christian said. When the man's eyes flicked away from the truck just a bit too quickly, he added, "Or maybe not."

The mystery man barely made it two meters beyond the tailgate when he lifted his hand to his ear. He was signaling someone or talking into a cuff mic. Either way…bad news.

As if on cue, the doors on a sedan a dozen cars behind them swung open in unison. Five men dressed for winter, the collars on their raincoats tilted up, their hats pulled low, exited the vehicle. Christian didn't need to see what was in the hands shoved deep in their pockets to know they were packing.

"I'm assuming you're all seeing this," Rusty said, carefully pulling the truck out of park.

"We see it," Emily assured him. "And what the hell? Who are they, and how do they know about us?"

"Your guess is as good as mine." Rusty shook his head. "What now?"

"Now we get the ruddy hell out of this line and turn back," Christian told him. "I don't know about the rest of you, but I don't fancy being stuck in this truck while whoever they are converge on us to do whatever it is they're here to do."

"Agreed." This from Angel.

"But what about Zoelner and Chelsea?" Emily looked startled. "They'll be waiting for us on the other side."

"Zoelner is nothing if not resourceful," Christian assured her. "They'll find their own way. Rusty?"

"Yeah?" Rusty's eyes met his in the rearview mirror.

"Get us out of here."

"Right." Rusty nodded and put the truck in reverse. They received a honk from the motorist behind them for their efforts. But after a three-point turn, Rusty had the big truck up and over the concrete median, heading away from the terminal.

Christian watched the not-so-subtle bloke blink in frustration as they motored past him. Then he watched the gent raise his hand to his ear again. This time, the movement of Not-So-Subtle's lips proved he wasn't giving a signal, but was, in fact, speaking into a cuff mic. As a unit, the five men in the raincoats turned back toward their sedan. Christian tried to get a look at their faces, but was thwarted by the tinted windows on the four-door. *Buggering hell.* He couldn't see the license either, because the car behind the sedan was nearly kissing its bumper. There was no way to tell if it sported government plates.

"We've got more company," Ace warned, looking into the passenger-side mirror.

Christian craned his head around to see a black SUV pull from beside the curb. This time he *could* see the license plate. "I don't like the looks of that," he muttered.

Emily turned around, her wavy hair slapping against his face and assaulting his nostrils with the smell of her shampoo. It was exotic. Like jungle flowers.

"*Why* don't you like the looks of that?" She looked a little wild-eyed.

Not for the first time, Christian wished she had stayed back in Chicago, safe and sound. Then again, the last few weeks, living with her in that tiny flat had been...

well, *memorable*. He wouldn't trade for anything the
night sleep had eluded them both and they had sat at the
kitchen table, drinking tea and talking—not arguing, not
taking swipes at each other, just *talking*.

"It doesn't look official," he explained. "No hazard
lights. Not government tags."

"Well, if it's not the officials coming after us, who
is it?"

"I don't want to find out."

"Neither do I," Ace said. "Rusty, punch it."

Chapter 44

EMILY'S ENTIRE DAY HAD BEEN A CARNIVAL RIDE OF ONE unlikely event after another. And now here she was involved in a car chase. A *car chase*, for crying out loud!

To make matters worse? She seemed to be the only person in the truck shitting bricks. Down to a man, her companions were as cool as proverbial cucumbers. Christian was the worst of them. There wasn't a tremor in his voice or a hitch in his delivery when he said, "We need to get off the motorway and ditch this bloody pickup truck."

"Ditch the truck?" She blinked at him as Rusty swerved around another car and sent her slamming into Christian's side.

To her dismay, he threw an arm around her shoulders to steady her. "It's the only way to lose our tail," he said.

"And once we ditch the truck? *Then* what?"

Rusty slammed on the brakes, leaving rubber on blacktop when a car pulled into his lane. She was lucky she was buckled in, or she would have gone sailing between the front seats and straight through the windshield.

Once she'd recovered, she demanded again, "What happens after we ditch the truck?"

"Not sure." Christian shrugged, looking completely blasé. "First things first."

"Right." She nodded. "Wonderful. Sounds like a plan. *Not!*"

"There!" Ace pointed through the windshield. "Take that exit."

Rusty crossed three lanes of traffic at a blistering pace. When she glanced over her shoulder, she saw the black SUV dart past them, unable to pursue without causing a twenty-car pileup.

Blowing out an unsteady breath, Emily realized she had dug her fingernails into Christian's thigh when he covered her hand with his and winced. "Little less pressure, darling. I think I might be bleeding."

"Oh!" She unstuck her nails from the denim of his jeans and gripped the seat in front of her instead. "Sorry. I—"

Her thoughts snapped off like bones brittle with age when Ace pointed to a road that led back into Folkestone. "Take that. And everyone keep their eyes peeled for a car we might steal."

"*Appropriate*," Angel corrected. "To steal something indicates we might think to keep it. We will merely be *borrowing* a car for a short while and—"

"There!" Ace cut him off. "That one."

Emily blinked through the windshield. They had turned onto a neighborhood street. Houses packed side-by-side sported postage-stamp-sized lawns, rosebushes, and the occasional tipped-over tricycle. "You mean the gray one? The Ford Focus? *Why?*"

"The Ford Focus is one of the most popular cars in the UK," Angel said, as if that bit of trivia was supposed to mean something.

"Given we're not certain what's going on, it's best if we blend into the crowd," Christian explained. *Bless him.* "Also, the vehicle comes standard with a Thatcham 2 security system, which means no alarm, just an immobilizer."

"An immobilizer?"

"Something that keeps common thieves from being able to hot-wire the vehicle."

"Good thing I am not a common thief," Angel said, not a shred of braggadocio in his tone, just a statement of fact.

The most popular car in the UK, Thatcham what-whozits, and immobilizers… Emily had always fancied herself a pretty knowledgeable gal, but obviously she was just a babe in the woods when it came to this stuff.

"Let me out at the curb there." Angel pointed. "Then drive around the block and wait. I will meet you there once I have the vehicle."

"Shouldn't we wait with you?" Emily asked, peering around, trying to see if anyone was in their front garden on this chilly March night. Thankfully, the block was quiet. The only movements came from the wind in the trees and a lone moth that seemed particularly intrigued by their right headlight.

"No." Angel said. "This pickup truck is too conspicuous. We do not want someone to look out their window and become curious."

"Right." She nodded. Curiosity was bad. Everyone knew what it had done to the cat.

Rusty pulled in front of the car they planned to steal… er…*appropriate*, and Angel hopped out. No sooner had the door slammed shut than Rusty was back on the gas and they were leaving Angel to quietly mosey toward the unsuspecting vehicle. With him gone, the heat radiating off Christian seemed amplified. So did the smell of him, that expensive earthy-sweet aroma of his cologne.

"How long will it take him to break in and hot-wire the thing, do you suppose?" Emily asked, her heart reaching speeds of a mile a minute.

"Not long." Christian hooked a thumb over his shoulder.

She turned to see that, inexplicably, Angel had

already jimmied open the door on the little Ford and was sliding into the driver's seat. As promised, no alarm accompanied his intrusion.

"Wow. I don't know whether to be terrified or impressed."

Rusty hooked a right, taking them around the block. When they reached a Y in the road, Rusty stopped the truck.

"And now we wait?" Emily craned her head around, gnawing on her lip and picking at a loose thread on the upholstery of the backseat. She rubbed the back of her neck and scooped her hair off her nape. It was hot. She was sweating. Unzipping her jacket helped. But only a little. She fanned her face.

"Yes. We wait," Christian said. "And stop fidgeting. You're making me nervous."

"You?" She sent him an incredulous look. "What about me? This is my first car chase. My first time running for my life. My first time stealing a vehicle."

"*Appropriating*," Ace corrected.

"If I hear that word one more time, I'm going to kill one of you."

"With what?" Christian asked, the twitch of his lips doing little to hide his amusement. She was glad *one* of them was having a good time. "We left all our weapons at Rusty's when we thought we were hopping an international flight."

"I'm creative. I'm sure I'll come up with something."

"Speaking of the weapons," Ace interjected, "do we dare go back and retrieve them?"

"Not tonight," Christian said. "Maybe not ever. If whoever these people are recognized Rusty's truck, chances are good they bloody well know where he lives. They probably have eyes on his house as we speak."

"So if we can't go back to Rusty's and we can't get to France, where will we go?" Emily asked, swinging around to face Christian.

"We could try our hand at a hotel," Ace suggested. "Check in using our fake passports."

"I shouldn't think so," Christian mused, rubbing his chin. "Still too public."

"So then, what?" Ace asked.

"We go to my uncle's."

Emily's chin jerked back. "Your uncle's? I didn't think you had family left over here."

"Why would you assume that?"

"Well, because…because…" She trailed off. The look on his face was like a line of police tape. It shouted DO NOT CROSS!

"He has a summer cottage on the coast in Port Isaac," Christian continued. "He won't knock off from London 'til June. So the cottage should be empty. We can hole up there until we get this cock-up sorted one way or the other."

"Sounds like a plan to me," Ace declared. "Okay, kiddies, hop out and grab your things. Angel is headed our way."

Emily glanced out the back window. Sure enough, the Ford Focus rounded the corner.

Christian pushed open the door, and the smell of salt-tinged air and threatening rain swooped into the truck. She followed him into the night and took her backpack when he handed it to her.

They had kept their gear in the bed of Rusty's pickup truck, and she had a fleeting worry that all their stuff wouldn't fit into the little four-door hatchback. And then a thought occurred…

"Rusty." She placed her hand on his forearm. "I'm so sorry I got you into this."

Rusty's ridiculously handsome face became even more ridiculously handsome when he smiled. "Don't worry." He covered her hand. "I haven't had this much excitement in years."

"But your truck. Your house." She shook her head. "You have to leave both behind until—"

"Just stuff, dollface. Just stuff." He used his key fob to lock his truck and turned toward the hatchback when it pulled up beside them.

"Shotgun!" Ace called, pulling open the passenger door. "Sorry." He turned to shoot Rusty an apologetic look. "But if I have to ride in the backseat with those two"—he motioned back and forth between Emily and Christian—"I might just kill one of them. Or *both* of them."

"And what makes you think I won't?" Rusty asked.

"Uh, because you're a nice guy?"

"I am that," Rusty said. Then added, "But you'll owe me."

"I look forward to the repayment."

Even given the direness of their situation, Emily was delighted to see the blush that spread over Ace's cheekbones. She didn't miss how quickly he ducked into the car.

Glancing at Rusty, she found him wearing a contemplative look. "In case it's not apparent, *he's* a nice guy too. You could do worse," she told him.

Rusty's eyes swung over to her. "Not that I don't love your nosiness, dollface, but maybe you should straighten out your own love life before you start meddling in mine."

"I don't *have* a love life," she assured him.

"No?" He glanced over her head.

When she turned to see what had snagged his attention, she saw Christian standing beside the vehicle looking like a Gucci ad on steroids. He was holding the door and his expression said, *Get your ass in the car, woman!*

For some reason, that bossiness caused a little trill to swirl low in her belly. She turned back to Rusty. "I don't know what you're talking about," she told him before flouncing into the backseat and settling her backpack between her feet.

Rusty and Christian followed her in, creating an Emily sandwich. And even though Rusty was drop-dead gorgeous, it was Christian's nearness that over-whelmed her.

"We need to call Chels and Zoelner," Ace said from the front seat. "Let them know what's going on."

"I'll do it," Emily volunteered.

Anything to take my mind off Christian…

Chapter 45

DAGAN CAME AWAKE IN THE MOST DELICIOUS WAY, WITH Chelsea kissing the place on his chest directly above his heart. The silly organ was her slave, so it answered by beating rapidly against his ribs in an effort to break through to her lips.

"Mmm." He rubbed her back encouragingly and slid his hand down until he could get a big handful of ass cheek. "Are we in France yet?" he asked groggily.

"Not quite. Ten more minutes or so."

"Mmm," he hummed again. "Want to put that time to good use?"

"What did you have in mind?"

"We could make out."

"With Gautier three feet away?"

"I hear nothing, *rien du tout*," Gautier called, proving he heard everything.

"See?" Dagan grinned.

Chelsea slapped his chest. In return, he slapped her ass, making her squeal. Even with his eyes still closed, he could feel her watching him. "In truth," she said, "I would love to spend ten minutes making out with you, but…"

"But what?" He continued to knead her butt. The next time he made love to her was going to be from behind. He wanted to watch her delicious derriere bounce while he thrust into her. Maybe he'd even give her bottom a slap or two. Not hard. Just enough to let her know who was boss.

The thought was enough to make him hard.

"But I need to talk to you," she said. "I have to tell you—"

"Ah, yes." He blinked open his eyes. Chelsea had her bottom lip caught between her teeth, and her hair was all wild and crazy, making her look so damned cute. Unfortunately, that look was back in her eyes. The one from Rusty's place. "Your big confession. Okay. Let me have it. Once again, Big Z is all ears."

She swallowed. "It's about Afghanistan."

That word shriveled his burgeoning hard-on. In contrast, the rest of his muscles stiffened. "Chelsea, I—"

"No, please." She placed a finger over his lips. "Will you let me finish?"

It was the last thing he wanted, but... "Yes. Okay."

She blew out a deep breath that ruffled the hair over his forehead. "When I heard you were handing over Abdul Waleed to Agent McShane before returning to the States, I went back and vetted him again."

He frowned. "Why? A whole host of analysts had already vetted him. Ted Edens, your boss and the head of Advanced Analytics, had already vetted him. *I'd* already vetted him. And Waleed gave us some really good Intel during the two years he was my asset. Why would you investigate him further?"

Chelsea's lips twisted. "He *sort* of gave you good Intel."

A sick feeling swirled low in Dagan's stomach. "What do you mean?"

"Waleed only revealed soft targets. Things that would convince you he was legit, but nothing that was ever truly actionable."

"That can't be right." Dagan shook his head.

"Think back. Did you ever actually catch a target? Find a hideout? Bust up a conspiracy?"

He searched his memory. "That bomb-making shop outside of Kabul. Waleed was the one to give us the location."

"And by the time you got there, the bomb makers were long gone."

"But we confiscated all their equipment, all their unfinished ordinance."

"Which they could have easily replaced. Which I'm sure they *did* easily replace."

That sick feeling swirling in his stomach turned into a tornado. He had known Waleed was a double agent. Of course he had. That had become apparent the day Waleed set off that suicide bomb. But to hear that he might have known *beforehand*? That the red flags had been there and he'd missed them? No wonder he had been fired the minute he set foot inside the director's office.

"So, yeah. That made me curious," Chelsea continued. "And me being me, I dug a little deeper."

Dagan screwed his eyes closed. He wasn't going to like what he heard next. That didn't stop him from asking, "What did you find?"

"I found out he was a second cousin twice removed from Mullah Zahed."

Dagan blew out a ragged breath. Mullah Zahed had been one of the most powerful and feared Taliban leaders before his capture, and he had been Waleed's *cousin*? "How did I miss that?"

"Not just you," Chelsea assured him. "Everyone missed it. Edens himself missed it. And now I know that was part of the problem. Edens didn't want it known he'd made a mistake. He didn't think it'd look good on his résumé. But, heck, I might have missed it too, had I not run across the guest list for Mullah

Zahed's daughter's wedding. Waleed's father attended, and that got me curious enough to go looking for the connection between the two men. It was really convoluted, but I eventually untangled all the threads and found the blood ties."

"Fuckin' A." Dagan ran a hand through his hair. He wouldn't have thought it was possible for the submersible to get any smaller, but the thing seemed to shrink around him. Then a thought occurred. "But, wait. You found this out *before* the handoff, right? So why—"

"And here's where my confession comes in," she said, her voice heavy with undisguised misery.

That sick, swirling feeling in Dagan's stomach ratcheted up from an F5 tornado to a full-force hurricane.

Chapter 46

"TWENTY-SIX HOURS BEFORE YOU WERE SUPPOSED TO HAND off Waleed, I went to Ted Edens and told him what I found," Chelsea said, her heart racing to beat the band.

"What did Edens say?"

She couldn't ignore that Dagan had gone as still as a statue carved from polar ice. It was a terrible change from moments before, when he'd been all warm hugs and roving hands. Was this a hint of things to come?

Love conquers all...

His words came back to give her hope. She clung to that hope as the memory of that day came pouring out of her head like that beat-to-shit piñata her father had strung up in a tree for her tenth birthday party...

"This is a stretch, Agent Duvall. Even for you," *Edens said, leaning back in his desk chair and folding his arms over his burly chest. His office smelled like breath mints and stale coffee. Neither scent did anything to soothe Chelsea's frayed nerves. "You can't judge a man by his family ties. Especially not over there, where everyone is related to everyone if you go back a generation or two."*

"That may be true. Maybe it's nothing. A coincidence."

"That'd be my guess."

She firmed her jaw. "But shouldn't we at least alert Agent Zoelner to the connection?"

Edens narrowed his eyes, studying her for a full

ten-second count. She had been working for the man for a few years, but she'd never gotten to the point where she could give him her unqualified respect. Edens was too much of a politician for her taste. It was no secret he had big aspirations, wanted to be the next director of the CIA. She couldn't shake the feeling that sometimes he acted for political reasons instead of strategic ones.

"We'll let Waleed's handoff go through first," he finally said. "We don't want Agent McShane to start his relationship with Waleed acting squirrelly. Assuming Waleed is legit and this flimsy connection to Mullah Zahed is just that, a flimsy connection, the last thing we need is Waleed getting suspicious or feeling unsafe. If he doesn't trust Agent McShane, he'll shut off his information pipeline."

Chelsea took exception to the word "flimsy." Yes, Abdul Waleed and Mullah Zahed were very distant relations. But in that part of the world, blood ran true no matter how far apart the branches were on the family tree. "Agent McShane is a professional. I hardly think he'll give Waleed any cause to doubt—"

"And can you say the same for Agents Walker and Moore? They're going to be there supplying backup for the handoff. Can you assure me they won't give themselves away if they suspect Waleed might be playing both sides?"

"I can't be one hundred percent certain of anything, sir. You know that. But—"

"I'll make note of your concern, Agent Duvall." Edens sat forward, placing his forearms on his desk and steepling his fingers. "But I've made my decision on this matter, and I expect you to respect it."

"Sir—"

*"Let's not fall into the Chicken Little trap and pro-
claim the sky is falling, huh?"*

*Chelsea gritted her teeth. "Yes, sir." Turning on her
heel, she marched from Edens's office, back straight,
arms stiff, sure that steam poured from her ears.*

"As you know," she told Dagan, coming out of the
reverie, "a day later the sky fell."

The dimness inside the sub didn't hide Dagan's
sawing jaw or the harsh light in his eyes. "And what did
you do then?" he asked.

His hand was no longer on her butt. She was pretty
sure he had it fisted against the yoga mat. With reluc-
tance, she pushed off him, settling herself with her back
against the cold hull.

Love conquers all…

Did it? She wasn't so sure.

"I stormed into Edens's office." She left out the part
about the tears of rage that had burned the back of her
throat. When she'd come in to work that day, the first
thing she'd heard about was the bombing, and for a
moment the whole world, *her* whole world, had gone
dark. Then she'd learned that Dagan was alive, and
relief and light had flooded into her. It had quickly been
tempered by the fact that while the man she secretly
loved had survived, three other valiant agents had not.
That fact would haunt her for the rest of her life. "I
screamed, 'I *told* you!' at him. Followed that up with 'I
warned you!'"

"What did he do?"

"He just sat there blinking at me, this blank expression
on his face. And then he asked me, 'What do you mean?'"

Once more, the memory of that day nipped at the
heels of her mind like a pack of angry dogs.

"Abdul Waleed!" she screamed at her boss.

"Calm yourself, Agent Duvall. You're being hysterical."

"Hysterical? Hysterical? Men are dead, sir! Men we might have been able to save, had we warned them!"

"I don't know what you're talking about."

She was so taken aback that she just stood there blinking at him. And then she suddenly understood. He was covering his own ass. He'd made the call to delay telling the agents about Waleed's connection to Zahed, and it had come back to bite him.

"I'll go above your head. I'll tell the director everything," she swore.

A terrible look came over Edens's face then. "And it will be your word against mine, Agent Duvall. I'll deny everything, and there's no way for you to prove otherwise. There's no paper trail, no emails or taped phone conversation. Tell me, do you have mental illness in your family?"

"Wh-what? You can't do that!" she raged. "You wouldn't dare!"

"Try me."

Her mouth hung open for a long moment, a million thoughts racing through her head. "Fine," she finally ground out, every blood vessel in her body expanding in fury. "It'll be my word against yours. And maybe you'll come out the winner in the end. But at least I will have cast doubt on you. With my credentials, I can find a job like that." She snapped her fingers. "But you'll never make it up to the big chair."

She turned to leave, determined to march into the director's office—or at least make an appointment with his secretary. As a lowly counterterrorism analyst, she didn't have the clout to just barge in on the man unannounced.

"Will you?" Edens asked before she could open his office door.

She swung back. "Will I what?"

"Find a job?" His smile was vicious. "Even with your credentials, I would think finding a new position would be difficult after I contact any would-be employers and tell them you're unstable and given to flights of fancy, always looking for ways to run the good names of your superiors through the mud."

Once again, her mouth hung open. Her heartbeat sounded loud in her ears.

"Go back to your desk, Chelsea." He no longer afforded her the courtesy of calling her "Agent Duvall."

"And I went," Chelsea told Dagan. "To my utter shame, I went. I knew he would make good on his promise. And I needed a job. I *still* need my job. Mom and I are still in so much debt, and the house…" The words had poured out of her. When the dam had finally burst, there had been no holding back. But now, self-loathing made her hesitate. "I didn't think Edens would get you fired. I don't know what I thought he would do, but it wasn't that. And then that day you came back…"

Dagan spoke, and the timbre of his voice was horrible. "The day the director of the CIA accused me of becoming complacent, the day he told me that no other agent would ever trust me or work with me again. The day he said he was left with no choice but to terminate my contract."

"Edens must have poisoned the well for you. I think he was scared that if you hung around, I would tell you the truth. And I wanted to tell you then and there," she swore. She never knew that anguish could tie one's stomach in knots. "I *tried* to tell you. But I-I was terrified of losing my job. Terrified of what it would mean for my mother and her happiness and her dreams and memories if I did. And there was no undoing what had been done. I just thought—"

"Edens died six months ago, Chels."

"Good riddance to bad rubbish."

"Why didn't you tell me then? When your job was finally safe?"

"Because you were working for BKI. You'd moved on. You'd gotten over it. You seemed happy. Avan was happy. I didn't think bringing up all that pain from the past was worth it. And I was so *ashamed* of having kept quiet for so long, Dagan."

"So then why the fuck are you telling me now?"

The submarine popped and groaned around them. They were changing depth. A sense of desperation grabbed hold of her. "Because…" She shook her head, searching his face, hoping to find some flicker of understanding. But there was nothing. "Because I can't start a relationship with you if there is this big, bad secret between us."

For long moments, he remained quiet, unmoving. When she couldn't take it anymore, she demanded, "Say something, Dagan. *Please*."

Only his lips moved when he asked, "What do you want me to say?"

"Say you forgive me for choosing my mother's home and memories and life's love all those years ago. Say you're not going to let this come between us. Say that love conquers all." Her tone was pleading, begging. She didn't care. When it came to this, when it came to *him*, she had no pride left.

He said none of that. What he said was, "I'm sorry."

Those two words might as well have been a death knell.

Chapter 47

Calais, France

DAGAN FELT LIKE HE HAD BEEN PUNCHED IN THE CHEST BY Tyson Fury.

He'd thought he knew heartbreak. His mother's cancer, his father's aneurysm, seeing Avan in the hospital looking like he was knocking on death's door. All of it had hurt him in ways he wouldn't have thought it possible to hurt. But this…this was *worse*. Because this…*she* was not the woman he thought he knew.

"We arrive," Gautier announced from the front of the sub. "I regret I cannot get closer, but the shore, she is not so far. Twenty meters, *peut-être*? No more."

"Dagan." Chelsea reached for him. "Please, I promise I'll—"

"Don't," he told her, a muscle twitching in his jaw. Another one was going to town in his right eye. "I can't right now. Just…" He shook his head. "Just leave it alone."

Her eyes were huge as she blinked up at him. He thought he saw her perfect mouth quiver, but he couldn't be sure because he quickly looked away.

When Gautier popped the top on the sub, Dagan inchwormed his way toward the front until he could see through the hatch to the stars shining overhead.

Huh. The world is still spinning.

He thought that odd considering *his* world, everything he thought he knew about Chelsea, everything he thought he knew about himself, had been blown to shit.

A series of vibrations buzzed in his pocket, alerting him to a waiting voice mail. He extracted his iPhone, thankful for the waterproof case, and glanced at the screen. It read *Unknown Number.* But the little asterisk beside the text told him it was someone from Black Knights Inc.

Without looking at Chelsea—he *couldn't* look at her; he was too confused, too dismayed—he held the phone to his ear and listened, his jaw sawing faster as each harried word entered his ear.

Thumbing off the device, he grabbed his backpack. "Change of plans," he told her.

"What do you mean?"

"That was Emily. She called to say they ran into some trouble. Looks like someone was waiting for them at the Eurotunnel terminal."

"How could anyone possibly know—"

"Same way they found out about you and me, maybe? Surveillance cameras? But the how doesn't matter. What matters is they're safe. They're headed to Christian's uncle's cottage in Port Isaac."

"Christian has an uncle?"

"Apparently so. Their plan is to lie low and wait until the heat dies down or until we can figure out what's going on. You and I are on our own for now. Get your pack ready. We have another swim in front of us."

"Dagan, we—"

"Chelsea, now's not the time."

"I know. I wasn't going to say anything about…" When she swallowed, he could actually *hear* the lump in her throat. "We need to call the others and fill them in on what's happened," she finished. "They need to know about Morrison and Spider."

Right. Of course. Why hadn't he thought of that? Oh

yeah. Because she'd dropped a bomb, and he was still reeling from the explosion. "Do it," he told her. "But be quick. I don't like sitting out here in the open. Makes me twitchy."

Chelsea pulled her phone from her back pocket. As she dialed, Dagan tossed his backpack through the hatch. It landed atop the sub with a hollow-sounding *pong*.

"Emily? We made it across," he heard Chelsea say, followed by, "No. No. We're fine. But Morrison isn't." Then she filled Emily in on Morrison's death, his revelation that he *wasn't* Spider, and the ensuing shoot-out with Surry. "Dagan thinks they used the CCTV cameras to track us. They're probably doing the same to you. Change cars often. *Away* from the eyes of those stupid cameras if at all possible, okay? And one more thing… y'all be careful over there." Her Southern drawl slipped out again, a testament to how little control she had over herself at the moment. Dagan refused to think too hard about that.

After she signed off, he pulled himself through the hatchway and sat atop the sub. The moon was half full and bright as a spotlight in the clear night. The air was warmer on this side of the Channel, but the metal skin of the vessel was absolutely freezing. It matched the ice that was quickly growing around his heart.

Shock was giving way to a cold, insidious kind of anger. *How could she have kept all that from me? How could she?* The question spiraled around and around inside his head, becoming louder each time. He understood the impossible position Edens had put her in. Hell, given the choice between family and a coworker, he'd choose family every damn time, too. But the *minute* Edens died she should have— He squashed the thought.

Shrugging into his backpack, he angrily accepted

Chelsea's when she handed it up to him. Despite everything, he couldn't ignore the jiggle of her breasts when
she wiggled her hips through the hatch. With the zipper
on her down coat open, and her wet sweatshirt plastered
against her front, her boobs were impossible to miss.
Inexplicably, he felt a frisson of awareness.

He still wanted her, damnit. He didn't know how
to consolidate *that* feeling with the icy fury gaining
momentum inside him. Looking for the answers in the
twinkling lights of the city perched beyond the beach
proved fruitless. All he saw was a distant clock tower,
the flicker of headlights on the streets, and the long
lines of hotels and condos that faced the water. When
he searched inside himself, what he found was just as
disjointed and even more confusing.

"I'll take that." Chelsea pulled her pack from his
lap. She shrugged into the straps and turned to Gautier.
"Thanks for the ride."

Gautier's shrug was classically Gallic. "I owed Angel
a great debt, *voyez-vous?* Now debt is paid."

Chelsea nodded but said nothing more before glancing at Dagan. He noticed she had as much trouble meeting his eyes as he had meeting hers. "Are you ready?"
she asked.

"Sure. I mean, I've spent all day treading water and
saving your ass. Why should I stop now?"

He realized how harsh his tone was when she ducked
her chin and blinked rapidly. Sighing, unsure if he was
more pissed at her or at himself or at a world where a
man like Ted Edens could make dumbass decisions that
took the lives of good men and make threats that put an
earnest young woman in an impossible position.

"Let's go," he said, ready to be back stateside so
he could sit down for a damn minute and *think* about

everything she'd told him and what it meant for him, for her, for *them*.

But just before they pushed from the top of the sub and slid into the choppy waters of the Channel for the *third* time that day, the hairs on the back of his neck twanged to life and his palms prickled.

Someone was watching…

Chapter 48

COLD.

That's what Chelsea felt both inside and out as she trudged up the beach after Dagan. Her teeth chattered. Her muscles clenched tight in an effort to generate heat. But it was the frosty chill of his words, the icy way he behaved, that blew through her heart like a winter wind.

Love conquers all.

It was a pretty lie. People believed it because they *wanted* to believe it. Because they wanted something to cling to, something to combat the fear that the only person they could truly count on was themselves.

For a time, she had dared to believe the pretty lie.

She was such a fool.

"Stay behind me," Dagan instructed in a harsh whisper.

From the pocket of his coat, he pulled the little revolver he'd taken off Morrison, flicked open the cylinder, and dumped the two remaining bullets into his hand. He blew through the holes of the cylinder to dry them and reloaded.

"What's happening?" she asked, the skin on her back crawling.

"Someone is watching us."

She wouldn't have thought after the day she'd had that a drop of adrenaline remained in her system. But she felt a spike of the stuff shoot through her bloodstream. It helped to speed her steps.

Pulling her glasses from where she'd stored them

in a zippered pocket on her jacket, she wiped the water from the lenses as best she could and slid them onto her face. The world came into focus, and the first thing she noticed was that light from the moon. It cast their shadows in long, inky streaks behind them, like they were being trailed by dark, malevolent specters. But other than that, she saw nothing. No movement. No *watcher*.

The word sent a chill down her spine that had nothing to do with the freezing water dripping from her clothes and her soggy backpack. Then she reminded herself that just because someone was watching didn't mean that someone wanted to do them harm. Heck, it could be a local or a tourist who'd spotted them lumbering out of the surf—and who *wouldn't* stop to watch that?

"Where?" she whispered. Sand stuck to the bottoms of her wet boots, making each step heavier than the one before it.

"Not sure." Dagan turned toward a parking lot nestled close to the beach. It was empty except for a panel van and one beat-up-looking Renault. The latter appeared to have left the assembly line sometime when Reagan was president.

"Not sure? Then how do you—"

"Instinct," he cut her off. "A sixth sense. Years of finding myself in the middle of someone's crosshairs. Whatever you want to call it. Someone is watching us. I can feel it."

"Okay, then." She swallowed the fear that rose in the back of her throat.

Just a local or a tourist, she reminded herself. Herself didn't answer back, which meant the chick remained glaringly skeptical.

"Shit," Dagan cursed, picking up the pace toward the

parking lot when a man in a long, dark raincoat crossed
the street and headed in their direction.

"The watcher?" she asked.

"Likely."

"He doesn't look too scary." She breathed a sigh
of relief. The man was bald and a good five inches
shorter than Dagan. Despite that, she would bet he was
pushing 250 pounds *dressed and hung*, as her daddy
would have said.

"Bonsoir!" The man raised a hand. "Nice night for a
swim, eh?"

His voice reminded Chelsea of an oil slick, all
sticky and dark. And *British*. There was no mistaking
that accent. She was instantly reminded of Surry and
Morrison. The hairs along the back of her neck lifted.
"Dagan—"

"Stay behind me," he hissed.

She didn't dare disobey, quickening her steps until
she was right on his boot heels.

"You lost?" Raincoat asked, still moving in a diagonal line toward them. And *that* was as much a warning
sign as anything. A normal person didn't watch two fully
dressed folks mysteriously emerge from the Channel at
night and then try to start up a friendly conversation.

"No," Dagan called. Then he added, "Stay where
you are!" when the man stopped his diagonal intercept
course and turned directly toward them.

"Don't think I will," Raincoat replied. Quicker than
Chelsea would have thought possible for a man of his
size, Raincoat dropped to one knee, pistol raised.

She barely had time to blink, but in that split second
Dagan tossed her onto the sand, flattened himself over
the top of her, and got off a shot before the other man
could. The *boom* of the little revolver so close to her ear

was deafening. It was immediately followed by a second head-rattling explosion.

Oh my Lord! she thought a little hysterically, two shots equaled two bullets. Their *last* two bullets.

Spitting sand from her mouth, she lifted her chin to see a bright-red patch of blood flowering in the center of Raincoat's chest where the halves of his London Fog flapped open. Even from a distance of fifty feet, she could make out the whites of his eyes as they rolled back in his head. He toppled sideways, his face half buried in the sand.

"Let's go!" Dagan grabbed her arm directly over her wound and yanked her to a stand. Pain lanced through her, but he didn't give her time to drag in a breath before he pulled her into a sprint. "We have more company!"

She glanced around and saw two men, one to the north and one to the south. They were both the length of a football field away, but they moved with a speed that left no doubt they were intent on closing the distance and doing it fast. If she wasn't mistaken, the moonlight glinted off a nickel-plated pistol in the hand of the one to the north.

"Gun!" she rasped, willing her legs to churn faster. *When did the beach turn to quicksand?* Her thigh muscles screamed with the effort, but every step seemed to get her nowhere.

"I know! Hurry!"

She was trying, damnit!

Without missing a step, Dagan reached down and snagged Raincoat's weapon as they charged by him. Five seconds later, her boots hit the parking lot's concrete surface and they ran toward the Renault. Dagan used the butt of Raincoat's weapon to smash the driver's side glass. His first blow only created a spiderweb crack

in the surface. The second blow was the charm. The
tempered glass shattered. He reached in and quickly
unlocked the door.

"Get in!" he yelled.

She had to crawl over the gearshift. The wet hem of
her jeans got stuck on something, but she managed to
unhook it and slide into the passenger seat. When she
turned, Dagan was already in the driver's seat ripping
the plastic covering from the steering column.

Her heart was going nuts behind her breastbone.
When she lifted a hand to adjust her glasses, she saw
how badly it was shaking.

In contrast, Dagan was as calm as a yoga instructor.
His fingers flew beneath the column, searching through
the various wires. When he found the ones he was looking for, he went to work on the insulation around the
wires.

She wondered why he hadn't chosen the van. Not
that it appeared extra speedy or anything, but at least it
looked like it had been serviced in the past few years.
The Renault on the other hand? Yeah, no. Then again,
the little subcompact was too ancient to come equipped
with an alarm or antitheft device, so perhaps it *was* the
better choice. She'd determine that if and when the
crusty thing started.

"Status report," he said, not looking up from the
column. He put the pistol he had taken from Raincoat
on the dash, and she noted that the gun black was worn
from the trigger. It was obviously a well-loved and
well-used weapon. That gave her the willies. "Chels!"
he barked. "Status report, damnit!"

"Huh?" She blinked.

"How close are they?"

"Oh, uh…" She peeked out the window. "The one to

the south is still fifty yards away. The one to the north…
maybe thirty."

"Okay. Duck down onto the floorboard. This is going
to be a close one."

Oh, Lord! Oh, God! Oh, Jesus! She wasn't sure if she
was really praying as she slipped out of her backpack
and folded herself as tightly as she could into the space
between the passenger seat and the glove box.

The car smelled like stale cigarette smoke and old
oil. Her face itched from the sand clinging to it. And
the taste of fear was sour on her tongue. It was odd the
things she noticed when she was seconds away from
being gunned down and—

Dagan sparked two wires together, and the Renault
coughed to life.

Hallelujah!

He wasted no time putting the car in reverse and pulling from the parking spot. He'd shifted into first gear
by the time the first bullet blew through the Renault's
metal frame and lodged into the middle of the passenger
seat. The passenger seat where she would have been
sitting if—

He gunned the little car, working the clutch and
shifting through gears. By the time he reached fourth,
another bullet slammed into the vehicle. This time, she
couldn't see where it hit. The back quarter panel maybe?
Which was good, right? It meant they were leaving the
shooters behind.

She peeked up at Dagan. She could see the muscles in
his jaw working even through the pelt of his beard. His
eyes were as hard as stone.

"Okay to come out?" she asked, her throat unbelievably dry. She swallowed, but she didn't have enough
spit left to do herself much good.

"Give it a few more minutes. I want to make sure we're not being followed."

Given the way he whipped the vehicle around corner after corner, she figured their route was too dizzying for anyone to track. But she obeyed him nonetheless.

One minute stretched to two. Two quickly became ten. Chelsea stopped counting when her left foot fell asleep and the material of her coat began to dry. The lights of the city gave way to the darkness of a country road. Only when trees whipped by the Renault on either side did Dagan visibly relax.

"Okay. You can come out now."

She'd been folded in a ball so long that it took some effort to climb into the passenger seat. Pins and needles went to work in her left foot as she glanced behind them expecting… What? She wasn't sure. But after everything, after being found at every turn, after feeling safe only to be accosted and shot at on *both* sides of the Channel, she wouldn't have been surprised to see headlights behind them and closing fast.

Fortunately, all that showed in the red glow of the taillights were the dairy cows in the fields on either side of the road. Their black-and-white sides looked like big bucolic Rorschach tests. After a while, Chelsea's breathing returned to normal. Her heartbeat soon followed suit, and she turned to Dagan.

"How the heckfire did they know where to find us?" She shook her head in disbelief. "How could they *possibly* have—"

"Surry saw the sub," he interrupted. "It's possible he was able to pass on the information before he died. And Calais is the obvious point of entry into France, so…" He shrugged. "It wasn't too much of a stretch."

"If this is all Spider's doing…"

"I'd bet my left nut it is."

"Then the man is faster, smarter, and deadlier than we gave him credit for."

"Which is why we need to get back home as quickly as possible. Pull up a map. I need you to navigate me to that private jet airport Emily talked about. What was the name of it again?"

"Paris–Le Bourget." She dug her phone from her pocket and brought up Google Maps.

For a long time, they sat in silence that was only broken when she told him to make a turn. It was a cutting emptiness she desperately wanted to fill.

Peeking over at him, noting how the lights of the dashboard created fascinating shadows over his hard, uncompromising face and how the wind from the shattered window and wide-open vents tousled his drying hair, she finally said, "Dagan, I just need to tell you that—"

"Chels, unless whatever is about to come out of your mouth has something to do with this mission or getting us to the airport, I'd appreciate it if you didn't talk. I need to think."

"I just wanted to apologize again and say how much I—"

He held up a hand, stopping her mid-sentence.

"Dagan, please. Just let me—"

He shook his head, and she bit down on her tongue. He'd closed his ears to her—likely his mind too. Trying to talk to him would be as helpful as carrying on a conversation with a brick wall.

The adrenaline that had raged through her system left an acidic residue behind. It strafed her nerve endings raw. After the day's twists and turns, shoot-outs and narrow escapes, the peace of the country road felt impossibly contradictory.

"I should probably call Emily and let her know what happened," she finally said. That fell into the first category of his mission-slash-directions stipulation, right?

He grunted his agreement, but she wanted more. She wanted to hear his voice. Needed to keep the lines of communication open. She knew how quickly silence could build on itself until it felt too big and wide and deep to overcome.

"Dagan?" She thumbed on her phone and dialed Emily's number. "Don't you think—"

The look he flicked her stung more than a slap to the face. He was on to her. He knew her game and wanted no part of it. As far as he was concerned, the lines of communication had been clipped, and there was no telling when or even *if* they would ever be repaired.

She blinked away the tears that stung her eyes. She would rather he scream at her, rail at her, call her names. At least then she would know what he was feeling. What he was *thinking*. At least then she would—

"You on your way to the airport?" Emily answered in lieu of a salutation.

"We are." Chelsea filled her in on what had happened at the beach. "Just thought you all should know."

"For the love of Fielder Jones." Emily sighed. "I'll be glad when you get back stateside and figure this mess out. If I have to spend too much time cooped up with these cretins, I—"

"Cretins?" Chelsea heard Christian say in the background. "It takes one to know one, darling."

"—Might just commit mass murder," Emily spoke over him.

"Once again," Christian said, "I ask you: With *what* weapons you plan to commit this mass murder since we've bloody well left everything that goes *boom* back at Rusty's?"

"And *again...*" Emily came right back at him. Chelsea could tell Emily had turned from the phone because her voice was fainter. "I'd like to remind *you* of two things. One, I'm very creative. Two, you have to sleep sometime." Emily's voice became louder as she spoke directly into the receiver again. "Tell me, Chels, do you remember the news story of that woman who waited until her cheating husband fell asleep before supergluing his dick to the inside of his leg? I've always appreciated her ingenuity and—"

"You are a complete nutter!" Christian wailed.

"Never said I wasn't." There was laughter in Emily's voice.

"Holy duck fuck!" Chelsea heard Ace shout. "Either you two cut the shit, or I'm going to call Don King and go ahead and make this an event."

There was a beat or two of silence following that outburst. Then Emily huffed. "Men... They're impossible." In a conspiratorial whisper, she added, "And British men are the worst."

"Uh-huh. Right. Keep telling yourself that, sister," Chelsea said. If her day hadn't put her in a terrible temper, and if she weren't terrified that she had lost Dagan for good, she might have enjoyed Emily and Christian's banter. As it was, it only gave her a headache.

"What is *that* supposed to mean?" Emily demanded.

"Nothing. I really need to go. Stay safe, Em. Stay away from the cameras when you can. Hopefully once Z and I"—was it her imagination or did Dagan flinch when he heard his nickname?—"are back stateside, we'll be able to get this mess cleaned up and it'll be safe to call you all home."

After they'd said their good-byes, and after Chelsea had returned her phone to her pocket, the car once again filled with silence. There was only the hum of the Renault's engine, the howl of the wind through the broken window, and the slight whistle of the heat blowing through the vents.

Chelsea was reminded of the Silence Charm Hermione Granger had used on a Death Eater during the Battle of the Department of Mysteries. When she couldn't stand it a second longer, she finally said, "Thank you."

Dagan didn't look at her, but thank goodness the Silence Charm had been broken. "For what?" he asked.

"For back there on the beach. For saving my ass. *Again*." For the record, she was still obeying his edict. She was only talking about the mission.

Muscles ticked in his jaw, causing the Beard to twitch. His moonshine voice no longer sounded smooth and distilled. Now, it was dark and harsh. "Just doing my job."

Annnnddd there they were again, words so cold they left a thick layer of ice around her heart.

She turned the vents more fully toward her, trying to get warm. It was a wasted effort. She would never be warm again. Dagan had taken the fire of his passion, the heat of his love from her, and all that was left was a cold, aching void.

Chapter 49

Chicago, Illinois

Ten hours...

That's how much time had passed since Chelsea hopped on the flight that had spirited her and Dagan across the Atlantic from Paris to Chicago. Ten hours of not sleeping, even though her eyes were filled with sand and her whole body was one big, exhausted ache. Ten hours of not talking because Dagan had claimed a sofa on the private jet, stretched out, and closed his eyes, effectively shutting her out.

Even after they had landed in Chicago and Becky Knight, a tiny wisp of a woman who had a penchant for lollipops and blowtorches—the latter no doubt developed over the years she had been building and designing the custom choppers that kept the Black Knights' covers intact—had picked them up from the airport and drove them to BKI headquarters, Dagan hadn't said more than a few perfunctory words to Chelsea.

And now? Well, now they were sitting in front of the bank of computers on the second floor of the old menthol cigarette factory that had been converted into the living quarters, a shop, and ground zero for all things BKI and clandestine, and Dagan continued to give her the cold shoulder. Anytime she tried to catch his eye, he quickly looked away, a muscle ticking in his jaw.

Everything Chelsea had feared for so long—losing his respect, his support, his friendship, and more recently his *love*—had come to pass. She had known it would hurt. But Lordy, she hadn't been prepared for just how bad it would be.

It felt like someone had ripped open her chest, torn out her heart, and tossed it on the floor. It was difficult to breathe. Difficult to think past the pain. Difficult to—

"This cockthistle doesn't know what's about to hit him," Ozzie crowed, his fingers flying across his keyboard.

Ever since she had planted the virus in Morrison's computer, BKI's computer whiz had engaged in a series of cyber battles with someone from either Morrison's camp or Spider's. And according to what Ozzie had muttered to her when she arrived and asked how he was coming along, his nemesis was good. *He's faster*, Ozzie had said. *But I'm smarter by at least two standard deviations*.

Now, even though Ozzie's brow was knitted in concentration, there was a smile on his face.

"Making headway?" Chelsea asked from the rolling desk chair beside him. Becky was occupying herself by cleaning a transmission on the conference table behind them, and Dagan was in the desk chair on Ozzie's opposite side.

"I'm almost in," Ozzie declared, and Chelsea's heart lurched. Maybe there was a way to salvage her mission yet. Maybe it hadn't all been for naught.

"You go get him, my hunka hunka burnin' lover," Samantha Tate, Ozzie's fiancée, said as she entered the room, steaming cup of coffee in hand.

She set the mug beside Ozzie's rattling keyboard, and Ozzie thanked her. Then, without taking his eyes off the screen, he lifted his mouth for a kiss. Samantha obliged, giving him a loud, smacking one before pulling a spare rolling chair up behind him so she could massage his shoulders.

There was such adoration in Samantha's eyes when she looked at her man, such love and respect. Chelsea had to glance away.

Samantha and Ozzie had an improbable love story. Samantha was an investigative reporter whose sole mission in life was to drag secrets into the light. And Ozzie was a covert operator who lived and worked cloaked in some of the world's deepest, darkest shadows. But somehow, someway, they made it work.

It was impossible for Chelsea to look at them and see happily ever after written all over their faces when she knew she would never have a happily ever after of her own.

As if sensing her distress, Peanut, the notch-eared, crooked-tailed tomcat that acted as BKI's mascot, placed his front paws on her knees and meowed up at her. His yellow eyes looked solemn, sympathetic.

A lump formed in her throat. Figuring she could use all the comfort she could get, Chelsea pulled the big cat into her lap. It took some effort. Peanut was far from a dainty thing. In fact, she'd put him at close to twenty pounds.

She reckoned her legs were sure to go to sleep in no time when he curled up into the familiar cat-loaf on her lap, all his legs tucked underneath him. But she didn't mind. Especially when he began to purr.

The sound was loud enough to compete with the noise the steel-and-chrome beasts made when Becky tested their engines down in the shop on the first floor. Chelsea found it soothed her as much as anything could.

You know, what with my heart lying on the floor.

"I got him!" Ozzie pumped a fist. "Take that, you sorry

sonofabitch!" His screen flashed from eye-crossing lines of code to reveal the classic Microsoft desktop screen.

"Is that Morrison's system?" Chelsea asked, scratching behind Peanut's ears. She leaned closer to the screen.

"You betcha." Ozzie nodded. "Now just let me…" He trailed off as he scrolled through the directory.

Unfortunately, there were no files named "Spider" or "Accounts that link me to Spider." But one file folder caught Chelsea's attention. She pointed to it. "What's that one? The one titled *Bad Things*?"

Ozzie clicked on it, and there was a collective gasp heard around the room. Becky, who had come to stand behind Chelsea's chair, whispered, "Dear sweet Jesus."

Bile climbed into the back of Chelsea's throat as one image after another flashed onto the screen. All of girls just entering puberty. All showing the subject either bound or gagged, or both. All so grotesque and heart-rending that Dagan's voice sounded shredded when he hissed, "Close out of there. For fuck's sake, Ozzie. I can't take any more."

Ozzie shut down the file, and for long moments no one said a thing. Even Peanut sensed the tension in the air. He stopped purring, and his ears flicked nervously.

"He's a pedophile." Chelsea was in shock. She'd known Morrison was a sick shit, but this… She'd never expected this.

"A dead pedophile," Dagan grumbled. "Which is the best kind, in my opinion."

"Fuckin' A" was all Ozzie said as he stared stony-eyed at his screen. Then he shook himself and leaned toward the keyboard once again. "Okay." He blew out a breath. "Okay, so there's *that*. And I…well, I don't have any words. Truth to tell, I'm a little nervous of what other horrors might pop out at us."

"Hopefully Spider's true identity and how he's tied to Morrison will pop out at us," Becky said.

"Right." Ozzie nodded and went back to scrolling through the computer directory.

Chelsea's phone came to life inside her pocket. When she pulled out her cell, the number for the director of the CIA glowed on the screen.

Back in Paris, she had called to let him know she was on the plane. But she had forgotten to phone him and tell him when she had landed and when she had made it to BKI headquarters. She blamed the oversight on emotional turmoil.

"Sir?" she answered, carefully dumping Peanut from her lap and walking away from the group gathered around the computer bank. "I'm sorry I forgot to—"

He cut her off. For a couple of seconds she listened, her heart pounding in her chest, then she said, "Of course, sir. Right away, sir," before thumbing off her phone.

Becky was the one to turn to her, a sleek blond eyebrow raised. "Well? I take it that was Director Russell. What does he have to say?"

Chelsea swallowed. "Given all the press back in the UK, and given it won't be long until Morrison's murder and my face are splashed all over the news stations *here*, he wants me back in Langley. He says I need to lie low until we can get this thing straightened out and clear my name."

"Probably smart." Becky nodded. "We'll keep you apprised of anything and everything we find."

"Thank you." There was a heartbeat in Chelsea's throat as she looked at Dagan's back. She desperately wanted him to turn to her, to say…something. *Anything.* But he didn't.

"I…uh…I could use a ride back to the airport. Director Russell has a plane waiting for me," she said.

Dagan *did* turn to her then. She hoped he would volunteer. If only she could get him alone, then maybe she could—

Her hope died on the spot when she saw his unblinking, incisive stare.

Becky glanced back and forth between them, brow furrowed. Finally, when it became obvious Dagan wasn't going to offer Chelsea a ride, Becky said, "I'll take you, Chels."

The backs of Chelsea's eyeballs were on fire when she managed a wheezy, "Thank you."

Ten minutes later, with Becky at the wheel, they drove through the big wrought-iron gates in front of Black Knights Inc. HQ. Chelsea felt like in place of her heart, there was a stone. It sat hard and cold in the center of her chest as she glanced in the side mirror at the big brick facade of the factory building.

Will this be the last time I see it? she wondered. *Will it be the last time I see him?*

The hard stone in her chest crumbled to dust at the thought.

Chapter 50

THREE DAYS LATER, DAGAN SAT ON THE LEATHER SOFA IN BKI's third-floor den, sipped his Goose Island IPA, and gave the CNN anchor on television half an ear as he waited for the most recent news to break. He hadn't seen Chelsea since she left Black Knights' headquarters to head back to Langley. But even though they were half a dozen states apart, he'd been unable to avoid her pretty face. It had been splashed all over the news.

Morrison's murder and Chelsea's "wanted" status had topped the headlines the world over. Speculation was wild. The newshounds were slavering over what few juicy details were available. But tonight, the whole truth—or at least the version the CIA director and the Black Knights had agreed upon—would be revealed.

"Breaking news!" the anchorwoman said right on cue. Her blond hair, styled in a sleek bob, barely moved when she pressed her earpiece and nodded. "We have an update on the Chelsea Duvall and Roper Morrison story."

Chelsea's photo appeared beside Morrison's on the screen. But Dagan's eyes were glued to only one of them.

Three guesses which one, and the first two don't count.

He wasn't sure where or when the picture of Chelsea had been taken. But she was in a small aluminum john-boat. The sun glinted in her golden eyes, and the smile on her face was pure and genuine and so...*Chelsea* that it made his chest ache.

"The CIA has just released a stunning statement," the

anchorwoman continued. Her eyes barely moved as she read the words streaming across her teleprompter. "They claim Chelsea Duvall, a former employee of the Bureau of Land Management and more recently media mogul Roper Morrison's personal assistant, is in fact one of their agents. According to a CIA spokesperson, Agent Duvall was sent by the agency to infiltrate Morrison's household and search for evidence tying the British billionaire to Pattani separatists in Thailand.

"The Pattani separatists are a terrorist group responsible for the 2016 bombings in the resort town of Hua Hin. They are also known to keep sex slaves and deal in the human trafficking of underage girls to the United States and the UK. The connection between Roper Morrison and the Thai terrorists was first discovered in the Panama Papers."

That was a lie. The Panama Papers had pointed from the diamond mine in Angola to Spider, which had *then* pointed to Morrison because, as it turned out, Morrison was laundering money for Spider's diamond mine venture—and many more of Spider's ventures—through his legitimate businesses. But it had been decided *that* would be kept on the down low. The evidence Ozzie found on Morrison's computer of Morrison traveling to Thailand to have sex with the underage girls the Pattani separatists kept in the middle of the jungle—when Dagan thought about that he wished *he'd* been the one to put the bullet in Morrison's sick, twisted brain—was the information the CIA had determined would be given to the press to validate their involvement in Morrison's takedown.

The anchorwoman continued. "The CIA spokesperson went on to say that when Morrison discovered Agent Duvall's true intent, she was forced to flee the country, taking along evidence she had collected of

Morrison's perversions. During her escape, Morrison and his employees caught up with her first in Folkestone, England, and then again across the English Channel in Calais, France. She had no other choice but to use lethal force to save herself from being captured and killed."

Lethal force. It was such a nice way of saying someone's guts or heart or brain had been introduced to a ball of lead traveling 2,500 feet per second.

"Two of the dead men, including former British SAS officer turned security specialist Steven J. Surry and an as-yet-unidentified man, were both gunned down by the same weapon. But the bullet fragment pulled from Roper Morrison did not match. When reporters questioned the CIA spokesperson about the conflicting sets of ballistics and whether that meant Agent Duvall had help from a third party during her escape, the spokesperson said, quote, 'That's classified information, which I'm not at liberty to discuss at this time.'"

The anchorwoman smiled, revealing a set of capped teeth so white they were nearly blinding. "So there you have it. Agent Chelsea Duvall, not a murderer and thief, but a true American hero. Stay tuned to CNN for more updates on this explosive story as they become available."

Dagan blew out a relieved breath when Chelsea's picture disappeared from the screen.

"So"—Ozzie spoke from behind him—"Chelsea's name has been cleared, huh?" Ozzie walked around the sofa, plunked beside Dagan, and twisted the top off a fresh beer. Through his jeans, Ozzie massaged the wound on his thigh that had come courtesy of an incendiary device and clinked the long neck of his bottle against Dagan's. "I'd say it's a job well done, but we still don't know who Spider is, so I'll just say it's a job *partially* done."

By the time Ozzie had managed to hack into Morrison's files and locate the accounts and transactions that seemed linked to Spider, all the money had been moved. To where? And by whom? And how? Those were the million-dollar questions.

"I take it that means you've had no luck locating any of the missing money or finding clues that might point us to Spider's identity," Dagan said.

"I haven't given up." Ozzie shook his head emphatically. "There are still a few more rabbit holes I can look down. I hope to have a lead soon. But I have to tell you, this Spider asshole is proving to be unbelievably crafty."

Spider's craftiness certainly wasn't lost on Dagan. After all, he'd spent months trying to bring the bastard down only to come up empty-handed. Well, not empty-handed, necessarily. Roper fuckin' Morrison was no longer in the picture—*or on this earth*. And that was something.

"Is anyone shaking the government trees over in the UK to see what monkeys fall out?" Dagan asked. "Neither Morrison nor Spider found us on their own that day. They had help."

"The director of the CIA knocked some heads together. According to Scotland Yard, they began reviewing CCTV footage the moment Morrison called with his claim that Chelsea had stolen something from him. Morrison being such an important and powerful man and all, they had jumped to help. But that's the most they'll cop to. I suspect Morrison had or Spider *has* some folks on his payroll over there. They're busy covering their asses." Ozzie dragged a hand through his messy blond hair. "But I care less about that and more about the fact that all these questions, all this attention, will make Spider go to ground."

"Just like the eight-legged abomination he is." Dagan squinted at the TV screen even though he wasn't paying attention to the fiber commercial that was playing. "But he won't stay there. He's too confident. He's been on top for too long. He won't like life at the bottom. He'll poke his head out eventually, and we'll be there to chop it off."

Ozzie nodded, but his expression remained unconvinced. Then he shrugged. "Speaking of people poking their heads out, now that the news about Morrison and Chelsea has aired, the heat will die down across the pond. The rest of the gang is planning to return stateside. The same charter pilot that brought you and Chelsea home is scheduled to bring them over in two days. And get this… That friend of Emily's who helped you all out over there is coming with them. Since we don't know exactly which authorities are in Spider's pocket, it's been decided this Rusty Parker guy would be safer here with us. At least for a while."

For the first time in days, Dagan felt a smile tug at his lips. "Ace will be happy about that."

Ozzie cocked his head. It reminded Dagan so much of Chelsea's "thinking pose" that he had to turn away.

"How's that?" Ozzie prompted.

"Huh?" Dagan had lost his train of thought.

"You said Ace will be happy about Rusty Parker being here."

"Oh, right. Well, I don't want to tell tales out of school…"

"Sure you do."

"But there were definite sparks flying between Ace and Rusty."

"No shit?" Ozzie's eyebrows disappeared into his hairline.

"No shit."

"Huh. Well…good for Ace."

"If you two are finished gossiping like a couple of frickin' schoolgirls…" Becky arrived in the doorway. "Zoelner, there's a phone call for you. Came in on the main line."

She handed him a cordless phone, and he looked at it in confusion. Who would be calling him at headquarters? Everyone who knew him knew to reach him on his cell.

He didn't try to disguise the curiosity in his voice when he said, "Hello? Who am I speaking with?"

"Agent Zoelner." A booming baritone sounded over the line. Dagan paid less attention to the voice and more attention to the "agent" in front of his name. No one had called him that in years. "This is Elliot Russell. Director of the CIA."

Dagan's stomach hit the floor right along with his feet. "What happened? Is Chels… I mean, is Agent Duvall okay?"

"She's fine," Director Russell assured him. Dagan blew out a ragged breath and tried to calm his pounding heart. He gave Ozzie and Becky a thumbs-up to wipe away the concern on their faces.

"Well, her cover is officially and eternally blown," the director added. "She'll never be able to do undercover work again, which means her job as the official liaison to BKI has been terminated. But other than that, she's fine. She'll go back to riding a desk somewhere, which she assures me will please you to no end. According to Agent Duvall, you never were too enthusiastic about her fieldwork."

"I was wrong about that, sir," he said. "Agent Duvall makes an excellent field agent. She's brave and decisive and—"

"That's good to hear," the director interrupted. "Too bad she's burned. But it's not Agent Duvall's future I called to talk to you about."

"No?"

"It's yours."

Dagan's chin jerked back. Did a needle scratch over a record somewhere? "Mine? What do you mean?"

"I mean now that President Thompson is out of office, and now that the Black Knights are in the midst of finishing their last assignment for him, I think it's time you started thinking about what comes next. A man with your skills would be wasted in retirement. Have you ever considered coming back to work for us here at Langley?"

"Come back to…" He shook his head. "I'm sorry. *What?*"

"Agent Duvall told me what happened with Ted Edens," Russell said, and Dagan stopped breathing. "She assures me if anyone deserved to be fired over that tragedy all those years ago, it was Edens for not taking action on reliable Intel and her for not coming forward to out her boss for his failings despite all his threats and accusations. Although, I'll tell you like I told her, she was pretty much stuck between a rock and a hard place. I'm not sure anyone walking in her shoes would have—"

"Sir?" Dagan's blood pounded in his ears. Chelsea had… She'd *told*? She'd risked her job, risked her reputation, perhaps risked losing the house she'd worked so hard to save for her mother and…*told*? "Are you really offering me my old job back?"

At this, both Becky and Ozzie leaned forward, frowns on their faces, unabashedly listening in to his phone conversation. Privacy wasn't a concept anyone at the shop held dear.

"Of course. You were always an excellent agent. Had I known what really happened all those years ago, you would never have been fired in the first place. Only an agent like Chelsea Duvall, with her tenacity and nose for connecting dots, could have been able to find the familial connection between your source and Mullah Zahed. I don't blame you for missing the link. But Edens made it seem like you had blatantly... Never mind. That's not important. The important thing is that your job is here if and when you want it. Oh, and one more thing..."

Then Director Russell dropped a bomb that left Dagan reeling. After he said his good-byes, Dagan sat in silence, his mouth hanging open.

"What?" Ozzie demanded. "Are you going back to work for the CIA?"

Dagan shook his head. "No, I...I don't know. I..." He couldn't go on. How could Chelsea have done that? How could she have... "I have to go." He pushed up from the sofa, looking around, his mind racing.

Becky's eyebrows slammed together. "Go? Where?"

"To DC. To Langley. I need to talk to Chelsea."

"But Chelsea isn't *in* DC or Langley."

He scowled at her. "Then where is she?"

Becky shot him a considering look. "First tell me what happened between you two in England."

Dagan crossed his arms over his chest and clamped his mouth shut, hoping his fiery stare was enough to convince her the subject was strictly off-limits. He should have known better. Becky was not easily intimidated. She just stared right back until he was forced to ask, "Why do you assume something happened between us?"

"Because you've been walking around here wearing a murderous expression for the last three days. And anytime one of us brings up Chelsea's name, you flinch."

She pointed at him. "See? You just did it again. So? What happened?"

"It's none of your business."

"It is if you want me to tell you where she is. Because I happen to like Chelsea. And I'm not sending you after her until I'm convinced you're going to be nice."

"I'm always nice."

"Bullshit." Well, she had him there. "When I talked to Chelsea—"

He stood up straighter. "You talked to Chelsea? When?"

"The day after she left."

"What did she say?"

Becky narrowed her eyes, regarding him for what felt like an eternity. He was so tempted to shake her and demand she answer that he had to stuff his hands in his front pockets. Someone started a buzz saw between his ears. Eventually she answered. "It wasn't so much what she said. It was more her tone."

"And what was her tone?"

"Sad."

The word was a bull's-eye arrow to his soul, piercing deep.

"So what did you do to her?" Becky asked.

"Why do you assume *I* did something to *her*?"

"Because you're a man. Which means you're inherently egotistical and pigheaded and—"

"Uh…" Ozzie raised his hand. "In the name of all good men everywhere, I object to that generalization."

Becky pulled a Dum Dum lollipop from the front pocket of her bib overalls—she'd been working down in the shop, which meant she was speckled in grease, paint, and a few metal shavings. Shoving the sucker in her mouth, she frowned around the stick at Ozzie.

"Fine. Point taken." Then she turned to Dagan. "Are you saying *she* was the one to do something to *you*?"

"You're damn right!" Was he shouting? *Why?* Oh, right. Because every cell in his body urged him out the door and on his way to find Chelsea. And Becky—nosy, irritating, *infuriating* woman that she was—was holding Chelsea's whereabouts hostage.

"So what did she do?" Becky raised a brow.

He struggled with himself for about five seconds before the whole sorry story poured out of him. He generally wasn't the kind of man to over-share, liked to consider himself more of the strong, silent type. But he'd been wrestling with what had happened for days, fighting all his contradictory feelings, and, God, it felt good to *tell* someone. To get it all out.

By the time he was finished, he should have felt drained and beaten. Instead, he was energized and more determined than ever to—

"Do you love her?" Ozzie asked, casually sipping his beer. The keen intelligence in Ozzie's eyes was anything but nonchalant, however. If Dagan lied, Ozzie would know.

"I thought I did." Anguish grabbed his heart and squeezed it in a fist. He ran a hand over his beard and shook his head. "No. I *know* I did. I still do, but—"

"No buts," Becky cut him off. "When it comes to love, there's no weakness in forgiveness."

Dagan blew out a blustery breath and stared at the ceiling where ducts and exposed piping created a lofty, industrial feel. The image of Chelsea's face, her gorgeous eyes pleading with him, flared to life in his mind's eye. "She's not the woman I thought I knew." It came out as a whisper.

"Of course she is."

"No." He shook his head.

Looking at Ozzie and Becky, his teammates, his *friends*, he begged them with his eyes to understand. Judging by Ozzie's mouth, which was in full-blown lemon-sucking disapproval mode, and Becky's stare, which was hot enough to blister paint, they *didn't*.

Becky spoke up. "She was put in an impossible position. If she had told the truth, Edens would have ruined her. You would still have been out of a job, because Edens would have had you fired to save his own ass. And honestly, if she hadn't been smart enough to look at the Intel in the first place and see the incongruities in the information your asset had passed you, you would've still been in the same boat. So I don't understand why—"

"I get it!" Dagan yelled, once again shoving his hands in his pockets, but this time it was to keep from pulling out his own hair. "And I could get past all of that. She followed a bad order that ended in a bad outcome, and her boss was holding a job she desperately needed over her head, so she kept her mouth shut. Believe me, I understand all of that. I *know* what it is to be responsible for a family member's happiness. I *know* what it's like to have to make a decision that goes against your better judgment because you're desperate for money. Avan and that whole mess with Senator Aldus ring a bell? Anyone? Anyone?" Ozzie and Becky just blinked at him.

"What I *can't* get past is her not telling me until after we…until after I…" His voice trailed off. "She should have told me once it was safe to. She *should* have. She was just too damned scared. And that's *not* the Chelsea Duvall I fell in love with."

For several seconds, the only sound in the room was

the murmur of the television. Another commercial was on, this one hawking a pain medication. Then, quietly Ozzie observed, "Shame and guilt make people do the damnedest things."

Becky was a little less subtle and hit Dagan over the head with "You don't really love her."

His heart skipped a beat. "What exactly do you mean by that?"

"If you really loved her, you'd kiss her tears and bumps and bruises the same way you kiss her lips. You'd stand by her side when she's at her absolute worst and doesn't think she deserves it. Real love is hard and messy and painful. Real love is sticking around when the ugly parts make you want to run away."

He opened his mouth. Closed it. Then opened it again. Before he could get in a word edgewise, Becky continued. "You thought Chelsea was perfect. You had her up on this pedestal. And boo-hoo, now she's fallen off, proved she's a human being. Poor you. But, you know what? If you really, truly loved her, you'd frickin' sac up and—"

"Becky." There was a warning growl in Dagan's voice. "Tell me where she is."

Becky's expression remained mutinous, but eventually she said, "She's home. In South Carolina. She told me she needed to spend some time with her mother. Said they had a lot to talk about."

"What's the address?"

"I don't know off the top of my head. But I have it on file somewhere."

"Good." He started for the door. "Get it for me while I'm packing my saddlebags." And then, to prove he *wasn't* egotistical and pigheaded, he added, "Please."

"Your saddlebags?" Ozzie called to his back. "Are

you planning to *ride* to South Carolina? That's a hell of a long way, and it's only fifty degrees outside."

"Well I have a hell of a lot to think about and sort through, don't I? And maybe the cold will help clear my damned head!"

Chapter 51

"Momma, will you please come sit down?" Chelsea patted the spot beside her on the porch swing. "You're making me nervous running around like a chicken with its head cut off. And you're making the installation men crazy, asking all those questions."

"Well, Chelsea Lynn, I just want to make sure they don't do any more damage than is necessary. Your daddy and I put up every one of these boards with our bare hands, and I—"

Chelsea looked at the trio of men in their matching blue coveralls and subtly put-upon expressions and stopped her mother right then and there. "They're professionals, Momma. They're going to do a wonderful job."

Her mother narrowed her eyes. Then, with a harrumph, she joined Chelsea on the porch swing. "Thank you," she said, accepting the glass of sweet iced tea Chelsea handed her.

They both pushed off, setting the swing gently rocking as the security system crew traipsed around the side of the house to pick out the locations of the cameras they would be installing. The evening air was crisp, ripe with the smell of the freshly turned earth in the flower beds and the tangy brightness of newly budding trees. Chelsea closed her eyes and breathed deeply, hoping the familiar smells of home would bring her a measure of peace. But instead, they just made her sad.

On second thought, that wasn't right. The smells of home didn't make her sad. She just *was* sad and—

"I know I'm a bit neurotic when it comes to this stuff," her mother said, cutting into Chelsea's thoughts. When her mom took a small sip of tea, the ice clinking against the glass competed with the tinkle of the wind chimes hanging in the corner of the porch.

"A *bit*?" Chelsea raised a brow.

"I just…" Her mother stopped and looked out over the front lawn.

Chelsea had always thought of this part of South Carolina as the land of swaying Spanish moss and white-columned homes. She adored it. Adored the crushed-shell driveways, the weeping willows, and the bright, cheerful azalea bushes that bloomed in the spring. But she didn't *love* it the same way her mother did—with everything she had, as if the place, the land, the *house* was a part of her, the marrow in her bones, the air in her lungs, the blood in her veins.

Watching the bright spark of contentment in her mother's eyes as they rested on the mailbox at the end of the drive, then alighted on the hummingbird feeders dangling from the live oak, then flitted to the pecan trees lining the fence, Chelsea wondered if, given the chance to go back in time and change the decision she'd made about Ted Edens and Afghanistan, she would have. Even now, she couldn't bear the thought of doing anything to jeopardize her mother's home and happiness. Still, she should have told Dagan the truth the minute Edens was dead.

Coulda, woulda, shoulda. She was plagued by that unholy trifecta.

"I know, Momma." She patted her mother's hand. "And I wish we didn't have to do this, but…" She shrugged.

Her mother smoothed a hand over Chelsea's head,
her dark eyes kind. "Didn't your boss tell you that this
man you've been huntin', this Spider character, would
be foolish to come after you, and by extension *me*, given
all the press?"

"It's not Spider I'm worried about. At this point, you
and I are small potatoes. Not worth his time, effort, or
exposure. But being in the news brings out the crazies.
I don't like the idea of someone fixating on me *or* you.
Because shit like that happens."

"Chelsea Lynn." Her mother tsked. "There's no call
for that kinda language."

Chelsea hid a smile at the familiar scold. "I need this
security system installed for my own peace of mind,
Momma. So I can sleep at night. I don't like thinking of
you by yourself in this house. I never have. And truth to
tell, I regret not having this done a long time ago."

Her mother patted her hand. "My sweet girl, regrets
are like pennies that have fallen down the cracks of the
sofa. Most times, they aren't worth collectin'."

Chelsea set her iced tea aside and regarded the
woman who had loved her since conception.

"What?" her mother asked.

"Are we still talking about the security system? Or
have we moved on to another subject entirely?"

Chelsea had come clean about everything, including Dagan. There had been shock on her mother's part,
of course. Then guilt, because her mother hated that
Chelsea had compromised her integrity to try to save
the house. That had been followed by great sadness
that Chelsea had lost the man she loved because of
the whole mess. And finally, Grace Duvall had gotten
mad. Mad at Dagan for not immediately seeing that
Chelsea had been in a bad situation and therefore

forgiving her on the spot. And mad was where her mother had stayed.

"I just think if he really cared about you the way you care about him, he'd understand why you did what you did and he'd be here by your side right now."

"Mom, I don't blame Dagan for not being able to get past this. You shouldn't blame him either. He's a really good man who values—"

She was interrupted by a familiar sound. It was a rumble like thunder, only constant and growing louder. She had worked with the Black Knights long enough to recognize the grumble of a good set of pipes. Turning toward the front of the property, she watched a sleek Harley chopper pull into the driveway.

The bike was named Redemption, a moniker that spoke to so much in Dagan's life. It was all silver and chrome, with an intricate dual exhaust system, a short stretch, and enough bling to blind the eye when it caught the sunlight dappling through the canopy of trees that bracketed the drive. But as beautiful as the motorcycle was, it didn't hold a candle to the man who rode it.

Chelsea's heart leapt in her chest. Her knees wobbled as she pushed to a stand and walked to the porch's top step to get a better look at Dagan as he motored toward the house, finally stopping the bike and cutting the engine.

She wouldn't have thought it possible, but in the five days since she'd last seen him, he'd grown more handsome. He wore faded and ripped jeans, a thick biker jacket, and steel-toed boots that looked impossibly heavy. After he toed out the kickstand and swung off Redemption, he turned to face them, taking off his helmet. The speckled sunlight shone in his dark, unruly hair and glinted in the sleek pelt of his beard. But his gray eyes, so stormy, so filled with hidden depths, were what held Chelsea's gaze.

Her body had gone numb the moment she saw him coming up the drive, so she barely felt her mother come up beside her and gently take her hand. She had no trouble hearing, however, when her mother gulped and murmured, "Oh my."

Chelsea smiled and shook her head. "You said it, Momma."

Chapter 52

BEAUFORT, SOUTH CAROLINA, WAS QUINTESSENTIAL SMALL-town America. When Dagan rode through it, his first thought was *Cue ol' Johnny Mellencamp*. However, the drive out to Chelsea's childhood home reminded him less of modern Americana and more of a throwback to a bygone era.

Large trees spread their branches over country roads. Big, gracious houses sat back from the lanes, their expansive lawns immaculately manicured, their white-columned facades congenial and imposing at the same time. It was beautiful country. And the moment he turned up the drive to Chelsea's mother's place, he began to understand…everything.

Unlike its neighbors, the Duvall house wasn't grand. It wasn't boastful. Quite the contrary, it was a small two-story cottage painted a cheery buttercup yellow. A wraparound porch sported various pieces of furniture arranged more for comfort than for style. The flowerpots lining the steps leading to the porch were mismatched, no doubt garage-sale finds that had been collected over the years. But what the place lacked in majesty, it made up in charm. It was a house that had been lovingly built and lovingly tended. It was a…*home*.

On the top step of that home stood the woman who had worked so hard to save it. One look at her, and Dagan's stomach filled with butterflies. She was so damn beautiful. So damn—

"Well, don't just stand there staring like a slack-jawed

dummy," the woman beside Chelsea declared, her hands going to her hips in a familiar Wonder Woman gesture that made the corner of Dagan's mouth twitch. "Come on up here and introduce yourself."

"Momma…" Chelsea scolded. But Dagan was quick to acquiesce. Grace Duvall didn't strike him as the kind of woman to be crossed.

"Yes, ma'am." He quickly climbed the steps. Once he reached the top, he extended his hand. "Mrs. Duvall, I'm Dagan Zoelner. I promised you I would come meet you. And I'm a man who keeps his word."

Grace tilted her head, regarding him intently. She was a beautiful woman. The lavender dress she wore paid homage to her dusky skin. Her cheekbones were high. Her brown eyes were large and almond-shaped. And her handshake was firm. Maybe a touch too firm?

"Are you, now?" She pursed her lips. "Well, that's good to know."

"Momma," Chelsea chastened again.

Grace dropped his hand, squared her shoulders, and took a deep breath. Her tone was a little less sharp when she said, "Well, I thank you for bringin' my Chelsea Lynn back in one piece."

"My pleasure." He nodded. *And my pain*, he thought. Because that crazy twenty-four hours in England had brought him a heaping helping of both.

Glancing at Chelsea, he noted the heightened color on her cheeks and the trepidation in her eyes. The way she looked at him, like he was seconds away from biting her head off, made his stomach ache. Maybe Becky had been right not to want to give him Chelsea's location. Maybe he *did* look like the Big Bad Wolf waiting to swallow Little Red Riding Hood whole.

He worked to soften his expression when he said,

"Chelsea, you look like you're recovering from all the excitement of this week."

Okay, and seriously? After all they had been through together, after all they had done to each other, after he'd ridden Redemption like a bat out of hell all this way, *that* was the best line he could come up with?

"I am." She nodded. "I hope you are too, Z."

If her husky sex-operator's voice was like velvet to his ears, then the hated nickname was like an ice pick. For a couple of seconds, they simply stared at each other until the silence between them was broken by a man in blue coveralls who came around the corner of the house asking, "Do you have a preference which end of the side porch you want the swivel camera mounted on?"

When Coveralls saw Dagan, he skidded to a stop. "Oh, hello." He doffed a dirty baseball cap sporting the logo for the Myrtle Beach Pelicans. "Sorry to interrupt, missus. Didn't know you had company."

"That's fine, Charlie," Grace said. Her brow puckered. "It was Charlie, wasn't it?"

"Yes, missus."

"Good. I'm usually terrible with names, but yours rang a bell because my daddy's great-uncle was a Charlie."

"It's as good a name as any, I reckon," Charlie said.

"Sure enough," Grace agreed.

Dagan couldn't hide his smile. Good ol' Southern charm on full display and dripping with banality.

"I'll come 'round and take a look here in a bit," Grace said. Charlie nodded, and after he disappeared back around the corner, Grace turned to pin Dagan with a keen-eyed stare. "Now, usually I'd cotton to the social niceties and make small talk with you before gettin' down to the nitty-gritty. But as you can see, I got a lot on my hands at the moment. So I reckon I'll just get to it."

"Momma—" Chelsea tried to cut in.

"No." Dagan stopped her. "That's okay." He nodded at Grace. "Go on and say whatever it is you have to say."

"Good." Grace dipped her chin. "I like a man who isn't afraid to let a woman speak her mind. So here it is. My Chelsea is a good woman. Not perfect, maybe. But none of us are. And you could do a lot worse than her, but I'm thinkin' you couldn't do much better."

Chelsea groaned. "Momma, please."

"No." Grace raised her hand. "No need to call me off. I've said my piece, and now I'll leave you two to talk."

With that, Grace turned and vanished around the corner of the porch. Dagan watched her go and considered the fact that she'd passed on more than her flashing smile and rhythmic, hip-swinging walk to her daughter. She'd passed on her smart, no-nonsense mouth too.

"Sorry about that." Chelsea shook her head. "Her rose-colored glasses are deeply tinted when it comes to me."

"As every mother's should be," Dagan said. It hurt to look at Chelsea. Looking at her made him want her. And wanting her made his love for her rise up so fast and so hard, it nearly choked him. Fearing that what he was feeling was written all over his face, he latched on to the first subject he could think of. "So what are you having done to the house?"

"Getting a security system installed."

Fear trickled down his spine. "What? Why? Has something happened? Have you heard something that leads you to believe you could still be a target?" He suddenly wanted to march around the corner and check Coverall Charlie's work. He'd seen and overcome many a security system in his day. He could give Charlie some pointers to—

"No." Chelsea shook her head. "Nothing. This is something I should have done a long time ago." He was surprised by the level of relief that rolled through him. "Z," she said, "why are you—"

"Will you please go back to calling me Dagan?" he interrupted.

"Oh-kay…" She licked her lips, and his eyes pinged down to catch the movement. A longing unlike anything he had ever known gripped him. Chelsea had a mouth that was something out of a wet dream. And now that he knew what she could do with it…

For the love of all that's holy!

"Why are you—" She tried again, but a drill whirred to life, which set off the dog next door. The big, rangy mutt ran to the row of bushes separating the two properties and started barking its head off. Which had Grace running out to shoo it away, yelling, "Git! Go on! Stop your fool barkin', you mangy mongrel!"

Once again, Dagan felt the corner of his mouth twitch.

"Let's walk down to the dock!" Chelsea yelled over the racket. "It'll be quieter down there!"

She lifted a hand as if to place it on his arm, and his breath hitched. If she touched him, he… Well, he didn't know what would happen. All he knew was that he had missed her touch like he would miss his own beating heart. But then she stopped, swallowed, and dropped her hand to her side.

Disappointment hit him over the head at the same time she waved him down the steps. She guided him around the side of the house where a little walkway had been created out of large, flat pieces of sandstone.

Once they reached the back of the property, he saw with his own eyes what before he had only seen on a map. Chelsea's childhood home backed up to a body of

water called Chowan Creek. But more than that, it had
an expansive view of Port Royal Sound.

To say the place was beautiful would be a disservice.
The only word Dagan could come up with that came
close to describing the view was *stunning*.

The wind smelled of wet earth and slowly moving
water. The afternoon sky was a deep robin's-egg blue.
And the sight of Chelsea, walking ahead of him in a soft
purple sweater and painted-on jeans, was the only thing
in the world he could think of that could compete with
the sheer, natural splendor surrounding him.

The boards of the dock were weathered but whole,
and the whir of the drill was soon eclipsed by the sound
of water lapping around the base of the pilings and the
tweedle-do-tweedle-do-tweet of a wren in a nearby tree.

They took a seat on the built-in bench at the end of
the dock. For a while, they said nothing, simply watched
the sunlight dapple the water and the wind push at the
creek. The space between them seemed filled with possibility. And, finally, he turned to ask the question that
had plagued him since his call with Director Russell.
But to his surprise, what came out of his mouth was
something else entirely.

Chapter 53

"How's your arm?"

Chelsea released a pent-up breath. Whatever she had been expecting Dagan to say, that wasn't it. The odd look on his face told her he was as surprised as she was by the question.

She lifted her arm and gave it a wiggle. "Almost as good as new."

"Good." He nodded without looking at her. Instead, he kept his focus on the undulating, sun-dappled surface of the creek and the crane fishing in the reeds along the far bank. "And all the press? Losing your anonymity? How are you dealing with that?"

She studied his profile, his straight nose, his high cheekbones, and his ridiculously thick eyelashes. Why had she never noticed before how long and sooty they were? Oh, right. Because usually when she looked into his eyes, she was too mesmerized by the swirl of his stormy irises to pay attention to anything else.

"I mean, it's not ideal, right?" she told him. "But it is what it is. *Qué será, será.* The fact that Morrison's depravities have been brought to light and the fact that BKI is a step closer to nailing Spider makes it worth it."

He nodded again. "And your mother? How is she handling all this?"

"Like she handles pretty much everything. With grace and aplomb and a few homespun anecdotes."

He laughed. The rumbling sound was as clear as moonshine and packed a wallop to match. Her heart, already thudding wildly in her chest, beat faster. "And how long are you planning to stay with—"

"Dagan, please stop." The shock of his arrival had worn off, and now the ache of his radio silence over the last five days was back in full force. Every day, every hour, every *minute* she had waited to hear from him. There had even been times when she had wondered if any of it had been real, or if she'd simply imagined the desperate way he had made love to her, the certainty in his eyes when he told ,that she held the key to his heart. Then she would look at her naked body in the mirror, and the proof of the former at least was there for her to see.

The love bite he had left on her inner thigh had faded from deep purple to soft pink. She was dreading the day it disappeared completely. Then the only evidence she would have of what they had shared would be the Dagan-shaped hole in her heart.

"I know you didn't come all this way to blow smoke up my ass," she continued. "So why don't you say whatever it is you need to say, or ask me whatever it is you need to ask me. Because right now the suspense"—*and the uncertainty*—"is killing me."

A crooked smile tilted his mouth. He tried to hide it by running a hand over the Beard. "Patience has never been one of your virtues, has it?"

"That, and I have a serious aversion to small talk and bullshit."

"Seems to run in your family." That crooked smile lingered for a second longer, then faded. "You told Director Russell what happened."

She swallowed. "Better late than never."

"And you told him that he should give me my old job back. And that if I couldn't work with you, given our history, then you would quit. You told him that I was far more valuable to the Company than you are."

"All true."

He searched her eyes. "Why, Chels? Why would you do that?"

She was tempted to drop his gaze and look out over the water. He'd always been able to see too much. But she owed him honesty. Not just the honesty of her words but the honesty of her eyes. So she held his penetrating stare without wavering. "Because I know you've been worried about your future, about what you'll do after Spider is apprehended and BKI shuts its doors. I put myself and the responsibility I feel for my mother ahead of you once. I refuse to do that again. You deserve your old job back, Dagan. You deserve… everything. Anything you want."

She desperately wanted him to tell her that what he wanted was *her*. But that's not what he said. What he said was, "And what will you do? Go to work for the DOD? They pay worse than the CIA."

"So I'll work a second job. I'm not too proud to bag groceries at the Piggly Wiggly. Besides, you're not the only one who thinks you need a little redemption. Right about now, I could use some too."

"You shoulder too much of the burden for what happened back then. I should have seen the red flags Waleed waved in my direction. Seen that the Intel he gave me wasn't actionable or important."

That sounded an awful lot like there was reason to… hope. Her breath stuttered in her lungs. "Waleed's success at becoming a double agent was a failure on the parts of *many* people. That doesn't change the fact that once *I* knew what was happening, I should have done something about it."

"You did. You told your direct superior just like you'd been trained to do."

"But afterward I should have done more. I should've gone over Edens's head. I should have told—"

"If you had told, your reputation and any chance of a career in the Intelligence Community would have been obliterated. Edens would have made certain of that." Okay, and that *really* sounded like a reason to hope. Tears she refused to let fall backed up behind her eyes. "I understand why you did what you did back then, Chels." Her chest was caught in a vise grip. "Hell, put in the same position with the same familial responsibilities and pressures, I would have done the same thing. But what I can't wrap my head around, what I can't seem to get past, is that you *kept* the secret even after Edens was gone. Why? Why didn't you tell me once your job was safe? Why the hell were you so...so..."

"Cowardly?"

"*Yes!*" he thundered, pushing to a stand and glaring down at her. His chest worked like bellows. His nostrils flared. She wanted so much to reach out and grab his hand that she had to curl her fingers around the edge of the bench and hold on tight. "The Chelsea I know and love isn't a coward. The Chelsea I know and love doesn't back down from confrontation. The Chelsea I know—"

"I was so ashamed," she cut him off. Now there was nothing she could do to hold back the tears. They flowed freely down her cheeks and plopped onto her sweater. "I had kept that secret for so long, and I was... I *am* so racked with guilt. I've always respected you so much, Dagan. I've always loved you so much that I couldn't bring myself to admit to something that I knew would make you look at me the way you're looking at me right now." A muscle twitched beneath his eye. "And I understand if you hate me for that weakness. I hate myself."

"I don't hate you."

The laugh that burst from the back of her tear-clogged throat was bitter. "Well, that's something, I guess."

For a long time, neither of them spoke. The only sounds were her sniffles and the soft *lap-lap* of the water beneath the dock. Then Dagan said, "You should have told me the minute Edens was out of the picture."

She nodded. "I know I should have. Hindsight being twenty-twenty and all that."

He blew out a gusty breath. "I'm mad as hell at you for not trusting me enough to tell me sooner, for thinking that I wouldn't understand the horrible position Edens put you in."

"And you have every right to be mad as hell."

"But you could have kept the secret forever. I would have never known. I would have gone on thinking that you…that we…"

"I couldn't let you love me without knowing the *real* me. Warts and all." She picked at the hem of her sweater. She couldn't look at him. She knew what came next. She knew he would tell her that this was something he couldn't get over. That she wasn't the woman he thought she was.

"You took a big risk going to Director Russell with the truth. He could have blamed you as much as Edens for failing to take action. He could have fired you on the spot and made sure you never got another job in Intelligence."

"It would have been worth it if it got you your job back. If it gave you the future you wanted."

"You really do love me, don't you?"

His image was blurred by her tears. "With all my heart. All my cowardly, weak, wide-open heart. I always have."

He nodded. And when he didn't say he loved her too, she thought she heard the sound of the first nail being hammered into the lid of a coffin. Inside that coffin was what remained of his feelings for her.

It hurt. It hurt so badly she almost wanted to die.

"You know," he said after a bit, "someone wise once told me that the past is written. That what's done is done. We can't change it. But the future? Well, that's unwritten. We can *choose* what happens."

And he would choose to leave her. It was there in his voice. There in his eyes. It took everything she had not to dissolve into a wailing puddle at his feet and beg him to reconsider.

"Babe?" Her breath caught at the endearment. Who would have ever thought she would be the kind of woman who liked being called *babe*? "Come here." He extended a hand to her.

The steadiness of his grip emphasized how badly her fingers shook. Pulling her to a stand, he gently cupped her face in his hands. As he searched her eyes, he got spooky-still. This was where he would tell her good-bye. This was where he would—

"Chelsea Lynn Duvall?"

"Yes?" she managed past the massive lump in her throat.

"I forgive you. I'm not going to let this come between us. I believe love really does conquer all."

They were the words she had begged him to say back in Gautier's sub. Words she had convinced herself she would never hear.

The sob that burst from her was loud enough to make the crane across the way take flight.

Dagan pulled her into his arms. He was so solid and hot and male against her. His leather jacket and his wind-kissed skin were the sweetest scents she'd ever smelled. And when she slipped her hands beneath his coat and wrapped her arms around him, the whole wonderful landscape of his back slid beneath her fingers.

"I love you," he breathed against the crown of her head.

She choked on her own *I love you* and tilted her chin back to stare into his mesmerizing eyes. A deep sense of contentment, of a love strong enough to last a lifetime, wrapped around her as warmly as the big arms that held her close.

And then Dagan did one of the many, *many* things he did best. He got carnal with her mouth.

Oh. My!

*Keep reading for a sneak peek of the next
Black Knights Inc. book*

Kirkuk, Iraq...

"WHO SENT YOU? WHAT DO YOU WANT?"

The policeman's accent made his words guttural
and hard, but they were nothing compared to the granite fist that smashed into Christian Watson's nose. A
geyser of blood gushed over his lips and seeped into
the cut on his chin that had come courtesy of the first
round of questioning.

Which had been...what? Twenty minutes ago? Two
hours?

Time slowed when you were getting the sodding shite
beaten out of you.

"My name is Christian Watson. I am a corporal in
Her Majesty's Special Air Service." He rattled off his
serial number before clamping his jaws shut. That was
all the information the Geneva Conventions required of
him. He would give no more.

Another blow drove deep into his gut, precisely
over the spot where the bullet had gone through. The

accompanying pain was a living thing that chewed at his intestines with hungry, needlelike teeth.

Dizziness and nausea crashed over him in undulating waves. He might have retched had the chair he was tied to not toppled backward with the force of the blow. When it collided with the floor in the tiny interrogation room, the sound his skull made as it bounced off the tiles was sickening, even to his own ears.

Darkness closed in on him, a malevolent specter hovering at the edge of his vision.

For the first time since he'd opened fire at the roadblock, fear tried to take root in his heart. He could not lose consciousness. Loss of consciousness was a loss of control. Loss of control terrified him worse than any corrupt Iraqi police officer ever could.

He struggled against his restraints, trying not to gag at the iron-rich smell of his own blood. He narrowly opened his one good eye to glare up at the policeman. His assailant wore a nasty smile. The hateful expression reminded Christian of a man from long ago. A man who inflicted pain for the simple pleasure of it. A man who—

The space around Christian shimmered and changed, melting into a new, more terrifying whole. Suddenly he was six years old, inside his boyhood room. Gone were the scents of blood and sweat and dry wind heavy with dust. They were replaced by the smells coming from the hulking shadow that loomed over him: whiskey and smoke, with an underlying hint of rot.

The shadow reached for him. Massive ham-hock hands curved into brutal, inescapable claws. Christian whimpered, scooting backward. But there was no place to go. Nowhere to run.

"Mummy!" he yelled, his voice hoarse with terror. "Mummy, please!"

But she would not come. It was too late. She was too far gone. He knew she would not come.

Orange light flickered in the darkness, licking flames into the brutal eyes of the shadowy man. Now he looked like what he was. Sadistic. Cruel. Evil incarnate.

Christian braced himself for what would come next. Even so, the first sizzle of fiery pain shocked him with its intensity.

Tossing back his head, he screamed…

"Wake up, damnit! Wake *up!*"

He bolted upright in bed. For a couple of confusing seconds, he didn't know where he was. *When* he was. There was only darkness and the lingering memory of agony. There was only… *Her.* Emily Scott. The woman who had crawled under his skin and made a home for herself. What was she doing here?

Tunneling up his nose was the exotic smell of her shampoo. It caused him to snap back to the here and now as if he'd been fired from a slingshot.

Buggering hell, he thought at the same time Emily said, "Holy fucking shit!"

He might have smiled—the woman had a mouth on her and it never failed to delight him—had the words she'd spoken not been thick with recently disturbed sleep and something more. Something he thought might be fear.

No doubt he'd been screaming his fool head off. Which would scare the piss out of a seasoned operative, much less a pretty pipsqueak of an office manager who had somehow managed to embroil herself in a mission she had no business being part of.

Buggering hell, he thought again, as remnants of the dream—correction: *dreams*—shuddered through him.

Months. That's how long it had been since he'd awoken in a pool of sweat, thrashing about as he tried to escape the ghosts of his past. He had hoped that perhaps he might finally have outdistanced them. Embarrassment and shame had him running a hand over his face. The growth of his day-old whiskers rasped against the calluses on his palm.

"Hey," she shook his shoulder as if uncertain he was truly awake. "You were having a nightmare." Her Chi-Town accent emphasized the *a* in all her words, making her sound tough. Which was funny, considering she looked about as dangerous as a baby bunny.

His words were harsher than he would've liked when he said, "No shite, Sherlock."

She drew back, taking the smell of her shampoo with her. His heart immediately hurled itself against his rib cage, as if it was trying to lessen the distance she'd put between them.

She huffed with exasperation, and he knew he should apologize. But the words stuck in his throat. He couldn't stomach the thought that she'd seen him like that.

So vulnerable.

So exposed.

So...*out of control*.

"You know," she said, not attempting to disguise the irritation in her voice, "a normal person would say, 'Thank you, Emily. Thank you for waking me up before I punched a hole through the bloody wall.'"

She'd donned an English accent. It was adorable. And total rubbish. She sounded more like a New Zealander than an Englishwoman.

"You're right," he admitted after taking a deep breath. "You're absolutely right. I'm sorry. Thank you for waking me."

His eyes had adjusted to the darkness so he could see she was wearing a familiar frayed pullover. Her brown hair was a rumpus of flyaway waves, and her face was scrubbed clean of makeup. If he weren't mistaken, she wasn't wearing a bra. He was fairly certain he could make out the subtle jut of her nipples through the thick fabric of her shirt.

Oh, bloody hell, he realized he was staring at her boobs. *Stop staring at her boobs.*

Right-oh. Problem was, not staring was a tall order since from the top of Emily's head to the tips of her unpainted toes, she was beautiful. Not beautiful like all those Hollywood starlets with their fake hair, medically enhanced bodies, and gallons of cosmetics, but beautiful in a timeless, effortless way.

Emily's slim figure was subtly curved. She had a pert nose, big dark eyes, and a lush mouth. If he had to put a label on it, he'd say she possessed an ingénue-esque air. It tended to cause a male stampede anytime she walked into a room.

Unfortunately, since the day he had met her, she'd made it clear she had no interest in him in *that* way. Certainly she enjoyed teasing him and taunting him. On a regular basis, she took strips out of his hide with the sharpness of her tongue. But when it came to nocturnal activities? Well, it was safe to say that she was the equivalent of a human stop sign. *Do not pass Go. Do not collect two hundred quid.*

Masochist that he was, that just made him fancy her more. As if to prove the point, his flag had already hoisted itself to half-staff.

"Do you want to talk about it?" she asked. Morning's first tender light chose that moment to filter in through the crack in the curtains. It glowed over the smooth, unblemished skin of her face, highlighted the beauty mark high on her right cheek, and showed the sympathy in her warm eyes.

"Talk about what?"

"Your nightmare."

He snorted. "About as much as I'd fancy having my bollocks shaved with a rusty razor blade."

For a moment she was silent. Then her lips curved up at the corners. "Whatever floats your boat, right?"

A joke. She was trying to tease the tension out of him. Which might have worked had she been anyone else. Had she *not* had such a hypnotic smile. He was afraid if he stared at it too long, he'd fall under its spell and be helpless to do anything but its bidding.

Glancing through the slit in the curtains, he eyed the sliver of view beyond. The rising sun cast the beach in a pearlescent glow. Golden rays turned the tops of the waves in the harbor pink and silver. It was a scene from his childhood. Back when his childhood had been…if not good, then at least *bearable*. Before it'd become a string of long, lonely days and terrifying nights.

"What time is it?" he asked, trying not to notice how his thigh touched her hip through the fabric of the quilt.

"Just past oh-six-hundred. You still have time to get more sleep."

"Not possible."

Her expression epitomized compassion. "Bad dreams do that to me too. I've found it helps if someone stays with me. You know, to sort of guard against the nightmare's return. Do you want me to stay with you?" Her head tilted innocently.

Good God, was she serious? He wanted her to stay with him more than anything. But he couldn't have her in his room, in his *bed*, without touching her. And since

in the world of unwritten rules, not touching a woman
unless she invited him to was underlined, bold, and in
all caps, she needed to leave.

"No. I'm fine. But thank you. Thank you for coming
to check on me. To wake me." He risked looking into
her eyes and immediately knew it for the mistake it was.
He was used to seeing a mischievous glint in her warm
brown irises, used to seeing derision or irritation or, hell,
occasionally even grudging respect. But what he was *not*
used to seeing was tenderness.

Not that Emily was unkind. Quite the contrary;
beneath her tough outer shell she had an incredibly soft
underbelly. Problem was, she rarely showed *him* her
softer side, choosing instead to give him all the sharp
edges she had honed while growing up in Chi-Town's
blue-collar Bridgeport neighborhood.

She placed a hand on his thigh and it immediately
brought him out in a sweat. "If you're sure you don't—"

"I'm sure." He was quick to cut her off.

"You're good at playing the tough guy, aren't you?"

He quirked a brow, made sure his expression was all
arrogance. "I don't have to play at it, darling."

Tossing her head back, she laughed. The sight of her
exposed throat combined with the low, husky roll of
her amusement had his flag hoisting itself to full-staff.
Bloody stupid appendage!

Emily lowered her chin to regard him, that hypnotic
smile still on her lips. "Let no one ever accuse you of a
lack of confidence, Christian."

He considered pretending he hadn't heard her, so
she'd say his name again. The way she pronounced it
always hit him like a shot of aged whiskey—warm,
potent, and intoxicating. But instead he went with, "You
say that like it's a bad thing."

"It's not. I like a confident man."

"Careful." He lifted a brow. "That sounded suspiciously like you just admitted to liking me."

She shrugged. It was a delicate, unconsciously graceful gesture. "Well, I don't *dislike* you."

Warmth unfurled in his belly. To distract her from the heightened color in his cheeks and the predatory gleam that had no doubt entered his eyes, he donned an expression of annoyance. "Damned with faint praise."

"Oh, it's praise you want? Well, I'm afraid you've come to the wrong woman. I'm bad at compliments."

"That's the understatement of the century." Although, truth be told, he'd heard her compliment their coworkers on many occasions. She was just beastly bad at flinging admiration *his* way.

Which was probably why his jaw slung open when she took a deep breath and blurted, "You have really pretty eyes."

Scriiiiiitch. That sound was a needle scratching across his mental record player. Did Emily Scott just say he had pretty eyes? Backup. Reset. Not just pretty eyes but *really* pretty eyes?

How odd she should think so. He'd always thought his eyes a bit…spooky. They were a strange color, somewhere between green and gold. Too light when paired with his tan skin and dark hair. Hadn't he been told as much? Hadn't his spooky eyes caused—

He crushed the memory and glanced around the room as if furtively searching for something. "Hang on a minute," he said.

A frown tugged at her pretty mouth. "What is it? What are you looking for?"

"The white bunny. I seem to have fallen down the rabbit hole."

She swatted his arm, not attempting to be gentle. "See? And that's why I don't compliment you. You don't know how to take it."

"I'm sorry. You're absolutely right. Let's try this again, shall we? You think I have really pretty eyes?" He fluttered his eyelashes for effect.

She groaned and pushed up from the bed. He felt the loss of her weight, the loss of her hip against his thigh, the loss of her exotic-smelling shampoo, in a place he dare not name. "And besides," she added, "your ego is big enough without me giving it the occasional stroke."

His breath caught on the last word. It seemed to hang in the air, pounding like a heartbeat.

If she noticed his sudden tension, she gave no indication as she sauntered toward the door. Turning at the threshold, she said, "Since you're not going to get any more sleep, how about you cook breakfast for the ravenous hoard, huh? I could use another hour of shut-eye."

She stretched her arms over her head and let out a mighty yawn. Her older-than-the-hills pullover inched away from the waistband of her pajama bottoms. A flash of pale, silky skin turned his mouth into a desert.

"Speaking of the ravenous hoard," he said, or rather rasped, "are they still asleep? Did I wake them?"

She glanced down the hall, her dark hair falling over her shoulder in a silky curtain he longed to touch. "The lights are off in their rooms. I think I was the only one who heard. You know, since we share a wall."

Ah, yes. The shared wall.

The wall he had stared at for the last five nights while they waited for things to get sorted so they could come out from hiding and return to Chicago. The wall he might have, just maybe, pressed his ear against a time or two in the hopes of hearing her…what? Snoring? Breathing? Pleasuring herself?

He stifled a groan.

"So?" She cocked a brow. "Will you?"

"Will I what?"

She frowned like his IQ had dropped fifty points in the last five seconds. Which, if he was being honest, it had. It *did*. Anytime she was in the room.

"Breakfast. Will you make breakfast? I know it's my turn, but—"

"Say no more." He lifted a hand. "It's done." Because even if breakfast duty was at the top of exactly no one's list, he was glad to assume the responsibility if it would get Emily out of his room. After having her so close for so long, he definitely needed some alone time with his John Thomas. "A traditional English breakfast it is," he added when she seemed to need additional reassurance.

She wrinkled her nose. "I can get on board with the sautéed mushrooms and the roasted tomato, but I've never understood beans for breakfast."

"They're good for your heart."

Even from across the dim room, he saw her eyes ignite with mischief. Emily liked to push buttons, do the unexpected, say things hysterically crass. He assumed it was because she enjoyed keeping the people around her off balance. "The more you eat, the more you—"

"For heaven's sake!" he scolded before she could finish the hideous children's rhyme. "Grow up, will you?"

Although, the truth was, he wouldn't change a thing about her. She drove him completely crazy. That was true. But she also made him laugh. And in his line of work—bloody hell, in his entire sodding *life*—laughter wasn't something that came easily.

"So stuffy," she complained. It was a familiar accusation.

"I'm not stuffy. I'm English, darling."

"My point exactly."

"Hurtful." He crossed his arms and thrust out his chin. If he weren't mistaken, her eyes alighted on his bare pecs, then traveled briefly over the sleeves of black, winding tattoos that covered his arms from his shoulders to wrists.

Is that interest I see in her eyes? he wondered hopefully.

He wasn't bad to look at. He knew that. Not that he had to fight the women away with a stick or anything, but neither did he have to look quite hard for a willing bed partner. Alas, whatever brief flicker of intrigue he thought he saw in her eyes disappeared before he had the chance to study it.

"Will you be happy to leave home today?" she asked, still lingering in his doorway.

"England isn't home," he assured her, his mood dropping into the loo. The only good to come of *that* was that his John Thomas followed suit. So, apparently there were two cures for his flag flying at full-staff. One, a swift rub and tug. Or two, talk of the country that had betrayed him. "It hasn't been for a long time."

She considered him for a moment more, then nodded and turned to go. Before she disappeared down the hall, she got in a parting shot. If he had known just how portentous her words would turn out to be, he might have stayed in bed with the covers over his head. "Someday you're going to tell me what happened here."

Port Isaac, Cornwall, England

Emily Scott was having a good day.

She'd pawned breakfast duty off on Christian. She was wearing her favorite sweatshirt, the one Paulie Konerko had signed after he helped the White Sox win the 2005 World Series. And she was on her way home. Back to the world of baseball and deep dish pizza, towering skyscrapers and a lake so big and blue it looked like an ocean.

Add to that the fact that she would no longer have to stay cooped up in a tiny cottage with four of the most testosterone-packed males on the planet, and she'd go so far as to say her day wasn't just good; it was Tony the Tiger *grrrreat*. Which was why she should have been prepared for things to start circling the drain. Long ago, it'd come to her attention that life liked to rise up and bite her on the ass when she least expected it.

Case in point: she found herself blinking in slack-jawed astonishment when two hours after she'd finished scarfing down Christian's delightful English breakfast—minus the baked beans, natch—he opened the front door of his uncle's cottage only to have a microphone shoved in his face.

"Are you Corporal Christian Watson?" a redheaded woman in a yellow pantsuit demanded. "Is it true you were the SAS soldier captured during the Kirkuk Police Station Incident?"

"Where have you been, Corporal Watson?" a man in a raincoat and cabbie hat demanded, holding up a digital recorder. "What have you been on about since you left Her Majesty's Special Air Service?"

Emily got a glimpse of half a dozen other people gathered on the cottage's front stoop—a honking

big camera was on the shoulder of one man—before
Christian slammed the door shut and twisted the lock.
His face was a thundercloud when he swung back into
the room.

"Bloody fecking hell," he snarled, then followed that
up with a string of profanity so blue it would make a
sailor blush.

Why did curse words sound better coming out of his
mouth? Oh, right. Because *everything* sounded better
coming out of his mouth. That accent! She was hard-
pressed not to fan herself.

Turning to the trio of men behind her, she found their
expressions mirrored her own. In a word: shock. In two
words: rampant curiosity. And in three words? Well,
what the fuck? came to mind.

"What in the ass?" Ace asked, adjusting the straps of
his backpack more comfortably on his broad shoulders.

They all had backpacks stuffed with the essentials
needed to flee the country: basic toiletries and a change
of clothes. Usually included in their "essentials" was an
array of handguns, knives, and other pointy or bangy
things which, when used correctly, resulted in death. But
they'd had to leave their arsenal behind during their initial attempt to hop the pond a few days prior. Emily had
wondered if the men felt naked without their customary
repository of combat blades and sidearms.

"I mean, seriously, what in the *ass*?" Ace repeated.
Colby "Ace" Ventura was a former U.S. Navy pilot
turned operator for Black Knights Inc., the covert government defense firm Emily had gone to work for after
she bugged out of the CIA. Although, in reality, it was
probably more appropriate to say the Black Knights had
taken her under their wings after the fiasco with her
former boss *forced* her out of the CIA.

"That's one way of putting it," she said to Ace before turning back to Christian. "Another way of putting it would be to steal the timeless words of Ricky Ricardo." She exaggerated her expression. "Christian…you got some 'splainin' to do." All those hours parked in front of the television as a kid watching reruns of *I Love Lucy* while her parents had been out doing who-the-hell-knew-what had apparently paid off.

Unfortunately, her flippancy was wasted on Christian. "Shite," he hissed, followed by, "Bloody fecking hell."

"You said that already," she informed him helpfully, trying to lighten his mood. When she thought of the vulnerability she'd seen in his eyes in that first second after she'd woken him from his nightmare, her silly, squishy, far-too-soft heart turned over. "Try something else. I like to go with bugfucking dickmunch or son of a bee-stung bitch. But I might also suggest—"

"Sod off, Emily." He glowered at her.

Really, Christian could glower like nobody's business because, and there was no subtler way to put this, he was a stone-cold fox.

Okay, so maybe he wasn't *handsome*. At least not in the traditional sense. His looks were more those of the high desert. Harsh. Dangerous. Stark. And like an oasis in the sand, his eyes glittered and shone.

Intensely masculine, that's what he was. Carnal. *Primal*. Six foot three inches of big bones and Superman hair. The kind of guy who was attractive not because he had perfect features, but because he oozed confidence and testosterone and power. A breaker of hearts. A slayer of vaginas. The kind of guy who got most women sweaty just by breathing.

Lucky for her, she wasn't most women.

Okay, so maybe she *was*. Because, seriously, *not*

lusting after his hot bod was kind of like saying to herself, *See that fat, furry little bulldog puppy? Do* not *think he's cute*. Still, whether or not she wanted to jump his bones was neither here nor there since she'd learn not to mix business with pleasure. Once bitten, twice shy, baby.

"Now is so not the time for your scathing wit," he added.

"No?" She lifted a brow. "And here I was thinking *any* time was a good time for my scathing wit."

"There are bloody reporters outside."

"Yep. Saw 'em with my own two beady eyes."

This time he gifted her with a put-upon grimace. Really, the man seemed to have a vast arsenal of sexy sneers and bone-melting scowls. And truth? She enjoyed each and every one of them. They gave her a glimpse of the real man beneath the carefully styled hair, the designer clothes, and the expensive whatnots. The man who was down and dirty, gruff and gritty. The man a part of her couldn't wait to meet.

It was the wild part of her. The careless part. The *crazy* part that didn't have a thought in its ditzy, horny little head except, *Yowza! Gimme, gimme, gimme!*

That was the part of her she tried like hell to ignore, choosing instead to focus on the *other* part of her. The sensible part. The reasonable part. The practical part that didn't dare give him any more sexy ammunition to use against her already panting libido.

"What do we do now?" Ace asked.

"Back door." Angel said, already turning. Angel was a former Israeli Mossad agent turned fellow BKI badass. Emily didn't know much about him; his past was even more shadowed than Christian's.

"Right. Good idea." She hustled after him.

Unfortunately, before they reached the back door, they heard the sound of voices coming from beyond it.

"Trapped," she whispered, her heart kicking into overdrive. She would have liked to think the sudden uptick was a product of their increasingly alarming situation. But the truth was, it was at least partly due to Christian having followed and come to a stop directly behind her, close enough that she could feel the blast of his body heat.

"This is bad," he muttered, taking a step back. She didn't know whether to be disappointed or relieved that he'd moved away.

"We need to stay calm," Angel insisted in that precise way he had. Jamin "Angel" Agassi's diction was perfect. But his voice? It was a wreck. Likely due to the fact that he'd had his vocal cords scoured to avoid voice recognition software after he left Israel. Talk about *ew*, not to mention *ow*.

"Right." Ace nodded. "Before we get too excited, we need to know what we're dealing with." He lifted an inquiring brow at Christian. "Is it true? Were you the one captured during the Kirkuk Police Station Incident?"

Emily turned to study Christian's face and saw the muscle twitching beneath his right eye.

"Yes," Christian said after a five-second beat. "That would be me."

"Holy hobbling Christ on a crutch," Ace swore, running a hand through his blond hair.

"What?" Rusty Parker, aka the only civilian in the group, asked. "What was the Kirkuk Police Station Incident?"

Rusty was a former Marine who had worked one summer as a CIA asset before he up and moved to England to become a charter boat captain. *Poor guy*, she thought now. She wouldn't have dragged him into this if she'd known just how much trouble she was going to cause him.

"Yeah." She nodded. "I'm with Rusty. What *was* the Kirkuk Police Station Incident?"

Christian shook his head. "We don't have time for this."

Christian, like so many of the Black Knights, was stubbornly closemouthed about his past. Most times, she didn't press. In her world, a smart woman allowed men like them their secrets. But this time, she felt compelled to push.

"Sure we do. Since our only exits are blocked by reporters, we have all the time in the world."

Christian blew out an exasperated breath that caused a whorl of hair to fall over his brow. It tried to distract Emily, but she refused to let it.

"Fine," he grumbled. "But let's bloody well make this quick, okay?"

"We're all ears," she assured him. "Fire away."

That muscle twitched beneath his eye again. It was joined by one in his jaw. "It was near the end of the Iraq War, after major hostilities had ceased and before the incursion of ISIS into the country. I was sent in to keep an eye on a group of Iraqi policemen who were running a crime unit with rumored links to corruption and brutality in the city. My job was to gather enough evidence against them to warrant a takedown."

"Oh, I remember reading about this." Rusty narrowed his eyes in thought. "There was a shoot-out at a roadblock, right?"

Christian nodded. "The policemen I was tasked with surveilling somehow found out about me. When I was leaving the city to deliver a situation report to my commanding officer, I was stopped at a roadblock. At first I thought I could talk my way out of it, yeah? But they pulled their weapons and started shooting. I pulled mine and did the same. Took a round to the gut that put me in bad shape. But before they managed to overwhelm me, I slotted two of the wankstains."

He said it so casually. *Before they managed to overwhelm me.* But Emily knew Christian. It must have been one hell of a fight.

"They took me to the police station where they questioned me for eight hours," he added. *Questioned.* Ha! A nice way of saying he had been interrogated and tortured. Visions of bludgeoning, waterboarding, and thumbs shoved into his wound bloomed in her mind. It was enough to have her breakfast threatening to reverse directions.

"Is that what you were dreaming about this morning?" she asked. If the hoarse screams that had jolted her from a dead sleep were any indication, Christian's eight hours in the hands of the Iraqis had been brutal.

The look he shot her was quick and definitive, the facial equivalent of *shut your trap*. But it was too late. Ace glanced back and forth between them, a shit-eating grin spreading across his handsome face.

"How would *you* know what he was dreaming about this morning, hmm?" Ace widened his blue eyes. "Is there something the two of you would like to tell us? Like, maybe you've finally had enough foreplay and it's time to get down to the main event?"

"Foreplay?" Emily scowled. "I don't know what you're talking about."

"Oh, sure you do. All that one-upping? The verbal sparring? That's foreplay, luv."

She waved a hand through air still tinged with the

smell of bacon and buttered toast. "Whatever. One-
upmanship is nothing more than good clean fun. And
maybe a little ego management on my part." She gifted
Christian with a squinty-eyed stare, indicating his height
with a gesture. "I mean, you've seen him, right? The
clothes. The hair. The smile. Someone has to keep him
grounded."

"Rrrright," Ace said, nodding his head.

She rolled her eyes and turned to Christian. "Tell him."

Christian lifted a brow that asked *Tell him what?*

She thinned her lips and widened her eyes. Her
expression said *Tell him I'm right.*

Instead of siding with her, Christian said, "Can we
please get back to the bloody subject? In case you've
forgotten, there are *reporters* outside preventing us
from catching our flight and getting the hell off this
sodding rock!"

Did he think their bickering was foreplay? She
didn't delude herself when it came to Christian. And
despite her protestations to the contrary, she *did* want
him. *I mean, who wouldn't?* But he'd given no indication he felt the same. In fact, he found her *as annoying
as a housefly.* His words. Not hers. Which was just fine
and dandy.

It was!

After all, there was that whole "not mixing of business and pleasure" edict she was determined to live
by. And even if there *wasn't*, the two of them were oil
and water.

He wore designer clothes and drove a Porsche. She
preferred yoga pants and sweatshirts, usually from the
discount rack at Target. There was an air of mystery
surrounding him, depths she dared not plumb. And she?
Well, she was pretty much an open book.

If she was simple, he was complex. If she was day, he was night. *A dark and stormy one*.

Acknowledgments

A story begins in the mind of an author and ends in the heart of a reader. But between Point A and Point B are a lot of people who do a lot of work to make that story the best it can be. I'm fortunate to have a wonderful team toiling away on my behalf.

Nicole, thank you for being my sounding board, my advocate, and my tireless cheerleader.

Deb, thank you for your diligence (and ruthlessness) with that red ink pen. My stories are smarter, stronger, and funnier because of your insights.

Beth, thank you for always pushing the publicity envelope. I appreciate all you do to "get the word out" about my books.

Dominique, Todd, Valerie, Sean, Susie, Rachel, Dawn, and all the other folks at Sourcebooks, thank you for doing the hard work so that I can sit back and have a blast at this author gig.

About the Author

Julie Ann Walker is the *New York Times* and *USA Today* bestselling author of award-winning romantic suspense. A winner of the Book Buyers Best Award, Julie has been nominated for the National Readers' Choice Award, the Australian Romance Reader Awards, and the Romance Writers of America's prestigious RITA Award. Her books have been described as "alpha, edgy, and down-right hot." Most days you can find Julie on her bicycle along the lakeshore in Chicago or blasting away at her keyboard, trying to wrangle her capricious imagination into submission.

To stay abreast of Julie's upcoming releases, sign up for her newsletter at www.julieannwalker.com.